P9-DFK-512

Praise for *New York Times* bestselling author Carla Neggers

"Only a writer as gifted as Carla Neggers could use so few words to convey so much action and emotional depth."
—#1 *New York Times* bestselling author Sandra Brown

"Neggers captures readers' attention with her usual flair and brilliance and gives us a romance, a mystery and a lesson in history."
—*RT Book Reviews* on *Secrets of the Lost Summer*, Top Pick

"*Saint's Gate* is the best book yet from a writer at the absolute top of her craft."
—*Providence Journal*

Praise for Caro Carson

"[Caro] Carson's romance is a humorous and heartfelt page-turner from the get-go. Her funny, genuinely touching and vibrant narrative sets the perfect pace with just a touch of Texas twang."
—*RT Book Reviews* on *The Bachelor Doctor's Bride*

"This romance is a real trauma twister, dealing with delicate social and political issues. The narrative flows and the characters shine."
—*RT Book Reviews* on *Doctor, Soldier, Daddy*

Carla Neggers is a *New York Times* bestselling author of more than sixty novels of contemporary romance and romantic suspense, including her popular Sharpe & Donovan and Swift River Valley series. Her books have been translated into twenty-four languages and sold in over thirty countries. Frequent travelers to Ireland, Carla and her husband divide their time between Boston and their hilltop home in Vermont, not far from Quechee Gorge. For more information and to sign up for Carla's newsletter, please visit CarlaNeggers.com.

Despite a no-nonsense background as a West Point graduate and US Army officer, **Caro Carson** has always treasured the happily-ever-after of a good romance novel. Now Caro is delighted to be living her own happily-ever-after with her husband and two children in the great state of Florida, a location that has saved the coaster-loving theme-park fanatic a fortune on plane tickets.

New York Times **Bestselling Author**

CARLA NEGGERS

WISCONSIN WEDDING

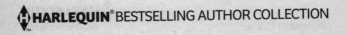

HARLEQUIN® BESTSELLING AUTHOR COLLECTION

ISBN-13: 978-0-373-28483-2

Wisconsin Wedding

Copyright © 2016 by Harlequin Books S.A.

The publisher acknowledges the copyright holders of the individual works as follows:

Wisconsin Wedding
Copyright © 1992 by Harlequin Enterprises B.V.

Special thanks and acknowledgment to Carla Neggers for her contribution to this work.

Special thanks and acknowledgment are given to Joanna Kosloff for her contribution to the concept for the Tyler series.

Doctor, Soldier, Daddy
Copyright © 2013 by Caro Carson

This edition published by arrangement with Harlequin Books S.A.

For questions and comments about the quality of this book, please contact us at CustomerService@Harlequin.com.

® and TM are trademarks of Harlequin Enterprises Limited or its corporate affiliates. Trademarks indicated with ® are registered in the United States Patent and Trademark Office, the Canadian Intellectual Property Office and in other countries.

Recycling programs for this product may not exist in your area.

Printed in U.S.A.

HARLEQUIN®
www.Harlequin.com

CONTENTS

WISCONSIN WEDDING   7
Carla Neggers

DOCTOR, SOLDIER, DADDY   253
Caro Carson

Also by Carla Neggers

Sharpe & Donovan

LIAR'S KEY
KEEPER'S REACH
HARBOR ISLAND
DECLAN'S CROSS
ROCK POINT (novella)
HERON'S COVE
SAINT'S GATE

Swift River Valley

THE SPRING AT MOSS HILL
A KNIGHTS BRIDGE CHRISTMAS
ECHO LAKE
CHRISTMAS AT CARRIAGE HILL
  (novella)
CIDER BROOK
THAT NIGHT ON THISTLE LANE
SECRETS OF THE LOST SUMMER

BPD/FBI Series

THE WHISPER
THE MIST
THE ANGEL
THE WIDOW

Black Falls

COLD DAWN
COLD RIVER
COLD PURSUIT

Cold Ridge/U.S. Marshals

ABANDON
BREAKWATER
DARK SKY
THE RAPIDS
NIGHT'S LANDING
COLD RIDGE

Carriage House

THE HARBOR
STONEBROOK COTTAGE
THE CABIN
THE CARRIAGE HOUSE

Stand-Alone Novels

THE WATERFALL
ON FIRE
KISS THE MOON
TEMPTING FATE
CUT AND RUN
BETRAYALS
CLAIM THE CROWN

Visit carlaneggers.com for more titles.

WISCONSIN WEDDING

Carla Neggers

CHAPTER ONE

WITHIN THE SEDATE, mahogany-paneled president's office of Pierce & Rothchilde, Publishers, Byron Forrester pitched a sharp-pointed dart at the arrogant face of his latest traitorous author. The dart nailed Henry V. Murrow smack in the middle of his neatly clipped beard. Byron grinned. He was getting pretty good at this! Now if Henry had been in the office in person instead of in the form of an eight-by-ten glossy publicity photo, Byron would have been a happy man. Only that morning Henry had called to notify him that he'd just signed a mega-deal with a big New York publisher.

"For what?" Byron had demanded.

"A technothriller."

"What, do you have a dastardly villain threatening to blow up the world with a toaster? You don't know anything about advanced technology. Henry, for God's sake, you haven't even figured out the telegraph yet."

"Research, my boy. Research."

Pierce & Rothchilde didn't publish technothrillers. Its specialties were expensive-to-produce coffee-table books, mostly about art, geography and history, and so-called literary fiction. Some of the latter was deadly stuff. Byron found Henry's books depressing as hell.

Technothrillers. From a man who'd been utterly defeated by the locks on Byron's sports car. "How does one exit from this contraption?" he'd asked.

Now he was calling himself Hank Murrow and planning to make a bloody fortune. Probably had shaved his beard, burned his tweeds, packed his pipe away in mothballs and taken his golden retriever to the pound.

"I wonder how much the fink's really getting."

Byron aimed another dart. Henry—*Hank*—had said seven figures, but Byron didn't believe him. He'd yet to meet a writer who didn't lie about money.

A quiet tap on his solid mahogany door forced him to fold his fingers around the stem of the dart and not throw it. He really wanted to. Henry had offered to send him a copy of his completed manuscript. Byron had declined. "It'll be more fun," Henry had said, "than anything that'll cross your desk this year." A comment all the more irritating for its probable truth. Byron had wished the turncoat well and gotten out his darts.

Without so much as a by-your-leave from him, Fanny Redbacker strode into his office. Trying to catch him throwing darts, no doubt. She regularly made it clear that she didn't think her new boss was any match for her old boss, the venerable Thorton Pierce. Byron considered that good news. His grandfather, whose father had cofounded Pierce & Rothchilde in 1894, had been a brilliant, scrawny old snob of a workaholic. He'd vowed never to retire and hadn't. He'd died in that very office, behind that very desk, five years ago. Byron, although just thirty-eight, had no intention of suffering a similar fate.

"Yes, Mrs. Redbacker?" he said, trying to sound

like the head of one of the country's most prestigious publishing houses.

Mrs. Redbacker, of course, knew better. Stepping forward, she placed an envelope on his desk. Byron saw her eyes cut over to Henry Murrow's dart-riddled face. Her mouth drew into a straight line of disapproval.

"It's tacked to a cork dartboard," Byron said. "I didn't get a mark on the wood paneling."

"What if you'd missed?"

"I never miss."

She inhaled. "The letter's a personal one addressed to you and Mrs. Forrester." Meaning his mother. Byron wasn't married. Mrs. Redbacker added pointedly, "The postmark is Tyler, Wisconsin."

Byron almost stabbed his hand with the dart, so completely did her words catch him off guard. Regaining his composure, he set the thing on his desk. Fanny Redbacker sighed, but didn't say anything. She didn't have to. It had been three months, and Byron still wasn't Thorton Pierce. He didn't even look like him. Where his cultured, imperious grandfather had been sandy-haired and blue-eyed and somewhat washed out in appearance, Byron took after the Forresters. He was tall, if not as tall as the Pierces, and thick-boned and dark, his hair and eyes as dark as his father's had been. For a while everyone had thought that despite his rough-and-ready looks Byron would step neatly into his grandfather's hand-tooled oxfords.

But that was before he'd ventured to Tyler, Wisconsin, three years ago. After that trip, all bets were off.

"Thank you, Mrs. Redbacker."

She retreated without comment.

Byron had forgotten his annoyance with Henry

Murrow. Now all he could think about was the letter on his desk. It was addressed to Mr. Byron Forrester and Mrs. Ann Forrester, c/o Pierce & Rothchilde, Publishers. At a guess, the handwriting looked feminine. It certainly wasn't Cliff's.

"Oh, God," Byron breathed.

Something had happened to Cliff, and now here was the letter informing his younger brother and mother of the bad news.

Nora... Nora Gates had found out who Byron was and had decided to write.

Not a chance. The letter wasn't big enough to hold a bomb. And the scrawl was too undisciplined for precise, would-be spinster Eleanora Gates, owner of Gates Department Store in downtown Tyler, Wisconsin. She was the *last* person Byron wanted to think about now.

He tore open the envelope.

Inside was a simple printed card inviting him and his mother to the wedding of Clifton Pierce Forrester and Mary Elizabeth Baron the Saturday after this in Tyler.

A letter bomb would have surprised Byron less.

There was a note attached.

Cliff's doing great and I know he wants to see you both. Please come. I think it would be best if you just showed up, don't you?
Liza

A hoax? This Liza character had neglected to provide a return address or a phone number, and the invitation didn't request a reply. The wedding was to take place at the Fellowship Lutheran Church. To find out more, presumably, Byron would have to head to Wisconsin.

Was that what Liza Baron wanted?

Who the hell was she?

Was Cliff getting married?

At a guess, Byron thought, his brother didn't know that Miss Liza Baron had fired off an invitation to the sedate Providence offices of Pierce & Rothchilde, Publishers.

Byron leaned back in his leather chair and closed his eyes.

Tyler, Wisconsin.

A thousand miles away and three years later and he could still feel the warm sun of a Midwest August on his face. He could see the corn standing tall in the rolling fields outside Tyler and the crowd gathered in the town square for a summer band concert. He could hear old Ellie Gates calling out the winner of the quilt raffle, to raise money for repairing the town clock. First prize was a hand-stitched quilt of intersecting circles. Byron later learned that its design was called Wisconsin Wedding, a variation on the traditional wedding ring design created by Tyler's own quilting ladies.

And he could hear her laugh. Nora's laugh. It wasn't her fake spinsterish laugh he heard, but the laugh that was soft and free, unrestrained by the peculiar myths that dominated her life.

He'd gone to Tyler once and had almost destroyed Nora Gates. He'd almost destroyed himself. And his brother. How could he go back?

Please come....

Byron had waited for years to be invited back into his older brother's life. There'd been Vietnam, Cambodia, a hospital in the Philippines, sporadic attempts at normality. And then nothing. For five years, nothing.

Now this strange invitation—out of the blue—to his brother's wedding.

A woman named Alyssa Baron had helped the burned-out recluse make a home at an abandoned lodge on a lake outside town. Was Liza Baron her daughter?

So many questions, Byron thought.

And so many dangers. Too many, perhaps.

He picked up his last dart. If he or his mother—or both—just showed up in Tyler after all these years, what would Cliff do? What if their presence sent him back over the edge? Liza Baron might have good intentions, but did she know what she was doing in making this gesture to her fiancé's estranged family?

But upsetting Cliff wasn't Byron's biggest fear. They were brothers. Cliff had gone away because of his love for and his loyalty to his family. That much Byron understood.

No, his biggest fear was of a slim, tawny-haired Tylerite who'd fancied herself a grand Victorian old maid at thirty, in an era when nobody believed in old maids. What would proper, pretty Nora Gates do if he showed up in her hometown again?

Byron sat up straight. "She'd come after you, my man." He fired his dart. "With a blowtorch."

The pointed tip of the dart penetrated the polished mahogany paneling with a loud *thwack*, missing Henry Murrow's nose by a good eight inches.

The Nora Gates effect.

He was probably the only man on earth who knew that she wasn't anything like the refined, soft-spoken spinster lady she pretended she was. For that, she hated his guts. Her parting words to him three years ago had been, "Then leave, you despicable cad."

Only Nora.

But even worse, he suspected he was the only man who'd ever lied to her and gotten away with it. At least so far. When he'd left Tyler three years ago, Nora hadn't realized he'd lied. And since she hadn't come after him with a bucket of hot tar, he assumed she still didn't realize he had.

If he returned to Tyler, however, she'd know for sure.

And then what?

"Miss Gates?"

Nora recognized the voice on the telephone—it was that of Mrs. Mickelson in china and housewares, around the corner from Nora's office on the third floor. For a few months after Aunt Ellie's death three years ago, the staff at Gates Department Store hadn't quite known how to address the young Eleanora Gates. Most had been calling her Nora for years, but now that she was their boss that just wouldn't do. And "Ms. Gates" simply didn't sound right. So they settled, without any discussion that Nora knew about, on Miss Gates—the same thing they'd called her aunt. It was as if nothing had changed. And in many ways, nothing had.

"I have Liza Baron here," Mrs. Mickelson said.

Nora settled back in the rosewood chair Aunt Ellie had bought in Milwaukee in 1925. "Oh?"

"She's here to fill out her bridal registry, but...well, you know Miss Baron. She's grumbling about feudalistic rituals. I'm afraid I just don't know what to say."

"Send her into my office," Nora said, stifling a

laugh. Despite her years away from Tyler, Liza Baron obviously hadn't changed. "I'll be glad to handle this one for you."

Claudia Mickelson made no secret of her relief as she hung up. It wasn't that Nora was any better equipped for the task of keeping Liza Baron happy. It was, simply, that should Liza screech out of town in a blue funk and get Cliff Forrester to elope with her, thus denying its grandest wedding since Chicago socialite Margaret Lindstrom married Tyler's own Judson Ingalls some fifty years before, it would be on Nora's head.

Five minutes later, Mrs. Mickelson and the unlikely bride burst into Nora's sedate office. Mrs. Mickelson surrendered catalogs and the bridal registry book, wished Liza well and retreated. Liza plopped down on the caned chair in front of the elegant but functional rosewood desk. Wearing a multicolored serape over a bright orange top and skinny black leggings, Liza Baron was as stunning and outrageous and completely herself as Nora remembered. That she'd fallen head over heels in love with the town's recluse didn't surprise Nora in the least. Liza Baron had always had a mind of her own. Anyway, love was like that. It was an emotion Nora didn't necessarily trust.

"This was all my mother's idea," Liza announced.

"It usually is." Nora, a veteran calmer of bridal jitters, smiled. "A bridal register makes life much easier for the mother of the bride. Otherwise, people continually call and ask her for suggestions of what to buy as a wedding gift. It gets tiresome, and if she gives the wrong advice, it's all too easy for her to be blamed."

Liza scowled. There was talk around town—not

that Nora was one to give credence to talk—that Liza just might hop into her little white car and blow out of town as fast and suddenly as she'd blown in. Not because she didn't love Cliff Forrester, but because she so obviously did. Only this morning Nora had overheard two members of her staff speculating on the potential effects on Liza's unusual fiancé of a big wedding and marrying into one of Tyler's first families. Would he be able to tolerate all the attention? Would he bolt? Would he go off the deep end?

"Well," Liza said, "the whole thing strikes me as sexist and mercenary."

Liza Baron had always been one to speak her mind, something Nora admired. She herself also valued directness, even if her own manner was somewhat more diplomatic. "You have a point, but I don't think that's the intent."

"You don't see anybody dragging *Cliff* down here to pick out china patterns, do you?"

"No, that wouldn't be the custom."

It was enough of a shock, Nora thought, to see Liza Baron with a catalog of Wedgwood designs in front of her. But if Liza was somewhat nontraditional, Cliff Forrester— Well, for years townspeople had wondered if they ought to fetch an expert in posttraumatic stress disorder from Milwaukee to have a look at him, make sure his gray matter was what it should be. He'd lived alone at Timberlake Lodge for at least five years, maybe longer. He'd kept to himself for the most part and, as far as anyone knew, had never hurt anyone. Nora had long ago decided that most of the talk about him was just that: talk. She figured he was a modern-day hermit pretty much as she was a modern-day spinster—by choice. It didn't mean either of them had a screw loose. Cliff, of course, had met Liza Baron and chosen to end his isolation. Nora had no intention of ending hers.

"If I were in your place," she went on, "I'd consider this a matter of practicality. Do you want to end up with three silver tea services?"

Liza shuddered. "I don't want *one* silver tea service."

Nora marked that down. "When people don't know what the bride and groom want, they tend to buy what *they* would want. It's human nature. It's to be a big wedding, isn't it?"

"Mother's doing. She's got half of Tyler coming. Cliff and I would have been happy getting married by a justice of the peace without any fanfare."

That, Nora felt, wasn't entirely true. Cliff no doubt dreaded facing a crowd, but would do it for Liza—and for her mother, too, who'd been his only real friend for years. But in Nora's estimation, Liza Baron relished being the center of attention again in Tyler. It wasn't that she was spoiled or snobby; she was still getting used to having finally come home to Tyler at all, never mind planning to marry and stay there. It was more that she wasn't sure how she was supposed to act now that she was home again. She needed to find a way to weave herself into the fabric of the community on her own terms. The wedding was, in part, beautiful vivacious Liza's way of welcoming the people of her small hometown back into her life. As far as Nora was concerned, it was perfectly natural that occasionally Liza would seem ambivalent, even hostile. In addition to the stress of a big church wedding, she was also coping with her once-tattered relationship with her mother, and all the gossip about the Ingalls and Baron families.

And that included the body that had turned up at the lake. But Nora wasn't about to bring up that particular tidbit.

She discreetly glanced at the antique grandfather clock that occupied the corner behind Liza. Of the office furnishings, only the calendar, featuring birds of Wisconsin, had changed since Aunt Ellie's day.

"Oh, all right," Liza said with great drama, "I'm here. Let's do this thing. The prospect of coping with stacks of plastic place mats with scenes of Wisconsin and a dozen gravy boats does give one pause."

Gates carried both items Liza considered offensive. Nora herself owned a set of Wisconsin place mats. She used them for picnics and when the neighborhood children wandered into her kitchen for milk and cookies. Her favorite was the one featuring Tyler's historic library. She didn't tell Liza that she was bound to get at least one set of Wisconsin place mats. Inger Hansen, one of the quilting ladies, had bought Wisconsin place mats for every wedding she'd attended since they first came on the market in 1972. Nora had been in high school then, working at Gates part-time.

They got down to business. "Now," Nora explained to her reluctant customer, "here's how the bridal register works. You list your china, silverware and glassware patterns, any small appliances you want, sheets, towels, table linens. There are any number of variables, depending on what you and Cliff want."

Liza wrinkled up her pretty face. She was, Nora saw, a terribly attractive woman. She herself was of average height and build, with a tendency to cuteness that she did her best to disguise with sophisticated—but not too chic—business clothes and makeup. She didn't own a single article of clothing in pink, no flowered or heart-shaped anything, no polka dots, no T-shirts with pithy sayings, damned little lace. No serapes, no bright orange tops, no skinny black leggings. She preferred cool, subdued colors to offset her pale gray eyes and ash-blond hair, which she kept in a classic bob. Liza Baron, on the other hand, would look wild in anything. Cast them each in a commercial, and Judson Ingalls's rebellious granddaughter would sell beer, Ellie Gates's grandniece life insurance.

"Nora, Cliff doesn't want anything. He'd be happy living in a damned cave."

But, as Nora had anticipated, in the quiet and privacy of the third floor office, with its window overlooking the Tyler town square, Liza Baron warmed to her task. She briskly dismissed anything too cute or too simple and resisted the most expensive patterns Gates carried. She finally settled on an elegant and dramatic china pattern from England, American silverplate flatware, a couple of small appliances, white linens all around, Brazilian knives and a special request to please discourage can openers. The stemware gave her the worst fits. Finally she admitted it was Waterford or nothing.

"Go for it," Nora said, amused. She tried to picture Cliff Forrester drinking from a Waterford goblet and found—strangely—that she could. Had someone said he was from a prominent East Coast family? Like most people in Tyler, Nora knew next to nothing about the mysterious, quiet man who lived at run-down Timberlake Lodge.

Liza slumped back in the delicate caned chair. "Is it too late to elope?"

"People would still buy you gifts."

Their work done, a silence fell between the two women. Despite her busy schedule, Nora was in no hurry to rush Liza out. The young woman had gone through a lot in the past weeks, and if the rumors circulating in the shops, restaurants and streets of Tyler were even remotely on target, she had more to endure. Falling in love with an outsider had certainly been enough to stimulate gossip, even undermine Liza's beliefs about what she wanted out of her life. In Nora's view, that right there was enough reason to steer clear of men: romance caused change.

It was as if Liza had read her mind. "You've never been married, have you, Nora?"

"No, I haven't. I like my life just the way it is."

Liza smiled. "Good for you. Have you ever been tempted?"

Nora's hesitation, she was sure, was noticeable only to herself. "Nope."

"Well, I certainly don't believe a woman has to be married to be happy or complete."

"But you're happy with Cliff."

"Yes." Her smile broadened. "Yes, I am."

Indeed, falling so completely in love with Cliff Forrester had already had an unmistakable effect on one of Tyler's most rebellious citizens. Liza Baron, however, seemed much more willing to embrace change than Nora was. She seemed much more at peace with herself than she had when she'd first blown back into town, if a little rattled at the prospect of a big Tyler wedding.

Nora shrugged. "Romance doesn't have a positive

effect on me, I'm afraid. It makes me crazy and silly...
I lose control."

Liza's eyes widened in surprise, as if she'd never
imagined Nora Gates having had anything approaching a romance, and she grinned. "Isn't that the whole
idea?"

"I suppose for some, but I—" Nora stopped herself in the nick of time. What was she saying? "Well,
I'm speaking theoretically, of course. I've never... I'm
not one for romantic notions." A fast change of subject was in order. "How're the renovations at the lodge
coming?"

"Fabulously well. Better than I expected, really,
given all that's gone on. You should come out and
take a look."

"I'd love to," Nora said, meaning it. As if marriage
and her return to Tyler weren't stressful enough, Liza
had also come up with the idea of renovating Timberlake Lodge, a monumental project Nora personally
found exciting. Unfortunately, the work had led to the
discovery of a human skeleton on the premises. Not
the sort of thing one wanted percolating on the back
burner while planning one's wedding.

"Anytime. And thank you, Nora."

"Oh, you don't need to thank me—"

Liza shook her head. "No, I've been acting like a big
baby and you've been so nice about it. The store looks
great, by the way. Your aunt would be proud, I'm sure.
You've added your own touches, but retained the flavor and spirit everyone always remembers about Gates.
When I think I'm living in the boondocks, I just walk
past your windows and realize there is indeed taste and
culture here in Tyler." She hesitated a moment, some-

thing uncharacteristic of Judson Ingalls's youngest grandchild. "Ellie Gates was quite a character. She's still missed around here."

"She is," Nora agreed simply.

"Well, I should be off." Liza rose with a sudden burst of energy. "I guess I'll go through with this big fancy wedding. If nothing else, Tyler could use a good party right now."

Now Liza Baron was sounding like herself. Nora swept to her feet. "You're probably right about that. I suppose you haven't heard anything more from the police?"

Liza shook her head. "Not a word."

Without saying so outright, they both knew they were talking about what Nora had begun to refer to as the Body at the Lake. The *Tyler Citizen* reported every new and not-so-new development in the case, but the rumors were far more speculative. Given her ownership of Tyler's only department store, her membership on the town council and her circumspect nature, Nora was privy to considerable amounts of local gossip, which she never repeated. Certainly *anyone* could have been buried at the long-abandoned lodge. Someone from out of town or out of state could have driven up, plucked a body out of the trunk, dug a hole and dropped it in. But townspeople's imaginations were fired by the idea that the body was that of Tyler's most famous—actually, its only—missing person, Margaret Alyssa Lindstrom Ingalls. People said Liza was a lot like her flamboyant grandmother. Bad enough, Nora thought, that Liza had to cope with having a dead body dug up in her yard. Worse that it could be that of her long-lost grandmother.

"I'll continue to hope for the best," Nora said diplomatically.

Liza's smile this time was feeble. "Thank you."

But before she left, she spun around one more time, serape flying. "Oh, I almost forgot. Cliff specifically wanted me to ask if you were coming to the wedding. You are, aren't you?"

"Well, yes, I'd love to, but I've never even met Cliff—"

"Oh, he's seen you around town and admires your devotion to Tyler and...how did he put it? Your balance, I think he said. He says if he has to endure a huge wedding, he should at least have a few people around who won't make him feel uncomfortable." Liza's eyes misted, her expression softening. She looked like a woman in love. "God knows he's trying. He's still uneasy around people—I guess you could call this wedding a trial by fire. Not only will half of Tyler be there, but there's a chance his family'll come, too."

"I didn't realize he had any family."

"A mother and a brother." Liza bit the corner of her mouth, suddenly unsure of herself. "They're from Providence."

"Providence, Rhode Island?" Nora asked, her knees weakening.

"Umm. Real East Coast mucky-mucks."

Byron Sanders, the one man who'd penetrated Nora's defenses, had been from Providence, Rhode Island. But that had to be a coincidence. That wretched cad couldn't have anything to do with a man like Cliff Forrester.

"Are they coming?" Nora asked.

Liza cleared her throat hesitantly. "Haven't heard.

From what I gather, our wedding's pretty quick for a Forrester, so who knows?"

"Cliff must be anxious—"

"Oh, no, I don't think so. He hasn't had much to do with his family since he moved out here. Nothing at all, in fact. He takes all the blame, but I don't think that's fair. He didn't tell them where he was for a couple of years, but when he did finally let them know, he told them to leave him alone. But they could have bulldozed their way back into his life if they'd really wanted to." She grinned. "Just like I did."

"But Cliff did invite them?"

"Well, not exactly."

Nora didn't need a sledgehammer to get the point. "You mean *you* did? Without his knowledge?"

"Yep."

Now that, Nora thought, could get interesting.

"I guess we'll just have to see how it goes," Liza added.

With a polite, dismissive comment, Nora promised Liza that she and her staff would steer people in the right direction when they came to Gates hunting for an appropriate wedding gift. Liza looked so relieved and happy when she left that Nora felt much better. Why on earth was she worrying about Byron Sanders, just because he and Cliff Forrester were from the same state? Rhode Island wasn't *that* small. No, that weasel was just a black, secret chapter in her life.

She tucked the bridal register under her arm to return to Claudia Mickelson. She did love a wedding—as long as it wasn't her own.

CHAPTER TWO

"I DON'T KNOW how Liza Baron can even *think* about getting married with this body business unresolved."

Inger Hansen's starchy words stopped Nora in her tracks. It was two days after Liza had sat in her office grumbling about feudalistic rituals while thumbing through a Waterford crystal catalog. As was her custom on Thursdays, when she gave piano lessons, Nora was moving toward Gates Department Store's rear exit shortly before five. She usually didn't leave until six.

Inger, the most imperious member of the Tyler Quilting Circle, went on indignantly, "That could be her grandmother they found out there."

Martha Bauer held up two different shades of off-white thread. It was just a show; she'd been buying the same shade for thirty years. "Well, I do wish they'd tell us something soon," she said with a sigh. "Don't you think they've had that body up at the county long enough to know *something?*"

"I understand that the body's a skeleton already," Rose Atkins, one of the sweetest and most eccentric elderly women in Tyler, said. "Identification must be a difficult process under such circumstances. And it would be terrible if they made a mistake, don't you think? I'd prefer them to take their time and get it right."

Nora agreed, and found herself edging toward the

fabric department's counter. Stella, the fabric clerk and a woman known for her sewing expertise, was occupied sorting a new shipment of buttons. Nora didn't blame her for not rushing to the quilting ladies' assistance; they knew their way around the department and would likely chatter on until the store's closing at six.

Inger Hansen sniffed. "In my opinion, the police are dragging their heels. No one wants to confront the real possibility that it's Margaret Ingalls they found out at the lake."

"Now, Inger," Rose said patiently, "we don't know for sure it's Margaret. The body hasn't even been identified yet as male or female."

"Oh, it's Margaret all right."

Martha Bauer discarded the wrong shade of off-white thread. "And what if it is?" She looked uncomfortable and a little pale. "That could mean…"

Inger jumped right in. "It could mean Margaret Ingalls was murdered."

"My heavens," Martha breathed.

"I never did think she ran away," Inger added, although in all the years Nora had known her she'd never given such an indication. "It just wasn't like Margaret to slip out of town in the cloak of darkness."

Rose Atkins inhaled, clearly upset by such talk, and moved to the counter with a small, rolled piece of purple calico she'd found on the bargain table. "Why, Nora, I didn't see you. How are you?"

"Just fine, Mrs. Atkins. Here, let me take that for you."

Off to their left, Martha Bauer and Inger Hansen continued their discussion of the Body at the Lake. "Now, you can think me catty," Inger said, "but I, for one, have always wondered what Judson Ingalls knew about his wife's disappearance. I'm not accusing him of anything untoward, of course, but I do think—and have thought for forty years—that it's strange he's hardly lifted a finger to find her in all this time. He could certainly afford to hire a dozen private detectives, but he hasn't."

"Oh, stop." Martha snatched up a spool of plain white all-cotton thread in addition to her off-white. "Margaret left him a note saying she was leaving him. Why should he have put himself and Alyssa through the added turmoil of looking for a wife who'd made it plain she wanted nothing more to do with him? No, I think he did the right thing in putting the matter behind him and carrying on with his life. What else could he have done? And in my opinion, that's not Margaret they found out at the lake."

Inger tucked a big bag of cotton batting under one arm. "Of course, I don't like to gossip, but whoever it was, I can't see Liza Baron and that recluse getting married with this dark cloud hanging over their heads. You'd think they'd wait."

"Oh, Inger," Martha said, laughing all of a sudden. "Honestly. Why should Liza put her life on hold? Now, would you look at this lovely gabardine?" Deftly she changed the subject.

Nora took a few dollars from Rose Atkins for her fabric scrap. As had been the custom at Gates since it opened its doors seventy years ago, Nora tucked the receipt and Rose's money into a glass-and-brass tube, which she then tucked into a chute to be pneumatically sucked up to the third floor office. There the head clerk would log the sale and send back the receipt and any change. None of the salesclerks handled any cash, checks or credit cards. The system was remarkably fast and efficient, contributing an old-fashioned charm to the store that its customers seemed to relish.

"Everybody's gone to computers these days," Rose commented. "It's such a relief to come in here and not have anything beep at me. Have you seen those light wands that read price stickers?" She shuddered; the world had changed a lot in Rose Atkins's long life. "You've no plans to switch to something like that, have you?"

"None at all."

That much Nora could say with certainty. In her opinion, computers didn't go with Gates's original wood-and-glass display cases, its Tiffany ceilings, its sweeping staircases and brass elevators, its gleaming polished tile floors. Tradition and an unrivaled reputation for service were what set Gates apart from malls and discount department stores. As Aunt Ellie had before her, Nora relied on value, quality, convenience and style to compete. At Gates, Tyler's elderly women could still find a good housedress, its children could buy their Brownie and Cub Scout uniforms, its parents could find sturdy, traditional children's and baby clothes. The fabric department kept a wide range of calico fabrics for Tyler's quilting ladies. There was an office-supply department for local businesses, a wide-ranging book section for local readers, a lunch counter for hungry shoppers. Nora prided herself on meeting the changing needs of her community. As far as she was concerned, tradition was not only elusive in a fast-paced world, it was also priceless.

The tube returned, and she slipped out Rose's change and receipt.

"Have you seen much of Liza Baron since she's come home?" Rose asked.

"She came in a couple of days ago to fill out her bridal registry," Nora replied. "But other than that, no."

Rose's eyes widened, no doubt at the prospect of wild, rebellious Liza doing anything as expected of her as filling out a bridal registry, but, a discreet woman, she resisted comment.

Behind her, Inger Hansen did no such thing. "I can't imagine Liza would want to do anything so normal. She's so much like her grandmother. You don't remember Margaret Ingalls, Nora, but she was just as wild and unpredictable as Liza Baron. It's odd, though. Your great-aunt and Margaret managed to get along amazingly well. I have no idea why. They were complete opposites."

"Ellie was always extremely tolerant of people," Martha Bauer put in.

"Yes," Inger said. Even tart-tongued Inger Hansen had respected and admired Ellie Gates.

"I'm sure it'll be a wonderful wedding," Nora said, half-wishing she hadn't delayed her departure to serve the quilters. Liza Baron and Cliff Forrester's upcoming wedding was indeed the talk of the town, but it was having an effect on Nora that she couldn't figure out. Was it because Cliff was from Rhode Island?

No. She'd put Byron Sanders out of her mind months and months ago. If the wedding was unsettling her it had to be because of the ongoing mystery of the identity of the body found at Timberlake.

Stella scooted behind Nora. "Here, Miss Gates, let me help these customers."

Nora backed off, and with Inger Hansen wondering aloud how Liza could have ended up with that "strange man living out at the lake," ducked out the rear exit.

Even if Liza Baron had been a fly on the wall during the past fifteen minutes, she wouldn't have cared one whit what the quilting ladies were saying about her and Cliff—she'd marry whenever and whoever she wanted. Liza had a thumb-your-nose-at-the-world quality that Nora appreciated. Nora wondered if *she* was ever the subject of local gossip. Not likely. Oh, her latest window display always received plenty of attention, and the time she'd added a wheelchair ramp to one of the entrances had gotten people talking about accessibility and such. And folks had talked when, after much soul-searching and calculating how few were sold, she'd ceased to stock men's overalls. But nobody, she was quite certain, talked about *her*. Her personal life.

"That's because it's dull, dull, dull."

But wasn't that exactly what she wanted?

The crisp, clear autumn air lifted her spirits. It was getting dark; the streetlights were already on, casting a pale glow on the bright yellow leaves still clinging to the intrepid maples that lined the perimeter of the parking lot. The feeling that life was passing her by vanished as quickly as it had overtaken her. *This* was life, at least hers. Small-town Midwest America. So it wasn't Providence, Rhode Island. So it wasn't wandering place to place with an elitist East Coast photographer who neither understood her nor the community she cared about. She belonged in Tyler. It was her home, and if it was Byron Sanders's idea of hell, then so be it.

He was a cretin anyway.

Coincidence or not, Cliff Forrester's own Rhode Island origins had gotten her thinking about the rake who'd almost ruined her life. For two days running now. She couldn't make herself stop.

Well, she had to. Rhode Island might be a small state, but the chances of Tyler's town recluse and a sneaky photographer having any knowledge of each other were remote. And Byron Sanders wasn't from any "mucky-muck" East Coast family.

He also knew to keep his size elevens out of Tyler, Wisconsin.

But he'd been her one love, and he remained her one secret. *No* one knew they'd been lovers. Not even Tisha Olsen over at the Hair Affair, who knew everything that went on in Tyler, or the quilting ladies, whose combined knowledge of the town's social history went all the way back to its founding during the great German immigration to Wisconsin 140 years ago. As far as everyone in Tyler was concerned, Nora was just like her great-aunt, the memorable Ellie Gates.

Only she wasn't. And she knew it.

So did Byron Sanders.

She was so preoccupied that she arrived at the doorstep of her 1920s house before she even realized she'd come to her tree-lined street. She'd inherited the house from Aunt Ellie. They'd lived together from the death of Nora's parents in a boating accident on Lake Superior when she was thirteen until Aunt Ellie's death three years ago, not long after Byron Sanders had moved on. In the house's quiet rooms and in Aunt

Ellie's quiet life, Nora had found peace and stability and hope.

She'd had the wide clapboards repainted last summer in the same cream color Aunt Ellie had chosen back in 1926. The trim was pure white. It was almost Halloween, but the porch swing was still out, the flower boxes planted with bright yellow mums.

With the house having been shut up all day, Nora left the front door open to catch the afternoon breeze while she went back to the kitchen. It was still thirty minutes before her first student arrived. Time enough for a cup of tea.

She'd made a few changes to the interior of the house, softening some of Aunt Ellie's relentless formality. She'd covered the furniture in pale neutrals and had added cotton throw rugs, Depression glass, quilted pastel wall hangings. There were two small bedrooms upstairs, one downstairs, a small library, a living room and a dining room that she'd converted into a music room, shoving the gateleg table up against the wall to make room for a new baby grand.

Nora, however, hadn't changed a thing in the kitchen. Its white cabinets, pale gray-blue walls and yellow accents didn't need changing so far as she could see. Her friends said she should get a microwave, but she hadn't yet succumbed. Before she died, Aunt Ellie had purchased a toaster oven. It still worked fine.

After putting on the kettle for tea, Nora sat at the kitchen table and looked out at her darkening yard. The bright leaves of the sugar maple had already fallen to the ground. Lately, birds had taken to fattening themselves at her bird feeders. Soon it would be completely dark. Winter wasn't far off.

She sighed. She loved autumn; she even loved winter. So why was she hovering on the edge of depression?

She fixed a proper tea: Earl Grey tea leaves, her English porcelain pot, her matching cup and saucer, milk in a tiny milk glass pitcher. A sterling silver spoon. Homemade butter cookies from her favorite bakery. She put everything on a teak tray, which she carried out to the music room.

And nearly dropped it all on the floor.

Moving with the speed and silence of a panther, Cliff Forrester took the tray from her and set it one-handed on the gateleg table. "I didn't mean to startle you," he said.

In his five years in Tyler, those were the first words Nora remembered his ever saying to her. She'd bumped into him on occasion at the hardware store, but Liza Baron's fiancé had made clear he didn't want to be disturbed at Timberlake Lodge. He wanted to be left alone. To heal his wounds and chase his demons or do whatever it was he did. Nora had heard all the rumors and possibilities. He was a tall, dark man. He didn't look like...how had Liza put it? Like his family were East Coast mucky-mucks.

"It's quite all right," she said, sounding stuffy even to herself. "I was expecting a piano student."

"You play?"

"Mmm, yes."

His brow furrowed. "I didn't know."

How could he have known? They'd never even officially met until now. "Would you care for a cup of tea? I made more than enough. I always end up having to throw out half the pot."

He shook his head. "No thanks."

And then he smiled. Nora found it an unsettling experience, but she couldn't pinpoint why. She felt no attraction to Liza's lover. It wasn't *that* at all. Then what? *Men in general,* she thought, disgusted with herself. *Tall, dark men from Rhode Island in particular.*

Too darned much thinking, she added to herself.

"Are you all right?" Cliff Forrester asked.

She nodded. "Perfectly."

"I gather you know who I am."

"Cliff Forrester. Yes, I think everyone in town knows."

The corners of his mouth twitched in an ironic smile. "I guess so. Look, I won't keep you, Miss Gates."

"Nora," she corrected.

"Nora, then." His dark eyes probed her a moment. "I came by because of Liza. She was grateful for the way you treated her the other day."

"I'd do the same for any of my customers, Mr.—"

"Cliff. And I think you would. Liza and I are…" He paused, seeming awkward, even pained. "We want this to work."

Nora thought she understood what he was trying to say. The Body at the Lake, the wedding, Alyssa Baron, Judson Ingalls, Liza's return to Tyler, the incessant gossip, long-lost Margaret Ingalls—it was a lot. And then there was Cliff Forrester himself. A recluse. A man uncomfortable around even small crowds. A man, it was said, afraid that something, someone, would trigger a bad memory and he'd crack. Hurt himself. Worse yet, hurt someone he cared about.

"Is there anything I can do?" Nora asked, instinctively wanting to help.

He seemed to relax, at least slightly. "If there's anything you can think of to help Liza through this thing, I'd appreciate it. She doesn't want to alienate anyone. She's trying."

Wasn't that what Liza herself had said about him? Nora found their concern for each other touching. This, she thought, was what love and romance were about. Two people coming together as individuals, not asking the other to change, not demanding perfection, not expecting fantasies to come true. Just loving and accepting each other and perhaps growing together.

"I wouldn't be interfering?"

"No."

He was, she thought, a man who knew his own mind. "Then I'll see what I can do."

His smile was back, or what passed for one. "Thank you."

"No need. It won't be long before Liza feels at home again in Tyler. She has family and friends, Cliff. They'll be here for her."

"I'm glad you already are," he said, and before she could respond, he was out the door.

Nora debated a whole two seconds, then went after him, catching him on the front porch. "Cliff?"

He turned, and there was something about him as he stood against the dark night—something both dangerous and sensitive—that hinted at his pain and complexity. Liza Baron hadn't solved all his problems. Nora suddenly wished she'd just sat down and drunk her tea instead of following him out. But what to do about it now?

She licked her lips. "Um—Liza mentioned that you're from Rhode Island originally. I was...well, I knew someone from Rhode Island once." She sounded ridiculous! "It was a while ago, but I—"

"Who?"

She swallowed. She'd never said his name aloud, not in public. "A guy by the name of Sanders. Byron Sanders."

Cliff Forrester remained stock-still on her porch step, staring at her through dark eyes that had become slits. Nora chose not to dwell on all the more lurid rumors about him.

"He's a photographer," she added quickly. "He did a series a few years back on Aunt Ellie. It was printed in one of the Chicago papers—"

"I'd like to see it."

"Well, I have a copy in my library—"

"Get it."

His words were millimeters shy of being an order, but there was a curious intensity to his tone, almost a desperation, that Nora detected but couldn't explain. Cursing herself for having brought up that cretin's name, she dashed to her study, dug out the scrapbook and ran back to the porch. Cliff Forrester hadn't moved.

She showed him the spread Byron Sanders had done on Aunt Ellie just weeks before she died. Picking the winner of the quilt raffle. At her desk in her old-fashioned office. In her rose garden. In her rocking chair on her front porch. In front of the department store she'd started, on her own, in 1924. Nora had every photograph memorized. It was as if each shot captured a part of Aunt Ellie's soul and together recreated the woman she'd been, made her come to life. Whatever his shortcomings as a man, Byron Sanders was unarguably a gifted photographer.

"This Byron Sanders," Cliff Forrester said, tight-lipped. "Is he a friend of yours?"

"No!"

His eyes narrowed. "Did he hurt you?"

She shook her head. Through Byron Sanders, she'd managed to hurt herself. She took full responsibility for her own actions. Which didn't mitigate her distaste for him. "No. I just remember he's from Rhode Island and wondered if you knew him."

"No," Cliff said. "No, I don't know Byron Sanders at all."

THE WAY BYRON figured it, he was dead meat. If Nora Gates didn't kill him, his brother surely would. Slumped down in the nondescript car he'd rented in Milwaukee, he watched Cliff head toward the center of town. He looked grim. Byron felt pretty grim himself. His jaw had begun to ache from gritting his teeth. He forced his mouth open just enough to emit something between a sigh and a growl.

No, I don't know any Byron Sanders at all....

It was all Byron had heard, but it was enough. His return to Tyler wasn't going to be all sweetness and light. Nora was already on the lookout for him, and now his brother had to have figured out that he'd been to Tyler before. Not a good start. When Nora found out that he'd lied, he'd be lucky to get out of town with all his body parts intact. When Cliff found out he'd sneaked into Tyler three years ago to make sure he was all right *and* had lied, he'd be—

"You're dead meat, my man," he muttered to himself.

He took heart that Cliff didn't fit any of the images that had haunted him for so long. He wasn't scrawny, scraggly, bug-infested or crazy. He looked alive and well and, other than that crack about his younger brother, reasonably happy. For that, Byron was grateful.

He loosened his tight grip on the steering wheel. Coming to Tyler ten days early had been his mother's idea. He'd phoned her in London, where she was visiting one of Pierce & Rothchilde's most prominent, if not bestselling, authors, one who'd become a personal friend. Anne Forrester was a strong, kind woman who'd endured too much. She'd lost a husband and had all but lost a son.

"But this note," she'd said, "leaves more questions unanswered than answered."

"I know."

"Do you suppose he really wants us there?"

"There's no way of knowing."

For years, Cliff had maintained that he didn't dare be around his family for fear of inflicting more pain on them. He didn't trust himself, not just with his brother and mother, but with anyone. So he'd left. Withdrawn from society. Turned into a recluse at an abandoned lodge on a faraway lake in Wisconsin. His absence, on top of her husband's horrible captivity and death in Cambodia, had been particularly difficult for Anne Forrester, but she was made of stern stuff and disliked showing emotion. She blamed herself to some degree for having let Cliff go to Cambodia to try and do something for his father. Blamed herself for not being able to do something to ease the pain of his own ordeal in Southeast Asia.

"You have no idea who this Liza Baron is?" his mother had asked.

"The Barons are a prominent family in Tyler."

Byron had chosen his next words carefully. "I remember meeting an Alyssa Baron. She's the woman who sort of took Cliff under her wing. Liza could be her daughter."

Anne Forrester didn't speak for the next two minutes. Although the call was overseas long distance, Byron hadn't rushed her. She needed to regain her balance. Rational and not prone to jealousy, she nonetheless had had a difficult time facing the fact that Cliff had allowed another woman to at least try to help him, where he'd only run from her. Even if Alyssa Baron was on the periphery of Cliff's life, she was at least in a small way part of it. His mother wasn't. But that, Byron knew, was precisely the point: far away, Cliff couldn't cause his mother—or his brother—further pain and suffering. Or so he thought.

"Maybe there's hope yet," she said finally, in a near whisper. "Oh, Byron, if he's happy...if he's *trying*..."

"I know, Mother."

"I can't get out of here until at least the first part of next week. What's your schedule like? I'm not sure we should both barrel in on Cliff for the wedding if we're not entirely certain he wants us there." She was thinking out loud, Byron realized, and he didn't interrupt or argue. "Unless there is no wedding and this is Cliff's way...well, that would be ridiculous. Not like him at all. He'd never play a trick like that on us, would he?"

"No," Byron had said with certainty.

"Would this Liza Baron?"

"I wouldn't think so."

"It's just all so...sudden. What if someone's using the wedding as a ploy to get us out there? You know, upset the applecart and see what happens?"

"It's a possibility," Byron had allowed, "but not a serious one, I would think."

Anne Forrester sighed heavily. "Then he *is* getting married."

In the end, Byron had agreed to go to Tyler ahead of time and play scout, find out what he and his mother would be walking into in ten days' time. None of the myriad excuses Byron could think of to keep him in Providence would have worked, so he didn't even bother to try. The truth was he'd do anything to see his brother again, even go up against Nora Gates. Hell, they were both adults. She'd just have to endure his presence in Tyler and trust him to keep quiet about their "tawdry affair" three years before.

She'd only, he recalled, talked like a defiled Victorian virgin when she was truly pissed off.

He'd half hoped she'd forgotten all about him.

Of course, she hadn't. Eleanora Gates wouldn't forget anything, least of all the man who'd "robbed" her of her virginity. She'd conveniently forgotten that she'd been a more than willing participant. And he hadn't told her he'd thought he loved her.

He exhaled slowly, trying to look on the positive. The shattered man his brother had been for so long—too long—seemed mostly a bad memory. For that, Byron was thankful. But Nora…

Before he could change his mind, he popped open his seat belt and jumped out of the car. She'd already gone back inside. Except for the masses of yellow mums, the front porch was unchanged from his last visit, when Aunt Ellie had still reigned over Gates Department Store. She'd been a powerful force in Nora's life. Maybe too powerful. Ellie had sensed that, articulating her fears to Byron.

"The store will be Nora's," she'd told him. "It's all I have to give her. But I don't want it to become a burden to her—it never was to me. If it had, I'd have done something. I never let my life be ruled by that store. Nora knows, I hope, that I won't roll over in my grave if she decides to sell. The only thing that'll make me come back to haunt her is if she tries to be anyone but herself. Including me."

A perceptive woman, the elder Eleanora Gates. Byron remembered feeling distinctly uncomfortable, even sad, although he'd only known the eccentric Aunt Ellie little more than a week. "What's all this talk about what will happen after you're gone?"

Gripping his hand, she'd laughed her distinctive, almost cackling laugh. "Byron, my good friend, you and I both know I'm on Sunset Road."

It was her self-awareness, her self-acceptance, that had drawn Byron to the proprietor of Gates Department Store—what he'd tried to capture in his photograph series on her. Aunt Ellie had been a rare woman. Her grandniece was like her—and yet she wasn't.

The front door was open.

Byron's heart pounded like a teenager's. Three years ago, Ellie Gates had greeted him with ice cold, fresh-squeezed lemonade and a slice of sour-cherry pie. What could he expect from her grandniece?

A pitcher of lemonade over his head? A pie in his face? Nora Gates didn't forget, and she didn't forgive.

Hard to imagine, he thought, reaching for the screen door, that she hated him as much as she did. She didn't even know who he was.

"Well, my man," he said to himself, "here's mud in your eye."

And he pulled open the screen door, stuck in his head and called her name.

CHAPTER THREE

"NORA," HE CALLED softly, only half-fearful for his life now that he was putting it on the line. "Nora, it's Byron."

He left off the Sanders and judiciously didn't add the Forrester. First things first. Remembering the screen door had a tendency to bang shut, he closed it behind him. Nora didn't come screaming out of some dark corner. So far, so good.

The small entry hadn't changed. To his right, the cream-colored stairs wound up to the second floor under the eaves. Three steps up, where the stairs made a right-angle turn, a window seat was piled with chintz-covered pillows, musty-looking library books and a well-used afghan. It was the sort of spot where Nora would like to curl up with a murder mystery on a rainy Sunday afternoon. Her idea of bliss. Until he'd come around, anyway. Then, for a little while, she'd preferred to curl up with him.

Calling her name again, Byron moved carefully into the living room, which had changed. The neutral colors, the informality, the American art—they were Nora's touches. Aunt Ellie's tastes had been more Victorian. She'd have been comfortable in the formal parlor of the Pierce family's Providence town house. Nora would have been stifled, even if the late-eighteenth-century mansion had been in Tyler. Of course, Byron had learned early on not to point out the differences between Eleanora Gates the older and Eleanora Gates the younger. Nora much preferred to hear of similarities.

The living room was separated from the dining room by a curved archway. There Nora had added a baby grand piano, definitely her own touch. He vividly recalled Aunt Ellie's happy amazement that her grandniece had any musical ability whatever. *"Didn't get that from me. Do you play piano, Byron?"*

He did. So did Cliff. There'd been years of required lessons. He hadn't touched a piano in ages. Wondering if he were completely mad instead of just half, he played a C-major scale, right-handed, one octave. As he'd expected, the piano was perfectly in tune. He added his left hand and went up another octave, then down two octaves, chromatically. All that drilling when he was a kid came back to him.

"Ricky?"

It was her voice. Even as his heart lurched, Byron snatched his fingers from the keyboard and readied himself for skewering.

"You really *have* been practicing, haven't you?" She sounded pleased and delighted, a mood due to end as soon as she caught sight of who was playing scales in her dining room. "That was wonderful! You're lagging a bit in the left hand, but—" She stood under the archway. "Oh, no."

Short of a knife at the throat, it was the sort of greeting Byron had expected. He moved back from the piano. "Hello, Nora."

If she'd changed, he couldn't see it. She was still as trim and quietly beautiful as she'd been three years ago, her hot, secret temper smoldering behind her pale gray eyes. She must have been upstairs changing. She had on purple tennis shoes, narrow, straight-legged jeans and a purple sweatshirt—neat and casual, but nothing she'd ever wear to the store. She was, he thought, a very sexy woman, all the more so because she didn't try to be.

He didn't fail to notice how she'd balled up her hands into tight fists. Apparently he still possessed the uncanny knack for bringing out the aggressive side of her nature—which she'd deny.

And he didn't fail—couldn't fail—to remember how very much this woman had once meant to him.

"You really are a bloodsucker," she said through clenched teeth. "Did you come here to photograph us small-town folk all aflutter over the Body at the Lake?"

"The what? Nora, I don't know what you're talking about."

"Always so ignorant and innocent, aren't you, Byron?" If her voice had been a knife, he'd have been cut to thin slices. But that was her way, at least with him, of repressing emotions she distrusted even more than anger—emotions like fear, love, passion. "Well, this time I happen to believe you. I think you're here for an even more despicable reason: Liza Baron and Cliff Forrester's wedding."

Byron almost choked. So she'd figured it out. She knew who he was. Now there'd be no explaining, no chance to plead his case…just his marching orders. Get out and don't ever come back. Damned without a trial.

But Nora went on in her chilly voice, "Another Rhode Island boy's getting married, and with his being a recluse from a big East Coast family, you thought you'd nose around. You're a leech, Byron Sanders. Pure and simple."

A bloodsucker and a leech. He was getting the point. First, she hadn't forgotten him. Second, she hadn't forgiven him. Third, she didn't know his photography days were over and he was president of Pierce & Rothchilde, Publishers. And fourth, she didn't know he was Cliff's brother. He had a chance—if a slim one—of getting out of Nora's house intact after all.

And an even slimmer chance of making her understand why he'd done what he had three years ago.

"Nora, I'd like to talk to you. Do you have a minute?"

"I don't have a *second* for you, Byron Sanders. If you think you can march into Tyler and into my life and expect anything but a frosty welcome, you've got your head screwed on upside down. Now get out before I..." She inhaled deeply, and her eyes flooded— which had to irritate her—and he could see the pain he'd caused her. "God, Byron, how could you come back here?"

Might as well get started by coming clean. "I was invited to Cliff's wedding."

"You were *invited*? By whom? Why?"

She was looking at him as if he'd just told her Cliff and Liza had invited a gorilla to their wedding. Byron didn't appreciate her incredulity, but he realized he'd set himself up three years ago to have Nora hate him. He could have told her everything. About Cliff, their father, his own demons—he hadn't done enough, hadn't saved his father, hadn't saved his brother, hadn't been able to stop his mother's suffering. Probably Nora would have been sympathetic. But she'd had her own

problems—Aunt Ellie's impending death, what to do
about the store, and about staying in Tyler. And there'd
been Cliff. Three years ago staying in Tyler hadn't
been an option for Byron, any more than leaving it had
been one for Nora. He'd come uninvited into a world
where his brother had finally found stability. Byron
couldn't destroy that stability. It wasn't the only reason he'd left, but it was an important one.

Still, he hadn't explained any of this to Nora. He'd
told her he was moving on, let her think he was nothing
more than an itinerant photographer, a bit irresponsi-
ble, wont to loving and leaving women. So she'd called
him a cad, a bloodsucker, a leech and the rest. Because
at the time that had been easier—for him and for her—
than admitting they'd broken each other's hearts. Three
years later, he'd chased away the worst of his demons,
but he wasn't about to risk hurting Nora Gates again.
If she needed him to be a cad, fine.

"This is just a courtesy call, Nora. I'm trying to
be nice—"

"The hell you are."

"You know," he said calmly, "for a woman who
prides herself on being something of a Victorian lady,
you have a sharp tongue."

She raised her chin. "I want you out of my house."

Byron sighed, leaning one hip against the edge of
her piano. "Nora, you have an attitude."

"Byron," she mimicked, "*you* have a nerve barging
into my house after what you did to me."

"What *I* did to you?" he repeated mildly.

She got the point and flushed clear to her hairline,
almost making him believe she was a maiden lady.

"What we did to ourselves," she corrected. "Now get out."

He switched tactics. Not that he wanted to prolong this scene and have her attempt to forcibly remove him, but he did have a nonrefundable return ticket to Providence for the Sunday morning after the wedding. If he was to survive until then, he needed to neutralize Nora Gates as a potentially explosive force.

Of course, the truth wasn't going to help that process. "Look, Nora, I know it must seem presumptuous of me to walk in here after all this time, but I knew if I rang the doorbell you'd never let me in."

"I never said you were stupid."

So far, reason wasn't working with the woman. "Then we'd have ended up having this discussion on the porch," he added, "which I know you wouldn't want. As I recall, you'd prefer to be a receiver of gossip than a subject of gossip—"

It was a low blow. He could see his words scratch right up her spine. "Leave, Byron. Slither out of my house and out of Tyler the same way you slithered in. I can't imagine that Cliff Forrester needs a friend like you."

Probably he didn't, but they were brothers, and that was something neither of them could change. "I haven't seen him in five years."

That wasn't strictly true. He'd seen Cliff three years ago. From afar. They hadn't talked. Byron had sensed that Cliff wasn't ready yet, might never be, and for his brother's sake he'd left.

Nora's clear, incisive gray eyes focused on him in a way that brought back memories, too many memories. Of her passion, of her anger. Of how damned much they'd lost when he'd left Tyler. "Did he invite you?" she asked, her tone accusatory.

"In a manner of speaking."

"What's that supposed to mean? No—no, don't tell me." She dropped her hands to her sides, then pointed with one finger toward the front door. Her precious self-control had abandoned her. "Out, Byron. Right now. You're worse than a cad. I don't know what your game is, but I'm not going to let you crash Cliff and Liza's wedding. Cliff's pulled himself together after an ordeal probably none of us in Tyler can imagine. He's *happy,* Byron. You are not going to play games with the man's head. You both might be from Rhode Island and maybe you do know his family or something, but you're not his friend. I know you're not. Cliff didn't even invite his own mother and brother to his wedding—Liza did. He doesn't even know about it, and if you tell him…" She gulped for air. "By God, I'll come after you myself. So you go on and leave him alone." She took a breath. "And leave me alone, too."

Byron had debated interrupting three or four times, but had kept his mouth shut. "Nora," he began reasonably, "you don't understand. I…"

"Out!"

"I didn't come here to bother you or Cliff."

"Now, Byron. Now, or I swear I'll—"

She didn't finish, but instead grabbed a huge book of Beethoven sonatas from the gateleg table. She heaved it at him. Byron ducked. The book crashed into the piano, banging down on the keys, making a discordant racket. Nora was red-faced.

Clearly this was no time for revelations destined only to make her madder. Byron grinned at her. "Bet you haven't lost your temper like that since I was last in Tyler."

"You're damned right I haven't!"

Then a big blond kid was filling up the doorway behind her. "This guy bothering you, Miss Gates?"

Byron could see her debating whether to sic the kid on him. *Yeah—throw him in the oven, will you?* But she shook her head tightly, and said even more tightly, "Not anymore."

This time, Byron took the hint. As he walked past Nora and through the living room, he heard the kid make the mistake of laughing. "Gee, Miss Gates, I guess you're stronger than you look. That book's *heavy.*"

"Chromatic scale, Mr. Travis. Four octaves, ascending and descending. Presto."

Byron decided not to hang around. But he had no intention of leaving Tyler. There was his brother to see, Cliff's fiancée to meet, a body at a lake to learn more about. And there was Nora Gates herself. Piano player, department store owner, would-be Victorian old maid. She was a woman of contradictions and spirit, and as he walked back to his rented car, it occurred to Byron that the past three years had been but a pause—a little gulp—in their relationship. It wasn't finished. There'd been no resolution. No final chord.

At least, he thought, not yet.

NORA DIDN'T CHARGE Ricky Travis for his lesson. In fact, for the first time since she'd had pneumonia six years ago, she cut a lesson short.

"You okay, Miss Gates?" Rick asked.

"I'm fine, just a little distracted."

"That guy—"

"I'm not worried about him. Don't you be, either."

He shrugged. "If you say so. I'll have the Bach down by next week. Promise. It's just hard with it being football season."

"I understand. It's not easy being both a talented musician and a football player at this time of year. But you've had a good lesson, Rick. It's not you. I'm just... well, it's been a long day." She rose from her chair beside the piano. "I'll see you next week."

"Sure thing, Miss Gates."

With Rick gone, the house seemed deadly quiet. Foregoing Bach and Beethoven, Nora put on an early Bruce Springsteen album and tried to exorcise Byron Sanders from her mind.

She couldn't.

She hadn't forgotten a single thing about him. He was as tall as she remembered. As strongly built and lithe, and every bit as darkly good-looking. His eyes were still as blue and piercing and unpredictable— and as dangerously enticing—as the Atlantic Ocean.

It would have been easier, she thought, if there'd been things she'd forgotten. The dark hairs on his forearms, for example, or his long, blunt-nailed fingers. But she'd remembered everything—the warmth of his eyes, the breadth of his shoulders, the way he had of forcing her not to take herself too seriously, even how irritating he could be. *Especially* how irritating he could be.

How had he learned about Cliff and Liza's wedding? It wasn't a secret, but how had an East Coast photographer heard that a Wisconsin couple was getting married? Maybe he *did* know Cliff—but Cliff had said he didn't know a Byron Sanders. Perhaps Byron knew the

Forresters, the mother and brother Liza had taken the liberty of inviting. Nora wondered if she should warn Liza about Byron.

Singing aloud with Bruce, she made herself another pot of tea and dug in her refrigerator for some leftovers for supper. If Sanders had shown up *before* Cliff had, she'd have pressed Liza's reticent fiancé a little harder about his fellow Rhode Islander.

Well, she thought, pulling a bit of brown rice and chicken from the fridge, *someone* was lying.

She made a tossed salad and warmed up her dinner. Really, what a terrific old maid she'd make. A pity the term was démodé.

The Spinster Gates.

It sounded deliciously forbidding. She turned off Bruce and tried to put her former lover—*arrgh, why couldn't he be less appealing?*—out of her mind. Sitting at her kitchen table, she found herself staring at her hands. They were ringless, still soft and pale. She remembered Aunt Ellie's hands in her final days: old, spotted, gnarled. Yet they'd possessed a delicacy and beauty that suggested she was a woman who'd lived her life on her own terms, a life that had been full and happy. She'd relished her family, she'd had many friends. She'd been generous and spirited and frugal, a model of independence and responsibility.

Once, over a similar supper of leftovers, Nora had asked Aunt Ellie if she ever got lonely. "Of course," she'd replied immediately, in her blunt, unswerving way. "Everyone does. I'm no different."

"But… I meant, did you ever wished you'd married?"

She'd shrugged, not backing away from so personal

a question. "At times I've wondered what it might have been like, but I've no doubt a married woman at times wonders what would have become of her if she hadn't married. But I have no regrets, any more than your mother had regrets about having married your father. I know and have known many wonderful men. I just didn't care to marry any of them."

"What about children?" Nora had asked.

Aunt Ellie had laughed. "My word, Tyler's filled with children. Always has been. You know, I believe sometimes when you don't have children of your own you're better able to appreciate other people's. You can do things for them and with them that their parents simply can't. You can enrich their lives. You don't worry about the same things. To be honest, Nora, I've never had the urge to bear children myself. I know that's hard for some people to believe, but it's the truth. But I've enjoyed having children in my life."

Indeed she had. Even before she'd come to live with Aunt Ellie when she was thirteen, Nora had loved her visits to the twenties house a few blocks from Gates Department Store. They'd bake cookies, go to museums, arts and crafts festivals, libraries. Aunt Ellie had taught her how to manage money and had instilled in her a sense of independence and confidence that continued to stand her in good stead.

She was stronger than she'd been three years ago, Nora reminded herself. She'd had time to adjust to the loss of Aunt Ellie and to becoming sole owner of Gates. She knew herself better. She knew that if Aunt Ellie had never yearned in any real way for marriage and children, she herself occasionally would. Every now and then, a man would even come along who tempted her.

She would survive Byron's reappearance in Tyler.

Once, of course, she'd figured out what he was up to.

Feeling a little like Agatha Christie's Miss Marple, Nora finished her supper and made her plans.

AFTER HASTILY REMOVING himself from Nora's house, Byron parked in the town square, put some change in the meter—which miraculously allowed him a full hour to mosey around—and found his way to the Tyler Public Library. It was located in a particularly beautiful, if run-down, turn-of-the century home. Given his own upbringing in a Federal-period town house and a center-chimney cottage on Nantucket Island, Byron found the preponderance of Victorian, Craftsman and Prairie architecture in Tyler refreshing.

Inside the library, which was old-fashioned and in desperate need of renovation, he tried not to draw attention to himself as he made his way to a stack of recent copies of the *Tyler Citizen*. He sat at an oak table in a poorly lit corner. Deliberately and patiently, he skimmed each edition of the daily paper, backtracking several weeks until he found the front-page article announcing the discovery of a skeleton at Judson Ingalls's Timberlake Lodge. The grisly discovery had been made when local construction chief Joe Santori and his crew struck the body with a backhoe while doing some excavation work; Cliff Forrester, the lodge caretaker, was called onto the scene. Apparently Liza Baron, Judson's granddaughter, was also up at the lodge at the time. According to the paper, Judson himself hadn't stepped foot on the property since his wife left him more than forty years ago.

Liza Baron.

Byron rolled the name around on his tongue and tried to remember. But no, he didn't recall a Liza Baron from his first visit to Tyler. He remembered Judson Ingalls, though. A taciturn, hardworking man, he was one of Tyler's leading citizens, owner of Ingalls Farm and Machinery. As Byron recalled, Judson's wife had been a Chicago socialite, unhappy in a small Wisconsin town.

Now why had he remembered that little tidbit of Tyler lore?

"Aunt Ellie," he whispered to himself.

In their long talks on her front porch, Ellie Gates had told Byron countless tales of the legions of friends she'd had over her long, full life. She'd mentioned Judson Ingalls's wife. "Margaret was a fish out of water here in Tyler, but we became friends, although she was somewhat younger than I. I'm afraid she didn't have too many friends here in town. A pity. She was such a lively woman. Of course, some of that was her own doing—but it wasn't all her own doing. In a small town, it's easy for people to develop a wariness of strangers, of outsiders." And she'd paused to give him a pointed look, as if she knew he was another outsider who'd fallen for a Tyler resident. "It's also easy for out-of-towners to act on their prejudices and figure a small town has nothing to offer, including friends."

Ellie Gates had believed in tolerance. She'd been an opinionated woman herself and forthright in stating her views, but she appreciated fresh thinking, a good argument and people's right, as she liked to put it, "to be wrong."

Her grandniece and sole heir was a good deal more stiff-necked. Nora Gates much preferred to deal with people who agreed with her.

Flipping back through the newspapers, Byron caught up with all the current Tyler news, as well as fresh developments regarding the body. He gathered that its presence at Timberlake Lodge had fueled much speculation in town. Without directly stating as much, the paper gave the clear impression that some towns-people believed the body was that of Margaret Alyssa Lindstrom Ingalls herself. Now all the authorities had to do was get busy and confirm that fact, and prove how she'd ended up buried at her husband's lodge.

So for the past five years, Byron thought, his one and only brother had been living right on top of Tyler's greatest unsolved mystery. Given all the horrors Cliff had witnessed in Southeast Asia, how had he reacted to finding a dead body under his feet? He'd come to Tyler to escape death and destruction.

He'd fallen in love, was what he'd done.

Byron shrugged. There was a certain logic in that, he supposed.

At one point, the *Citizen* had printed a grainy pic-ture of Liza Baron, for no solid reason Byron could figure out except that she was Judson Ingalls's grand-daughter and had finally come home. So this was the woman his brother planned to marry. She was attrac-tive in a dramatic, grab-you-by-the-short-hairs way. Byron guessed that she would be bold and direct with her loves and hates.

A few days later, the paper had dredged up an old

photograph of Margaret Ingalls. Apparently she'd been quite the party animal. Putting the two photos side by side, Byron saw a strong resemblance between grand-mother and granddaughter.

There was no picture of Cliff. No quotes from him, as there had been from Joe Santori, about having dis-covered the body. "Cliff Forrester couldn't be reached for comment," the paper said. Which might have meant anything from they couldn't find him to he'd chased them off with a shotgun.

Byron suddenly wished he hadn't agreed to sneak into Tyler and play scout for his mother—or for him-self. He'd done that once, completely on his own, with disastrous results. There were too many unknowns. Cliff's being involved with a Tyler woman Byron had anticipated. And he'd have to have been a complete idiot not to know he was in for a fight with Nora Gates. But a dead body? A dead body that could belong to the grandmother of his future sister-in-law?

Best, he thought, to hold off for a bit before phoning his mother in London and reporting the news.

But that wasn't what was really eating at Byron and he knew it.

He was bothered by the big unknown, the one that had gnawed at him for three long years. How would he react if he ever saw Nora Gates again?

He shoved the newspapers back where he'd found them and left the library, walking quickly to his car. It was fully dark now. Cold. There was a stiff breeze. The square was quiet. Byron already had his car door open, but he shut it softly. He had another five min-utes on his meter.

After crossing the street, he walked down to Gates

Department Store, a fixture on Tyler's square since Ellie Gates had opened the three-story building in the Roaring Twenties, using an unexpected inheritance from an uncle back East. People had been surprised she'd risked her money on a business venture instead of putting it safely in the bank so she could lead a ladylike life. They'd doubted she'd be able to stay in business, never mind make enough profit to fill three floors with merchandise, or attract enough customers from Tyler and surrounding communities to support a full department store. But she'd proved them wrong, her sense of style, service and tradition finding a large and loyal following.

Gates closed at six o'clock, except for Thursdays and Fridays when it stayed open until nine. Its window displays were often mentioned in Wisconsin travel guides, regional magazines and newspapers, a "must see" in Tyler. They were Nora's brainchild. Aunt Ellie had done the usual perfunctory displays, but not her grandniece. Nora's were elaborate and creative, playing on the history and charms of her corner of the Midwest.

The current display featured Halloween, complete with witches, pumpkins, black cats and skeletons, but also a touch of whimsy: two figures, a boy and girl, dressed as children of Swedish immigrants, bobbing for apples in a wooden bucket; a puppy stealing a caramel popcorn ball from an overflowing bowl; a cheerful-looking ghost peering out of a closet. It was a montage of scenes that were warm, nostalgic, funny, spooky. Busy owner of Gates or not, Byron thought, Nora had to have been personally responsible for such an imaginative window.

A gust of Canadian air went right through his slouchy jacket and chamois shirt. But instead of moving along the street, Byron remained in front of the department store window, staring at the children bobbing for apples, trying not to remember....

A hot, muggy August afternoon, his first in Tyler. Byron hadn't come to Wisconsin to take pictures. For him, then, photography was only a hobby. He'd come to see his brother. Cliff had retreated from society two years before and Byron wanted to reassure himself that his brother was alive, functioning, living a life he needed to live, on his own terms. For Cliff's sake, Byron had come to Tyler unannounced, on the sly, without fanfare. He didn't want to do anything—*anything*—to upset the precarious balance his brother had established for himself. But if Cliff needed him, if he was in any danger of hurting himself or anyone else, Byron felt he had to know. If necessary, he would have intervened.

His first stop in Tyler had been the square, his first stop on the square, Gates Department Store. He'd wanted to get a feel for the town in which his brother had taken up residence, if as a recluse.

Nora had been in the window, working on a back-to-school display that featured Tyler's original settlers heading across the fields to their one-room schoolhouse. Already Byron had been feeling a little better about where his brother had landed. Tyler, Wisconsin, wasn't a weird, gritty, hole-in-the-wall town where he'd find Cliff living in some gutter. It was picturesque and homey, a real community, with farms, businesses, schools, a hospital, a sense of history and pride. The people ran the gamut from the working poor to the well-to-do; it wasn't just an upper-class or a working-class town. Those things mattered to Byron, although, even now, he couldn't have said why.

Nora had worn her hair longer then. With a thick braid trailing down her back, and wisps of ash-blond hair poking out, she'd looked as old-fashioned and fresh-faced as her nineteenth-century figures.

She'd spotted him and smiled politely. He could tell she'd already pegged him as a stranger.

That night, pretending to be a freelance photographer, he'd had dinner with her and Aunt Ellie at their twenties house a couple of blocks from the square. Things had snowballed from there. Although still technically the sole owner of Gates Department Store, Ellie Gates was ninety and in failing health, and left most of the day-to-day management up to her grandniece. And, to his delight, Byron had discovered that Nora was hardly an eighteen-year-old kid. In fact, she was thirty, unmarried and determined to stay that way. He'd admired her independence, her spirit, her energy, her devotion to her hometown and her sense of humor and tolerance. He hadn't, however, expected to fall in love with her.

He hadn't guessed she was a virgin. And she hadn't told him until the last moment, in the tent at the lake outside town where he'd camped. Afterward, she'd insisted she had no regrets. It might not even have been a conscious lie. Byron's own regrets had nothing to do with making love to Nora Gates, of having loved her and dreamed of having a life with her, but everything to do with having himself been so damned blind to what was going in her life. He'd been preoccupied with his own problems—Cliff, their father, his own pain and guilt over their suffering. He hadn't seen, until it was too late, that Nora Gates was letting go of the last person she had in the world, a woman who'd meant everything to her. That Aunt Ellie was ninety and had never pretended she'd live forever wasn't the consolation Byron, in his blindness, had anticipated. She had been a force in Nora's life, and Nora had been trying to find a way to carry on without her.

They'd picked a hell of a time to fall in love.

Two weeks after that first night together, he'd left Tyler, knowing Nora thought him, incorrectly if not unreasonably, a cad and a heel and a scurrilous East Coast rake. Nora Gates was as inventive in her insults as in her window displays, only a good deal less charming. But he'd known her anger toward him had been, in a peculiar way, a relief to her. A consolation. She'd fallen—blindly, temporarily—for the wrong man. In her odd world, that was better than having fallen for the right man.

"This isn't your first trip to Tyler," a quiet, familiar voice said next to him.

Byron turned slowly, and for the first time in five long years, he faced his brother. Cliff seemed to have materialized out of the darkness. For a moment, Byron wondered if he was just imagining him. But the lines in his brother's face were too real—the dark, narrowed eyes, the touches of gray in his hair. He was a different man from the one Byron had known, neither the eager, determined young man who'd gone off to Southeast Asia after their father nor the broken, potentially explosive man who'd tried, and failed, to come home. This Clifton Pierce Forrester was grown-up, changed by the suffering he'd witnessed and endured, but whole at last. With a photographer's visual acuity and a brother's instincts, Byron made his assessment and was confident he was right.

He also knew his brother was royally pissed off.

"Cliff," he said, barely able to say more.

"Yeah." Cliff remained rigid and unmoving, performing his own assessment of his younger brother. "You came to Tyler to spy on me. You've done it before."

Byron neither confirmed nor denied the accusation. "I'd like us to talk, Cliff."

"Nora said you called yourself Byron Sanders."

"It's the name I used professionally," he said with heroic equanimity. "I used to take photographs."

Cliff's hardened face remained expressionless. "Nora asked me if I knew a Byron Sanders. I figured she meant you."

"And you said you didn't."

"That's right."

"Why not?"

"Because I wasn't sure I do know you."

Byron nodded. He and Cliff had always, at minimum, been honest with each other. If everything else had changed, the tough honesty between them hadn't.

Then Cliff added, in a voice so low his words were almost lost to the wind, "And because you're my brother."

"Nora," he whispered in the dark of a moonless summer night. "I love the sound of your name." Slowly, purposefully, he moved his palms across her bare breasts, already inflamed by his touch. "I love the feel of you." And he kissed her, run-

ning his tongue along the sharp edges of her teeth, into the secret corners of her mouth. "I love the taste of you."

She was nearly delirious with wanting him. She'd never realized such aching passion was possible, not for her. It made her forget everything but him. Pressing her hands against his strong hips, she drew him to her, moaning at the feel of the rough hairs of his chest against her, the taut muscles of his abdomen, his long, long legs.

"I want to feel you inside me," she whispered.

"Are you sure?"

"Yes," she breathed.

"There'll be no going back. We can stop, but you won't ever be—"

She smiled. "A virgin again?"

But he was serious.

She pressed him harder. "Love me, Byron."

Nora awoke sweating and panting—not, in her opinion, a moment too soon. She snatched up the water glass she kept by her bed and took a huge gulp. Water dripped down the sides of her mouth and spilled onto her sheets.

"Whew," she said, and laughed a little.

It had only been a dream. *Thank God.* She switched on the small pottery lamp on her antique nightstand. She was alone in her brass bed, cozy under her down quilt and Egyptian-cotton sheets. She wasn't in a musty old tent making love to Byron Sanders.

Feeling awkward and embarrassed, although there were no witnesses to her dream, she flipped on her radio to a predawn classic jazz program. Benny Good-man's clarinet playing filled the silence. She fluffed up her pillows and leaned against them, knowing she'd never get back to sleep. She didn't want to sleep if her subconscious was going to betray her like that again.

She didn't want to dream about that man.

"Dream, my foot," she muttered.

Unfortunately, it had been a memory.

Benny Goodman hit a high, clear, impossible note. Nora threw back the covers and jumped out of bed. It was chilly in her room. Just as well. A good shot of cold air was what she needed. She wasn't one to turn up the heat until the pipes were in danger of freezing. Not bothering with a robe, she headed for her bath-room down the hall, where she allowed herself the luxury of a space heater. She turned the water on in the tub to let it get good and hot, then switched on the shower. Of course, after that dream, she should prob-ably take a cold bath.

So far she was failing miserably as Miss Marple, and not only because Agatha Christie's intrepid hero-ine would never have had such a steamy dream. Before heading to bed, Nora had disguised her voice, pretend-ing she was from back East, and had checked all the ob-vious places in and around Tyler where Byron Sanders might have decided to rest his untrustworthy head. He wasn't registered anywhere. Had he pitched his reek-ing tent on private property? Well, if he was in Tyler, she'd find him. He wasn't going to do anything—not one single thing—to disrupt Cliff Forrester and Liza Baron's wedding.

"It's not your problem, you know," she said aloud to

herself. "Aunt Ellie always warned you against meddling."

Nora could hear her great-aunt at her most imperious. "Meddling," she'd said on numerous occasions, "is too often one of the great temptations of the single woman."

But Nora knew Byron Sanders. He wasn't nearly as upright and honest and sensitive as he came across on first impression. How could she stand back and let him work his charms on an unsuspecting Cliff and Liza? *They'd* end up in a spread in a Chicago newspaper.

If any two people could take care of themselves, she knew, it was those two. But still, it was her *duty* to find out what the weasel was up to.

And she would. Come morning, she'd track him down, for sure.

CHAPTER FOUR

BYRON SAT ON a battered Adirondack chair in a clearing along the shore from Timberlake Lodge, the sun sparkling so brightly on the water it hurt his eyes. He'd planned to stay in a motel in the next town, but Cliff had found him an old tent at the lodge and let him pitch it on an out-of-the-way stretch of lakefront. With hardly a word, Cliff had disappeared for the night. He'd reappeared shortly after sunup, bearing stale doughnuts and a thermos of piping-hot black coffee, more from duty, Byron suspected, than from a desire to be nice.

Now Cliff was standing on a rock, staring out at the lake. Byron drank from the thermos cup and dipped his plain doughnut into the coffee to soften it. Even as kids, Cliff hadn't been picky about food. Byron wasn't, either, but he did prefer fresh doughnuts.

So far, neither had had much to say. Byron had opted against trying to explain his trip to Tyler three years ago—one attempted explanation in the past twelve hours had already backfired. And from Cliff's reaction to seeing his younger brother in town, Byron guessed Miss Liza hadn't yet confessed she'd shot off an invitation to her future in-laws. Byron wasn't going to step into that particular pile of warm Wisconsin dung. Nor did Cliff initiate any conversation. How had he come to fall in love? What had his life been like the past five years? What were his plans now that he was getting married? Answers would have to wait. Byron was patient. It was enough, for now, that he and his brother were together by a beautiful lake on a cool, bright morning in Wisconsin.

"Are you going to tell me about you and Nora Gates?" Cliff asked without turning around.

Byron sipped his coffee, feeling it—or guilt—burn a path to the pit of his stomach. He'd never told anyone about his brief, fiery, insane affair with Nora Gates. He'd promised her. She'd insisted on calling it, derisively, his "fling."

Cliff interpreted his brother's silence in his own way. "This isn't good, Brother."

"No."

Looking around at Byron, Cliff asked, "Does she hate your guts?"

"Apparently."

"Because of the photos?"

"That's one reason."

"I can't imagine Nora Gates hating anyone," Cliff said thoughtfully, "but when she asked about you…" He sighed. "Dammit, Byron, did you break that woman's heart?"

"That woman," Byron said, popping a soaked piece of doughnut into his mouth, "doesn't have a heart capable of breaking. Don't let her fool you. She needs your sympathy about as much as a badger does. You know what she eats for breakfast, don't you? A five-pound bag of nails. Guaranteed. Check it out yourself."

Cliff frowned. "She's not that kind of woman."

"That, Brother, is what she wants everyone in Tyler to believe. She has the tongue of a witch."

Overhead, in the distance, he could hear the seemingly chaotic honking of a flock of Canada geese. Winter was coming to Wisconsin. The geese knew when to clear out. Pity, Byron thought, he lacked their good sense.

His brother's mouth twitched in what Byron decided passed for a smile these days. "Do you care about her?"

"Cliff, I have to warn you, you're treading on thin ice even bringing up the subject. What did or didn't happen between Nora and me three years ago is between us. I can't talk about it. If I did, she'd hunt me down like a rabid weasel and put me out of her misery."

His brother's smile almost blossomed, then faded abruptly. It seemed suddenly as if he'd never smiled before and never would again.

"Are you and Nora friends?" Byron asked.

"Not in any normal way."

And Cliff's eyes, hinting of the years of pain and self-imposed isolation and loneliness he'd endured, reached Byron, reminding him that his brother had come a long, long way from where he'd been five years ago, ten years ago. And there was healing still to be done—for him, for Byron, for their widowed mother. Had Liza Baron made his tortured life a thing of the past? But if Cliff encouraged Byron to talk, listened intently, he avoided himself as a topic of conversation. Cliff was guarded about his upcoming marriage, the life he'd been leading, where he planned to go from this point, even the body that had been dug up not too far from where they now sat. Byron knew he needed to continue to be patient.

And he wanted to hear Cliff's views on Nora Gates. It was crazy, he thought, but there it was.

"You could say," Cliff went on, looking out at the glistening lake, "that Nora's one of the people in Tyler I've admired from afar. Until yesterday afternoon, I'd never even spoken to her. But I've seen her around town, heard about her from time to time from Alyssa Baron, read about her in the newspaper. She's her own person. She sits on the town council and is active in various local charitable organizations. She has strong views on certain issues and she's direct, but she manages to be gracious at the same time. People listen to her, even when she's saying something they don't want to hear, because they know she cares about them and Tyler."

Byron knew his brother spoke the truth, but couldn't help recalling that saintly Nora Gates had thrown a book of Beethoven sonatas at him. If she'd had any kind of arm, she'd have knocked him out.

"I doubt she takes to liars," Cliff added.

The geese were directly overhead, flying in picture-postcard formation against a sky as clear and blue as any Byron had seen, from Maine to Florida to California to Alaska. He could think of worse places to end up than Tyler, Wisconsin. His mahogany-paneled Providence office, for one, he decided wryly. He drank more of his coffee, the warmth of the plastic cup finally penetrating his fingers. It had been a chilly night. He was used to camping out in every type of weather, although there'd been something eerie about pitching his tent not far from where a body had been mysteriously buried for who knew how long. And his memories of Nora Gates, both past and current, hadn't been conducive to sleep. But it was simpler to blame the weather.

With the sun climbing higher, sitting outside wasn't

so bad. Anyway, Cliff hadn't invited him into the lodge.

"I lied to Nora about who I was," Byron said, "because I was afraid of what would happen if word got out that Cliff Forrester's brother was in town."

"If I found out, you mean?"

Cliff's tone was deadly calm, even neutral, but Byron sensed the regret, the guilt, the uneasy resignation. "You did what you had to do, Cliff," he said carefully. "So did I."

Bending down suddenly, Cliff snatched up a small rock, straightened and skipped it across the calm lake. Yards out, it disappeared in spreading concentric circles. "Father taught us that," he said, his back to Byron. "Remember?"

"I remember."

Cliff turned, his expression harsh and unyielding in the bright sun, maybe more so than he meant it to be. But his eyes looked as if they were melting. Byron was almost seared by his brother's torment. "I thought this would be easier."

Byron tossed the last of his coffee into the grass. "Me, too."

"Liza..." It was the first time Cliff had mentioned her directly. He turned back to the lake, where the last of the concentric circles had vanished, leaving behind a glasslike surface. "She thinks all things are possible. Sometimes I get to thinking that way, too."

"Cliff—"

"She told you and Mother about us, didn't she?"

"You'll have to talk to her about that."

"She would, you know. She's meddlesome like that—the kind of woman who'd teach a kid to swim

by pitching him headfirst into the water." He sighed.
"But this time she went too far. I don't know if I'm
ready for this."

"That's why I came early. To see if you were. She
can't understand what it's been like, Cliff. No one can."

He nodded.

"If you're not ready to see me, I'll leave. Now, today.
Mother won't come at all. It's your call."

Cliff was silent. Then he said, "Tell her who you
are, Byron."

Back to Nora Gates. Cliff, apparently, would go
only so far in articulating his innermost thoughts.
Byron smiled thinly. "That might mean the end of me."

"And if you want to stay," Cliff said, his face expressionless, "then stay."

"I'll see how today goes. As for Nora— I'll tell her
the truth after the wedding."

"Before."

"She's invited?"

Cliff jumped from his rock, landing as silently as a
panther. "Half the damned town's invited."

For a moment, Byron dismissed his troubling
thoughts about Nora Gates. She was a strong woman,
a survivor. He didn't need to coddle her. He remembered every second of their time together, wishing like
hell he didn't. He *had* loved her. And he'd tried, amid
his own pain and confusion, to do the right thing, even
as he'd lied to her and ended up making her hate her.
But through knowing her, through knowing Aunt Ellie,
he'd learned that before he could help anyone, commit
to anyone or anything, he had first to save himself.

It was his brother, once again, who worried him.
"Are you going to make it through this thing?"

"I will. For Liza's sake."

"She wants a big wedding?"

But Byron had stepped over the line. The mask dropped into place, covering up the raw, exposed parts of himself that Cliff preferred to deal with on his own. He looked out past Byron to the lodge. "Company."

"Work crew?"

"Nope." And because the mask was in place, because he was the big brother and didn't need anything from Byron, Cliff managed one of his twitching smiles. "That's Nora Gates's car."

Byron followed his brother's gaze, but could only make out a champagne-colored BMW. Far too racy and expensive for frugal, demure Nora Gates. "Where?"

"The BMW."

"That's no Victorian old maid's car."

Cliff grunted. "And you think you know everything about Nora Gates."

NORA HAD DRESSED conservatively for her trip out to Timberlake Lodge, not for Liza's sake—Liza greeted her in jeans and a Tyler Titans sweatshirt—but for her own. Her reliable double-breasted wide-wale charcoal corduroy jacket, her black wool gabardine trousers and her stark white cotton shirt reminded her that she was smart, successful, responsible and perfectly capable of handling most anything, including the return of Byron Sanders to Tyler. It would not be a repeat of three years ago. She would keep a level head, unsettling dreams or no unsettling dreams.

"Nora," Liza said, obviously surprised. "Well, hi— what on earth brings you out here?"

"I hope I'm not too early. It's such a beautiful morning I thought I'd take a ride out. The place looks great."

"Doesn't it, though? Come on inside— I'll give you the grand tour."

"I'm not disturbing you?"

"Not at all. I was just stewing about this wedding getting out of hand, and Joe Santori isn't around this morning so I can't pester him. Cliff's off somewhere. It's just me and the cobwebs right now."

Liza's infectious cheer helped Nora recover her own steady manner. They climbed onto the old lodge's formidable porch, which overlooked the beautiful lake. The long-abandoned lodge was a grand dinosaur of a place, but Nora, as a member of the Tyler town council, was thrilled to see it being renovated. It was a pity the discovery of a body on the premises had put a damper on things.

"Stay all morning if you want," Liza said. "I've got nothing special planned, except a phone call to my mother tactfully reminding her that it's my wedding, not hers." She smiled guiltily over her shoulder. "She's such a sweetheart, though. We're both under a lot of strain. I keep telling myself she means well—"

"And she just wants you to do the right thing."

Liza's smile broadened into a grin. "Isn't that true of all mothers?"

"I'm sure it is," Nora said softly. Her own mother had been dead for twenty years.

"Oh, drat, me and my big mouth again. I'm sorry, Nora. I forgot—"

"It's all right. Gosh, Liza, I can't get over how much you and Cliff have accomplished in such a short time."

Her small faux pas behind her—Liza Baron wasn't

one to beat herself over the head for long—she breezed through the front door into the entry. She seemed cheerful and content, if also somewhat hyper and over-whelmed by all that was going on in her life. Nora thought she could understand. Never mind finding a dead body in your yard, one, no less, that might be that of your long-lost grandmother. Never mind com-ing back to your hometown to live. As far as Nora was concerned, falling head over heels in love as fast and furiously as Liza Baron had with Cliff Forrester would turn anyone's life inside out. Even if Liza *was* used to doing everything fast and furiously. From her own glaring romantic mistake, Nora was convinced that if there was one area in life where a woman should al-ways act with great deliberation and extreme caution, it was in affairs of the heart. A woman should take her time about falling in love. Shop around. Be careful. Romance was not an area in which to be precipitate. If she was feeling reckless, Nora would head to the race-track before she would dial Byron Sanders's number.

"Anything in particular that brings you out here, or did you really just seize the moment?" Liza asked.

"I guess I wanted to see how you were doing."

She shrugged. "On the whole, I'm doing great. A little nuts maybe, but I've never been happier."

Something only someone madly in love would say. Nora had felt that way when she'd thought she was in love with Byron Sanders. She'd learned, in the years since, that she could be just as happy out of love, if not happi*er*. It was a matter of perspective and self-disci-pline. People in love always thought they were happier than people who weren't. In her opinion, that kind of thinking was just…hormones.

"Have you ever been up here before?" Liza asked.

Nora pulled herself out of her introspective mood. "I trespassed once or twice when I was a kid—hunting wildflowers, as I recall. And I've canoed by a number of times."

"You and Aunt Ellie used to go canoeing together, didn't you? She was something else. Damn, she used to make my grandfather mad sometimes. But she'd always remain so calm and composed. Granddad told me once that he wanted to get her mad enough to spit nickels, but I don't think he ever succeeded. She just refused to let him get to her. You're a lot like her, Nora. You don't let people get to you, either."

Nora kept her expression neutral and refrained from comment, wondering what Liza Baron would think if she'd witnessed her throwing a book of Beethoven piano sonatas at her ex-lover just last evening. Fortunately, Ricky Travis wasn't a big mouth or the story would have been all over town by now. If his little brother Lars, another of Nora's piano students, had caught her, she might as well have taken an ad out in the *Tyler Citizen* announcing the news. Lars did like to talk.

"Your grandfather must be thrilled with how the lodge is shaping up," Nora said, deftly changing the subject.

"Oh, I think he would be, if we hadn't..." She waved a hand awkwardly. "You know."

The Body. Nora nodded sympathetically, sorry she'd brought it up, even indirectly. But Judson Ingalls's lodge, where his wife had had so many of her wild parties in the late forties, was showing fresh potential, new life. No one but Cliff Forrester had lived in the place since Margaret Ingalls had left her husband in 1950. And now, of course, Liza and her daily influx of renovators. Her creative spark was evident in the ongoing work, in the choice of walls she'd had Joe Santori knock down, in the colors she'd chosen, in her attention to detail, even in the way she'd made the spare furnishings and torn-up rooms seem downright homey.

"What do you think of my rug?" Liza asked as they passed over a small Oriental rug in the entry. "Neat, huh?"

"It's beautiful."

"I found it up in the attic when Cliff and I—well, when we were still stalking each other, you might say. I think it's a real Oriental, not a fake. Cliff's not so sure. Look at those colors, though. I don't know if you can get that rich burgundy from a fake. I don't really care, except if it's real, my grandmother might have bought it on one of her infamous shopping trips."

Nora, who treasured her own family heirlooms, was intrigued. Margaret Ingalls was on the minds of just about everyone in Tyler; Nora wanted more insight into the woman Aunt Ellie had believed was rather misunderstood by the townspeople. "Did you ask Judson or your mother about it?"

"No, not yet. Margaret's not the best subject of conversation to bring up right now. And I'd hate Granddad to make me take up the rug just because she might have bought the damned thing—you're never sure how he'll react. You know what an old curmudgeon he can be."

One, however, who adored his irrepressible granddaughter Liza. Nora had never pretended to fully understand the Ingalls family. But Liza seemed reluctant to say anything further about her grandfather.

"And I'd ask Mother," she went on, sighing, "but she hasn't had much of anything to do with the lodge since she was a little girl. Of course, I wasn't even born when my grandmother hit the road—I have to remind myself that she was my mother's mother, not some stranger." She made an exaggerated wince, as if she'd just caught herself doing something naughty. "I'm sorry, I don't mean to bore you with all this stuff. Anyway, it's no big deal. There's so much junk squirreled away around here I got excited when I found the rug, but it's probably just junk, too. Oh, well, I like it, regardless. I'm going to have it cleaned and appraised, but I thought I'd wait until the dust settles around here." She gestured broadly toward a partially destroyed wall as they made their way to the kitchen. "Literally."

Long-lost rugs, sawdust, a rambling, run-down lodge—near chaos seemed to suit Liza Baron, which, Nora thought, was so unlike herself. She preferred order and stability. But in the kitchen, freshly renovated, she saw another side of her new friend, because its unexpected coziness—the rag rugs, the splashes of color, the chipped pottery teapot filled with autumn wildflowers—had to be Liza's doing. She'd added character and charm to what, with its long stainless steel counters and stark white cabinets, could have been an institutional-looking kitchen. Nora could imagine Liza and Cliff having dinner together at the battered pine table. The two of them, she suddenly saw, were completely right for each other.

"Hey, what do you say to a cup of hot coffee on this chilly autumn morning?" Liza offered cheerfully, already pulling two restaurant-style mugs down from an open shelf. "I tried to talk Cliff into building a fire to take the nip out of the air, but he was off like a bat out of hell at the crack of dawn. That man. I'll never figure him out." She grinned over her shoulder, reaching for the coffeepot. "Guess that'll make our life together all the more intriguing."

Nora smiled. "You have a way of jumping headfirst into the future, don't you?"

"It's the only way I know how. Cream and sugar?"

"Just black," Nora said absently, sitting down at the table. She herself plotted and plodded and eased her way into the future, tried to predict it as much as possible, relied on short-term and long-term goals.

Liza set the steaming coffee in front of her and sat down. Nora finally became aware of her probing, curious stare. "Is something wrong?" Liza asked.

"No! No, not at all." Nora sat up straight and tried the coffee. "Hazelnut, isn't it?"

"Hope you like it. I only make it when Cliff's not around. He hates it."

"It's lovely. You and Cliff are so different—"

"Yep. Keeps life interesting. Nora…" Liza squinted, her expression a reminder of her astuteness. Given her rebellious, outrageous side, people often tended to underestimate her intelligence. "Nora, did Cliff put you up to coming out here?"

"Actually…"

"I'm not going to get mad. I told you, he thinks highly of you. He's that way—makes up his mind quickly about people."

Nora sighed. Naturally. People generally did think "highly" of her. But wasn't that what she wanted? If she had a choice, she'd prefer to inspire respect, not passion. *Why not both?* That was dangerous thinking, the sort in which she'd indulged when Byron Sanders came to Tyler for the first time.

"Well, yes," she said, "he asked me to give you a hand in whatever way I could, but I was going to do that anyway, especially after I saw you in the store the other day. I gather with everything going on you haven't really had much chance to touch base with your old Tyler friends."

"Not really, no," Liza said, dumping a heaping teaspoon of sugar into her mug of coffee. "My best friend from high school lives in Chicago these days and the rest…" She shrugged. "As you say, there hasn't been time. I suppose a few will turn up at the wedding. Mother handled most of the Tyler invitations. RSVPs keep pouring in…." She trailed off, looking uncharacteristically preoccupied and unsure of herself. "Do you think we're overdoing it? Or at least me? None of this wedding stuff's Cliff's doing—the hoopla, I mean—but I'm trying to pull it off in no time at all. It's a lot to handle."

"Yes, it is, but if a big wedding is what you want," Nora said diplomatically, "then it's what you should have."

Liza groaned, throwing up her hands. "I don't know anymore if it *is* what I want. Maybe I'm trying to please too many people. You know what I mean? Mother's lassoed one of her friends into having a bridal shower for me. Can you imagine? It's supposed to be a surprise, but when I started yapping about how relieved I am there wouldn't be time for that sort of thing, she told me."

Liza shook her head, and Nora refrained from comment as she drank more of the hot, flavorful coffee. She would just let her new friend articulate her worries and frustrations...before she found a subtle way to introduce the subject of Cliff's fellow Rhode Islander.

Wrinkling up her face, Liza continued, "I hate the idea of going through with a shower. Every nosy old prune in town'll be there—you know, those women who've never even had a man but feel free to offer advice." She stopped herself all at once, blushing furiously, something not a few in Tyler would have paid to see. "Nora, I'm sorry. I didn't mean—"

"It's quite all right."

"No one *ever* called your aunt Ellie a nosy old prune, and I'm sure it'll be the same for you—oh, God, I'm just making it worse."

But Nora, who'd never minded being compared to Aunt Ellie and who well understood the ramifications of being an old maid, started to laugh, imagining what Liza Baron would have to say if she'd been privy to Tyler's youngest spinster's steamy dream just a few hours ago. Liza stared at her, obviously confused and embarrassed, and then sputtered into laughter, too.

"Look," Nora said finally, really *liking* Liza Baron as a person, "why don't I talk to your mother and find out what she has in store that she wouldn't want you to know? If it's anything dreadful—and I'm sure it isn't—I'll do what I can to spare you any unpleasant surprises. I'll also offer to lend a hand, since this can't be all that easy on her, either."

"Oh, Nora, I couldn't let you go to all that trouble—I was just going to put my foot down with Mother and tell her to cancel."

"What, and spoil everyone's fun?"

"Showers are so—"

"Sexist and mercenary," Nora supplied, recalling Liza's forceful opinions on bridal registries. "Another feudalistic ritual."

Liza's bright, pretty eyes were glistening with amusement. "Right. And I don't intend to have any bridesmaids, either."

"I'm sure that's a perfectly legitimate decision. Traditions sometimes need a fresh look—or even to be abandoned altogether. But I like to look upon bridal showers and bridesmaids not as being about pots and pans and male power and dependence and such, but about sisterhood."

"No kidding?"

"Sure. When these things work, they're a celebration, an affirmation of who we've been as a community of women in the past and the possibilities and hope for what we can become in the future, as individuals, in our roles as wives, mothers, grandmothers, aunts, sisters."

"I'll have to mull that over," Liza said dubiously. "You do have a way of putting a nice spin on things, Nora Gates."

Nora shrugged. "Everyone loves a wedding."

"I know, and I've been thinking of so many of these wedding traditions as a burden—you know I'm a rebel at heart. It's my nature to question everything that's 'expected.' But it's refreshing to consider the meaning behind all these traditions. You *don't* have to talk to my mother, however."

"But I want to. Really."

Liza narrowed her eyes. "You mean it, don't you?"

Nora smiled. "I wouldn't mislead you on something this important. A bridal shower shouldn't be an imposition and it shouldn't be trivial—it should be fun."

"You're right."

"And a shower would help you get your feet wet—so to speak—before the wedding. You know, see your mother's friends and some of your old friends before you and Cliff—"

"Are waltzed up the aisle," Liza finished, grinning suddenly. "Okay, I get your point." But her grin vanished, her beautiful eyes darkening. "*Do* you think Cliff and I are rushing things?"

"It's not my place to say—"

"I don't mean about falling in love. That's happened. Nothing and nobody can undo that. I mean the wedding. People have hardly had time to adjust to my being home, never mind to my marrying the town recluse. And they don't know Cliff."

"Look," Nora said, comfortable in her role as confidante, "everyone in Tyler knows you do things in a whoosh. A couple of weeks' notice for your wedding is about all anyone who knows you would expect."

Liza downed half her coffee in a big gulp. "You wouldn't do it this way."

"I'm not you, Liza."

But Nora couldn't help thinking—*again*—of Byron Sanders. If their short-lived affair hadn't been a spontaneous whirlwind of lunacy, she didn't know what was. And there'd been a time when she'd thought nothing and no one could have pulled them apart. But that was over, an incident she didn't care to repeat because it *wasn't* her way of doing things. Whirlwind love affairs—even one that endured—were not her style.

She went on, "You need to do what's right for you without—"

"Without getting myself tarred and feathered and run out of town," Liza said good-naturedly. "I'm glad Cliff got you to come out here. For one thing, it shows he's thinking about me—which I *know,* but it's always nice to have it demonstrated. For another thing, it's a relief not to have to go through these wedding 'traditions' alone. I know I have Cliff and Mother—and Amanda and Jeffery, of course, but—"

"But fiancés, mothers and siblings don't help when what you really need is a friend."

Liza nodded. "Sisterhood, right? Honestly, Nora, from anyone but you that kind of talk'd sound downright radical. Hey, you want to say hi to Cliff? He should be around outside somewhere."

"If I won't be intruding."

"Not at all."

Nora rose to take her empty coffee mug to the sink, as Liza went on, "If you ask me, Cliff needs more intrusion. People in Tyler have been tiptoeing around him for too long, and there's just no need. You know, he'd had almost nothing to do with the human race for years and years until I barreled into his life."

She seemed quite pleased with herself as, standing next to Nora, she dumped out the rest of her coffee. Liza Baron was confident that she and Cliff Forrester were right—*meant*—for each other. Any of the upheaval their romance had caused for him and for herself was well worth the struggle, the change, the need to adapt and adjust.

Three years ago, Byron Sanders could have been smug about having barreled into Nora's life. But there was a difference. Cliff Forrester's life had needed stirring up. Nora's hadn't.

And it still didn't, she thought.

And, she added silently, there was another big difference: Liza Baron and Cliff Forrester loved each other.

"Come on," Liza said, "I'll take you through the back. There's a path down to the lake. I think that's where Cliff went."

They cut through a small sitting room off the kitchen and went out onto the veranda, which offered one of the old lodge's many spectacular views of the lake. With her usual boundless energy, Liza made a beeline to a narrow, beaten path that wound through the overgrown yard down toward the lake, as blue and clear as the autumn sky. The grass, knee-high along the path, was dotted with goldenrod and asters, and there were pale birches, the odd gnarled pine and clumps of sumac. All the more brightly colored leaves—the reds, burgundies and vivid oranges—had fallen to the ground, leaving only those of the more muted colors, yellows and soft oranges, clinging to the trees.

Nora screwed up her courage. "Have you heard from any of Cliff's family or friends in Rhode Island?"

"Oh, I only invited family—just his mother and younger brother. His father's dead. I don't know any of his old friends."

So Byron Sanders *hadn't* been invited to Tyler. The lying fink. How had he found out about the wedding? From the Rhode Island Forresters? The mother or the younger brother must have blabbed to someone who'd blabbed...well, Byron would be on the receiving end of any manner of gossip and news. He was that way. If the reclusive Cliff Forrester did indeed come from a prom-

inent East Coast family, Byron could have himself
quite a coup if he managed to photograph his wedding.

"How long has it been since Cliff's seen his family?" Nora asked casually.

Liza was getting well ahead of her. "Five years at
least," she said over her shoulder. "Why?"

"I was just curious. Sorry if I seem nosy—"

"No, that's okay. You don't seem nosy." Liza stopped
in the middle of the narrow path until Nora caught up
with her, a matter of thirty seconds. Nora was intensely
aware of her new friend's scrutiny. "You do seem a little... I don't know, nervous or something."

"I'm not—"

But Nora stopped, feeling her face drain of all color.
Up ahead, probably on the same path, or not bothering with a path at all, two men were walking toward
them. One clearly was Cliff Forrester. The other, just
as clearly, unless Nora had gone completely off her
rocker, was Byron Sanders.

"Hey, there!" Cliff called, waving.

Spotting him, Liza beamed and waved back. A
woman in love. "What're you up to? Who's that with
you?"

"I can't hear you. Wait there and we'll join you."

Liza frowned, her hands on her hips as she peered
down toward the lake and the two men. "That's not
one of Joe Santori's crew, is it?"

"I don't think so," Nora said, gritting her teeth.

Then the two men came up over the rise and she
could see Byron's dark hair glistening in the sun, the
hard edges of his face, his strong, even gait. The prospect of such ignominy, of having to deal with this man
again, and in front of two friends—two potential vic-

tims of Byron Sanders's wiles and charms—thoroughly unsettled and annoyed Nora.

She thought she saw him smiling.

The cad. Had he just recognized her? Did it amuse him to know he threw her off balance? Did he *enjoy* making her miserable?

I won't give him the satisfaction, she thought.

But as the two men came closer, Nora found herself muttering an oath Aunt Ellie certainly had never taught her.

Liza glanced at her, eyes twinkling. "Gee, Nora, I didn't think you had it in you."

Nora could feel the color returning to her cheeks. "Sorry. I'm just…it's possible I know this guy."

"No kidding?"

Then they were approaching and Nora gritted her teeth, saying nothing, refusing even to look at Byron Sanders. She felt his presence, though. It was just that way with her and him—one of those uncomfortable realities, like poison ivy and root canals.

"Hi, Cliff," Liza said. "Who's your friend?"

"He's not a friend."

Nora's eyes shot up. Cliff was looking pointedly at Byron Sanders. Had he found out what a two-faced weasel his fellow Rhode Islander was? Had he— With a brief, dark glance at Nora, Byron stepped forward, stretching out his hand. "Hello, Liza," he said in his most suave, debonair voice. "It's a pleasure finally to meet you."

"Oh, yeah? Who are you?"

Only Liza.

"My name's Byron," he said, with no detectable catch in his voice. "Byron Sanders Forrester."

Nora's knees when weak.
Liza said, "Then you're…"
"Yes. I'm Cliff's brother."

CHAPTER FIVE

GIVEN THAT SHE had an audience, Nora managed to keep her mouth shut and not go for the bastard's throat. She prided herself on her ability to make a quick recovery and hold back her emotions under the most trying circumstances, but this was beyond trying. She knew she must look shocked, pale, stiff, furious. But at least she wasn't in the process of committing a felonious act of violence.

"It's great to meet you, Byron," Liza said, not a little unnerved herself. Nora could see her glancing sideways at her husband-to-be, who hadn't, of course, known his brother was invited to their wedding. "When did you get here?"

"Yesterday."

Byron, Nora observed, was the only one who didn't look as if he wanted to strangle someone. He was used to sticky situations, however, and wasn't a man who could be easily analyzed from his outward appearance.

"Do you need a place to stay?" Liza asked. "Cliff and I have tons of room at the lodge—"

"That's okay. I'll manage."

Her hands locked into fists, Nora struggled to retain her composure. Had Byron squealed to his brother about their affair? There were too many dangers, too many questions.

Cliff moved close to his fiancée. "I promised Byron something to eat."

"Sure," Liza said. "Nora, would you care to join us? We could have an early lunch."

Nora would rather have joined a public snake roasting. "No, thank you." She sounded hoarse and a bit overcome even to herself. She cleared her throat. "I need to get back to the store. It's good to see you, Cliff." She made herself turn to the dark-eyed weasel. "Good to meet you, Mr. Forrester."

Because she was trying to be grown-up and not betray her true feelings, the way she said "Forrester" was frosty but not icy-sharp.

Cliff must have noticed. "Come on, Liza. You and I need to talk."

"About what?" Liza asked innocently.

"You know."

Never one on whom subtlety worked with any degree of regularity, Liza frowned. "I don't get it."

With a sigh of love and exasperation, Cliff took her by the elbow and hustled her off.

Nora tried to follow them, but Byron stopped her with one soft-spoken word. "Stay."

In the ensuing silence, Nora could hear the rustling of the breeze in the grass and in the woods beyond the path. She could hear birds, the distant honking of geese and the quiet lapping of lake water on the rocky shoreline nearby. Her ex-lover hadn't made another sound. She would have wondered if he'd slithered off to a sunny rock, but she could see his shadow. She refused to look at him. First she had to get a grip on herself.

Finally, he said, "I couldn't think of any decent way to tell you."

"Of course not. Decency isn't your style."

"I don't blame you for being angry."

He didn't go on, but waited for her to respond. She kept her silence. She couldn't yet allow herself to indulge in a full reaction. She might start screaming or cursing at him. She might jump him. Worse, she might cry. She'd hate that. The absolute worst, however, was not knowing what she'd do. And that was how it had been from the start when she was around this man: she couldn't count on being sensible. She couldn't always predict how she'd react.

"Cliff is…" Byron broke off with a grunt of frustration and, Nora guessed, out-and-out irritation. She didn't care. What did he want her to do? Look up at him angelically and say all was forgiven? If he was annoyed with her for her stony silence, with himself for the deep, dark hole he'd dug for himself, then good. She had no sympathy. But he went on quietly, in that gentle voice of her dreams, "Cliff's my only brother, Nora. He's been through a hell I can't even imagine. I had to come back."

"Yes," she said stiffly, in her most holier-than-thou old maid tone. "I suppose so."

"Sanders is my middle name."

It had a nice ring to it. Byron Sanders Forrester. One of your good upper crust East Coast names. No doubt he knew how to sail and play lacrosse. Probably had a pair of horn-rimmed glasses tucked in a tweed coat pocket somewhere.

When she didn't respond, Byron added, "My paternal grandmother was a Sanders. From Boston. Cliff's named for my mother's side of the family—Clifton Pierce Forrester. It's just the two of us. We were raised

in Providence. The Pierces have been there almost
since the Puritans banished Roger Williams from Massachusetts in 1636 and he came to Narragansett Bay."

By now his tone was only half-serious, but Nora
neither smiled nor relaxed. She wished she trusted
herself to be as spontaneous as Liza Baron was. But
Byron wouldn't charm her. Not this time. "Liza said
that Cliff's from a prominent East Coast family."

"That would be the Pierces."

She heard a wry bitterness creep into his voice,
prompting her to look at him square in the face. Immediately she wished she hadn't. The man was still,
after three years, one handsome devil. If she'd known
she'd be seeing him again, she would have prayed to
her fairy godmother to turn him into a frog. At the very
least, she'd have hoped that she'd take one look at him
and ask herself what all the fuss had been about three
years ago: how could she have fallen for someone as
transparently rotten as he was? He was so obviously
wrong for her. Not even sexy. Sort of lazy and worn-
out looking.

But that wasn't how she'd reacted. If wrong for her
on other counts, the man who'd swept her off her feet
three years ago still possessed the roguish sexiness
and charm that had drawn her to him so disastrously.
She could no longer try to blame bad timing. Aunt
Ellie wasn't dying anymore and she wasn't reexamin-
ing the choices and assumptions she'd made about
her own life. She was stable, satisfied, successful. In
a word, she was happy.

And still damnably, irreversibly, it seemed, attracted
to Byron Sanders. And not just physically. Their attraction to each other had never been purely physical.

She and Byron Sanders, in a very real way, had been kindred spirits and—

She seethed. Byron Sanders *Forrester*. She'd have to remember. She couldn't allow herself to forget that he was a liar, if a dangerously irresistible liar.

He didn't turn away from her, but met her probing gaze straight on. His eyes were as dark as his brother's, with fine, almost imperceptible lines spraying out from the corners. They were memorable eyes. But where she'd once found only unshakable confidence and humor, she now detected hints of pain and regret, hints of complexity. He wasn't *just* a cad or a rake, and she knew it. Perhaps, deep down, she'd always known it.

"They were publishers," he said, still talking about the Pierces. "My great-grandfather and a friend of his founded Pierce & Rothchilde, Publishers, more than a hundred years ago. They moved to their present location in Providence in 1894. The Rothchildes got out of the business in the twenties. Cliff and I are the last of the Pierces."

And Cliff was a near-recluse, Byron an itinerant photographer. Pierce & Rothchilde was one of the most prestigious publishers in the country. Nora was intrigued by the questions and potential conflicts those facts presented, but she'd already made up her mind. "I don't need to know anything about you or your grandmother Sanders or the Pierces or the Forresters. I really don't."

He sighed. "I know you don't. I guess I just don't know what the hell to say to you."

"Goodbye would be nice."

"All right. Goodbye, Nora."

But it wasn't good enough. Nora got three steps
back up the path and knew she needed satisfaction.
The man had slept with her and she hadn't even known
his real name! She whirled back around, the sun almost blinding her.

"Unless you can uproot a tree," Byron said calmly,
"there's nothing handy for you to throw at me."

He was maddening. How did he know what she
was thinking? What she was feeling? She tilted up
her chin, hanging on to the last shreds of her dignity.
"Does Cliff know about us?"

"He knows you don't like me."

"But I never indicated…"

Byron grinned. "You aren't as good at hiding
your emotions as you think, Miss Gates. But you can
relax—he doesn't know why you dislike me so much."

"What did you tell him?"

"Nothing."

"He just thinks I dislike you because of the series
on Aunt Ellie?"

Byron shrugged, his eyes clouding, his expression
unreadable. "I don't know what he thinks."

Nora exhaled at the blue autumn sky. "I could strangle you, Byron." But the truth was out, and at least it
explained—even excused—his presence in Tyler. It did,
in fact, have nothing to do with her. She looked back at
him. "And that's only the half of it."

"I'm sure," he said. His tone was neutral, but she
saw the lust—the damned amusement—in his eyes.

"Don't you get any ideas, Byron Sanders Whoever.
You don't mean any more to me than a bag of dried
beans."

"Remember the fairy tales, Nora. Jack's beans turned out to be magic."

"You're making fun of me."

"I'm not—"

"You never did take me seriously—*my* hopes, *my* dreams, who *I* am. You were only interested in your photography career and a little quick, convenient sex with an unsuspecting small-town woman."

Byron's mouth twitched, but apparently he was smart enough not to smile outright, given that there were uprootable trees in the vicinity. "Nora, it wasn't a little sex, it wasn't quick, that wasn't all there was to our relationship, and you're about as much the stereotypical unsuspecting small-town woman as Cliff and I are the stereotypical East Coast blue bloods." He paused while she came to a full boil. "I'd like to explain why I lied to you."

"You don't owe me an explanation, and frankly I don't require one." She looked at him for a moment, daring him to respond, but he didn't. What could he say? She was proud of her cool tone. She had to prove to herself that his remarks about their love life wouldn't get to her—at least so that anyone would notice. "All I ask is that you keep what we…*were* to each other to yourself."

And she started back up the narrow path, wondering what she would tell Liza. Because now, for sure, she wouldn't become involved with the wedding festivities. She didn't even want to attend the ceremony with Liza's future brother-in-law there. It was just too dangerous. Even if she trusted him—which she didn't— she didn't, in a very different way, trust herself. Seeing

Byron Sanders Forrester all dressed up for his brother's wedding just might do her in.

"I owe Cliff the truth," Byron said behind her.

That did it. Nora swung around, marched down to Byron and slapped him hard across the face, just as Katharine Hepburn slapped Humphrey Bogart in *The African Queen,* Aunt Ellie's favorite movie. Before she turned around and flounced back up the path, she noticed the red handprint on Byron's cheek. It just wasn't in her to feel sorry for him. He owed Cliff the truth. What about her? She'd spent three years thinking—

Well, she wouldn't think about Byron Sanders *Forrester* anymore.

"You know," he said, not far behind her, "you always act like an insulted Victorian virgin when you're mad. It's a good defense mechanism. But I don't believe it."

She ignored him.

He had to speak a little louder for her to hear him. Thank heaven Joe Santori and his crew weren't lurking about, eavesdropping. "I think you'd like to do a hell of a lot more than slap my face."

Like what? She almost panicked.

"*I* think," he yelled, "that what you'd like to do right now is skin me alive, and what grates is that you know I know it."

Skin him alive. Yes, that was it. That was just exactly what she wanted to do with him.

She whirled around, stepping backward. "Skin you alive and throw your bones to the wolves, you cad!"

He grinned. He wasn't marching in fast little steps the way she was, but moving deliberately, his long legs eating up the distance between them. She wished she'd worn her running shoes and jeans instead of her conservative businesswoman's outfit. She couldn't see his eyes against the bright sun. Three years ago, they'd told her what he was thinking, even feeling. Or at least she'd thought they had. She'd only seen what she'd wished to see—which wasn't like her. She prided herself on her ability to look life straight in the eye.

"I've never met anyone like you, Nora Gates," he said, still grinning.

She scoffed. "You told me that three years ago."

"Meant it."

"Then it was the one thing you said that you did mean."

"Oh, I said a lot of things I meant. But I don't blame you for being skeptical. Nora, the past is past. Let it go. I don't want my presence in Tyler to be a thorn in your side. You don't need to avoid me. I won't—" He broke off, his dark, dark eyes resting on her. "I won't let what happened three years ago happen again."

She didn't say a word. Could she believe him? Was that what she wanted to hear from him? "What happened and didn't happen wasn't just up to you, you know."

"Oh, really?"

"Byron..."

"No one needs to know that we were lovers three years ago. I just mean that I owe Cliff the truth about why I was in Tyler, what I did, why I left. He doesn't need to know the sordid details about us."

He'd said it so easily. As if being lovers with someone was no big deal. Probably the country was dotted with his ex-lovers. Nora raised her chin. "You're Cliff Forrester's brother. Everyone in Tyler's madly curious about him and his relationship with Liza—she's from one of the town's more prominent families. He's been a recluse out here for years and years. You're going to be well scrutinized."

"I expect so."

"Has it occurred to you that someone might recognize you as the photographer who did the series on Aunt Ellie?"

"It's possible, but—"

"Then not only will people be asking you questions, but they'll be asking *me* questions as well. Did I recognize you? Have I talked to you? Did I know you were really Cliff's brother?" She gulped for air, tense and irritated, just imagining what could be in store for her. "You've put me in one hell of a position."

"I'm sorry," he said.

His apology seemed genuine. What did she want from the man? Any other woman discovering an ex-lover back in town wouldn't go nuts at the prospect of people finding out about their long-dead relationship. It wasn't as if she'd been married to another man when Byron had burst into her life.

"I weighed all the pros and cons when I decided to come to Tyler," Byron said.

"And you came anyway."

"He's my brother, Nora. I had to come."

"Just keep your distance," she told him.

"Okay."

"And don't tell anyone *anything*. I value my reputation in this town."

"Your secret's safe with me."

"Scout's honor?"

He winced at the acid in her tone. "I'm not making fun of you."

"Yes, you are."

"Nora..."

"What you are doing, Byron, is belittling me. And I object. Vociferously. You don't have to understand me, but do not belittle me."

He sighed. "Nora, for the love of God, if I took out a billboard and announced that Nora Gates and I fell in love three years ago and it didn't work out, do you honestly think anyone in Tyler would give a damn?"

She squared her shoulders. "I swear, if there was a rock handy the coroner would be examining *two* bodies found at Timberlake Lodge! We did *not* fall in love. We—"

"Okay. I'll put on the billboard that Nora Gates isn't a virgin and I know it because I slept with her. Or should I be more explicit?"

"I'm just saying—" her whole body was on fire! "—that whatever it was we had together, it had precious little to do with love."

"Then it had to do with sex. I'll put that on my billboard."

"Dammit, Byron!"

"Don't 'dammit' me, Nora. Just tell me what you really do want."

"I want you not to exist!"

"No can do."

"Then at least..." She groaned, wondering what she did want. "At least respect me. I don't want my friends and customers—my community, Byron—to know that I...that you..."

"You did. I did. We did. Nora, nobody but you will care."

"That shows how little you know about Tyler."

Byron didn't relent. "Maybe it shows how little you know."

His tone was soft and seductive, so serious she would have thought he cared and understood, but experience had taught her otherwise. "I'll take full responsibility for my actions," she said tightly, "but don't you judge me, Byron *Forrester*. I'm not the one who talked a dying old woman into spending so many of her last days having her picture taken. I'm not the one who cynically swept a vulnerable small-town girl off her feet. I'm not the one who said Tyler wasn't for him and slithered out of town. I'm—" She stopped, staring at him. "What're you looking so incredulous over?"

"You," he said.

"Me? Byron, aren't you *listening?*"

"Yeah. I'm hearing every word, sweets. Just one question—what vulnerable small-town woman did I cynically sweep off her feet?"

Nora called him something that, coming from her, would have raised Liza Baron's eyebrows and dropped the jaws of half the people in Tyler. Aunt Ellie wouldn't have been shocked; it was her favorite thing to call randy neighborhood dogs who ran amok in her bushes.

Byron Forrester just laughed.

It was the same laugh that had awakened her from too many dreams over too many months. A laugh that she hadn't made up, but was real. Byron wasn't a fantasy.

"Relax, Nora," he said. "Lots of women fall for cads."

"I don't."

"You did. At least for a little while."

If she stayed there, she *would* skin him. Or fall for his roguish charms all over again.

"But I promise," he went on, "that I won't tell anyone you were human once for a few weeks. I'll keep your secret, Nora." Then his eyes darkened, and he added, "Until you decide you want to tell the whole world yourself that you're human after all."

Spotting Cliff and Liza out on the lodge's veranda kept Nora from an appropriately physical reaction. She wasn't a violent person. She wasn't even remotely homicidal. She just wanted Byron Sanders Forrester out of her life.

But his brother was about to marry one of Tyler's first citizens.

Byron, Nora thought miserably as she trudged up the path, pretending she hadn't heard that last gibe, would haunt her *forever.*

As BYRON WATCHED Nora in full retreat, a sudden, brisk wind blew off the lake and chilled him to the bone. It was like a parting shot from the owner of Gates Department Store, warning him to keep his distance.

Well, he thought, too late.

"Coffee's ready," Liza Baron yelled from the porch. "Lunch'll be ready in a bit."

Byron was torn. Given his reception, he wished he'd ignored Liza's invitation to the wedding and had waited to hear from Cliff himself. The least he could have done was to have worked up the guts to tell Nora the truth last night. Not that she'd given him the chance. There'd been the book of Beethoven sonatas, the beefy piano student. His own unexpected reaction to a woman he'd slept with for a couple of weeks one past summer—which was how he'd tried, mostly unsuccessfully, to think of her the past three years. Standing in her dining room last night, watching her just now in the cold light of day, he'd remembered how very much he'd loved her. Leaving her with so much unsaid, with all the promise of what they could have been together unfulfilled, had been one of the hardest things he'd ever had to do. And also one of the most important. If he'd stayed, he'd have risked destroying any hope for Cliff.

"What to do, what to do," he mused, watching the sunlight catch the cool shades of Nora's hair, making it shine.

He wondered if he would be doing everyone a favor—including himself—if he just headed back to his campsite, packed up and got the hell out of Tyler.

"Are you coming?" Liza yelled.

"In a minute."

And he trotted back to his musty tent, threw things into his nonexecutive-looking duffel in a flurry of purpose and action. Then came the cry of geese and another chilly gust off the lake, and he collapsed on Cliff's rock and thought, the hell with it. What was waiting for him back in Providence? Another smarmy phone call from another author who actually wanted to make a living at his writing? More dubious looks from Mrs. Redbacker? More mornings tossing darts? No, he thought. He wanted this time with his brother. He wanted to get to know Cliff Forrester all over again.

And Nora Gates.

He wanted this time with her, too. God help him, but he wanted to get to know her all over again, just to find out if what he was feeling right now was real. If what he'd done three years ago *had* been right for her, too.

He sighed, skimming a rock out onto the lake. What he was feeling right now was regret. For the lies, the choices he'd made, the time lost. And desire. There was no question he was feeling a good dose of desire for the gray-eyed woman he'd loved so many, many months ago.

He was also damned hungry, he thought, climbing stiffly to his feet.

By the time he joined Cliff and Liza on the veranda, Nora was long gone and they had put together a simple but fabulous lunch. There was ham and Wisconsin cheese on locally made sourdough rye bread, sliced fresh tomatoes—the last vine-ripened tomatoes of the season, which Liza herself had tucked away—and leftover cranberry-apple crisp, made, of course with Wisconsin cranberries and apples.

It was almost—but not quite—too cold to eat outside.

"Nora left?" Liza asked.

Byron shrugged, trying to seem neutral on the subject of Nora Gates. "Apparently."

"You two chitchatted quite a while. She knows you?"

"Me?"

"Yeah. She thought she recognized you."

"Did she?" He stabbed a slice of tomato with a fork. "She didn't say anything. Mostly we talked about the geese."

"Uh-huh."

Liza didn't sound convinced. Cliff eyed his brother, then looked away. "I've got a few things I need to get done." Without another word, he took off with his sandwich and a cup of coffee.

If Liza was annoyed by her fiancé's abrupt departure or her future brother-in-law's sidestepping her questions, she gave no indication. She did not, Byron decided, have a suspicious, devious mind. He already found himself admiring her energy and optimistic nature, and it was easy to see how much she was in love with his older brother.

Unfolding her long legs from under her on her wicker chair, she planted her feet on the newly painted veranda floor. "So, Byron," she said, "do you think your brother's going to string me up for sending you and your mother that invitation?"

"Did he say he would?"

She grinned. "No, but I got the drift."

"I'd have warned you I was coming, but you didn't include an address or number—"

"Intentionally. I figured I'd just strike the match and see if I could start a fire. You want some more coffee?"

She was, obviously, a woman who didn't look back. "No, thanks, this is fine."

"Cliff didn't tell me he saw you last night."

She spoke without defensiveness or anger. She was a confident woman, too, and sure of Cliff's love for her. Whatever Cliff's reasons for ducking out, they had nothing to do with his relationship with Liza Baron. That was rock solid. Byron had been concerned his brother might have fallen for a woman who'd pity him and indulge his isolation, who'd coddle him and exacerbate his problems. Liza Baron, however, was clearly not that kind of woman.

"We needed to talk first," Byron said.

"Have you?"

"Some. Not enough."

Liza nodded. "I guess you two seeing each other for the first time in so many years must be about as unsettling as my coming back to Tyler to live and all. And it's gotta be a lot tougher."

Byron didn't speak. It *was* tough to see Cliff—and Nora—and not know how it would turn out.

"How come you're here so early?" Liza asked baldly.

"Let's just say I'm on an advance scouting mission."

Liza slapped what must have been another tablespoon of spicy mustard onto her sandwich. "In case Cliff was marrying some fruitcake or had gone nuts altogether?"

Byron smiled. "Something like that."

"Well," she said, jumping to her feet, "we're both probably crazy as hell, but not in the way most people think. Byron…" She paused, suddenly serious. "Byron, I'm worried about Cliff—that I'm making him bite off more than he can chew at one time. Mother says I need to go easy, but then she so obviously wants this big wedding—and then *I* go and meddle in Cliff's relationship with his family. I mean, not too many weeks ago he was living up here like a damned timber wolf."

"I can leave," Byron said.

"No, that'd be the worst thing you could do. The horse is already out of the barn, as the saying goes. I mean, you're here, Byron." She looked in the direction Cliff had gone and said, almost to herself, "I ache for him sometimes." Then she turned to Byron and smiled, her eyes shining with tears. "And he hates it."

"What do you want me to do?"

"For starters, move out of that damned tent. Looks

terrible to have you camping out at the lake. People will think you're another recluse like Cliff and the whole damned Forrester family's nuts. We've got to find you a regular place to stay until the wedding."

"I don't mind camping—"

"*I* mind. The gossip mill in this town's grinding me and my family to pieces enough without having my future brother-in-law washing his face in the lake. Can you imagine the morning of the wedding? This is going to be one fancy shindig, you know. It just won't do to have you show up smelling like a musty old tent."

Byron laughed; Liza did have a way about her. "I won't stay here with you two, so don't even try that one on me again. In fact, I wasn't planning to stay at all. The wedding's not until next Saturday." He thought of his nonrefundable ticket and his Yankee soul almost rebelled, but he added, "I'll come back."

Liza frowned, scrutinizing him. "Business to tend?"

"No, but—"

"Then stay. Unless," she said, obviously well aware she wasn't being told everything, "there's some compelling reason you can't."

The reason had just gone screaming back to town. No, Byron thought, not screaming. Not Nora. She did everything purposefully, deliberately. He'd bet she'd never gone over the speed limit in her life. The one time she'd been out of control had been with him, which was why she hated his guts. And also because he'd behaved rather badly toward her, but that was another matter.

His momentary distraction had given Liza enough time to come up with an impulsive idea. "Hey—why don't I ask Nora to put you up? She's anxious to give me a hand, and from what I hear she's a great hostess. She lives alone, so she loves to have company."

Byron didn't believe it necessarily followed that one who lived alone loved to have company, but he didn't disabuse Liza of that point. "Nora Gates, you mean?" he asked as innocently as he could, considering he'd not *that* long ago slept with the woman. Nevertheless, he wasn't an altogether inefficient liar. "I could never ask her—"

"I could. Leave everything to me."

"People could get the wrong idea—"

"Good!" Liza was grinning, warming to her solution. "It'd do Nora's reputation a world of good to have a little dirty talk circulating about her. Gosh, people have already started calling her Aunt Ellie. You never knew her, but she's a legend in Tyler. She started Gates Department Store. Nora takes after her, but she's... I don't know, she's *not* Aunt Ellie. It was just the two of them for so many years, and now Nora's alone...." Her voice trailed off, as she nodded to herself. "Yeah, I like this idea. I'll let you know what she says."

And she was off, serape flying. In another minute, Byron heard her white T-bird roar to a start.

"She's tough when she latches on to an idea," Cliff commented, coming onto the veranda.

Byron set his empty cranberry-apple-crisp plate on the lunch tray. "Nora will choke on her teeth when Liza asks her to put me up."

Cliff raised his dark eyes to his brother. "Don't be too sure. I saw the way she looked at you. What went on between you two three years ago?"

"Doesn't matter. Right now she'd like nothing better than to have my head stuffed and mounted on her dining room wall."

Cliff gave a small smile. "Not your head, I think."

"Very funny." But his brother was perhaps more astute than Byron wanted to admit. Nora Gates could have forgiven any number of transgressions, any number of things he might have done to her. But he hadn't done any number of things. He'd made love to her. With her. He groaned just thinking about it. "It won't work, Cliff. You and Liza don't need me here. I shouldn't have come back until I knew for sure you were ready."

"I'm ready. Liza knew before I did." Cliff plopped down in her chair. "The question is, are you?"

Byron didn't answer. "Why didn't you stay for lunch?"

"Needed to think. Things are just shy of getting out of hand around here. I needed to get a grip. The wedding's enough of an ordeal...the crowds..." Expressionless, he looked out at the lake. "I didn't expect you. Even less you and Nora." He looked at his brother. "I had no idea you were here three years ago."

"You weren't supposed to."

"You were protecting me?" he asked bitterly.

Byron shook his head, wanting to explain, but Cliff had already jumped to his feet and was heading off the veranda. "I don't want to argue," Byron said.

"Then don't. Come on, I'll show you around the lodge."

Byron didn't budge. "What about Nora? Cliff, she'll never agree to put me up. Liza will want to know why—"

"Liza can be very persuasive when she wants something." Cliff smiled that twitching smile. "Look at me."

"What is it about Tyler that breeds such women?"

"Long, hard winters, I think."

"You don't believe Nora will turn Liza down?"

Cliff shook his head. "If nothing else, she'll want to save face."

"Well, you're crazy."

"So people say."

But Clifton Pierce Forrester, Byron could now see, was not in any way, shape or form mentally unbalanced. Which wasn't to say that his years of suffering and isolation hadn't taken their toll. So had the recent activity around him—the people activity. Byron guessed that a part of his brother wanted to bolt, and perhaps only his overwhelming love for Liza Baron was keeping him from finding another place to hide, retreating from the world he and Liza were building for themselves.

Instinctively, abruptly, Byron knew that Cliff needed him to stay in Tyler. Just as, three years ago, he'd known that Cliff had needed him to leave. No, not just leave. Never to have come at all. It was a fine distinction, but one that mattered. Whether Cliff would see that or not, Byron wasn't prepared to say.

He found himself giving in, nodding. "Okay—let's have the grand tour of where you've been hiding all these years."

"Not hiding," Cliff said. "Healing."

CHAPTER SIX

It was late October in Wisconsin and night came early. Too early as far as Byron was concerned. Parked outside Nora Gates's house, he checked his car clock. It wasn't even seven yet. He had the whole damned evening still ahead of him.

"She said she'd be glad to have you over," Liza had told him victoriously upon her return to the lodge. She hadn't even been gone an hour. "You're to be at her house for dinner at seven sharp. See, didn't I tell you? Gosh, she's just the *nicest* woman."

Byron had wondered if he were Nora's intended main course. Roasted publisher. He knew writers—and a few editors—with Pierce & Rothchilde who'd share such a fantasy.

He thought Nora Gates was a lot of things, but *nice* wasn't among them.

His brother had been no help. "You and Nora have things you need to settle. Maybe it's a good idea to throw you two together for a while."

Byron had laughed. "Cliff, that's like throwing a spider and a fly together to see if they'll get along. They just won't. It's a matter of nature."

"Who's the fly and who's the spider?"

Byron left his gear—which Cliff had shoved at him when he'd told him to go, confront Nora like a man, not a fly—in his rented car. The wind had kicked up and it was damned cold on Nora's pretty tree-lined street. He walked up onto the front porch. It was such a peaceful place. Why the hell was he looking for booby traps? *You made her hate you. Now reap what you sowed.*

A tall, skinny boy, probably about thirteen, was shuffling out the door. "I promise I'll do better next week, Miss Gates. I haven't had much time to practice with it being footfall season."

"Lars," Nora said, "you're not on the football team."

From the looks of him, Byron thought, he never would be. "I know," the kid said, "but I watch practice every chance I get. I want to go out for the team next year."

"We all have a variety of interests, Lars," Nora, still out of view, said patiently. "The trick is to find a balance that works. You're wasting your parents' money and your time—and, I might add, a considerable amount of natural talent—if you don't practice."

"Right, Miss Gates, I understand. I'll do better."

As Lars came out onto the porch, Nora moved into the doorway, holding open the screen door. She had on charcoal-gray corduroys and a roll-neck charcoal-gray sweater. With her hair swept up off her face, she looked controlled, in charge of her world and very, very attractive. "I hope you do because—" She spotted Byron and straightened up, stiffening noticeably. "Oh, you're here."

All in all, it was the sort of greeting he'd expected.

"Who're you?" the kid asked boldly.

"My name's Byron Forrester."

"He's my houseguest," Nora put in, without enthusiasm. "Byron, this is Lars Travis, one of my piano students."

The kid's eyes had lit up. "Gee, Miss Gates, I had no idea— I mean, everybody in town thinks you don't… that you'd never…"

"Mr. Forrester is in Tyler for Liza Baron and Cliff Forrester's wedding next Saturday," Nora said, spots of color high in each of her creamy cheeks. "With Timberlake Lodge being renovated, I agreed to have Byron stay here. He's Cliff's brother. Now, Lars, don't get any ideas."

"No, I won't, Miss Gates. I just was surprised because I didn't think you knew any men."

And he scampered off the porch, all bony arms and legs, before Nora could strangle him.

She watched the kid go with narrowed eyes. "I'm doomed. Lars has the biggest mouth in town next to Tisha Olsen and maybe Inger Hansen, and he has very peculiar ideas about me. You'd sometimes think I'm not human."

"Isn't that what you want people to think?" Byron asked casually.

She transferred her piercing gaze to him. "You're not going to make this any easier, are you?"

"You didn't have to take me in."

"I realize that."

"Then why did you? If it's just because you didn't want to disappoint Liza, you can damned well forget it. Nora…dammit, I'm tired of thinking you've got a stiletto tucked somewhere and are going to do me in at any moment. I came to Tyler three years ago, I fell for you, you fell for me, I neglected to tell you my real name, and now I'm back. I can't change history."

"I'm not asking you to," she said softly, "and I didn't agree to take you in just so I wouldn't disappoint Liza." She smiled mysteriously. "And I don't have a stiletto hidden on me."

"A blowtorch?"

"Too big."

"Nora…"

"Come inside, Byron. It's getting cold out. Where are your bags?"

"Nora, I won't stay if you—"

"I'm doing this for myself, Byron," she said, cutting him off. "Not for you, not for Liza, not even for Cliff. Nobody manipulated me or talked me into anything. If you'll recall, I do know my own mind. Now, I've got dinner in the oven."

She walked briskly past him down to the street and reached into the passenger seat of his car, pulling out his disreputable-looking duffel. She made a face. When he was traveling on behalf of Pierce & Rothchilde, he took matching monogrammed bags. Mrs. Redbacker insisted. Nora would have approved.

She carried the duffel back up onto the porch as if it were something dead and smelly she'd found out on her street. Byron didn't offer her a hand. Some things Nora Gates just preferred to do herself.

"You'll have to move your car," she said.

"Neighbors might talk?"

"The street sweepers are doing a special leaf pickup tomorrow."

"Nora…" He leaned against a porch column. "Thanks."

In the harsh light of the porch, he could see the tiny lines at the corners of her eyes and where her raspberry lipstick had worn off, but she looked better than she had three years ago. Not as gaunt, not as uncertain of her own future. He'd have told her so if it wouldn't have infuriated her to have him notice such things. She liked to think men only respected her. And mostly they did. But sometimes they thought about her in other ways, too. Anyway, he did.

He held open the screen door for her. She didn't complain. "I'm putting you in the front bedroom upstairs," she said. "It gets nice morning sun."

"I was expecting the torture chamber."

She shot him a look, but he thought he detected a hint of amusement in her pale eyes. "A pity I don't have one."

"Going to skewer me in my sleep?"

"I'm not going near you in your sleep," she said, dashing inside before he could see if she'd blushed. Not that there was much chance of that. Their lovemaking didn't embarrass her nearly as much as it ticked her off, challenging her most cherished beliefs about herself. She *wasn't* another Aunt Ellie.

She dumped his bag on the bottom step leading upstairs. It was heavier than it looked, and she was breathing hard, as much from the tension of having him there, he felt, as from exertion. "I'll get dinner on the table. You can find your way?"

"I remember," he said in a low voice.

"Maybe," she said starchily, "it would be better if you didn't."

"No. It wouldn't."

His sincerity seemed to have no discernible impact on her. She marched off to the kitchen, leaving him to fend for himself. The front bedroom was the guest room and always had been, from the time Aunt Ellie had had the house built. Nora had moved into the back bedroom overlooking the gardens and yard when she was thirteen. It was where she and Byron had made love, after Aunt Ellie had gone into the hospital. She'd made it home to die. By then, Byron had left Tyler.

The guest room hadn't changed, the senior Eleanora Gates's fussier taste in evidence. The curtains were filmy lace, the bed a four-poster with a lace dust ruffle, lace coverlet, lace pillow shams. There was a tiger-maple bureau with a matching mirror, and an Oriental rug of vivid roses and blues.

Byron couldn't resist: he went across the hall and had a peek. Nora obviously had moved downstairs, and her old room was completely different. It was as if she'd wanted to exorcise the girl she'd been there, the woman she'd become. She'd installed two twin beds, covered with utilitarian quilts, and painted chests, a painted trunk and a children's table and chairs set up with teddy bears at a tea party. Nora had said she'd make a great aunt. Apparently not having any nieces and nephews of her own hadn't stopped her. What had Liza said? People in town were already starting to call her Aunt Ellie. That was fine, if it was what Nora wanted.

He thought better of tossing his duffel up on the lacy bed and instead shoved it into the closet, which had potpourri sachets hanging from hooks. He'd unpack later, if at all. If worse came to worst, he'd find himself a park bench.

Down in the kitchen, Nora had set the table with a simple but tempting meal of roast turkey breast, baked acorn squash and tossed salad. Byron could smell apples baking in the oven. His stomach flip-flopped on him; he hadn't had anything like this in his life in years. Ever since his return to Pierce & Rothchilde three months ago, he'd found himself relying on Providence restaurants and take-out gourmet.

"You didn't have to go to any trouble on my account," he said.

"I didn't. I always make proper meals for myself, and I set the table every night. Just because I live alone doesn't mean I don't lead a civilized life."

"Whoa, there. Don't forget that I live alone, too."

"In a tent," she sneered.

Byron raised a brow. "You've been keeping track of me?"

"The store carried your last book. Naturally I couldn't resist a peek at your bio—which I presume wasn't *all* lies?"

A year ago, he'd had a slender volume of his photographs published by a small press—he'd refused to pull any strings at Pierce & Rothchilde. The distribution was nil and there wasn't a chance that it would have been accidentally or casually picked up by a department store with a small book section. It would have had to have been special-ordered. But given that Nora was putting him up—and had a carving knife in her hand—Byron decided not to press the issue.

"It wasn't any of it lies," he said, sitting in the chair she pointed at with her knife.

"Your name—"

"I used Byron Sanders as a pseudonym, that's all. It's a common practice."

"The bio said you'd spent the previous two years crisscrossing the country and some of Canada and Mexico, living out of your van and a tent."

"Pretty much true."

She set down her knife and laid slices of steaming turkey on a small platter, which she set in the middle of the table. "Byron Sanders is 'pretty much' your own name, too, but it hardly tells the whole story."

"Do you ever let anything go?"

"Seldom."

"By 'pretty much' I only mean that I also had the family place in Providence." He lifted half an acorn squash, dripping with butter and brown sugar, onto his plate. "My mother's away frequently, and it's…spacious." Telling her it was a mansion, he decided, would further undermine the myths Nora had created about him and would not, given the timing, be wise. "So it's not as if I had no place to go but my van and tent."

"I see. Can't let life get too tough, huh?"

He frowned. "Nora, if you don't lighten up you're going to get indigestion. And give me indigestion while you're at it."

But she smiled suddenly, her entire face brightening. It was the way he most liked to remember her, when she was at her most captivating. He'd never really understood what made Nora Gates smile. "Byron, I was kidding. A bit sensitive about this family place, hmm? Must be something. But I don't care if it was designed by Charles Bulfinch, has the best view of the Atlantic in Providence and is the next fanciest thing to the Ritz on the East Coast. As Aunt Ellie used to say, it makes no never mind to me."

Byron chose not to tell her how damned close she'd come to describing the Pierce house on Benefit Street in Providence, Rhode Island.

Her expression turned serious. "The book...your photographs were wonderful, Byron. I mean that."

"Thank you."

Despite its modest sales, his book had won a couple of prestigious awards, individual photographs other smaller rewards. His subject had been fathers and sons. He'd traveled from small town to big city, in search of the extraordinarily ordinary. And he'd found it, time and time again. His work, his years of being on the road, neither a Pierce nor a Forrester, had helped him make himself whole again.

"When you came to Tyler," Nora said, sitting across from him, "you weren't a professional photographer, were you?"

"I'm still not."

"Then what did you...what do you do for a living?"

She asked the question as if she already knew she wouldn't like the answer. Anyone else, Byron thought, would have squirmed having to face those incisive eyes. But Nora Gates didn't intimidate him; none of the little ways she kept people at a comfortable distance—or men, anyway—worked with him.

Which still didn't mean she'd like his answer.

"I was president... I *am* president of Pierce & Rothchilde, Publishers."

She didn't throw anything. She just leaned back, fork in hand, and narrowed her eyes at him.

"What are you doing?" he asked.

"Trying to picture you in pinstripes."

"Oh, pinstripes are much too racy for P & R."

"But..." She scooped a piece of squash onto her plate, stabbed some turkey. "Then I assume you have a business background or some sort of training."

He nodded matter-of-factly. "A Harvard M.B.A. Being the great-grandson of Clifton Rutherford Pierce—P & R's founder—hasn't hurt any, either."

She inhaled, and he could see her revising her thoughts. First, she'd had to adjust to his being the younger brother of the reclusive man up at Timberlake Lodge. Now she had to adjust to his not being the disreputable, uneducated, incorrigible heel of a photographer she'd imagined he was three years ago. Mostly it *had* been her imagination; he'd never told her all that much about himself. He hadn't lied so much as omitted pertinent details.

"You quit to do your book?" she asked.

"I took a leave of absence after I came to Tyler."

"For how long? I mean, are you going back?"

"I have gone back," he said.

"So you're president of one of the most prestigious publishing houses in the country?"

There was no way around it. "Yes."

"Well," she said, and muttered something about having forgotten the cranberry sauce. She got a small bowl from the fridge and sat back down, changing the subject to the fate of the Tyler Titans, the high school football team, in their latest game, and how Ricky and Lars Travis were both talented pianists but so different. Finally, she looked at him and said, "Harvard, huh?"

"Yep."

"Well, that makes everything easier."

"How so?"

"You're not the man you were three years ago. You're someone else. You're Byron Sanders Forrester, East Coast blue blood, amateur photographer, president of Pierce & Rothchilde, Publishers—I don't know.

You're just not the Byron I saw staring at me in Gates's window that summer. I guess…" She paused, swallowing a piece of turkey. "I guess in a way that Byron doesn't exist."

He leaned back. "Nice try, Nora."

"I beg your pardon?"

"It won't work. You can't erase me. You can't press a damned delete button and just eliminate me." He pushed back his chair and leaned over the table, so that he could almost feel her breath on him. "I am the same man who slipped your bra off that night in the tent. It was lace—it had a front clasp. I'm the same man who kissed the little mole on your stomach. I'm the same man who went skinny-dipping with you in that swimming hole in the stream—"

"Stop!"

"I'm the man who made love to you, Nora Gates."

She jumped to her feet. "Leave the dishes. I'll—"

"I'm not a dead file you can just clear out of your cabinet."

"I'll do them when I get back. I take a fitness walk most evenings."

He turned around in his chair so he could see her sneak across her kitchen. "I'm not somebody you made up one summer."

She smiled coolly, distantly. "Make yourself at home— I won't be long."

She was already at the kitchen door. Byron tilted his chair back on two legs. "You know," he said, not cool, not distant, "you should be thanking your lucky stars I do exist. In fact, you're damned lucky I turned up in Tyler again."

Only her eyes—as always—betrayed her intensity. "I fail to see why."

"Because, Miss Gates," he said, "you're trying to become something you're not."

"And what, pray tell, is that?"

"Your Aunt Ellie."

He could see her swallow. "You're wrong."

"Am I?" he asked gently.

"Yes." She looked away. "Anyway, we're not discussing me. Three years ago, you tried to be something you weren't. Don't try to resurrect Byron Sanders now. It won't work."

"I don't know," he mused, setting his chair back down on four legs. If she wouldn't talk about Aunt Ellie, he couldn't make her. "That haughty way you talk... I think you've been spending too much time rereading Jane Austen and the Brontë sisters."

"You can be such a jerk, you know that?"

"That's better. Thought you might call me an 'incorrigible rake' or a 'dastardly fellow'—"

He didn't see it coming. He was still thinking Jane Austen when he noticed the cookbook flying through the air; she'd snatched it from a shelf by the door and launched it before he could react. It missed by far fewer inches than the Beethoven had.

Byron laughed, reassured. He'd thought for a second that mentioning Aunt Ellie had only reminded Nora that she wasn't behaving the way she figured she ought to behave. But if she was back to throwing things, she was at least letting her emotions, however raw, rip. "Look at it this way—my being here will improve your aim."

And she was off, wishing out loud that her life *did* have a delete button so she could send him into the electronic ether. Byron was unreasonably glad that she at least wasn't neutral on the subject of her ex-lover.

Suddenly he was ravenous. Reaching across the table he grabbed Nora's plate and finished off her dinner. Then, half to annoy her, half because he'd been taught to be a proper guest, he did up the dishes.

But that wasn't the only reason he did them. Washing the dishes was one way of staking out territory in whatever relationship they were to have in the days until Cliff and Liza's wedding—and beyond. He wasn't just Nora's guest. He wasn't an old friend. And he sure as hell wasn't somebody who hadn't *existed* one August three years ago. He was a man who'd loved her, and there was no way either of them could deny it.

There was no way, either, he thought, scrounging in her kitchen drawers for aluminum foil, that he could deny it would be all too easy to fall in love with Nora all over again. What was it about the woman?

He found the foil, then tripped over the book she'd pitched at him. It was a low-fat, low-everything cookbook. Snatching it up, he grumbled aloud that there wasn't *anything* about that unforgiving prude that should attract a solid, reasonable, nonself-destructive man such as himself. Was she just a challenge to him? Did he want her only because she'd made herself so damned unattainable?

"You are out of your mind, my man," he muttered. "You've no business wanting that gray-eyed witch."

But then he could see those gray eyes fill with unspoken pain, with loss and grief, and love, when he'd mentioned Aunt Ellie, and nothing, he knew, would ever be simple or easy when it came to his feelings for Nora Gates.

AFTER HER TENSE and overlong day, Nora returned from her brisk three-mile walk relaxed, if also tired and cold and a bit chastened. She could warm her hands in a pan of dishwater and soothe her soul with a good book and an early lights-out. But Byron had already done the dishes. He'd even slipped her cookbook back into its slot on the shelf. Looking at its torn cover reminded her of her fit of anger, but that was over now. She wouldn't let him get to her like that again.

She found him in the study, where he had a fire going in her brick fireplace. He was sitting on the carpet in front of the fire, his long legs stretched out in front of him, just staring at the flames. He seemed unaware that she'd come in.

"Thank you for doing the dishes," she said.

He glanced up at her; she hadn't moved from the doorway. "You don't have to thank me. How was your walk?"

"Invigorating." She licked her lips, suddenly unsure if she should go any further. She'd done some thinking on her walk. A lot of thinking. "I haven't been very grown-up about your being back in Tyler. I mean, throwing things *is* a bit puerile...."

"Puerile? Haven't heard that word in years. Look, Nora, I don't mind honest emotion—in fact, I'm glad you can be yourself when you're around me. And you'd never get so out of control as to hurt me...."

She almost smiled. "You always have been an optimist. I do admire that about you—and your sense of humor. Most of the time, anyway." She cleared her throat, wondering if launching down the perilous path of being amiable with Byron had been a smart idea. But here she was. "You've made it clear that your lying about your name had nothing to do with me—that things you didn't tell me three years ago were…well, you know. It's over. I see no reason why we can't go on from here and at least be civil to each other."

"I haven't thrown anything at you."

He did know how to upset her equilibrium. "That's true, but you can't deny that you've deliberately tried to provoke me."

"Okay. I won't deny it."

"Byron…" She sighed, breaking off. "Never mind. I've had a long day. If you don't need anything from me, I'd like to turn in, do some reading."

"Jane Austen?"

"Byron…!"

He smiled. "Sweet dreams, Miss Gates."

She did not have sweet dreams. She dreamed about him again. Aunt Ellie was still alive, grinning her toothy grin as Nora and Byron made dinner together, laughing and chopping carrots as if the three of them were a happy, if unorthodox, family. Spinster businesswoman, orphaned niece, wandering photographer. The dream made no sense. It took place in the present, although Aunt Ellie had been dead for three years, and she'd seemed to like Byron, enjoy his company, although how could she? He'd lied to her, too. But the discrepancies didn't strike Nora until she woke up with a start, heart pounding, for the dream had ended—abruptly—with Byron kissing a silver band on Nora's finger.

"Perish the thought."

It was rather like coming to amid a nightmare in which one was tumbling from an airplane without a parachute.

Throwing on her chamois bathrobe, she was out in the kitchen before she remembered that part of her dream was true: Byron *was* back in Tyler. And in a fit of madness, she'd agreed to have him as her house-guest.

"Oh, Lord."

He had a pot of coffee on already and was digging in her refrigerator, plaid shirttail hanging out over jeans that after years of wear fit comfortably over the muscular contours of his hips and legs. He was barefoot. He grinned a good-morning over his shoulder, and she saw that his hair was still tousled from sleep. His jawline was a sexy shadow of dark beard. He looked every bit the rakish photographer, but she quickly adjusted her image. He was the president of an East Coast publishing house. He'd been born with the proverbial silver spoon in his mouth. To him, Gates Department Store—Aunt Ellie's labor of love, her dream, her creation—was probably quaint. Nora realized, with a pang, that she didn't know this man—that she had no right to hate him.

"Eggs for breakfast?" he asked.

"I don't eat eggs and you don't need to make me breakfast."

"Egad, what's this? Eggs in a bottle?"

"It's an egg substitute. Byron, I don't permit house-guests to rummage at will in my refrigerator."

He pushed aside her liquid egg substitute as if he'd found a moldy leftover. "What do you usually eat in the morning?"

"Oatmeal and raisins. Now out—"

"Okay." He rose, making her kitchen seem smaller with his size and the sheer force of his presence. Nora wasn't used to having anyone around in the morning, not even a cat. When she had guests, she kept them out of the kitchen until she had breakfast ready. "Oatmeal it is. No raisins, though. You use brown sugar?"

She shook her head. He hadn't buttoned his shirt all the way and what buttons he had done up were crooked. It was impossibly sexy. She could see curls of dark hair poking out. "I'll cook," she said.

"Nope. You sit. It's Saturday morning and I've put you through hell the past two nights." He laughed. "Bad choice of words. 'Yesterday and the previous evening' sounds less scandalous, hmm? I won't judge your nights."

"Are you making fun of me?"

He poured her a cup of coffee and set it on the table, although she'd yet to sit down. "Never."

"Ha."

"You take your coffee black, right?"

"I'm surprised you remember."

He looked at her. "You shouldn't be."

At that, it was either sit or get out of there so she could collapse in private. She couldn't stand around feeling out of place in her own kitchen. She tried the coffee. It was strong enough to pave a driveway, probably exactly what she needed. Byron got out the oatmeal, measuring cups, a pan. He studied the carton, frowning.

"Recipe's on the inside of the top now," she said.

"Ahh. Haven't made oatmeal in a while."

"You eat eggs every morning?" Then she remembered his background. "Oh. I suppose you have a housekeeper."

"No housekeeper, and I don't eat eggs every morning. I'll often grab a bagel or a muffin or just make toast."

In his tent, the morning after they'd first made love, they'd shared little boxes of cereal. They'd cut the boxes open with his jackknife and poured the milk inside and eaten with plastic spoons. It had been the most romantic breakfast Nora had ever had. Sometimes she wished she could forget it.

"What're you doing today?" he asked.

"I'll stop by the store. Then I have some errands to run. You?"

"I need to see Cliff—he's got to be rattled with all that's going on."

"This business with the body can't have helped matters. I wish the Tyler police department would tell us *something*. The rumors...well, they're unpleasant."

Byron's pot of water had come to a boil. He dumped in a couple handfuls of oatmeal, stirred, contemplated the pot, then dumped in a bit more. Nora had made oatmeal hundreds of times, and although she did have the recipe for a single serving memorized, she measured every time.

"Would you tell me what the rumors are?" he asked.

"I hate to repeat gossip."

"That's why everyone tells you everything."

"Not everyone. Those who expect some little tidbit in return tell me nothing. Gossip is a currency for some people." But that wasn't anything Byron didn't know, or cared about. She was just babbling because it was morning, she'd dreamed about him, and he was making oatmeal for her in her own kitchen. "You want to know because of Cliff?"

Byron nodded, and while he kept an eye on the

cooking oatmeal, stirring it occasionally, Nora told him what she knew people were saying around town about the Body at the Lake. That it could be Margaret Ingalls. That Judson might have known more than he was letting on. That she'd been murdered. That she'd never run away.

"If nothing else, people say she wouldn't have abandoned Alyssa the way she supposedly did," Nora said.

"That's Margaret's daughter?"

"And Liza's mother."

"Considering what Cliff's been through," Byron said, dumping scoops of oatmeal into two pottery bowls, "this all could cause him to have a relapse. It could stir up nightmarish memories for him."

"Nightmarish memories of what?"

He stared at her. "You don't know?"

She shook her head. "Byron, nobody in Tyler knows anything about Cliff. Lots of people thought he was certifiable until Liza came back. Not a few wonder if—" She stopped herself.

"If Liza's making a mistake?"

"It's just talk."

Byron nodded. "With the added strain of a big wedding and my being here, our mother planning to show up…"

His voice trailed off, but Nora, abandoning thought of getting him to tell her what exactly Cliff Forrester had endured, finished for him. "You're afraid Cliff could throw in the towel—find another Tyler in which to hide."

"I think he's afraid of it, too. Yesterday he started to give me a tour of the lodge, but he couldn't finish.

He…he just walked away and started chopping wood. Post-traumatic stress disorder isn't always predictable."

"But he loves Liza."

Byron looked at her. "Exactly."

Nora frowned. "I don't get it."

"I know you don't." He plopped a bowl of oatmeal in front of her. "Come on, let's change the subject and eat breakfast."

He sat across from her with his box of brown sugar. She fetched the raisins. Then, sitting back down, she suddenly couldn't stand it anymore. "Byron…your shirt. It's buttoned crooked."

He smiled and reached across the table. "Your robe," he said a little hoarsely, touching its frayed neckline, "is coming undone."

At first she assumed he meant the fabric was getting frayed and worn, but then she realized he meant the tie. It had sagged into her lap, her robe falling open, exposing the filmy pale mauve lacy nightie she'd secreted from the lingerie department after a Valentine Day sale. Her salesclerk had speculated that it hadn't been sold because it was just too racy for Tyler women.

"I think I will try a little brown sugar on my oatmeal," she said.

And Byron Sanders Forrester had the gall to laugh.

CHAPTER SEVEN

WITH ITS SAGGING shutters and peeling paint, Timberlake Lodge looked downright spooky under the gathering clouds. The wind had picked up. Gusts kicked
up dust and fallen leaves. Even for October it was cold.
Cliff's truck was parked outside, but not Liza's T-bird.
Byron could smell the lake in the fresh country air. He
knocked on the front door and waited, the cold penetrating his jacket and navy sweater. Lunch on the veranda today would be out of the question.

There was no answer. Given the size of the place,
Byron wondered whether anyone inside would hear
his knock. He tried the door, which was unlocked,
and pushed it open. Such liberties were getting to be
a bad habit.

No cookbooks or Beethoven sonatas came flying
out at him, but that wouldn't be Cliff's style.

*"You don't understand, Byron. I could hurt some-
one."*

"Who?"

*"You. Mother. I just don't know. I don't... I can't
trust myself anymore."*

Byron had tried to reassure him. *"I know you, Cliff.
You'd never lay a hand on Mother. As for me—I can
hold my own with you, big brother. You don't have to
worry."*

His brother's eyes had never seemed so impenetrable. *"How can you know me? I don't know myself. That's the whole point, Byron. I just don't know anymore what I would or wouldn't do. That's why you can't trust me. It's why I have to leave."*

"Let me visit."

"No."

"Cliff, don't shut us out."

"I have no choice."

For two years, Byron had kept out of his brother's life. Then, three years ago, he'd come to Tyler, just to see him, and he'd known Cliff had made the right decision, at least for himself. His only hope was time. Yet, even now, with him on the verge of marrying, Byron wasn't sure his brother wanted him back in his life.

When no one answered his call, he shut the door and walked back down the porch, ignoring the blustery wind, the sprinkle of rain, the wrenching in his gut. Being back in Tyler reminded him all too vividly of how close he'd come three years ago, of how much he'd lost. He'd had so much in his grasp—his brother, a woman he'd loved, stability. And he'd let them go. Cliff, Nora, Tyler itself. He'd left thinking they were gone forever. He'd missed his chance, even if he'd had no choice but to leave.

"Hey, Brother."

He spun around, and there was Cliff, leaning on an ax handle. Sweat poured off him despite the cold, and there were wood chips in his hair. Byron noticed the holes in his jeans, the bald spots in his chamois shirt. His brother the recluse. But even as kids, Cliff had worn whatever was handy.

"I was just giving up on you," Byron said.

His brother's dark eyes flickered. "Not you, Byron. You'd never give up on me." He pulled out a folded black bandanna and wiped the sweat off his forehead. "Liza's off to town. She's got some woman sewing a wedding dress for her. You know, she makes a show of hating all these wedding traditions, but I think deep down she's having a ball."

"You?"

Cliff shrugged. "Seeing her happy is important to me. I'll do what I need to do." He swung the ax onto his shoulder. "Come on, let's take a walk."

The prospect of an imminent rainstorm didn't seem to bother him. For all Byron knew, his brother hadn't started sleeping in the lodge until Liza arrived. They headed out across the driveway toward the lake. The occasional sprinkles had increased to a fine mist.

"How're you and Nora getting on?" Cliff asked, leading the way.

"I lived through the night."

He hadn't slept much, however. He'd lain amid the lace and fluff thinking about how sexy and beautiful Nora had looked standing on the study threshold. Freshly showered with her almond-scented soap, he'd stared wide-eyed at the ceiling and let himself remember every detail of the first time they'd made love, in his tent too long ago. He'd let himself remember how much he'd loved her. How painful it had been to leave. Yet how could he have stayed? Even Aunt Ellie had understood his dilemma. And for the first time, Byron thought he himself truly understood if not what his brother had been through, at least the suffering he'd endured when he'd come home that one time and known he couldn't stay.

"Cliff—she has good reason to hate me."

They'd come to the lake, its waters gray and choppy, a warning of the impending storm. Cliff started along a narrow, rocky path that wound along the shoreline. "I figured as much."

"I promised never to tell anyone what happened between us three years ago."

"Then don't."

Byron sighed. "Thanks. I thought you might insist."

"Nope. I might be something of a hermit, Brother, but I'm not a fool."

Cliff turned off the path and walked out onto a decrepit boat dock, one with more boards missing or rotting than intact and solid. Byron followed, stepping where his brother had stepped. Fat drops of rain struck him on the head and hand. Cliff didn't seem to notice. He squinted, looking out at the lake.

"If you hurt her...break her heart again..." His jaw set and he glanced over at Byron. "That wouldn't sit too well with me."

Byron wondered where his brother got his ideas about Nora Gates, considering he'd never even spoken to her until the night before last. Other than Aunt Ellie, Byron bet he knew Tyler's would-be spinster better than anyone. And if he'd broken her heart three years ago, he'd also made it more tolerable for her by giving her reason to hate him.

"Hell, Cliff," he said, avoiding articulating his true mixed-up feelings, "Nora isn't about to let herself fall for anyone. She's got her heart under lock and key. So far as I can see, I did her a favor by leaving Tyler when I did. Ask her yourself. I'll bet she'll tell you the same thing."

Cliff shook his head. "Then you're both deluding yourselves."

"Everyone in town knows she doesn't want anything to do with romance—"

"Doesn't matter. Until a few years ago—" Cliff looked again at his brother "—presumably when you came to town, Nora Gates was sure of herself, knew where she was going, what she wanted out of life. The past few years, she hasn't been the same and I don't care what anybody says. You could look at her and tell she'd lost some of her spark, some of her sense of purpose. Not a lot. She's a survivor. But you could tell she'd had a look at the dark side of life."

Meaning me, Byron thought. "Nah, Cliff, I don't buy it. She's been grieving for her aunt. She'd lost the last close relative who really cared about her. Of course she's been floundering a little. If Aunt Ellie were still alive and I'd hit the road—hell, Nora would have set off fireworks in her front yard."

Cliff looked unconvinced. "Did you leave before or after Aunt Ellie died?"

"Before."

His brother was silent.

"It's what Nora wanted."

"So she'd say."

"Don't underestimate her, Cliff. She knows her own mind. Besides, I thought you didn't want to know the details. If she finds out you've guessed we…that we had something going…"

"She'll have your head."

"And more," Byron added.

Cliff smiled his almost-smile. "She forgets you're my brother. I know you. You were bound to fall for a woman who'd scare the hell out of you." He gave Byron a pointed look. "And naturally you wouldn't notice until it was too late."

Meaning, Byron thought, that Cliff knew he and Nora had made love because Byron was too damned stupid to *not* have made love to her. A change of subject was in order. "Rain's picking up."

"We need it," Cliff said. He swung his ax down off his shoulder, standing it on its head and leaning on the handle, his toes hanging over the edge of the dilapidated dock. "You left three years ago on account of me?"

Byron almost lost his balance at the guilt in his brother's voice, the deeper meaning of his question. He shook his head, being as frank and truthful as he possibly could. "I know what you're saying and no, Cliff—God, no. I don't know how the hell I can explain this, but when I came to Tyler, I saw you only a couple of times and—"

"You spied on me."

"Yeah, sort of."

Cliff squinted out at the lake. "You used to do that when we were little kids. I'd go off with a friend, and next thing I knew, we'd find you up some tree with your binoculars."

"Spies were big in those days. When you caught me, there was hell to pay."

"Lesson didn't take."

Byron grinned. "You didn't always catch me."

His brother didn't look at him. "So you came to Tyler, spied on me and decided I was a brick short of a load."

"No," Byron said, serious now. "What I decided,

Cliff, was to respect your wishes and leave you alone. I didn't count on the rest."

"Nora."

"And Aunt Ellie."

"The pictures," Cliff said, understanding. "Nora showed them to me the other night. They're good, Byron. More than good. Not that you need me to tell you."

"It's always nice to hear." Byron, too, found himself staring out at the lake, part of it lost now in the mist and increasing rain. So far, his jacket wasn't soaked through, but his jeans were damp, his hair starting to drip. "Taking those pictures...knowing Aunt Ellie, knowing she was dying—and Nora, seeing how much she was grieving... Then you, living alone up here..." Byron looked up at the sky as the rain came harder now, pelting his face. "It was too much. I had nothing to give to anyone. I was empty, Cliff. Just empty."

"Not empty," Cliff said hoarsely. "Hurting too much yourself."

"I wanted to whisk her off and live happily ever after, but...hell, I couldn't make Aunt Ellie young again, I couldn't undo what you'd seen and done in Cambodia, I couldn't bring Dad home. I've never felt so damned helpless. Maybe that's what I needed, to really feel that emptiness, acknowledge that I had my own demons to confront. I don't know. I was so damned afraid of doing the wrong thing—making Aunt Ellie's last days worse, sending you over the edge, making Nora incapable of carrying on alone. It was hell."

Cliff nodded. "I know. It's a lot easier to hurt people and see them hurting if you don't care about them.

Byron, you left because you needed to become whole again yourself."

"That's what Aunt Ellie said."

"She was right."

Byron shook his head. "I should have been stronger. I hadn't seen the things you'd seen, I wasn't dying, I wasn't losing the woman who'd taken me in after my parents were killed. God, Cliff, I failed you all."

"That's what Dad said in the end," Cliff said softly, rain streaming down his face, among his tears. "The villagers told me. He set high standards for himself, too. It was painful, knowing how much he'd done, how hard he'd tried, that he'd died thinking he should have done more. Byron, you did your best. Now let it go."

"I could have gone to Southeast Asia with you."

"No."

"If we'd gone together—"

"It wouldn't have made any difference to Dad or to me. And what would Mother have done? Let it go, Byron. For God's sake, don't torture yourself over what you didn't do."

"Have you let go of what you saw, what you did?"

Cliff hesitated, then answered, "It's a part of me. It no longer controls me."

Byron moved shakily off the dock, choosing his steps carefully. He could hear Aunt Ellie, feel her gnarled, cold hand squeezing his. *You have to know who you are, Byron, before you can give yourself to anyone."*

Slipping on the wet, soggy wood, he jumped onto a rock, then onto firm ground, Cliff right behind him. "You didn't explain any of this to Nora?" his brother asked.

"She had enough problems of her own without taking on mine, too."

"What if she wanted to?"

"She didn't. She's leading the life she's always wanted to lead."

"You're sure about that, are you?"

"She is. That's what counts."

"What about you? Are you leading the life you want to lead?"

Byron left the path. The rain was coming down hard now, and he opted for the shortest route between two points, one being where he was, the other being his car. Suddenly he wanted to be alone. "It seemed right to get off the road. I've done some things I'm proud of at P & R. Mostly, though, the job's incredibly routine."

"And you don't fit in."

"Hell, I don't fit in anywhere," he said without rancor.

"Come on," Cliff said, clapping one hand on his brother's shoulder, "let's go back up to the house, get a cup of hot coffee. I know right now you probably are itching to be alone, but that's the last thing you need. Trust me on that one, Brother. Maybe Liza will be back. She's guaranteed to cheer us up."

Byron smiled. "It's good to see you happy."

"Yeah." His brother's dark eyes danced. "It's even better to be happy."

As Cliff had predicted, Liza's T-bird was parked crookedly in the driveway behind the battered truck her grandfather let him drive. She had rock and roll playing on the kitchen radio, the volume turned up high, and was scooping dollops of orange dough into muffin tins. A big pot of coffee was already in the works. She announced pumpkin muffins would be ready in twenty minutes, then, looking around at the rain-soaked brothers, she shook her head.

"You two been talking serious, nasty stuff, huh? Well, shake it loose. Byron, you can get yourself a towel and dry off, and I'll pour you a cup of coffee in my special travel mug, which I most definitely want back."

"You kicking my brother out?" Cliff asked.

Liza grinned. "Sending him on a mission."

Byron was getting suspicious.

"I saw Nora at Barney's just down the road. She rode her bicycle and it's raining cats and dogs out now— I'd have offered her a ride myself, but I'd already blown past her before it registered that it was her out there among the pumpkins and her BMW wasn't with her. Anyway, Byron, you can go fetch her back here for coffee and muffins."

Cliff sat at the table, looking amused. "Liza can be very dictatorial."

"I'm in a rented car," Byron said, thinking that he had to be the last person Nora Gates would want to have rescue her from the rain.

Liza waved off both their remarks as she scraped the last bit of dough from her wooden spoon with her finger. "Oh, so what? Look, Nora doesn't have her head screwed on straight today if she's off hunting pumpkins on a bicycle. And never mind the rain, how's she going to carry pumpkins back in town on a bike?"

Cliff didn't answer and Byron chose not to, seeing how he wasn't, as far as Liza Baron was aware, supposed to really know the somewhat eccentric owner of Gates Department Store.

"Unless what they're saying in town is true," Liza said, popping the muffins into the oven.

Byron's eyes met Cliff's, but neither man spoke.

Liza was having a great time for herself. "Martha Bauer—she's doing my dress for me—says she saw the photographer who did the picture series on Aunt Ellie at the library the other night. Then Tisha Olsen reminded her that his name was Byron Sanders. Then Ricky Travis's little brother, Lars, said something to somebody who told Inger Hansen who told Martha that Nora has a man staying at her house. From his description, Martha figures it was her photographer. Then *she* talked to somebody else—I hope I've got this all straight—who remembered seeing Nora and some man who fit Byron's description having lunch together a few years ago, but who'd dismissed it, thinking he had to be a salesman or something, given that Nora would never be caught dead *dating* a man."

Without a word, Cliff got up, pulled open a drawer and got out two towels, one of which he handed to Byron. The other he used to wipe his face as he watched his fiancée.

Byron swallowed hard. "So people are gossiping about Nora?"

"Oh, my, yes," Liza said delightedly. "Lordy, I missed lots of good stuff while I was away. Now everybody's got it figured out."

"Got what figured out?" Cliff asked.

She grinned. "That Byron and Nora were lovers!"

A HALF MILE from Barney's, which had the most extensive selection of pumpkins in or around Tyler, Nora was drenched to the bone and shivering and absolutely

certain she'd lost her mind. What had she been thinking when she'd climbed on her bike to go pumpkin
hunting in the rain? Even if it hadn't been raining then,
she'd known it *would* rain. She listened to the radio
weather report every morning.

She recognized Byron's rented car in her handlebar
mirror and hoped she was the last person he'd expect to
see, bicycling in the rain with a pumpkin tucked under
one elbow and a flimsy camouflage poncho whipping
out behind her in the wind. Her sweatshirt, turtleneck,
bra, underpants, jeans—everything was soaked. And
even as small as her pumpkin was, it felt like a lead
weight and made steering more difficult and the ride
home even more torturous. But she had her pride. She'd
gone to Barney's for a pumpkin, and by God, she'd go
back with a pumpkin.

She tucked her head inside her poncho hood, but
Byron's car pulled up just ahead of her. Unless she
wanted to get run over, she had no choice but to stop.

Byron rolled down his window. "Forget your car?"

"No, I—I planned it this way."

"A bike ride with a pumpkin in the driving rain,
forty-mile-an-hour winds and fifty-degree temperatures?"

If it was fifty out, she was home under her down
comforter. "You don't have to believe me."

"I lie to save my skin, you lie to save face. It's the
fundamental difference between us. Want a ride?"

Rain was pouring off her nose. "No, thank you."

Byron frowned, looking handsome if not entirely
dry himself. "My instincts tell me to let you drown or
freeze—whichever comes first—but I have orders to

bring you back to Timberlake Lodge for coffee and pumpkin muffins."

How tempting. Maybe Cliff would build a fire. Liza could lend her dry clothes. But she shook her head. "I have more errands to run."

"Like that? You'll get a reputation."

She would, too. It was the Byron Sanders Forrester effect. "Liza sent you? I wondered if she spotted me." A strong gust of wind blew the rain hard into her face and almost knocked her off her bicycle. *I'm nuts,* she thought. *Completely bonkers.* "I've got to run along."

Byron sighed. "Nora, quit cutting off your nose to spite your face and get in the damned car."

"My bicycle—"

"Leave it in the ditch. You can come back for it later."

"Someone will steal it."

"In this weather? Besides, you couldn't get three bucks for that bomb at a flea market. How old is it?"

"I don't know— Aunt Ellie picked it up for me at a garage sale when I first came to live with her. It was pretty old then."

The driver's door swung open, and Byron got out of the car, grumbling. "I can't believe I'm discussing how old this rusting hunk of junk is while you're out here freezing your lovely behind off. Now, in the car."

She tilted up her chin, her poncho hood falling down her back, not that it had been doing any good. Her hair was dripping. "I won't have you order me about."

"Then consider it a plea. Liza won't give me coffee and muffins if I come back without you."

"Horrors."

"Come on, Nora."

"As you wish, but— Byron, I think my fingers are stuck."

He covered her frozen hand with his, its warmth immediately penetrating the stiff, purple fingers practically glued to her handlebar. She let him take her pumpkin. She began to shiver uncontrollably as she pried her fingers loose. Byron didn't let go of her hand.

"I feel like an idiot," she said, coughing.

"It's that kind of day."

She peeled off her poncho before getting into the car; Byron balled it and shoved it on the floor in back. "I must smell like a wet dog," she said when she climbed next to him in the front.

He smiled. "Just so long as you don't have fleas. Be tough to explain to the rental car folks."

"If you don't mind—coffee and pumpkin muffins sound great, but I'd prefer just to go home."

The rain was coming down now in sheets, and her bicycle crashed over in the wind. Byron collected it and jammed it in the back seat of his car. What had she been thinking when she started pedaling home? At the very least, she should have stayed at Barney's. Maybe, deep down, she'd wanted Byron to rescue her. She'd guessed he was out at the lodge. She'd seen Liza's T-bird streak past her. *I'm not that kind of woman. I left Barney's because I thought I could get home before the worst of the storm hit. Don't make more of this than there is.*

"You okay?" Byron asked.

"Just wet and cold."

He set her pumpkin on the seat between them and started the car. "What's the pumpkin for?"

"This one, not much. I was checking what Barney

had in the way of jack-o'-lantern pumpkins. I do a
Halloween party every year. Byron, I'm getting your
car all wet."

"It'll have time to dry, not that I'd give a damn if
it didn't. I wish I had a blanket or something to give
you—"

"We'll be home in just a few minutes."

"Right. You're sure you don't want to go back to
the lodge? It's closer."

She looked out the passenger window. "I'm humiliated enough as it is."

Byron sighed. "What the hell's so humiliating about
getting caught out in the rain?"

When she didn't answer, he pulled out onto the road,
but, mercifully, headed toward town rather than turning back toward Timberlake Lodge. Nora tried to relax,
but she couldn't. She was too cold, too tired, too aware
of Byron so close beside her. She was used to doing
things right. Taking care of herself. She didn't need
him. She didn't need *anyone*.

"Thank you for the ride," she said finally.

Byron looked at her, his expression virtually impossible to read. "It wasn't my choice." Then he smiled ir-
reverently. "That's supposed to make you feel better."

"So I won't think you were being nice to me on
purpose?"

"Seems to annoy the hell out of you when I try."

She said nothing, uncomfortable with the note of
wistfulness she detected in his voice, even as his eyes
and smile remained hopelessly irreverent. Instead of
trying to explain her jumble of contradictory feelings,
she pulled off her drenched sweatshirt. Immediately
she regretted what she'd done. The turtleneck under-

neath wasn't of the highest quality, the thin, pearl-gray fabric becoming translucent when wet. She could see the lines of her lace bra, and the outline of her nipples, hard with the cold, the rain, the awareness of the solid man beside her.

"Nora...a week of this..."

There was no point in denying the obvious any longer. "I know."

They arrived at her house. Byron parked along the curb, and before he had the engine turned off, Nora shot out of the car, unlocked the door and dashed into her room. She peeled off her wet clothes. Despite her purple fingers and toes and her goose bumps, her body felt as if it were on fire. She couldn't remember anything so erotic as feeling that hot and that cold at the same time, at least not in the past three years. If Byron Forrester walked into her bedroom right now, she'd pounce. There was no question in her mind.

"Nora," he called from out in the hall, "are you all right?"

"Fine!"

"If there's anything I can do, let me know."

Oh, Lord! She grabbed fresh underwear—the most utilitarian she had—and put on iron-gray drawstring sweatpants that would have made Marilyn Monroe look like a truck driver. Then she got out a black turtleneck and her father's old Black Watch wool hunting shirt and put them on, letting the tails hang down over her hips. She found some wool socks that were about as sexy as organic compost, then combed out her hair. The extremes of hot and cold had melded into a pleasant feeling of dry, cozy warmth.

She found Byron building a fire in the study. See-

ing him on one knee, leaning over the birch logs and
kindling as he watched the flames take hold, was like
striking a match to a drought-stricken prairie. As the
fire spread, the flames licking the wood, rising blue-
edged and hot, Nora could feel herself begin to burn.

"You're still in your wet clothes," she said.

He climbed to his feet. "I'll go change."

She nodded, stepping out of the doorway so he
could get past her without touching her. If he did, she'd
go up as fast as the kindling.

But he stopped on the threshold. "It won't work,
you know."

"What won't work?" she asked innocently, fearing
that she knew what he was talking about.

"The woods-woman look. Believe me, if I wanted
you soaked to the bone in a camouflage poncho and
the driving rain, I want you now."

And he ducked out fast, before she burst into flame
by pure spontaneous combustion. She was so damned
hot she had to take off the watchplaid shirt and push up
the sleeves of her turtleneck. Who needed a real fire?

She made a pot of coffee and heated up a couple of
applesauce-nut muffins she'd stuck in the freezer earlier in the fall, then got out her Halloween tray with the
pictures of pumpkins on it, two orange paper napkins
and plain white mugs and plates. In a few minutes,
she was back in the study, everything nicely arranged.

Byron joined her. She wondered if getting into dry
clothes had had a similar effect on him and if he was now
more composed. He didn't look as if he were hanging by
his fingernails to the last shreds of his self-control. The
fire was burning well and good sense seemed restored.
Outside, however, the storm raged on.

"Should I call Cliff and Liza?" she asked.

"No, I think they'll figure it out."

"Well... I wouldn't want them to get the wrong idea."

"Nora—"

He broke off, but she'd spotted the knowing concern—the I-know-something-I-wish-I-didn't in his eyes—and prodded him. "What is it?"

He shook his head. "Nothing. Tell me about your Halloween party."

Sitting on the floor, Nora leaned back against her couch and stretched out her decidedly unsexy legs toward the fire. Byron sat cross-legged opposite her. He'd put on dry jeans and a dark blue shaker-knit sweater that somehow made her believe he could be the president of an East Coast publishing house. He, too, had skipped shoes. The fire crackled. The study was small, with just a couch, a glass-fronted bookcase, a couple of caned chairs and a tub table. It was where Aunt Ellie had best liked to read.

"About seven years ago," she said, "Aunt Ellie and I decided to have a Halloween party for our neighborhood—adults as well as children. Aunt Ellie always considered Halloween a bizarre custom. She just didn't get trick-or-treating. But she loved bobbing for apples, haunted houses, ghost stories, jack-o'-lanterns. She didn't approve of having a bunch of mercenary kids in dime-store costumes pounding on our door for free candy."

Byron smiled. "And I'm sure her opinion of Halloween was no secret."

"Hardly. She was starting to get real curmudgeonly about the whole thing—to the point of wanting to turn out the lights and pretend we weren't home—until I suggested a party. Only homemade costumes—they didn't have to be fancy—were allowed. I ordered all kinds of materials for the store—face paint, false noses and teeth, hats, sequins, feathers—the works. And we'd do all the old-fashioned stuff, like bobbing for apples, spooky ghost houses, making popcorn balls. It was great fun. Aunt Ellie dressed up as a witch—warty nose, croaking voice, poison herbs and all. For the first two years nobody knew it was her. They all thought she'd gone to visit her friend in Milwaukee when I had my party. She just loved that."

"And what were you?" Byron asked, his eyes on her.

She felt the warmth rise into her cheeks. "A gypsy."

He laughed. "Eleanora Gates, who's never lived anywhere but Tyler, Wisconsin, as a gypsy. That *is* a fantasy. Did you read palms?"

"Of course."

"And have a crystal ball?"

"One year I did. Lars Travis broke it."

Byron was silent for a minute or two, and Nora found herself unable even to guess what he was thinking, yet very much wanting to know. Was he imagining her in her gypsy costume? Remembering past Halloweens when he and Cliff were children? For three years, she'd thought she had him all figured out. To her, he was a wanderer, a cad, a womanizer, a man of talent and vision who would never commit to anything but a fleeting image he could capture on film. Now all bets were off. He might have been some of those things, or none. She didn't know who Byron Sanders Forrester was, what made him tick.

"After Aunt Ellie died," she went on, "I wasn't sure

I wanted to continue our Halloween party tradition. But that first Halloween—she'd only been dead seven weeks—I found myself at Barney's buying up pumpkins, and I came home and made jack-o'-lanterns and popcorn balls and... I don't know, people just showed up. I never sent out a single invitation. It was almost like Aunt Ellie had gotten us together, just to prove we could—or at least I could—carry on without her. I remember putting on my costume and feeling so alone. She was gone." Nora glanced over at Byron, her throat tightening. "You were gone. And there I was, dressing up like a kid for Halloween. But I could feel her spirit with me, telling me to buck up and get on with my life. So I did."

"What costume did you wear that night?" Byron asked.

Nora didn't expect that question. "What?"

"What costume? It's important."

"My gypsy costume. I've worn the same one for years."

He nodded. "Good."

"What were you thinking?"

"I was afraid you'd taken over Aunt Ellie's role as the Halloween witch."

Breaking a warm muffin in half, Nora let Byron's words sink in. Had she considered donning Aunt Ellie's black crepe dress and wax warts? Had she wanted to be Aunt Ellie that night?

"You're like her in many ways," Byron went on, "but you're not her. You're yourself, Nora. You have to live your own life."

"I know that."

"Yes, maybe you do. If you'd worn Aunt Ellie's witch's costume that night—"

She smiled. "I'd still have made a lousy witch. She was taller than me, remember? Besides which, my gypsy costume's a lot more fun to wear than Aunt Ellie's warts and poisons. I get rhinestones, a racy little embroidered top, lots of makeup…it's fun. And believe me, people wondered who the gypsy was for a while, too. I think people thought Aunt Ellie and I both had either gone nuts or had been spirited off by goblins."

Byron poured himself a cup of coffee. "How little and how racy?"

"What? Oh…" She grabbed a small couch pillow and threw it at him, but he caught it with one hand. "You have a nerve, Byron Forrester."

He grinned, unapologetic. "When's your party this year?"

"Tuesday evening."

"If I'm still around, what'll you do with me? I haven't dressed up for Halloween in years. A lot of years."

She gave that one some thought. "Well, you'd make a damned good goblin. Wouldn't even take that much imagination. But I think most likely I'd just dress you up as a skeleton and stick you in a closet. Appropriate, don't you think?"

"Let's not talk about nerve," he said, climbing to his feet.

"Where are you going?"

"Thought I'd run up to the lodge for a little while. It looks as if the weather's breaking— I'd like to let Cliff and Liza know what happened to us."

"Okay."

He hesitated. "Nora, I'm sorry I left the way I did three years ago, with so much unsaid. I let you believe some pretty unpleasant things about me. I thought I was doing the right thing."

"Maybe you were," she said, almost inaudibly.

"I don't know, but I...well, I've been wondering if I shouldn't leave Tyler for now. Come back just in time for the wedding."

"Why?"

"Because of you. Nora, I don't want to mess up your life. I want to respect your choices— I do care about you, you know." He smiled. "Why else would I tease you the way I do?"

She swallowed, her throat tight, and wished she could just go on hating him. But she couldn't. She wasn't sure she ever had. He hadn't been half as mean to her three years ago as they both were pretending. He'd told her he had to leave Tyler. He'd explained he knew she couldn't go with him. He just hadn't explained why he couldn't stay, and had let her believe that she hadn't meant enough to him. And he'd never asked her to go with him. Of course, she hadn't offered.

He left her alone in the study, the fire dying down, his muffin untouched, his coffee still steaming. Nora wiggled her toes inside her socks. She was nice and toasty. With Byron gone, she could do a few things around the house.

She wondered if he'd be back for dinner.

Well, it wasn't that hard to whip up something for two. She was used to it from her days with Aunt Ellie. If he showed up, he showed up. If not...

If not, she'd eat alone, as she had almost every night for the past three years.

CHAPTER EIGHT

THE CUCKOO CLOCK in the study was striking midnight when Byron tiptoed into Aunt Ellie's old bedroom down the hall from the kitchen. He'd just come in. He had enough damned pumpkins for every man, woman and child in Tyler. Barney, who had to be 105 years old, had known a soft touch when he saw one. Byron had listened to the weather reports. It was going to rain all day tomorrow, and even with Liza's bridal shower in the middle of the afternoon, that made for one hell of a long Sunday ahead. Byron planned on carving a lot of pumpkins.

Cliff had already told him he needed space tomorrow. Liza could play the sweet bride-to-be and unwrap a dozen toasters, but he needed time alone to think. Byron understood. They'd called London from the lodge, talked to their mother. By the time Byron got on the phone, she couldn't stand it anymore and had burst into tears. Cliff knew. She'd held it together for him, but listening to Byron's end of the conversation, he'd figured out what was going on.

"I wish I could undo all the suffering I've caused her," he said when Byron hung up.

"She wishes she could undo what you've suffered. None of us can, Cliff. Let it be enough that we want to."

Cliff had twisted his hands together. "I'm close,"

he'd said in a choked whisper. "So damned close. If I lose it again…"

But he hadn't finished, retreating out into a very cold, very dark night, and Liza, white-faced, had joined Byron in the kitchen. It was painful to see such a vibrant woman look so worried and scared.

"I'm canceling the wedding," she said. "It's too much for him."

"Don't, Liza. Not yet. Let me get out of here and see if he doesn't rally—"

"No…no, Byron, you're just not getting it. It's not you. It's crowds, the prospect of really thinking about the future. Cliff's used to living just for today. He hasn't thought about tomorrow in years, if that makes any sense. I'm making him. With me, he has to think about a big wedding, becoming a part of my family, having a family himself one day. The stress of you and your mother—that's only a small part of what he's going through." She threw up her hands and let them flop down to her sides. "I'm just asking for too much too soon."

"Is there any other way?" Byron had asked, rhetorically. "Half measures don't work in a relationship. It eventually comes to a point of all or nothing."

Liza had looked at him knowingly. "Is that what happened with you and Nora?"

"I promised I wouldn't tell."

She hadn't pushed, instead throwing on her wild serape and heading out to find Cliff. Byron admired her courage, her unshakable love for his brother. They'd already triumphed. The rest—the wedding, the painful Forrester family reunion—was just logistics. When they both saw that, they'd be fine.

Byron had tried pitching Cliff's old tent. It leaked. Then the wind blew it down. And he'd known he wouldn't stay out all night, anyway. He had to go back to Nora's little twenties house with the mums on the porch.

"Nora?"

"So it is you." She sat up in bed, only her silhouette visible in the dark room. He noticed she had a night-light. Living alone didn't come that easily to her. "You're lucky I don't sleep with a gun under my pillow."

"I just wanted to let you know that I'm back."

For a few seconds she didn't speak. Then she said, "Okay."

"Pleasant dreams."

"Thank you." He started out, but she stopped him. "Oh, Byron. I'll make breakfast in the morning. I bought eggs."

He couldn't help a small grin. "Knew I was coming back, did you?"

"No," she said quietly. "No, I really had no idea."

That did it.

He took three long strides across her dhurrie-carpeted floor and grabbed her by the forearm, not hard. She could have pulled away if she'd wanted to. He drew her toward him, careful not to lose his balance and fall onto the bed. If he did, they were doomed.

In the dim, pale glow of her night-light, her eyes were liquid and luminous, and he recognized the painful loneliness in them, because it was the same agony he'd felt night after night for the past three years. Even as he'd known he was doing what he had to do, even as he'd structured a good life for himself, he'd wake up nights knowing that his life could have been more than it was. It was like that for Nora, too. He knew it. Her life was good. But it could be more than it was, and on dark, lonely nights, she knew it, too.

And so he kissed her.

Her lips tasted of his best dreams, and when she kissed him back, moaned softly against him, he knew he'd wake up in his brother's collapsing, leaking tent. This couldn't be real. He slid his tongue into her mouth, stroked the sharp edges of her teeth. He felt himself hardening. Her tongue circled his, tasting, testing. To steady himself, he grabbed her by the waist. It almost did him in. His fingers dug into the flimsy fabric of her little nightgown, felt the hot, smooth flesh underneath. It was no dream. If he had dreams as real as this, he'd never wake up.

But he made himself let go, stand up straight.

"Next time," he said, his voice hoarse, tortured with wanting, "know I'll be back."

"I SEE YOU fell for Barney's routine."

Nora was sitting at the kitchen table, watching Byron bring in his twelfth pumpkin, which he plopped on the counter with all the others. She hadn't seen so damned many pumpkins since *she'd* fallen for Barney's routine.

Byron leaned against the counter, crossing his arms over his muscular chest. "How does it go?"

"He's getting old, doesn't think he'll plant any pumpkins next year."

"He'd hate to see his last crop used for compost," Byron added, grimacing.

Nora grinned. "He uses his pumpkin money—"

"To buy heating oil for winter."

"That's a switch. Last fall it was heart medicine. The routine works best on tourists. He doesn't even try it on townspeople anymore."

"It ever work on you?"

"Once."

"Aunt Ellie?"

"Never. She went to school with Barney, said he tried at lunchtime to sob-story his classmates out of their desserts. He does grow nice pumpkins, though."

With a dubious grunt, Byron turned around and pulled two knives from her magnetic rack. She admired the way he moved. So far, they'd been friendly with each other, if careful to keep plenty of breathing room between them. She hadn't gotten to sleep last night until after dawn. It wasn't because she'd actually regretted having fallen for his charms. She was honest enough with herself to admit she'd wanted him to kiss her. It was, instead, that she'd enjoyed their kiss too damned much. She'd lain awake because she'd wanted more. She hated the wanting, but it was, she thought, extremely difficult to deny.

"They'd look nice lined up on your porch for your Halloween party," Byron said, pointing at the line of small, medium-size and large pumpkins. "I'll even buy the candles for you."

"I thought you weren't going to be here."

He shrugged, not looking at her. "Changed my mind."

She hadn't asked him where he'd gone last night, why he'd come back. "Any particular reason?"

"No place else to go."

"Weak, Byron. Very weak."

He handed her a knife, which, given his deliberately inadequate answer and the cocky, sexy way he looked at her, was brave of him. She set it purposefully on the table and got up and fetched a pumpkin, a smooth, deep orange one of medium size. It would make a perfect jack-o'-lantern. Setting it on the table, she made sure it was steady and sliced into it with her knife.

"We'll need newspapers for the guts," she said. "The recycling bin's just inside the cellar door." He went after them. When he had the cellar door open, she added, "And Byron, you don't have to tell me anything you'd rather not tell me. You're just my houseguest. You're welcome to stay through Liza and Cliff's wedding."

He returned with a stack of newspapers, which he slapped onto the table. "You know," he said in a low voice, his eyes even darker than they'd been last night, "when you go Victorian virgin on me, it just makes me want you more."

"Cad," she said, unable to hold back a smile.

He grinned. "Count on it."

Naturally he chose the biggest pumpkin, but it was slightly misshapen and had a golf-ball-size growth on one side. He patted it as if it were a prize piglet.

Continuing from where she'd stabbed into her pumpkin, Nora carved a neat circle for a lid, which she gently lifted, intensely aware of Byron's eyes on her. She wondered if rich East Coast publishing types ever made jack-o'-lanterns, as kids or as adults. Suddenly she was madly curious about his life, his upbringing, everything about him.

"I had dinner with Cliff and Liza last night," he said abruptly. "Cliff's on edge—he tries not to show it, but it doesn't take a genius to see that I've opened a can of worms by coming here. And I can't just up and leave. I need to be here."

"For his sake?"

"Yeah, even if he doesn't know it. But for my sake, too. We've had a long, hard row to hoe, Cliff and I. It's time we got it done." He ran his fingers over the circumference of his pumpkin, as if he were a surgeon and this a delicate operation. "Our mother's flying in from England on Thursday."

"She lives there?"

"No, she's visiting a friend—a Pierce & Rothchilde author, actually. She hasn't seen Cliff in five years. And in the past three years, I haven't...well, I haven't made her life any easier."

Nora set her pumpkin cap gently on the table. "Byron, I know Cliff's lived in Tyler for years, but he's kept to himself. No one but Alyssa Baron—and now presumably Liza—understands what drove him into his isolated life up at the lodge. As I said before, you don't have to tell me. I just want you to know that I, too, am in the dark."

He nodded, but said nothing.

"Do you know how to carve a pumpkin?" she asked.

"I haven't done one since I was a kid. Why, are there rules?"

"No, but it's one of those things that's not as easy as it looks. My first one usually comes out looking like Frankenstein's monster."

"Well, it's Halloween."

He seemed distracted, studying her with those mesmerizing eyes. She could almost feel the sandpapery roughness of his beard stubble against her cheek, against her breasts. Licking her lips, she scooped out pumpkin guts and seeds with one hand.

"My father was held prisoner and killed in Cambodia. Cliff was there. There was nothing he could do. He ended up staying, got caught up in the Khmer Rouge horrors, the killing. God only knows what all he saw. He did what he could, was almost killed himself, got out." With the tip of his knife, Byron drew a light line around the top of his pumpkin. "Our family hasn't been the same since."

"Your father was in the military?"

"Air Force. Mother was supposed to have fallen for someone who'd have liked to run Pierce & Rothchilde—she could have run it herself but nobody thought of that at the time—but she didn't. We did the Air Force routine for a while when we were young, until Dad volunteered for Vietnam. Then Mother took us to Providence to wait out the war. Only he never came home."

"I'm sorry," Nora said.

"Yeah."

"Does Cliff blame himself?"

"He did."

"And you? Do you blame yourself?"

Byron stabbed into his pumpkin. "I could have done more for both of them."

Using her free hand, Nora scraped pumpkin goo from her palm and fingers, slapping it onto the newspaper. Body Found at Abandoned Lodge, the headline read. "And your mother?" she asked, keeping her voice neutral.

"She's truly an amazing woman. She doesn't blame herself, Cliff, or me—or Dad. She's accepted what happened. Right now, she just wants to see both her sons happy."

Nora smiled. "Who can blame her?"

"At least Cliff's well on his way."

"When my parents died," Nora said, walking over to the sink for a paper towel, "I was absolutely positive it was my fault. I don't think I've ever been as sure of anything in my life. It was illogical—I had nothing to do with planning or executing their boating trip—but my guilt had nothing to do with logic. Everyone tried to talk me out of how I felt, until I came to live with Aunt Ellie. She just let me feel whatever I felt. In time, the guilt went away."

"Do you still miss them?"

"Yes. The missing never does go away. I wouldn't want it to. I miss Aunt Ellie, too. I always will."

Byron nodded, not with understanding, she thought, but with acceptance. "I think you and my mother would get along."

"I hope to meet her."

"Oh, you will. I plan to stick around until the wedding. I figure," he said carefully, "the gossip about us will only get worse if I keep leaving and coming back. People'll think something really is going on between us. If I stay, maybe they'll realize I'm just a houseguest after all and you're only doing Cliff and Liza a favor by putting me up."

Nora narrowed her eyes. "What gossip?"

"You know small towns."

She scowled. "Well, you don't, Mr. Forrester. I've never been a subject for that sort of gossip in my life, so you needn't worry."

But he seemed worried, hacking at his pumpkin haphazardly, bound to make a mess.

"Byron—is something wrong?"

"No."

"If it's our...our kiss last night, you needn't worry about that, either. I certainly wasn't an unwilling partner, but I was merely...well, I was curious as to how I'd respond should you...should *we* kiss again. But now I know."

He set down his knife and glared at her. "Are you trying to tell me our kiss was a damned *experiment?*"

"Not an experiment. A test."

"Well, did you pass? Did *I* pass?"

She pursed her lips, carefully slicing out the pumpkin's eyes. It was a delicate maneuver and she didn't want to make a mistake. Having Byron Forrester's dark gaze pinned on her didn't help her concentration. "Now, Byron," she said, "let's be adults about this. You know we were bound to kiss, just because of our history. Now it's done with. We know what it'd be like kissing each other again because in a small fit of insanity we've gone ahead and done it. The mystery's over."

"The hell it is." He tore off his pumpkin's cap, which he'd failed to cut clean through in places, but what didn't come easily he just ripped out. "I'll have you know, Nora Gates, that I wasn't wondering what it'd be like to kiss you again."

Now, she thought, who was doing the self-deluding? "You weren't?"

"No."

Then she got his full meaning and felt her knees weaken.

"As far as I'm concerned," he said, "nothing's done with and the biggest mystery yet remains."

"I see," she said primly.

He grinned. "I'm on to you, Miss Gates. You drag out your Victorian virgin act whenever I hit a nerve."

"Let's get these pumpkins carved."

He laughed. "Let's."

She turned the radio to a live broadcast of *Madame Butterfly,* which Byron vetoed, so they compromised on jazz. In the time Nora carved three pumpkins, Byron did two. His first wasn't too bad, just rather uninspired. The second looked like something out of a science fiction movie.

"Kind of grisly, isn't she?" Byron said.

"She?"

"Looks like a woman to me."

Her three, of course, were perfect jack-o'-lanterns. They could have been carved from a mold. She displayed them side by side on the counter.

"Mine have character," Byron said.

"Yours will scare the neighborhood dogs."

"Count on it. By the way, what time is Liza's shower?"

"Oh, God, I almost forgot! I've got to get ready—would you mind cleaning up? Don't worry about the rest of the pumpkins, we can just set them out... I'm going to be late, and I promised Liza."

Byron coughed. "Nora, wait."

She stopped in the kitchen doorway, listening. All morning she'd felt he had something on his mind, but she decided not to prod him.

"Have a good time."

Whatever it was, he wasn't going to tell her now. "Thank you, I'm sure I will."

She didn't catch his muttered comment as she raced upstairs to get dressed, wishing she'd kept her promise to Liza to find out what her mother had in store for her. But since Liza Baron was the one who'd thrust her future brother-in-law onto her, Nora figured she'd understand.

BYRON KNEW THERE'D be hell to pay.

While Nora was off at her bridal shower, he considered all the various things he could do to make his life easier when she got back. There had, of course, been no convincing Liza that the gossips were wrong and he and Nora hadn't been lovers. Only under certain circumstances—this one qualifying—did Byron consider a strategic, outright lie noble.

"Liza, that's just gossip," he'd said. "Nora Gates has never wanted a man in her life."

Liza was unpersuaded. "She's never wanted to get *married*. That doesn't mean she doesn't want to have a little sex now and then."

Cliff, judiciously, had kept out of the discussion.

"Lordy Lord," Liza had gone on, clearly delighted, "now I can't *wait* for my bridal shower. If anyone can drag the truth out of Nora, it'll be the quilting ladies."

Given his role in the gossip in question, Byron had believed it was his duty to warn Nora what she was in for, but with their talk about his family, her parents, Aunt Ellie—with her damned perfect jack-o'-lanterns and her gorgeous, haunting gray eyes—he'd skipped any warning. He could have justified his cowardice by claiming that he'd believed Liza was exaggerating and that the quilting ladies—they sounded like an intrepid lot—would exercise good manners. But the truth

was, he'd kept his mouth shut because Nora, a hothead
from way back, had access to too many knives, several
newspapers' worth of pumpkin innards and a whole
line of pumpkins. Byron valued his head.

Still, he debated cleaning her refrigerator, making
dinner, carving the rest of the pumpkins, even having
at the odd thing it might be handy to have a man around
to fix. He'd checked for faulty wires to mend, plaster
to patch, squeaky hinges to oil, dried up paintbrushes
to rejuvenate. But everything in the Gates household
was shipshape. Finally he'd said to hell with it and had
caught the first quarter of a football game on the an-
cient television in the study.

At five o'clock the cuckoo was calling the hour and
Nora came home screaming bloody murder.

Byron flipped off the game—it was a rout anyway—and pulled his feet off the couch just as Nora
stormed into the study.

She looked great. Decidedly annoyed, but gorgeous.

"You heel," she snarled.

She pulled her handwoven chenille scarf from
around her neck and threw it at him. Then came her
hat, also handwoven, and her peacoat, which she more
or less slammed at him because it was too heavy and
bulky to really throw. All the while she screamed,
"You bastard, you knew!"

What he should have done while she was out, he
decided, was nail down everything in the house, given
that sooner or later she was bound to run out of clothes
to throw at him.

"You *knew* I'd be interrogated at that shower."

Off came a conservative black pump, which missed
him by a yard.

"You knew half the damned town thinks I slept with you."

Off came a second black pump, which missed him by a good deal less than a yard.

"You bastard, you knew and you didn't warn me!"

She was down to her sleek two-piece heavy cotton long-over-short knit outfit and black-tinted stockings. "I have no quarrel," Byron said, "with your tossing the rest of your garments at me, but I think it's something you might regret. We do have a certain relentless attraction for each other, you know."

Her hair was wild. "I've been humiliated."

"How so?"

"Inger Hansen... Martha Bauer... Tisha Olsen, Liza—" She gulped for air. "They all know. The whole town...*arrgh!*"

Byron plucked the scarf off a pottery lamp with wildflowers pressed into its shade. "You're sure they know?"

"Oh, yes." Her eyes bored into him; he could feel the holes. "And they do give a damn. They haven't had such a juicy bit of gossip since the body was discovered at Timberlake Lodge. They haven't had such an *amusing* bit of gossip since they used to sit around trying to identify the rich guests Margaret Lindstrom Ingalls would invite to her wild parties. They *loved* the idea that I might have slept with a reprobate like you!"

Considering he was president of Pierce & Rothchilde, lived in a house on the Providence Benefit Street walking tour, Byron thought her calling him a reprobate was stretching it somewhat. Probably, he thought, Nora knew this, too. "Nora," he said, "you *did* sleep with me."

"I refused to confirm that fact." She folded her arms over her breasts and panted, her anger having required a good deal of exertion. "No one in this town will ever look at me in the same way."

"Hoist by your own petard, m'dear."

She glared at him. "And what's that supposed to mean?"

"It means," he said, "if you hadn't tried to hide our affair, the gossips in town wouldn't have had anything to find out about you. It's not as if they're spreading vicious lies. They're merely spreading the truth. We *did* sleep together." He shrugged. "Actually, as I recall, we seldom slept."

With a panting glare, she blew out of the study.

"So," Byron called, "was everyone relieved to know you're human or what?"

The whole house shook when she slammed her bedroom door.

His answer, he figured.

Always one to take his life in his hands, Byron walked down the hall to her bedroom and tried the door, but, no fool, she'd locked it up tight. "I wish I had it in me to feel sorry for you," he said, "but I don't. You can be mad at me for not having warned you, but if I had, you wouldn't have gone this afternoon, which would have been a mistake. And go ahead and feel humiliated if you want. But I won't feel sorry for you. What people have deduced about us is true."

She yelled, emphatically, "*Was* true."

"If you'd unlock your door," he said, unable to resist, "we could take care of the past tense."

Something hard struck the bedroom side of the mercifully solid wood door.

"Nora, admit it. Ever since you saw me in your dining room the other night you've been thinking about what we had three years ago, how good it was. You wouldn't have wanted to go through life having missed that chance and you know it."

He could hear her pounding across her floor. She tore open her door, her hair sticking out everywhere, her breath coming in gasps. "There's a tent in my garage. Get it and get out."

"You're just upset—"

"No, Byron, I'm not upset. Take a good look at me. Do I *look* upset? No, I look angry. Furious. And not just with you. With myself. You're right. I set myself up for this afternoon. I should have kept my hands off you three years ago, I should have pretended I didn't know who the hell you were. I thought…" She gulped in more air, her voice rasping because she'd been yelling so much. "I thought I was above being a subject of gossip. All that does is make me a better target—a juicier subject—if anyone does find out the slightest irregularity about my life."

Byron leaned against the doorjamb. "I'm not sure I like being called an irregularity."

She almost smiled. He *knew* she did. But then the anger was back, darkening her face, and she was calling him a bastard and banishing him to the garage for her tent.

It had to be a hundred years old. He could see doughboys camped in it on the Western Front. It stank worse than Cliff's did.

"If Mrs. Redbacker could see me now," he muttered. Hell, if the Pierce & Rothchilde board could. This was worse than the dartboard on the mahogany paneling.

For three years he'd lived on the road, but his van and tent had never smelled.

The rain had finally ended, but it was still damp and chilly outside, and very dark even though it wasn't even six o'clock. He was hungry. But he'd endured worse conditions.

Not that he had any intention of letting Miss Nora off scot-free for her bad temper. Was it *his* damned fault people in town were on to them?

He could have gone to the lodge, or found a motel or roominghouse, or even driven to Milwaukee and stayed in a proper hotel. He did have options. But this wasn't about options: it was about calling Nora's bluff. She couldn't keep hiding behind her hot, secret temper.

Her yard was bordered with flowers and shrubs, and had a nice little birdbath and bird feeders here and there. That left plenty of room for the flea-bitten World War I tent. He held his nose, shook it out and got to work.

In two seconds, Nora's bedroom window popped open. "What do you think you're doing?"

"Pitching the tent."

"Not here!"

"Why not here?"

"You're being deliberately obtuse. I want you off my property and out of my life!"

She'd poked her head out the window, but she'd combed her hair and, he could see, changed into one of her flowing caftans. Her heart just wasn't in her anger anymore.

"Do you, Nora?" he asked.

"No," she said abruptly, and banged her window shut.

He figured that was as good as he'd get in terms of an invitation to come inside again.

But on his way back to her garage with her tent, he ran into Liza Baron. "My God, Byron," she said, startled, "I thought you were a burglar. What're you doing out here?"

"Checking out Nora's antique tent."

"Yuck, it's disgusting."

"No kidding. What's up?"

"Nothing much. Is Nora around? I just wanted to thank her for going out of her way to make the shower such fun. She knew I was dreading it, but she was right on the money—it really was a kick, in large part thanks to her. I've never seen her so animated."

"I was under the impression," Byron said carefully, "that she didn't have a good time."

"Well, that's news to me. She was the life of the party."

Byron could imagine such a thing, even if Nora herself never could. "What about the gossip about her and me?"

"Oh, *that*. Well, she was terrifically good-natured. Inger Hansen did rib her a little unmercifully— I mean, the idea of Nora Gates having a torrid affair with anyone is front-page news in Tyler, but with *you*…" She laughed, clearly loving the notion herself. "People will be talking about that one for years to come."

That, Byron suspected, would come as no surprise to Nora, though not as a fact to be welcomed.

"And I'm not sure Inger really realizes you two actually *slept* together."

"Now, Liza, you never have heard me confirm—"

She waved him off. "Being a man, Byron Forrester,

you haven't denied it, either. Come on, I'm not stupid.
Neither are most people in town. Gosh, Nora can't
think people haven't been speculating about her sex
life for *years*. Even before I left town there was talk—"

"I wouldn't tell Nora that if I were you," Byron
put in.

"Honestly, Byron, for someone who slept with her,
you sure don't have much notion of what Nora Gates is
like. She's one of the most mature, level-headed people
I know. She's not going to let a little harmless town
gossip upset her, especially when it's true." She started
up the front porch steps. "You coming?"

"Let me get rid of this tent. I'll be along."

And when Nora answered the door, he heard her
laugh and say, "Oh, Liza," as if she were the most reasonable person in the world and hadn't just bombarded
her houseguest with half her wardrobe and sent him
out into the cold, cruel night.

Byron stuffed the tent back into its place in the garage where it could spend the next hundred years. "Oh,
sweetheart," he said to himself, "you don't know it, but
all you're doing is raising the stakes."

And the gossips, he thought, be damned.

CHAPTER NINE

MONDAY MORNING NORA did better. Work helped restore her equilibrium. She acted—felt—like a grown-up and the formidable businesswoman she was. She treated employees and customers with her customary respect and reserve, and they responded. There was no indication that the gossip circulating in town had penetrated Gates Department Store.

Until Lucille buzzed her from the book department. "Miss Gates, I have a man here who wants to see you."

Her tone suggested it was a *man* man, not a salesman or customer. Since she was at work, removed from the trials going on in her home, Byron Forrester didn't leap onto her list of possibilities. In fact, no one did. For her that was a happy state of affairs. She assumed Lucille herself was reacting to the man's asking to see the boss.

"Who is he?" Nora asked.

"He hasn't given me his name. Let me see… Oh, excuse me, sir, Miss Gates hasn't agreed to see you. Sir!" Lucille sighed. "He's on his way up. Shall I call Horace?"

Horace was the daytime security guard, and now that she knew it was Byron Forrester bounding up to her office, Nora imagined what he might tell Horace to get him to back off.

"No," Nora said, "I'll handle this one."

"I thought you might want to," Lucille said, her meaning impossible to miss.

With considerable effort, Nora kept her response professional. Then she buzzed her assistant, Albert Shaw. "Albert, I wanted to let you know that a friend of mine is on his way up. Send him right in, won't you?"

"Is this the brother of that guy up at Timberlake Lodge, the one who's staying with you?" Albert asked.

Despite their many virtues, Nora thought, small towns did have their flaws.

She had just enough time to reapply her lipstick before Byron Forrester strolled into her office, breathtaking in his slouchy jacket, shaker-knit sweater and wool pants. The weekend storm had blown out the mild weather of the end of last week and brought in clear skies and winterlike temperatures. Nora herself had worn a smart steel-blue wool suit to the store.

"'Morning," he said in a drawl that sounded more Georgia than New England.

Nora leaned back in her chair. "Lucille implied that you had an urgent need to see me."

He grinned. "Oh, I have an urgent need, but it's not just to see you."

She sighed. It had been like that since Liza's brief visit last night. Double entendres, teasing remarks, sexy looks. The gloves were off. Byron was making it crystal clear that he wanted to go to bed with her and all she had to do was give the nod and it was done. She'd decided she must have hit him with something in her rampage after all. Or her banishing him to the wilds of Wisconsin, even if he'd tried pitching her tent in her own backyard, had scrambled his brains. Clearly, her anger had lacked its intended effect. Instead of pushing him away, it seemed only to have drawn him to her. He'd seen her at her worst and now seemed to want her more than ever.

Either that, or he was just rising to the challenge she presented.

Well, let him.

Still, if he weren't so damned attractive himself, so sexy and easygoing and yet mysterious, resisting him would have been a hell of a lot easier. As it was, it was fast becoming one of the major challenges of her life. She could feel the ache—a physical longing that was so acute, so real it was almost painful—spreading from between her legs to her breasts, her nipples, her mouth, the tips of her fingers. Every part of her was sensitized, electrified.

And he hadn't even touched her.

"Byron, I'm working. It's a very busy day. What is it you want?"

"Besides to make mad passionate love to you?" His voice was light and teasing, but his eyes were not. "How 'bout spiriting you off to lunch?"

"I can't. I have a meeting."

"In my whole life, I've attended maybe two meetings that couldn't have been postponed or canceled altogether."

"You must be a treat to work for."

He walked over to the window and looked down at the town square, still, in these days of shopping malls, an attractive and active downtown. "I can see Narragansett Bay from my office."

She tried to imagine it. "Must be nice."

"Yeah, it's a great view."

"Do you like your work?" she asked, suddenly very much wanting to know.

"It has its moments." He hadn't looked up from the window. "I don't live for Pierce & Rothchilde. My work is my work, not my life."

If his comment was a dig at her and her commitment to Gates, she couldn't tell. "What about your photography?"

He shrugged. "I haven't picked up a camera in the three months since I ended my leave of absence and took my place at P & R."

"Is that a loss for you?"

"Not for me, no." Looking around at her, he seemed all at once the tall, well-built, well-educated, handsome East Coast blue-blooded executive. "I've felt some pressure from critics to continue—so I can trip up one of these days and they can lambaste me, I think. But I chased all the demons I wanted to chase. The rest are going to stick around forever. We're used to each other."

Nora recalled the photographs in Byron's book, the fathers and sons he'd captured on film. In context with his life, they made even more sense to her—were even more heart-wrenching and, in some ways, optimistic. If Byron Sanders Forrester could look back with such love and hope at a relationship that had ended so painfully, so tragically for himself and particularly for his older brother and father, then, surely, others could look beyond the wounds of their own past to the future. Byron had never been the shallow, insensitive cad she'd tried to make herself believe he was.

"Actually," he went on, "I don't mind being a publishing executive. I'm just not sure I want to continue as a publishing executive at Pierce & Rothchilde."

"Because of your family?"

"No." He smiled at her, moving away from the window. "Because they don't do technothrillers."

She didn't get it.

Byron laughed. "I'll have to introduce you to Henry—I should now say Hank—Murrow one of these days. All I'm saying is that Pierce & Rothchilde has a tendency to believe its own press, always a dangerous thing. They take themselves too seriously. They need to loosen up. It's like your place here. Gates has found a nice balance between quality with a capital Q and keeping its feet planted firmly on the ground. P & R too often focuses narrowly on quality—which becomes elitist. A technothriller, for instance, can have quality."

"With a capital Q?"

"Absolutely." He was warming to his argument now. "Why does Gates carry cotton dusters?"

Nora answered without hesitation. "Because our customers—some of our customers, particularly the elderly women—want and need them."

"And they're good quality, sturdy cotton dusters."

"Sure."

"But they're still cotton dusters. There, you see? I rest my case."

Nora thought she knew what he meant, but Byron Forrester, Harvard M.B.A. or not, did have a unique perspective on business.

"Now," he said, "lunch?"

"I still can't."

"A stubborn woman you are, Eleanora Gates the Younger." He planted his palms on the front edge of her desk and leaned over until his face was mere inches from hers. "Thinking what it'd be like for us to make love on your blotter, aren't you?"

The thought had occurred to her. "Byron…"

"We will." His voice was husky, his eyes liquid and midnight-black. "Some night after the place's closed up we'll come in here, lock the door and make love until dawn."

Then he was gone, and it was several minutes before she could breathe again.

That evening, she came home to a quiet, if not orderly, house. Byron had been cooking. In addition to a sink full of pots and pans, he'd left a note.

> I made curried pumpkin soup. It's in the fridge.
> It's horrid stuff, but don't blame me. I got the
> recipe from one of your healthy cookbooks. I'm
> off to the lodge for dinner. See you tonight.
> B.

He hadn't exaggerated about the soup. It was truly dreadful. The recipe, however, wasn't the culprit; he'd used homemade puree that he'd cooked insufficiently and, worse, had neglected to drain. The soup was lumpy and stringy, and she found a seed. He'd also put together a salad, however, that was wonderful.

By seven, she was off to a closed meeting of the Tyler town council. As usual, it began with an animated discussion of the latest victories of the high school football team and its chances for a title, then moved on to what was happening with the Body at the Lake, hopes for doing something about the deteriorated condition of the public library, and—the only real business at hand—the problems in the police department. Nora did her best to concentrate.

"Belton's giving up its police department," Johnny Kelsey was saying; Belton was a nearby town, also in Sugar Creek County. "They've gone to just having a sheriff's substation. It's saved them a ton of money."

Alyssa Baron, who seemed even more distracted than Nora, frowned, her hands twisting together in her lap. Talk of the mysterious body discovered on her father's land had upset her more than usual. Ordinarily she was sharp-minded, acutely interested in the affairs of her town. "I don't know if I like the idea of having to rely on the county for all our police protection. Tyler has always been independent. Nora, what do you think?"

At the moment, Nora was working up enough interest to give a damn. Just a week ago nothing had compelled her more than every little going-on in Tyler, Wisconsin. "I don't know as we have much choice."

"With Paul retiring," Johnny said, "the timing couldn't be better."

Paul Schmidt was Tyler's longtime police chief. Nora nodded, but she had her reservations. "Has anyone talked to Brick?"

Alyssa winced. Johnny sighed. Sometimes it wasn't easy being on the town council. Tough decisions had to be made. Good people got hurt. Likely enough, Brick Bauer would be one of them. He was the obvious choice to replace Paul Schmidt as Tyler police chief. If Tyler went to a sheriff's substation, Brick would suddenly be working for the county, not the town.

"He's a good man," Alyssa said.

Johnny nodded. "Nobody wants to see Brick get the shaft, but he knows it's not personal."

"Becoming a county employee," Alyssa added thoughtfully, "could actually help his career, I suppose."

But, as it was with Nora, Tyler had always been Brick's first love. She remembered when he'd moved to town; he'd been in high school, a Robert Conrad type a couple of years younger than she. He could have gone to Milwaukee or even Chicago to advance his career, just as Nora could have, if she'd been interested in big department stores. But that wasn't what she'd wanted. What about Brick?

"I know the needs of the town come first," she said. "I'm sure Brick knows that, too."

"But," Alyssa finished, "he's a part of this town and we need to be open, direct and sensitive."

Johnny Kelsey sighed, but nodded in agreement. "Sometimes I wonder why I ever ran for this job. How 'bout you, Nora? You're a born politician." He grinned. "Except you have integrity. No skeletons hanging in your closet."

Obviously, she thought, he hadn't been privy to recent gossip. Feeling her cheeks burn, Nora refused to meet Alyssa Baron's eye.

"Going to run for the state legislature one of these days?" Johnny teased.

Nora laughed. "Now when would I do that?"

"Good to see you smile, kid," he said. "I was beginning to think you were taking this police substation thing too seriously. We'll work it out. Brick won't get the shaft."

The meeting adjourned not long after, the decision

on the police department problems temporarily postponed. Alyssa Baron followed Nora outside, where it was dark and downright frigid.

"Can I give you a ride home?" Alyssa asked.

"I don't mind walking...."

"Oh, you'll freeze. Look, my car's right here."

Sensing Alyssa was reluctant to be alone with herself just yet, Nora climbed into the passenger seat of her sister-councillor's expensive car. Alyssa pulled on thin leather driving gloves. She was so different from Liza, Nora thought, that it was almost eerie.

"I know Liza didn't notice yesterday afternoon," Alyssa said, turning on the ignition, "but I did. Nora, I'm sorry if any of this talk about you and Byron Forrester has caused you embarrassment. Liza...it just doesn't occur to her that a woman not much older than herself would be less than amused by such gossip."

Nora was taken aback, but resisted her impulse to deny that anything so silly as local talk could upset her. She was tired of pretending she had no feelings. "Thank you for noticing, Alyssa. You're right— I was embarrassed, but only at first."

Alyssa pulled out into the dark, quiet street. "Then there's no truth to the rumors?"

"About Byron and me? Well, no... I mean, yes, there's truth to them."

Alyssa Baron was silent.

"Three years ago," Nora said, staring out her window, "Byron came to Tyler to make sure Cliff was all right. He didn't intend to contact anyone in town—he just wanted to check on his brother and get out."

"But he met you."

"He told me he was a photographer. One thing led

to another and I invited him to dinner. Then he met Aunt Ellie."

Slowing for a turn, Alyssa didn't take her eyes off the road. "The pictures."

Nora exhaled. "For a long time I was convinced he used her."

"I can't imagine anyone taking advantage of Ellie Gates."

"They spent a lot of time together. And I spent a lot of time with Byron. Then he left and a few weeks later Aunt Ellie died."

"How awful for you," Alyssa said with genuine sympathy.

Nora looked at her. "I wasn't thinking just of myself. For the past three years I've told myself I should have seen what Byron was and warned Aunt Ellie, spared her...." She trailed off, unable to finish.

"Spared her what, Nora?"

"Having to spend so much of her last weeks with someone who saw her as quaint, as a subject for a series of photographs that would advance his career. That's what I've thought for the past three years. I'm not sure I was right."

Alyssa almost missed her next turn and had to brake hard, at least by her standards. "Nora, you amaze me sometimes. You have a tendency to look at all the wonderful things Aunt Ellie did for you without even considering the wonderful things you did for her."

"She never wanted marriage or children, but I came along—"

"You came along and enriched her life. She was already close to seventy when your parents died. She had the store and many, many friends, but you were her only close relative. She taught you what she knew about business. Don't you think that gave her tremendous satisfaction and solace? And you gave her constant companionship and true devotion in her old age. You were never a burden, Nora. How many times did she tell me you kept her young? You made her keep moving—she couldn't give up."

"She'd never have given up."

"Maybe. Maybe not."

Nora swallowed, her throat tight. "I used to think she'd live forever."

"At one time or another I think we all thought that of Aunt Ellie," Alyssa said, smiling wistfully. "I remember when I was a little girl— I must have been tiny because Mother was still around. She took me to Gates Department Store to buy handmade chocolate angels Aunt Ellie had special-ordered for Christmas. She was standing behind the glass counter herself and she seemed old even then." Alyssa paused, her expression warm and nostalgic. "Not old, really. Timeless."

They'd come to the house Aunt Ellie had had built for herself, back even before she was officially an old maid. Alyssa pulled her Mercedes alongside the curb.

"Honoring Aunt Ellie," she said, "doesn't mean you have to become her."

"Thank you, Alyssa. You've been awfully kind, considering the stress and strain you must be under. I know I can be hard on people—"

Alyssa laughed softly. "Oh, Nora, you're so much harder on yourself. People in this town look up to you and you try to fulfill all their expectations. But Aunt Ellie dared to be herself. Let that be an example to you." She shifted the car into neutral, her foot on the brake. "I had dinner tonight with Byron, Cliff and Liza. Actually, Byron and Liza. Cliff didn't stick around."

Nora could hear the concern in her older friend's voice, but withheld comment.

"Liza's my first child to get married. I want her to be happy and to have a memorable wedding." Alyssa hesitated. "And I know she believes in trial by fire. She thinks I've been too protective of Cliff and that he needs to jump feetfirst back into society. But a big church wedding..."

"You're worried Cliff might have a relapse," Nora said.

Alyssa's nod was almost imperceptible. "He hasn't been around people in a long, long time."

"Do you think Byron's being here is a help or a hindrance?"

"I don't know."

"And their mother—she's arriving on Thursday."

"Yes." Alyssa sighed, her foot slipping off the brake; the car rolled forward. "He desperately wants to see her again."

"But..."

"But I'm worried. Liza, the renovations, the—the discovery at the lodge. Now the wedding and Byron... It's a lot for a man who only a few weeks ago most people in Tyler thought was a burned-out recluse beyond redemption."

The past weeks, Nora thought, couldn't have been easy on Alyssa Baron, either, and perhaps she was projecting some of her own anxiety onto her daughter's fiancé. Discovery of the Body, whatever the ultimate results, had to have stirred up memories of Alyssa's mother's departure from Tyler when she was just a little girl. Nora had lost both her parents at a young age, but at least she'd known what happened to them. Alyssa didn't have that small consolation. For all she knew, Margaret Ingalls could still be alive.

Or, Nora thought dismally, lying on some slab in a morgue, awaiting identification.

"I'll talk to Byron," she offered.

Alyssa smiled her sweet, nonjudgmental smile. She was too kind a person, Nora thought, to suffer. "Thank you."

BYRON HAD A fire raging in the study. Nora could feel its warmth from the doorway. She sank against the painted doorjamb, and it occurred to her that she'd never really wanted to live alone. Until she was thirteen, she'd had her parents. Then there'd been Aunt Ellie. For a few weeks—or days, really—she'd had the promise of a life with an itinerant photographer. Only since Byron's departure from Tyler and Aunt Ellie's death had she lived alone. They'd been fulfilling years. She'd coped with plumbing problems and a foot of snow in her driveway and the odd bat swooping into her bedroom. But she liked coming home to a warm fire and a warm body in the house.

Spotting her, Byron smiled. "You look done in."

"It's been a long day, but I like to keep busy."

She kicked off her shoes and walked across the thick carpet in her stocking feet, then hiked up her skirt a bit and sat cross-legged in front of the fire. Byron had his shoes off, too. His feet were bare, his toes almost touching the flames. He had his ankles crossed. She noticed the length of his legs, the snug fit of his jeans on the hard muscles of his thighs. He had his shirt pulled out, the bottom wrinkled where it had been tucked in. He'd pushed up his sleeves. There was something inordinately sexy, Nora thought, about the man's forearms.

"I made a couple of long distance calls on your phone," he said. "Seems Pierce & Rothchilde can't get along as swimmingly without me as they believed."

"Do you find that reassuring?"

"Not in the least."

Leaning back on her elbows the way he was, she stretched out her legs, but because they weren't as long as his they didn't quite reach the fire. "Does it worry you, then?"

"Nope." He seemed confident of his answer. "I do my job. So did the woman I replaced. If I stay, I'll continue to do my job. If I leave, someone will take my place. It's a mistake to believe you're indispensable." He shrugged. "It's also arrogant."

"I'll bet your great-grandfather didn't feel that way."

"Good ol' Clifton Pierce? He wasn't nearly as married to the company as his son, my grandfather, Thorton Pierce, was. The old bastard never even retired. Died at his desk."

"Aunt Ellie died at home," Nora said, "but she never officially retired."

"Big difference."

Nora stared at the flickering flames, failing to see his logic.

"Aunt Ellie didn't live to work, Nora. She worked to live. Gates Department Store was her life's work and she loved it, gave it her all. But she also loved Tyler, and you. She had her friends, her hobbies. She was a whole person. That's what my series of photographs on her was all about."

"This," Nora said, not too nastily, "from a man who knew her all of two weeks."

"Two and a half weeks," he corrected amiably.

"She never knew you'd misrepresented yourself."

For a full minute, Byron said nothing. Nora listened to the crackling of the fire and the soft ticking of her cuckoo clock, keeping her eyes on the man stretched out beside her. Finally, he said, "Yes, she did."

"You told her you were Cliff's brother?"

"She guessed. Said we had the same eyes."

Nora rolled over and rose up on her knees, peering into Byron's eyes. "You do. But how would Aunt Ellie have known what Cliff's eyes looked like?"

"She'd seen him a couple of times around town. She was a highly observant woman. She was also a tad suspicious. *And* she'd badgered Alyssa Baron into telling her what she knew about the weirdo living out at her father's abandoned lodge. So I was already neck-deep before I'd even opened my mouth."

Not certain how to react, Nora sat down again. "She never told me a thing."

"Like the younger Eleanora Gates, the older Eleanora Gates didn't repeat gossip or confidences."

It wasn't in Nora to be angry with Aunt Ellie for not having shared with her all she'd known and deduced. But *Byron* could have told her! She glared at him.

He got the message. "Nora, I know what you're thinking. It was up to me to tell you the truth about myself and I didn't, simple as that. If it's any consolation, Aunt Ellie understood my decision to leave Tyler when I did, if not the way I did. Cliff had his demons. I had mine. You had yours. We all needed the past three years. We weren't ready for each other."

"And now?"

"Now," he said, turning to her, his eyes reflecting the orange glow of the fire, "Cliff has found Liza. And I'm not letting him off the hook this time— I'm not backing off, no matter how hard it is for either or us. He's my brother. As for you, Miss Nora…" He smiled, moving closer. "I'm very ready for you."

It was another of his deliberate, incorrigible remarks designed to make her aware—intensely aware—of the way she'd responded to his kiss the other night, the boundless passion they'd shared three years ago. She was not unmoved.

"Is this," she said, refusing to inch away from him even as he inched closer, "your way of distracting me from demanding reimbursement for your phone calls?"

His eyes danced, or else it was the flickering of the flames. "I think you're the one trying to do the distracting."

"Do you miss Providence?"

"No."

"Do you feel the same way about Providence as I do about Tyler?"

"No."

"But you've been there two hundred years," she said.

He laughed, the flames still dancing in his eyes. "I haven't."

"You said the Pierces…"

"Actually, the Pierces have been in Providence for more than three hundred years. They've had their house on Benefit Street for only two hundred."

Nora tried to imagine it. "Those are serious roots."

"Cliff and I are the last direct descendants of Clifton Pierce—"

"The founder of Pierce & Rothchilde."

"Cofounder. There are other Pierces in Providence. We both love the Pierce house and I guess Providence will always be home, but I've traveled too much and have had too many varied experiences to sink down 'serious roots' there."

"Or anywhere else?"

He looked at her. "Not necessarily."

She smiled. "There, you see? I have distracted you."

"No," he said in a low voice, touching her mouth with one finger, "you haven't."

His touch, as brief and light as it was, rekindled the desire she'd managed to keep at a slow, quiet burn through her dinner of salad and stringy pumpkin soup and her routine meeting of the Tyler town council. If she'd bypassed the study and gone straight to bed, as common sense had told her to do, she'd have dreamed about him. Now she knew she wouldn't have to rely on dreams.

"That's okay," she said. "I haven't distracted myself, either."

"I wondered."

His lips grazed hers. It was just a small kiss, a taste. It had the effect of a small spark on a very short fuse. Nora sizzled. Unfolding her legs, she sat up straighter than he was, her chest at his eye level. He unbuttoned just one button of her pale lemon silk blouse. She glanced down and could see the lacy edge of her bra, her breasts straining against its stretchy fabric.

"Byron, I don't want to dream about you tonight."

He looked up at her. He was propped up on one elbow, turned on his side, his head at a different angle, so that the flames no longer danced in his eyes. "What do you want?"

With a hand that trembled only slightly, she unbuttoned three more buttons on her blouse. They were small buttons, shaped like pearls, and not that difficult to work. In a few seconds, she slipped the blouse from her shoulders. She could feel the silk drop onto her hips and the heat of the fire on her exposed skin, which glowed in the orange light. Her nipples were hard against her lace bra. She reached around to unclasp it, but Byron stopped her, instead reaching around himself. With one hand, he unfastened the hook. The fabric fell loose. He slipped one strap off her shoulder and then the other, until her breasts were free. She shook the bra off her arms and watched him watching her.

"You have your answer," she whispered.

And he rose onto his knees, his mouth, already open, reaching hers. His tongue was hot, wet, insistent. She got to her knees as well. He caught her breasts with his palms, moaned softly into her mouth as his tongue plunged deeper. Slowly, he moved his hands down her sides, around to the small of her back. She pressed herself against him, feeling the warmth of his shirt against her bare breasts. Now she, too, moaned.

"I never thought this would happen to me again," she whispered. "Not twice in one lifetime."

He answered with her name, spoken hotly against her mouth as his hands slipped into the waist of her skirt, sliding inside her underpants and stockings, down lower until he was cupping her buttocks, lifting her against him. His fingers went lower, deeper, probing, exploring.

They melted together to the floor.

"I want to see all of you," he said hoarsely. "To touch you everywhere."

Happy to comply, she unzipped her skirt in back, arching up slightly, but then he seized the hem and slowly, erotically, pulled the skirt down over her hips, her thighs, her ankles. He cast it aside. Breathing hard, he made shorter work of her panty hose. She lay on the carpet in just her lace bikini underpants, her feet very close to the fire. She doubted she looked much like a stern, Victorian old maid.

"I thought I'd never want you more than I did three years ago," Byron said, his voice low, hoarse with the desire that made him hard and taut all over. "But I do. Nora, there's never been anyone in my life even remotely like you. I knew when I left Tyler I'd never forget you—and I never did. I never will."

She helped him with his own clothes then, lifting his shirt over his head, resisting the sweet agony of pressing her breasts to his chest. First things first. He wasn't wearing a belt with his jeans. They came off with little effort. Underneath he wore deep purple underpants; they barely contained him.

"I thought all East Coast blue bloods wore striped boxers," she said.

"Not this East Coast blue blood."

And in a matter of seconds, he wore nothing at all.

Hooking his thumbs into the elastic waist of her underpants, he slid them down her thighs, over her knees, down her shins, her ankles and off.

He looked at her for a long time, seeing all of her.

And he touched her, tentatively at first, as if making certain they hadn't plunged together into the same dream. Nora had never experienced anything so deliciously erotic. And he did what he'd said he'd wanted to do, touching her everywhere.

After that, he tasted her everywhere.

And she him.

Then she was drawing him onto her, into her, and because it had been so, so long, it hurt a little, but it was a welcome hurting, and he held back just long enough, although she could see that it was an effort. But then there was no holding back. It was as if the fire at their feet had spread over them, consumed them, until they were red-hot coals, burning everything they touched.

It was a long, long time before they burned down.

When they did, Nora gathered up her scattered clothes and dashed to her bedroom, leaving Byron dead asleep in the study.

She looked at her reflection in her antique mirror. At her love-swollen lips and reddened breasts, at the places where she could still feel his touch on her.

"Some old maid you make," she said, not lightly at all.

And she locked her door, so as not to tempt fate or a Rhode Islander in the form of Byron Sanders Forrester.

CHAPTER TEN

NORA AWOKE TO the clanging of pipes, the hissing of her radiator and a warm haze enveloping her. In a few minutes she was sweating under her quilt. In another minute, she was on her feet, pulling on her robe and stomping to the kitchen. She stopped at the thermostat in the hall.

"Seventy-two!"

Incredulous, she found Byron in the kitchen. Even as it struck her how oddly right he looked at her counter, she noticed he had on running shorts and a Boston Marathon T-shirt. No shoes, no socks. He smiled a good-morning at her and cracked an egg on the side of her medium-size stainless steel bowl.

"I've *never* had the thermostat up that high, even in the dead of winter," she told him. "I'm surprised the furnace didn't blow up."

Byron began whistling some obnoxiously cheerful tune. "You really are such a genial soul in the morning. As far as I'm concerned, Miss Nora, if you leave a man sleeping stark naked on your study floor with your thermostat set at a notch above frigid—"

"Sixty is a perfectly reasonable nighttime setting."

"Tell that to my vitals."

He'd cracked another two eggs into the bowl. That made at least three. Was he expecting guests for break-

fast? Just what other liberties did he intend to take
with her home?

"If," he went on blithely, "you'd tossed a quilt over
me or put another log on the fire, I might have resisted
the impulse to turn up the heat to a humane level."

"I don't mind you turning up the heat, but seventy-
two?"

He cracked another egg into the bowl. "It's a nice
round number, guaranteed to thaw certain frozen body
parts. And I didn't turn *up* the heat. I turned it *on*. A
fine but critical distinction."

"Easterners," Nora said, and sat down at the table,
since it didn't look as if Byron needed any help just
yet. If the kitchen had been any warmer, she'd have
needed a fan. "What are you making?"

"A frittata."

"A glorified omelet. How many eggs are you using?"

"Enough. I'm not using all the yolks."

"Are your frittatas better than your pumpkin soup?"
she asked dubiously.

He grinned. "My frittatas will melt in your mouth."

It wasn't an exaggeration. While he worked his mira-
cles with her eggs, she made toast and coffee, breaking
out her mocha java beans, and set the table with Aunt
Ellie's best English stoneware breakfast dishes. Nora
was warm in her chamois robe, so she went back to her
bedroom and changed into her lightweight waffle-weave
cotton robe, which, ever the optimist regarding Wisconsin weather, she hadn't put away yet for the season.

"I'll let you have your way with my thermostat until
I head off to work," she told Byron upon her return to
the kitchen for cleanup.

His dark eyebrows went up. "Oh?"

"Byron! Are you going to act like an eighth-grader again today? I can't say anything without your twisting it around into something dirty."

"What's so dirty about any of my remarks?"

"You know what I mean."

He squirted way too much dishwashing liquid into her sink. "Are you going Victorian virgin on me again?"

"Now that," she said, almost under her breath, "would be a neat trick, wouldn't it?"

And after cleanup, they ended up making love, laughing and teasing each other, on the lace coverlet of the bed in the front guest room. Byron spirited her there while she was supposed to be getting ready for work, on the pretext that the radiator didn't work. She had a look. It worked fine.

"It was probably slow heating up," she said, "because it hasn't been on since early spring. I like a cool house."

"Do tell. Instead of turning up the heat I should have crawled into bed with you at dawn. Let you warm up my cold body parts."

She shrugged. "It would have been cheaper."

He crossed his arms over his chest. "I tried, you know. Your door was locked. Sort of like closing the barn door after the cows've gotten out, wouldn't you say?"

"More like," she said, "after the bull had been on a rampage."

At which point he'd pounced, flinging her onto the bed and tickling her unmercifully, until she was howling with laughter, screaming for him to stop before the neighbors called the police and Brick Bauer himself came to see what was up. "Then I'd have to vote against the sheriff's substation to keep him quiet, and there goes my reputation...."

Byron had silenced her laughter.

Quite efficiently.

And made her late for work for the first time in twenty years. When she told him, he applauded. "On your way out," he said, "turn down the heat. It's hotter'n hell in here."

He did have a way of getting her to not take life—and herself—too seriously. Given the tragedies of his own life, it was a remarkable gift.

It was just her luck to run into Inger Hansen in the Gates Department Store parking lot. "I was just coming in to look for something for Liza for her wedding," she said, peering closely at Nora. "You look flushed, Nora. Are you ill?"

"No! Really, I—I ate a big breakfast."

And she held back a silly giggle, imagining what immature, crude, *funny* rejoinder Byron Forrester would have ready. He was, she thought, a decidedly unsettling influence on her life. And a potentially wonderful *part* of her life. But she couldn't think about romance and such now. There was a Thanksgiving window to plan, the Christmas season to prepare for—plenty of work to be done.

On her way up to her office, however, she stopped at the book section to see what Gates carried from Pierce & Rothchilde.

Not a single title.

She and Byron were, she thought, hardly for the first time, from very different worlds.

"So," CLIFF SAID, "You're setting her up for a broken heart all over again."

Byron could feel his brother's tension. Cliff was standing in front of him on the veranda, where he'd gone with a cup of coffee. They'd spent the morning and early part of the afternoon together in the lodge, which, when the renovations were complete, would be an incredible place. Mostly they'd talked about the past. And the implications of having discovered a body on the premises. On the surface, Cliff was avoiding speculation until he had concrete information. But underneath, like so many in Tyler, he was worried. If the body *was* that of Margaret Lindstrom Ingalls, how had it gotten there? What did his future grandfather-in-law know? How would his future mother-in-law, a sensitive and perhaps somewhat emotionally fragile woman, react? And Liza, Byron thought. How would Cliff's future wife react? Could they continue to live at the lodge where her grandmother might have been murdered?

Then there was Cliff himself. He'd already seen far too much murder and destruction, far too many families torn apart. With his big church wedding just days away, he had to be feeling the stress.

It was easier, Byron realized, for Cliff to focus on his younger brother's somewhat suspicious love life.

"Cliff, she's an adult," Byron said patiently. "She doesn't need your protection. And I *do* care about her."

Cliff looked around at him, his face unyielding, even ravaged, speaking volumes about how difficult the transition from recluse to ordinary human being still was for him. That he couldn't have done it without Liza's unconditional love—and his unconditional love for her—was crystal clear. "Nora Gates has to live in this town after you've gone. So do I."

Byron sighed. He had no good response, if only because he'd stopped believing in crystal balls. He didn't know what the future would bring. He did know, however, that he'd never loved anyone—now or three years ago—as much as he loved Nora Gates. But was love enough?

Cliff looked out toward the lake. It was a bright, clear, crisp Wisconsin afternoon. The weekend rain had whipped most of the remaining leaves from the trees, leaving them suddenly bare, their gray branches and trunks outlined in sharp focus against an achingly cloudless sky. Only clusters of rust-colored leaves and a few fading yellows clung to the odd tree. In town, more leaves had held on through the wind and rain. But it was very cold. Before he left Nora's house, however, Byron had lowered the thermostat, not to sixty, but to a reasonable sixty-five.

"I don't know," Cliff said, squinting at the sparkling lake. Coming up next to him, Byron could see the pronounced lines at the corners of his brother's eyes. They were eyes, he thought, that had seen too damned much of humanity's dark side. "Sometimes I think Forrester men are destined to break the hearts of the women they love."

Byron tensed. "Cliff, don't."

"Look at Mother. How she's suffered for having loved Dad."

"She married a military man. There was a war. They knew what they were doing. Cliff, you're not Dad. Liza isn't—"

But Cliff turned abruptly, the strain he was under,

just for an instant, rising to the surface. "Liza and I are forever. That doesn't mean I won't break her heart. And you, Brother. You're more like Dad than you want to admit. I'm like the Pierces. I like to sink roots. Tyler's a good place. I can stay. But you? You like to wander."

"I've done my wandering."

"Have you?"

"For three years."

"Now you're back at Pierce & Rothchilde. And you hate it."

Byron said nothing.

Cliff's mouth twitched. "Mrs. Redbacker still there?"

"She'll go out like Grandpa Thorton."

"Feetfirst," Cliff said.

"I like the job. I've got weekends for wandering."

"You still take pictures?"

Byron shrugged. "Always."

His brother's only response was a small nod as he sipped his coffee, still steaming faintly.

"I don't think," Byron said, choosing his words with care, "that Nora will regret what's happened between us, regardless of what the future brings. And it's not just what I want and who I am, you know. It's also a matter of what she wants and who she is."

Cliff kept his coffee mug close to his mouth. "And right now you contradict what she thinks she wants and who she thinks she is."

"In a nutshell, Brother," Byron said, "that's it."

WHEN NORA CAME home from the store a couple of hours early to prepare for her Halloween party that evening, she found Byron in her bedroom checking out his glow-in-the-dark skeleton costume in her full-length mirror.

"Good Lord," she said, "where did you find *that?*"

"That's classified information."

There was nothing like it at Gates. It was a black knit unitard—including feet—with a skeleton outlined on the fabric in white fluorescent paint. He looked positively eerie.

"I have white face paint, too," he said.

"Gross."

"There's a hood and a mask, but they're a bit much, don't you think?"

He held them up. They were more than a bit much, so he received no argument from her. All day, she'd worked hard and diligently to keep in mind that she was a woman who didn't focus exclusively on the moment. She always kept in mind the past and the future—where she'd been, where she was going. When she was with Byron Forrester, the past seemed unimportant and the future elusive, something that would take care of itself. But that was dangerous thinking, she'd told herself. And it wasn't her.

But he was so damned sexy in his sleek skeleton costume.

"Ahh," he said with considerable relish, "if only the Pierce & Rothchilde board could see me now."

His hair was wild and dark, and he had plaster dust in his cuticles, a couple of scraped knuckles. He'd spent the day, she remembered, at the lodge with Cliff. She found it strange, yet curiously right, that two brothers from the East had ended up in Tyler, Wisconsin. One definitely to stay, the other probably not.

But she wouldn't think about Byron's leaving right now. "Any calls to Rhode Island today?"

"Only from. Seems my pal Hank Murrow was a bit premature in gloating about his technothriller megacontract. Now he wants us to buy some dreary tome he's written."

"It's not good?"

"Oh, no. I'm sure it's great."

Nora made no pretense of understanding the publishing industry, or Byron Forrester's attitude toward it. "What about his technothriller?"

"Who knows? It's not what P & R does." He pulled at the neckline of his skeleton suit. "God, I'm about to suffocate in this thing. It's like being encased in a giant rubber band. How was the store today?"

"Busy."

"Gearing up for the Christmas rush already?"

She nodded, unable—or at least damned unwilling— to take her eyes off him. She'd worn a navy wool gabardine coatdress with chunky silver jewelry to the store, distracted periodically all day by images of Byron slipping it off her when she got home. Now here he was in her bedroom.

"The party's not for another three hours," she said.

Naturally he read more meaning into her statement than she'd intended. "Oh?"

"I was just reminding you—"

"In case I didn't want to run around in my glow-in-the-dark skeleton costume for the next three hours or in case I had other plans in mind?"

She snapped her mouth shut. "I just thought you might get hot." Then she added, because he was determined to give her no rest, "In your skeleton suit."

"It is a bit close. Here, give me a hand—there's an invisible zipper in the back. Stand aside, though. When I peel this thing off it'll snap back down to Ken doll-size."

He did have a point.

He'd also neglected to tell her how little he had on underneath his costume. Not that there'd been much mystery.

"Are you blushing?" he asked, highly entertained.

"Men have no modesty."

"Mustn't generalize. Besides, there's nothing here you haven't seen…aha, so that's it! You're not the least embarrassed, Miss Nora. That's pure *lust* I see in those beautiful gray eyes of yours." He slid his arms around her and drew her close. "You are beautiful, you know."

"No one's ever told me—"

"That's because they were afraid you'd clobber them if they did. You do have a temper."

"Only with you." He had her in such a tight embrace she could do nothing with her arms except slip them around him; he had a strong, smooth back. "You seem to bring out…not the worst in me, I think, but whatever it is I'm feeling, good, bad, or indifferent. I'm afraid I'm not very good at censoring myself when I'm around you."

"That's good, isn't it?" he asked seriously.

"It's not like me— I'm usually more controlled. But yes, I think it's good. I don't hold anything back when I'm with you. I just can't seem to be…well, circumspect."

"I'm glad."

"And you?"

He smiled. "What you see is what you get."

She knew it was true. Even three years ago, when he'd neglected to tell her the whole truth of who he was and why he'd come to Tyler, he still had been his own person. Most of her negative feelings toward him for the past years had stemmed not from what he'd done or said, but from what he'd let her—deliberately or otherwise—believe about him, from her own suppositions, deductions, prejudices. He was more centered now, more balanced, but the irreverent sense of humor was still there, the sexiness, the energy, the optimism. He'd needed those three years on his own. So had she. But he was still the Byron she'd loved three years ago. And he'd loved her. She was sure of that now.

"I'm not holding back on you," he said, without her prompting. His smile had faded, in its place an expression of warmth and gravity. "I've never known anyone like you. I've never felt for anyone what I feel for you. I doubt I ever will."

She draped her arms over his hard, bare shoulders. She could feel her lips part, inviting him, but she didn't wait for his response. Instead she tilted back her head and kissed him lightly on the chin. "The first time I saw you on the street outside Gates," she said in a low voice, "I knew you'd change my life. It was just there, a certain knowledge. I didn't know how or why or in what way, but I knew you were meant to be standing out there on that sidewalk while I was doing that window. And I don't even believe in fate."

"I felt the same way."

She nodded. "I believe you."

"Nora—"

"Byron, I want you to know that I do trust you. I'm not saying I know what's going to happen to us. I don't know where we'll go from here. But I do know that the past—what I used to think about you—what I *needed* to think…" She paused, wishing she could be more articulate, wishing she could explain how certain and yet mixed-up she felt. "I just believe you now."

His arms tightened around her, and he seemed unable to speak. Their mouths were very close. She let her tongue flick against the edges of his teeth, into his mouth.

And he responded, in action if not in words. Lifting her, he carried her to the bed. Halfway there her shoes fell off. He kissed her deeply, his tongue plunging far into her mouth, its sensual rhythm a promise of what was to come, a promise of much more than sex. Her dress was hiked up to midthigh. When he laid her on the bed, it hiked up to her waist.

Finally, he managed to whisper her name. It was enough.

She assumed he'd start by removing her dress, or stand back so that she could, but he didn't. Already his eyes were dusky with passion. He peeled off her panty hose, purposefully taking her underpants with them this time. The air in the bedroom was cool on her overheated skin. She didn't object.

Starting at her ankles, he slid his hands, alternating between his fingertips and palms, up the insides of her legs. She ached with anticipation. A small moan escaped when he came to her inner thighs, betraying her longing. He paused just for a moment. She was almost overwhelmed with a need that was sensual, earthy, so very real.

He touched his fingers to where she was dark and moist. She arched for him, cried out for him not to stop, but he drew back, all the way to her ankles again, where he followed the same trail with his tongue, until he was back to where she was wet and dark and aching, and this time he stayed. In seconds she was a volcano erupting, spilling out molten lava, and at some point he dispensed with his underpants, entering her with a heat that matched her own.

"I love you," he whispered. "I think I always have."

And she believed him.

Finally, when they became aware of the world again, Nora noticed the clock. "My party!"

They had to scramble. Together they lined up the jack-o'-lanterns they'd made on the front porch and got them lit, put on the spooky music, tucked ghosts and goblins and shrunken heads here and there, filled a tub with water for apple-bobbing, loaded bowls with mountains of treats. At last Byron sauntered off to put on his skeleton costume, and she retreated to her bedroom, where she quickly smoothed out her bed and put on her layers of makeup, her jewelry and the filmy, gaudy fabric.

"Good God!" Byron said, staring at her when she joined him in the living room. "How many years have you been dressing like that?"

"It's the same costume I always wear. My rendition of a gypsy—"

"Well, if there's a single person left in Tyler who still believes your Victorian virgin act after seeing you in this getup, I'll swear you're as pure as the virgin snow myself."

"What? I'm *not* a gypsy." She laughed, loving how he teased her—how he refused to take her too seriously. "It's sort of a sexy costume, I realize, especially for me, but—"

"Sort of?"

If the proverbial doorbell hadn't rung, in another minute there'd have been a gypsy and a glow-in-the-dark skeleton making love on the living room floor.

By six-thirty, Nora's house was packed. People who didn't ordinarily come to her annual Halloween party took advantage of her open invitation and showed up. She figured most of the newcomers had stopped in to get a glimpse—quite literally—of the skeleton in her closet. Byron seemed to enjoy popping out of the entry closet, scaring the daylights out of little kids. Then, of course, charming them.

People came and went; others lingered. Nora tried introducing Byron as her houseguest, who'd be staying through Cliff and Liza's wedding on Saturday, but he refused to say he was anything but a skeleton in her closet. It made for many widened eyes.

"You always have this many people at this thing?" he asked, pulling her aside.

"Not half. Everyone wants to see what you look like. It's not easy to tell with the face paint. The clingy costume doesn't leave much of the rest of you to the imagination."

He grunted. "I should have dressed as a pirate and kidnapped you, given them all something to talk about."

"They have plenty to talk about as it is."

His eyes turned serious. "Do you care?"

She smiled. "If talk's the only punishment, it's well worth the crimes I've committed."

"And to think," he said, laughing, "we've only just begun our crime spree."

Later, when the little kids had gone home, Nora put on her favorite Halloween music, *Night on Bald Mountain,* and broke out the hot mulled cider and the pumpkin rolls—no strings or seeds included—she'd made ahead and frozen. They were filled with layers of cream and nuts, then sprinkled with sifted powdered sugar. They'd been Aunt Ellie's favorite. Nora also had her biggest pottery bowl brimming with warm cinnamon applesauce.

Into this quieter, homey part of her Halloween festivities, Liza Baron walked, pale and scared, wearing a huge denim jacket that had to be Cliff's. Someone started to tease her about not wearing a costume. But she didn't smile in her vivacious way, and her big eyes wouldn't focus. Nora quickly set down her tray of mugs filled with steaming cider.

But Byron was already on his glow-in-the-dark feet, grabbing his future sister-in-law as she stumbled into the music room. "Liza, what's wrong?"

She looked at him, the tears spilling down her white cheeks. "It's Cliff." She almost collapsed, but Byron was there. "He's gone."

CHAPTER ELEVEN

BYRON TOOK THE next flight East.

He'd told Liza—and Nora—that he thought he knew where his brother was headed.

When his plane touched down at Logan Airport in Boston, he got his car out of long-term parking and drove to Providence, arriving very late. It seemed he'd been gone for years, yet it had been less than a week. He called Nora from the kitchen phone in the Pierce house on Benefit Street, half-expecting his grandfather to sneak around the corner and whack him with his cane for slouching. Thorton Pierce had been a brilliant publisher and a formidable grandfather. He had never taken—or, to be fair, tried to take—Richard Forrester's place. He'd made no secret of his mystification over his son-in-law's choice of a military career, particularly when there was a war on.

Nora picked up on the first ring.

"Any word from Cliff?" Bryon asked, just in case.

"None."

"I didn't expect there would be. Is Liza with you?"

"Yes. Alyssa talked her out of staying at the lodge alone, especially…well, you know."

The mysterious dead body discovered on the premises. It had to give anyone, even the irrepressible Liza Baron, pause. Byron nodded grimly, aware of his own solitude in the elegant town house. It was well after midnight, but Nora sounded fresh and alert, one of Tyler, Wisconsin's rock-solid citizens, a responsible woman who could be counted on in an emergency. In addition to wanting to make love to her night and day, Byron did also admire her.

"There's nothing more I can do tonight," he told her.

"I know," she said, more for his sake, he felt, than for hers. "Cliff's a grown man. It's not as if he's likely to be in any danger."

Liza, in fact, had given no indication whatever that Cliff had flipped out. Despite the strain he'd seen in his brother earlier in the day, Byron was inclined to believe her assessment. But what Liza hadn't articulated—and what he knew she most feared—was that Cliff Forrester had up and left her the same way, for the same reasons, that he had left Rhode Island and his mother and brother so many years before. *Liza and I are forever. That doesn't mean I won't break her heart.* Cliff's words of less than twenty-four hours ago.

But Byron thought he knew, finally, something that Cliff, even after his years of isolation, was only beginning to figure out. His stress and need and fears in these days before his marriage to the woman he loved weren't about cold feet. They weren't about his reluctance to face crowds or his fear of flipping out and hurting someone, even Liza.

No, Byron thought, looking in his refrigerator for something to eat. He found a shriveled apple and a beer. He chose the beer. It hissed when he unscrewed the cap.

Cliff's stress and need and fears were about Colonel Richard Forrester of the United States Air Force. They were about a man who'd died in captivity a long, long way from home and about the son who'd tried—and almost died—to save him. Ultimately, they were about confronting who Clifton Pierce Forrester had been, as a brother and a son, as a boy and a young man. They were about all of those things, Byron knew, because he was there himself, coming to terms, at last, with the past. Accepting what was.

He sipped his beer, but it didn't taste right, and he broke out the last of his grandfather's private stock of brandy and poured himself a glass. He went up to the top floor of the grand, historic house, where he had his studio. Or, more accurately, what was supposed to be his studio. Since his return to Pierce & Rothchilde, he'd had precious little time for photography or anything else.

Aunt Ellie, he thought for no particular reason, would have loved the sweeping staircases, the eclectic furnishings that reflected the best in American craftsmanship, from the 1790s when the Pierces were shipbuilders, to the 1990s when they were publishers. Byron didn't know what they'd be in the year 2090.

"Snooty publishers," Aunt Ellie had called Pierce & Rothchilde in her outspoken manner. She loathed anything in herself or anyone else that smacked of elitism.

The house was warm. Upon leaving for Wisconsin, Byron hadn't thought to turn the heat down from its usual sixty-eight-degree setting. Now...well, it was obvious to him that nothing would ever be the same. Like his last trip to Tyler, Wisconsin, this one had changed him forever.

In his studio, Aunt Ellie grinned her toothy grin from behind a glass-fronted counter on the first floor of Gates Department Store. Beside her, smiling demurely, was her grandniece and namesake, Nora. Byron had had the picture blown up and framed. It was his favorite of all the shots he'd taken that hot Wisconsin August, one he'd held back from the series the Chicago paper had published just before Aunt Ellie's death, launching the photographic career of Byron Sanders. Eleanora Gates had seldom left Tyler in her long lifetime, but she'd seen so much, knew so much. *The best gift you can give someone you love is the gift of being your whole self. Don't give yourself to Nora in pieces, Byron. She can't put you back together. No one can but you. If you ask that of her, you'll destroy yourself. And you'll destroy her.*

He raised his brandy snifter to her. "You were a wise and kind woman, Miss Eleanora Gates."

And he dialed Mrs. Redbacker's home number, because it was Tuesday night. She'd be with her mother, alternating as she did with her siblings to keep the elderly lady out of a nursing home, and he was guaranteed to get her message machine. Which he did. He left instructions for her, then finished his brandy in the company of Aunt Ellie and her grandniece, and went downstairs.

In his mail—delivered by a housekeeper he hadn't yet mentioned to Nora—he found a thick padded envelope that looked suspiciously like a manuscript. Didn't anyone know the difference between a publisher and an editor these days? He didn't have time to *read*.

"Aw, gee."

It was Henry "Hank" Murrow's technothriller. There was a note attached. "Thought you might want to have a look to see how stupid New York publishers really are."

Having nothing better to do until morning and
knowing he'd never sleep, Byron started to read. After
page three he knew that New York publishers weren't
nearly as stupid as ol' Hank wanted to believe. But he
did keep reading.

At least worldwide mayhem was a distraction from
thinking about Cliff.

And Nora Gates.

"Oh, Nora," he whispered, hoping for a dose of her
pragmatism and can-do spirit. He'd need them.

LIZA PACED BACK and forth from the living room,
through the music room, down the hall to the kitchen
and back until dawn, then collapsed for a few hours on
the study couch. When Nora asked if she needed anything, she pulled in her lips in a look of pure Ingalls
stubbornness. "The bastard could've left me a note."

Never had Nora seen anyone as worried about someone and yet as strangely confident that everything,
in the end, would be fine. She'd watched Liza's ini-
tial panic settle into a slow burn of frustration. But
whatever Cliff's agenda, his love for Liza Baron was
a given. That was settled. Nora considered it bizarre.
Cliff Forrester had cut out on Liza just days before
their wedding, she might for all she *really* knew never
see him again—and yet there was no doubt in her mind
that he loved her. Then what the devil was love? Who
needed it?

Love, Nora had thought uncomfortably as she
dragged herself off to bed, was a peculiar thing. But
she'd known that for years. Look at how she felt about
Byron. It was the most mixed-up jumble of feelings any
person could possibly want to endure. Her hopes and

longings and needs and dreams all suddenly seemed to revolve around that dark-eyed Easterner, and made for lots of tossing and turning. She ached for him. She hurt for him. She wanted for him. She wanted him to be happy, to be everything he could be, needed to be. He had definitely turned her world upside down.

But life was easier when her world was right side up.

In the morning, she called Albert first thing and told him she wouldn't be in today. "I'm not surprised," he said. "I had coffee at the diner this morning and heard that Cliff Forrester had bailed out on Liza Baron. Word is she's hiding out at your place."

"She's not hiding. She's staying with me until we know more."

"Then the rumors are true?"

Too late, Nora realized she'd been had. She was in the awkward position—one she usually studiously avoided—of having to comment on gossip instead of merely hearing it. She'd seldom confirmed or denied a Tyler rumor. "Albert, you know I don't comment on other people's personal affairs."

"Well," he said, undeterred, "at least tell me if the wedding's still on. Will folks be lining up at the door to return wedding gifts?"

"They shouldn't be," Nora said crisply, changing the subject before hanging up in relief a few minutes later.

If only Byron would call again. She and Liza needed information. An update. Any scrap of fresh news they could hang on to. But the phone was annoyingly silent. And she couldn't call him. He'd neglected to give her his number. She'd tried Rhode Island information even before she'd called the store.

Liza had come into the kitchen. Her hair was tan-

gled and sticking out at odd angles, and her eyes, ordinarily so clear and bright, were puffy and red from
insufficient sleep. She'd borrowed a flannel nightgown
from Nora that came to well above her ankles. She was
barefoot, but Nora wasn't worried, since she'd kept the
thermostat at whatever "humane" temperature Byron
had settled on.

"Good morning," Liza said.

"'Morning. Coffee?"

She smiled weakly. "Just inject it directly into my
veins. Anything new?"

Nora shook her head.

"What's that I smell?"

"Corn muffins."

"Nora, you didn't have to—"

"I was up early. It gave me something to do." While
waiting for the phone to ring, she thought, but she was
unwilling to let Liza know the extent of her own emotional involvement in the Forrester brothers' goings-on.

Liza sat at the table, and Nora brought her a mug
of steaming coffee. The way things were going, she'd
get used to having company for breakfast and would
never want to go back to oatmeal alone with CNN and
the *Tyler Citizen*.

"I *hate* waiting," Liza said suddenly, visibly squeezing her coffee cup, her impatience nearly palpable.

"It's not my long suit, either."

"Why the hell would Cliff go to Rhode Island?"

"Byron could be wrong—"

"But he's not. You know he's not." She exhaled,
setting her mug down hard. "Cliff's told me zip about
his life in Rhode Island. I've got the highlights, but
he hasn't talked a whole lot about what his childhood

was like, what he did *before* he went to Southeast Asia. He's got stuff to settle with his family and I...well, I'm not part of that."

Nora poured herself a cup of coffee, took a sip. "Do you regret having invited Byron and Mrs. Forrester?"

Liza shook her head adamantly. "No, this had to come out and get done sooner or later. And you know me—better sooner than later. What that family's been through can't have been easy. Cliff's taking a big step. I wish I were a part of it, but...if we're going to be everything we want to be to each other, he's got to do it all, come to terms with all he's got to come to terms with. I can't dictate what he needs to do and doesn't need to do. I just hope..." She sighed, blowing on her coffee, not meeting Nora's eyes. "I just hope he hasn't run away because of this big wedding we've—*I've*—got planned. I would've thought he'd tell me if it was too much."

"Surely he would have," Nora said.

"Yeah, I guess. But everything's moved so fast..." She shrugged, her words coming in bursts, her concentration not at its best. "If it's Rhode Island...you know, if his family's been there for hundreds of years and he wants to go back there to live, I'm game."

"You'd move East?"

"Sure."

"But your needs and wants count, too."

"Yeah. They do. They just don't happen to include living in Tyler forever and ever. I mean, I can. It'd be great. But I can leave, too. If Cliff *has* to be somewhere, that's okay by me. I've been thinking he has to be at the lodge. Now maybe I'm wrong." She frowned. "Am I making sense? It's like you, Nora. You *have* to be in Tyler. I don't know what Byron wants, but I'll bet he doesn't need to be in Providence the way you need to be in Tyler."

Nora wasn't sure she liked the implications of what Liza was saying, which were that she was inflexible and stuck in her ways. But she focused on the other implication. "Liza, I know you think that Byron and I...that we..."

Liza's grin, even with her disheveled appearance, held some of its old devil-may-care spirit. "Oh, give it up, Nora. You and Byron *are*. It's so obvious."

The oven timer buzzed, and Nora, glad for the distraction, got out the muffins, dumping them onto an old, bent cooling rack Aunt Ellie had had forever. She got out the butter and honey, heaped the muffins onto a platter, and brought them to the table, where she sat across from Liza.

"You couldn't live in Rhode Island, could you?" Liza asked.

"I've never even been there."

"What do you think Cliff's up to?"

Nora shrugged. "Marriage is a milestone. No matter how willingly one goes into it, it's got to make anyone think about the past—where one's been. I'd guess Cliff's making his peace, with whatever drove him to Timberlake Lodge in the first place, the choices he's made, what he's done. Not just in Southeast Asia. Before that."

Dropping a piping-hot muffin onto her plate, Liza asked softly, "You don't think he's running?"

"No, frankly, I don't."

She dipped her spoon into the honey. "Maybe I've asked too much of him too soon."

"No more," Nora said confidently, "than he's asked of you or either of you has asked of yourself."

Liza nodded, not so much in agreement as in acknowledgment that she understood what Nora was trying to say, and she looked thoughtful, contemplating Nora's words.

Then she said, "You know, the bastard *could* have left me a note."

Nora smiled. "Yes, he could have. And Byron could have called again by now."

Liza watched the honey drip from her spoon onto her split muffin. "I've never been to Rhode Island, either."

Nora got up, tore a scrap of paper from the notepad by her phone, sat back down and pushed it across the table to Liza.

"What's this?" Liza asked.

"The times of today's flights from Milwaukee to Boston and Providence."

This time, Liza's smile reached her sparkling eyes. "You, Miss Gates, are far more devious than you look."

IT WAS A CLEAR, sharply cold New England morning in late autumn. As he walked onto the quiet, isolated stretch of Nantucket Island beach, Byron could smell the salt in the air, feel it on his skin. The wind off the Atlantic penetrated his bones. In the distance, the sea gulls swooped and croaked. These, he thought, would always be the sights and smells and sounds of home. Which was why he'd known his brother would come here.

He could see Cliff walking slowly along the ocean's edge, his shoulders hunched against the cold.

Byron hesitated, then moved across the white sand.

And in his mind, he could see two small boys and their father running across the sand, discovering tide pools, scooping up shells, chasing waves. He could hear the father's laughter. It was clear and strong and filled with love and hope. The two boys responded with hoots and squeals. For the boys and their father, and their mother who would join them later for a clambake, Nantucket was a retreat, a place of peace and beauty where they could be together without the pressures of the outside world—of war, family, commerce, reputation. On Nantucket, they preferred to live simply, in harmony with the rhythms of the sun and the tide.

Then Byron was standing beside his brother, and he could see that the two boys had become men. And he knew that the father was gone and had been for too long. Cliff didn't look at him. He didn't speak. He and Byron continued along the beach together.

Finally, Cliff said, "We all did our best."

"Yes," Byron said, "we did."

"It wasn't enough to save Dad."

"No. There was never any way it could be. But he knew that. He didn't expect it."

Cliff nodded, looking out at the choppy ocean that was so impossibly blue, so impossibly beautiful, under the cloudless sky. "I know he knew."

For a while longer, they walked in silence.

Then Cliff said, "I couldn't save everyone I wanted to save in Cambodia."

"You saved more than most, Cliff. More than anyone could have asked you to save."

Cliff's gaze cut toward his younger brother; the bright sunlight revealed every line, every scar, a harsh reminder of the years that had passed, the time they'd lost. "Until Liza, I'm not sure I ever really understood what it must have been like for Mother to lose both of us, Dad and me."

"She didn't lose you, Cliff."

"I know that now. I didn't for a long time."

They walked into the wet sand where a wave had receded, making footprints that wouldn't last. Cliff seemed unaware of the cold. Byron zipped up his leather jacket.

"You'd knew I'd be here?" Cliff asked.

"Yeah."

He nodded, not needing to know how Byron had known. It was enough that he had. "We were all at our best here. I had to come before I walked down the aisle on Saturday. I had to know I could."

They started back across the empty beach.

A woman was coming toward them, over the same ground Byron had come, moving slowly, uncertainly. Her head was wrapped in a flowing challis scarf against the increasingly fierce wind. If it didn't die down, Byron thought, the plane he'd chartered would be grounded and even the ferry wouldn't run.

But then, beside him, Cliff whispered hoarsely, "Mother."

And she recognized him, too, and hesitated, and Byron could feel his brother's pain that his own mother would hold back when she saw him. But, for a time, that was what he'd wanted, what he'd needed. Now it wasn't.

He grinned suddenly and waved.

Even with the wind, Byron could hear their mother's cry of happiness and relief. Cliff was moving faster. Byron hung back. This was their moment.

Their mother's scarf had come undone, trailing down her back, and she wasn't the young woman who'd tried to explain to her sons their father's sense of duty when he'd gone back to Vietnam for yet another tour, who'd tried to give them hope and stability in their grandfather's historic house in Providence during those difficult years, first of absence, then of uncertainty, finally of loss. Anne Forrester had grown older since her husband had gone off to war, never to come home, even to be buried. But she'd retained her strength and courage and humor. Byron could sense those qualities, even as he saw tears glistening on her cheeks.

Then Cliff caught up with her, and he held her, and both mother and firstborn son were still and silent, and crying, in the autumn wind.

"HOLY COW," LIZA BARON said as she and Nora stood in the reception area of the very sedate, very plush Providence offices of Pierce & Rothchilde, Publishers. "Cliff wasn't kidding when he said his family were East Coast mucky-mucks."

Nora doubted those had been Cliff's exact words, but Liza did have a point. She couldn't imagine a better symbol of East Coast blue bloods than the beautiful brownstone headquarters of one of the most prestigious publishing houses in the country. Mrs. Redbacker, Byron's intrepid assistant, came out to greet them, reluctantly bringing them back to the offices of the president.

"Mr. Forrester is away this week," Mrs. Redbacker said.

Liza, in her serape and leggings and much more herself now that she was *doing* something, spoke up.

"I know. He went to Wisconsin for his brother's wedding. I'm his almost sister-in-law."

Mrs. Redbacker nodded, as if outrageous Liza Baron was about what she'd expected. Nora, in a more conservative outfit of wool pants and plaid blazer, took in the antique furnishings, the computer, the fax machine, the steely-eyed portraits of Clifton Rutherford Pierce, Cofounder, and Thorton Pierce, Past President, above the marble fireplace mantel. And for three years she'd thought Gates Department Store was as close as Byron had come to corporate America. She gritted her teeth. The man did have a way of setting her off.

"So Byron hasn't been around today?" Liza asked.

Mrs. Redbacker sniffed. "No, he hasn't. And I'm sorry, but I don't expect him."

Liza frowned, in no mood for anyone to tell her anything she didn't want to hear. They'd checked at the airport in Milwaukee and then again in Providence—she'd vetoed flying into the bigger airport in Boston, which was farther away—but there was no word, anywhere, from either Byron or Cliff. Not at the lodge, not at her mother's, not on Nora's phone, not at the store. This did not sit well with Liza. It was sitting less and less well with Nora.

Nora tore her gaze from the two Pierce portraits and smiled at Mrs. Redbacker as she would at a dissatisfied Gates customer. "That is a surprise," she said calmly, "because Mr. Forrester—Byron—asked us to meet him in his office."

She glanced at Liza, hoping her friend would realize what she wanted: she had to see Byron's office. She might never get another chance. And it could tell her so much about this man who'd wormed his way into her life, into her mind and heart. She wanted to know everything about him, regardless of what the future held.

"He did?" Mrs. Redbacker asked, not expecting an answer. "Well, I suppose it's entirely possible."

Her tone was unmistakable; she thought she'd make a better president of Pierce & Rothchilde, Publishers, than Clifton Pierce's great-grandson and Thorton Pierce's grandson did. Possibly she thought almost anyone would. There was no rancor in her voice, just the long-suffering of an assistant devoted to her company more than to a particular personality slated at birth to run it. Mrs. Redbacker seemed not to resent or dislike Byron Forrester as much as she simply believed he wasn't where he belonged. Nora had employees herself who were more loyal to Gates and its meaning to the community than to her personally. And Aunt Ellie's longtime personal secretary had retired just before her boss fell ill, at which point Nora had hired a full-fledged assistant in Albert Shaw. Not that it would have mattered; most people regarded her as another Aunt Ellie.

Clearly Byron was not another Clifton or Thorton Pierce.

Which Nora found curiously heartening.

She decided to intervene. "Byron and I are old friends."

Mrs. Redbacker narrowed her eyes. "Oh?"

"He did a series of photographs on my great-aunt three years ago," Nora said, trying to stick to the truth as much as possible. "He's an award-winning photographer, you know."

"I'm aware of that." Mrs. Redbacker's tone was a little too sharp for Nora's tastes. It wouldn't be easy to get past her. She narrowed her eyes. "What did you say your name was?"

"I didn't, but it's Nora. Nora Gates."

Liza warmed to the project. "We're here to pick up something for Byron from his office. It's a special gift for Cliff. His brother. You know—"

"Yes," Mrs. Redbacker said. "I know all about Cliff Forrester."

Liza snorted. "You don't believe us!"

Mrs. Redbacker sighed. "To be perfectly honest, I don't know what to believe. Mr. Forrester—Mr. Byron Forrester—did leave something in his office for Miss Gates. But I understood I was to send it to her." The very experienced assistant, clearly out of her element, turned to Nora. "If you're Nora Gates of Gates Department Store, Tyler, Wisconsin."

"I am."

"Well, then, come along. It's a photograph of an elderly woman—your great-aunt, I believe—and some girl. I'll show it to you and you can decide if you want to take it with you or have it sent to Wisconsin."

Liza was grinning. "Yeah, that'd be great."

Nora, however, found herself unable to speak, and silently followed Liza and Mrs. Redbacker into the elegant office of the president of Pierce & Rothchilde, Publishers.

"MY PERSONALITY WAS probably more suited to running this place than yours," Cliff said as he and Byron headed down the cream-colored corridor to the office occupied by a Pierce for most of the past century. "But it wasn't meant to be."

"It's not a bad job."

"It wasn't a job to Grandfather. It was a passion—the way Gates is for Nora."

Byron nodded. "That's to be respected, unless it interferes with a person living a full life. Anyway, my passions lie elsewhere."

"Photography," Cliff speculated.

"For a few years, yes. But I don't want to make a job of it. I like it as something I can do when the muse strikes, so to speak."

They'd come to his office.

In the outer room, Mrs. Redbacker was speaking to a slightly paunchy security guard. "I don't believe they're in any way dangerous, but they…well, they just won't *leave*. They insist Mr. Forrester is bound to show up sooner or later. One or the other Mr. Forrester, they say. They keep calling him but get no answer. If they did, I suspect they'd go harass him at his home. Why, I do believe they'll *sleep* here if he doesn't return. And it's after five now!"

"I'll talk to them," the guard said.

Cliff hung back, amused. "Sounds like you've got company. Do your thing, Brother."

Imagining boycotters and protesters of various descriptions—someone could be found to disapprove of virtually any book on any given publisher's list—Byron stepped forward, trying to look presidential. "What's up, Mrs. Redbacker?"

She was clearly flustered, an increasingly frequent state during his three-month tenure at Pierce & Rothchilde. "Oh, I'm so *glad* you're here." Which had to be a first. "Early this afternoon two women barged in here. One claimed to·be your brother's fiancée and the other seemed quite respectable and normal at first, and I...well, I fell for their act, I must admit. They're in your office now. They've been there for hours, and they won't leave. They...they're playing *darts,* Mr. Forrester."

"Darts?" Byron repeated.

Behind him, Cliff said, "Liza couldn't hit the side of a barn."

Byron grunted. "I'll bet Nora could take the eyes out of a bull at a hundred feet."

"Ol' Granddaddy Pierce is probably doing flips in his grave."

"Both ol' Granddaddy Pierces," Byron said.

"Think we should leave 'em to security?" his brother asked.

"It's a thought."

Then his office door swung open, and a dart came flying out, landing with a precise thwack on Mrs. Redbacker's bulletin board, just inches from Byron's head.

"I think," Cliff said, coming up beside him, "your lady's pissed off."

"Mine? *You're* the one who skipped out on your fiancée three days before your wedding."

Then another dart whizzed out of the inner sanctum of the president of Pierce & Rothchilde, Publishers. It thwacked against the wall near enough to Cliff for him to know he was the intended target, but the plaster wouldn't hold it and it fell onto the floor.

Mrs. Redbacker had ducked behind her desk. The security guard was looking to Byron for guidance. With some effort, he remembered he *was* the boss. He grabbed the dart off the bulletin board. Cliff got the idea and snatched up the one on the floor.

Apparently the two interlopers in Byron's office got the idea, too, and slammed the door shut.

"You two can go on home," Byron told his assistant and security guard.

He and Cliff waited until the two had retreated, Mrs. Redbacker with a frosty good-night, the guard without a word.

Then, darts in hand, the two brothers took their grandfathers' office in a frontal assault.

CLIFF ADMITTED HE should have left Liza a note. He said he should have called. He said he loved her with all his heart and soul.

She relinquished her cache of darts.

Byron allowed he should have called with an update, as promised, although he figured his bumpy flight to Nantucket and his absorption with his mother and brother a good excuse for not doing so. So as not to irritate Nora further, he didn't mention anything about loving her.

She did not, however, relinquish her cache of darts. And she seemed to have the much bigger cache.

"I ought," she told Byron, "to pin your stinking hide to your mahogany paneling."

"Me? What'd I do?"

With great exaggeration, she let her gaze fall on the framed photo of her and Aunt Ellie looking like two peas in a pod, a photo Mrs. Redbacker was *supposed* to have wrapped and sent via overnight express by now. Of course, she'd had to cope with a sit-in most of the afternoon.

"What's the problem?" Byron asked, really not sure.

"You've had this picture for *three years?*"

Clearly she wasn't pleased. "Yes."

"On your studio wall?"

"Not the whole time. I only had it framed and hung on my studio wall three months ago, when I came off my leave of absence from P & R."

"It's a picture of Aunt Ellie," she said stonily. "Part of your series on her."

"Yes—"

"I never saw it."

"No—"

"I'm in it."

Byron considered that obvious and decided he'd better not comment.

Nora was rigid, darts clenched in her fist. "What," she said angrily, "if you'd walked into *my* house and found a picture of you and Aunt Ellie on *my* wall and I said, yeah, I've had it hanging around for *three damned years* but it's just a picture of Aunt Ellie and I never even noticed you."

Thick-skulled Yankee though he might be, Byron finally got it. "Nora, you—"

"Obviously," she interrupted, really angry now, "I've never had the impact on you and your life that you've had on mine."

"Nora, if you're suggesting you don't mean as much to me as I mean to you, you—"

"I said impact, Byron. I said nothing about whether it was a positive or negative impact."

She was definitely not in a mood to have him say anything more about loving her, which he most definitely did.

"How could you have had that picture for *three years?*"

And, not a woman to hold back anything from him, as she'd pointed out, she started pitching darts at nothing in particular—not even aiming at him—and he and Cliff and Liza all ducked, Byron knowing he'd never get through to her while she was throwing-things mad.

At which point Anne Forrester walked into his office, looking fresh and happier than he'd seen her in years. She and her sons had agreed to meet at P & R and then go out to dinner as a family, for the first time since Cliff had left for Southeast Asia so many years ago.

"Mother," Byron said, "I'd have warned you, but—"

"You must be Liza," she said to Nora, smiling. "I heard you were a live wire."

Nora was clearly mortified. She set down the rest of her darts on Byron's desk.

"No, Mother," Cliff said, trying not to laugh, "*this* is Liza."

And Liza, who, unlike Nora, could never stay mad for long, rushed out of hiding to greet her fiancé's mother. Anne covered for her mistake with her usual good grace, giving Byron a look out of the corner of her eye. It was one of those I'm-your-mother looks. *Who is this woman and what have you done to make her so mad?*

This time, Byron knew the answer. He'd fallen in love with her, was what he'd done. Madly, passionately, forever.

And she'd fallen in love with him. Maybe just as madly, surely just as passionately, and possibly even forever.

By Nora Gates's account, definitely a crime punishable by darts.

CHAPTER TWELVE

ON FRIDAY MORNING, Gates Department Store went on a low-level alert as Anne Forrester paid a visit. By eleven o'clock Nora had word that not since Margaret Ingalls, had Gates sold so much "pricey stuff," as Albert put it, to one person in a single hour. By noon a debate was raging whether the wealthy East Coast blue blood had beaten the missing Chicago socialite's record, taking into account inflation. The mother of the town's recluse, Mrs. Mickelson reported, had even purchased a set of Wisconsin place mats.

When Nora returned from her midday sweep of the three floors of her department store, she found Byron Forrester with his size elevens propped up on her rosewood desk.

"I think I'll buy you a dartboard for your office," he said.

He was never going to let her forget perhaps the most embarrassing moment of her entire life. Cliff, Liza, Anne Forrester—they'd all seen her out of control. Since attacking Byron in his own office with his own darts, Nora had become more subdued, shell-shocked from her peek at his life in Providence. He'd put them all up at the Pierce town house on Wednesday night, calling in his housekeeper to make dinner, change beds, put out fresh towels. Quite sure of himself, Byron had shown Nora his studio, his darkroom, a part of his soul, and she'd realized, with a deep pang of emotion she didn't understand, that he and his family had stronger roots in the East than she did in Tyler. For three years she'd thought of him as an itinerant photographer, rootless, uncommitted, a wanderer and a rake. But that wasn't the real Byron Sanders Forrester.

On Thursday morning, they'd all flown back to Wisconsin. Liza, proving herself truly Judson Ingalls's granddaughter, grumbled about how much money all this flying around was costing. Like Nora, Cliff was quieter and more contemplative. Anne Forrester was radiant and gracious; Nora had liked her immediately. In Milwaukee, Cliff and Liza had headed for Tyler in his pickup, which he'd left in the airport lot. Nora had driven home alone. Byron had rented another car and driven back to Tyler with his mother, whom Nora, thinking it was a sensible idea, had invited to stay with her.

"I won't be distracted," Byron had told her as she'd left the airport.

"I'm just trying to be helpful."

"No, you're not. You're just trying to avoid being alone with me before the wedding. Doesn't matter. There's always after the wedding."

"What about your nonrefundable ticket home on Sunday?"

He'd smiled. "I can absorb the loss."

Good son that he was, he'd moved to the back bedroom, which Nora had set up for her younger guests, and let his mother have the front bedroom. No sleeping naked in the study, no predawn visits to Nora's room. Setting her alarm, Nora had gotten up early and made oatmeal and fresh apple muffins, which went over well with Anne Forrester. Byron had picked the raisins out of his oatmeal.

Now, in his charcoal-gray sweater, wool trousers and his herringbone jacket, he removed his feet from her desk. "This place hasn't changed since Aunt Ellie's day."

"There was no need," Nora said, remaining standing behind her desk.

"If it ain't broke, don't fix it?"

"Precisely."

He nodded, his eyes resting on her in a probing way, reminding her of his photographer's acuity, and their mad sessions of lovemaking. In another minute, she'd have no choice but to sit down. "Perhaps I should have had a little more of that attitude when I took over at Pierce & Rothchilde. I wanted to put my stamp on the place."

She shrugged. "That's a normal impulse, I think."

"Of course, the reverse can be true—you can be too afraid of change."

She'd thought he'd go on, but he didn't. She had nothing to add. The silence between them, however, was uncomfortable. *I have to remain strong. I have to remember who I am.*

"What'd you think of Providence?" he asked casually.

Too casually, Nora thought. He wanted to know. He wanted to talk, to listen, to understand. Finally, she had to sit. "I had no idea…it's obvious you and your family have deep roots there. When you went on the road three years ago…" She sighed, wishing she could articulate her still-jumbled feelings. "It must have been a difficult choice."

"To leave my dartboard and barracuda of an assistant?"

"Well, your executive style may be a bit unusual, but—"

"But I'm a Pierce," he finished for her.

She nodded. "Yes, and your family's been in Providence for generations. That means something."

"What?"

"That's not for me to say."

"Bingo. It's not. It's for me to say. I'm not just half Pierce. I'm also half Forrester."

"Pierce & Rothchilde is an important company."

"So's Gates."

"In Tyler, yes. But Pierce & Rothchilde has a wide impact. It's recognized internationally as a quality publishing company and—"

"So?"

"So it's *important*."

"What, you want to run it?"

She groaned. "No! Byron, I'm trying to be serious."

"Okay." He nodded at her and paused a few seconds before going on, "I care about P & R, but I don't need to run it. I can continue to sit on the board and I'll still own stock, but it doesn't matter to me if I remain president—and I daresay it doesn't matter to most of the people under me. Just because a Pierce almost always has sat in the president's office doesn't mean one always must. If Mother wants, she can take over. She says she's too old, but that's hogwash."

"Then you don't feel obligated to stay on?"

"I did at one time. I don't anymore."

Looking away, Nora said in a low voice, "You think I feel obligated to run Gates."

"No, I don't," Byron said gently. "My grandfather instilled a sense of obligation in me. He hadn't had a son himself, Mother married the wrong man and God forbid a Pierce woman should do something as distasteful as work. Cliff...well, you know what happened to him. So there was me. It wasn't the same for you, Nora. That's one of the things so precious and wonderful about Aunt Ellie—she didn't make you feel you *had* to take over Gates when she was gone. You're here by choice."

Nora looked around her, at the simple, tasteful furnishings Aunt Ellie had bought so long ago, at the framed pictures of Gates Department Store in its early days. She could hear the traffic down on the town square and smell autumn in the cool air coming through her window, which she'd cracked open despite the gray, blustery weather.

"And you love Tyler," Byron said.

She nodded.

"You don't see me sitting on the Providence city council."

"But..."

"But we've been there three hundred years. Sorry, love, but I just don't feel the burden of that. We moved around a lot when we were kids—why the hell do you think my mother married someone in the military?"

Then Albert buzzed, telling Nora that Anne Forrester had finished her shopping. "I've arranged to have her purchases delivered directly to your house."

Had she actually beaten Margaret Ingalls's record?

"Well!" Anne said, coming into Nora's office, looking slightly flushed and very content after her Wisconsin shopping spree. "What a delightful store you have here, Nora. I'm afraid I left Rhode Island in such a whirlwind, and then with having been in London, I had a number of things I needed. I'm so relieved I could find everything here. Byron, have you gotten your brother a wedding gift yet?"

Byron grinned at her. "My presence isn't enough?"

She pursed her lips, obviously accustomed to her younger son's sense of humor. "I bought them a dozen Waterford goblets—Liza did have them marked in her bridal registry. It's difficult after all these years to imagine Cliff sitting down to a set table, but I suppose..." She shrugged, smiling. "Liza Baron does have a way with him."

With that, both Byron and Nora could agree. Nora said, "I'm glad you liked Gates. If there's anything else we can do for you, don't hesitate to ask."

"Oh, you've done far too much already. And it's truly a wonderful store. We're off to Timberlake Lodge for lunch. Won't you join us, Nora?"

Nora didn't give herself a chance to think, but shook her head immediately. "I have a million errands to run—and I need to be back here at one for a meeting. But thank you. Have a good time."

Anne Forrester rushed along, but Byron lingered. He shut Nora's office door and walked back to her desk, leaning over it. "You can't avoid me," he said. "You can't distract me. And I won't leave Tyler until I know you don't want me in your life, because, Miss Eleanora Gates, I very much want to be in yours."

Then, with Albert buzzing her, he kissed her hard on the mouth, and it was just as well her lipstick had rubbed off hours ago or Anne Forrester and Albert and everybody at Gates would have known everything. Which, she thought, might have been just as well.

"ARE YOU GOING to tell me what's going on between you and Nora Gates?" Anne Forrester asked her younger son, following him onto the porch of Timberlake Lodge.

Byron shrugged. "It's tough to explain."

His mother gave him a small smile. "In other words, no, you're not going to tell me."

Inside, the lodge was warm and surprisingly cozy, with a fire going in the kitchen fireplace. Amid the renovations, Liza and Cliff had put together a lunch of curried corn chowder, fresh sourdough bread and carrot-raisin salad. Byron could smell apple pie baking in the oven. Alyssa Baron was there, and Liza's sister, Amanda, and her brother, Jeffrey. Judson Ingalls was noticeably absent. The lodge, Byron remembered, wasn't his favorite place. But it couldn't have been easy for Alyssa, who'd lost her mother at such a young age, to be there, either.

"I should have had a rehearsal dinner," Anne whispered to Byron.

"Cliff would have croaked."

"As my dear father would have said, this wedding is all so *irregular*." She smiled broadly. "But I don't give a damn. It's so obvious Cliff is happier than he's ever been." Then her smile faded, and she turned to Byron, her eyes narrowed. "Now if you'll get your life straightened out, I'll be a contented woman."

Byron grinned. "Once a mother, always a mother."

"Nora Gates—you'd better do right by her, Byron Sanders Forrester. While I was shopping I overheard talk about you two. Quite a considerable amount of talk."

"Don't tell Nora. She likes to think she's above being a subject of gossip."

Anne Forrester sniffed in her upper-crust way. "That only makes her a juicier target, I'm afraid. I gather her romantic life—or lack thereof—has been a topic of quite considerable speculation over the years. She's something of an independent sort, rather like her great-aunt, but at least several elderly ladies in the fabric department—have you seen the range of calicos Gates carries?—think that Nora is avoiding romantic entanglements whereas Aunt Ellie simply wasn't interested."

Mercifully, Liza spotted them and burst forward, taking her future mother-in-law by the hand and introducing her to her family, thus sparing Byron, a grown man, from having to listen to his mother discuss what people of Tyler were saying about him and the would-be old maid owner of Gates Department Store behind their backs. He certainly wasn't going to corroborate any of the gossip. First, it wasn't his place. Second, Nora would likely have his hide. Third, they'd find out soon enough. In due time, the people of Tyler—the whole world—would know how much he loved Nora Gates. He was willing to tell them right now. But he respected Nora's ambivalence, her fears, her resistance to change, her need to make that decision for herself. He respected her enough to let her decide when she wanted to admit to the world that she loved him. Because she did. Byron *knew* she did.

CLIFF WAS NOWHERE to be seen. After saying his hellos and being introduced all around, Byron found his older brother out on the veranda.

"I can't wait for this circus to be over," Cliff muttered.

Byron could sense his discomfort. "Going to get through it?"

"If it's what Liza wants. I've already gotten what I want—my life back."

If his brother seemed more at peace after his excursion to Rhode Island, it was also clear to Byron that he didn't enjoy being in the public eye, that the people-activity of his wedding—being something of a spectacle, the burned-out recluse marrying Judson Ingalls's granddaughter—continued to take its toll. He wasn't in danger of flipping out. He just didn't *like* what was happening.

"Sometimes," he said, "I feel like grabbing her and getting the hell out of here."

"Hey, you guys," Liza called from the door, "lunch is on."

Byron clapped a hand on his brother's shoulder. "Tomorrow morning it'll all be over."

Cliff nodded grimly. "My tux arrived this morning. Can you imagine?"

Byron couldn't. But it wasn't his place to tell his brother and future sister-in-law that they were going about their wedding all wrong, trying to please everyone but themselves. And when it came to romantic advice, Byron supposed he did lack a certain credibility.

At least, he thought somewhat more optimistically, for the time being. Who knew what tomorrow would bring?

FRIDAY NIGHT WAS QUIET, cool and rainy, and Nora spent it deliberately alone, before a fire in her study. She'd made herself a cup of hot cocoa and had dug out one of her favorite Agatha Christie mysteries, featuring the indomitable Miss Marple. Byron and Anne Forrester had taken Cliff and Liza and Liza's family to dinner. They'd invited Nora to join them. She'd declined with thanks, on the grounds that she had piano students. But she was not a Forrester. She was not a Baron. She was not an Ingalls. She was not a member of the wedding party. There was no reason Miss Manners would support her presence at the dinner, except as Byron's date.

Alone in her study, Nora tried to get in touch with the life she'd had since Aunt Ellie died, before Byron's second visit to Tyler. Peaceful evenings. Independence. Freedom. Time and space to think and reflect.

The cuckoo clock struck ten, and she counted each cuckoo as she blew on her steaming cocoa, feeling its warmth on her fingertips and mouth. It was almost erotic. A reminder, if a strange and unexpected one, of making love with Byron on her study floor.

"Independence doesn't mean solitude," Aunt Ellie had lectured more than once over the years. *"I'm an independent woman—but so was your mother, who was married and had a child. I might not be married, and I have no children, but I'm not alone. Even before you came to live with me, Nora, I never considered myself someone who 'lives alone.' I have too many friends and neighbors—I'm too involved with people—to feel isolated."*

Even after three years, Nora missed her great-aunt's wisdom and solid presence.

But it was her mother, now, who came to her mind.

She'd been a quiet, hardworking woman who'd died far, far too young. In her grief, Nora had wanted never to inflict the kind of loss she'd endured on anyone. Life with Aunt Ellie only reaffirmed her determination never to marry, never to have children, never to let anyone get close enough to be hurt.

Someone pounded on her front door, startling her from her introspective mood. She went into the entry.

It was Liza, smiling tentatively, nervously. "No emergency—the Forrester clan's splitting a bottle of champagne before the festivities tomorrow. I ducked out. Nora, I need a favor. Actually, it's more than a favor."

"Sure."

"Be my bridesmaid tomorrow."

Leave it to Liza Baron not to beat around the bush. Taken by surprise, Nora invited her back to the study, where she threw a log on the fire while Liza, with her usual restless energy, paced.

"Look," Liza said, "you're the best friend I have in Tyler right now. I wasn't going to bother with a bridesmaid—my sister didn't mind being spared—but you've been so incredible, I'm not sure Cliff or I would have made it through this week without you. I know I brought a lot of this stress and strain on myself by inviting the Forresters and opting for a big wedding, but I'm glad I did. I have no regrets. And I'm so grateful for all you've done. You've been there for me."

Nora wasn't so sure she'd been there for anyone this past week, including herself, but she didn't argue. "I'm very flattered, Liza, but I don't have a dress—"

"You own the best store in town, Nora."

"Yes, but—"

"But it's short notice and you don't do much on short notice." Liza stopped pacing a moment and smiled. "Remember what you said? Bridesmaids are about sisterhood. Nora, please. I want you to be by my side tomorrow morning."

Nora sighed, touched by Liza's offer of real friendship. Then she, too, smiled. "What color should I wear?"

Liza being Liza, she had an answer. "Got anything in burgundy?"

AT TEN O'CLOCK Saturday morning—just an hour before his wedding—Clifton Pierce Forrester was out at the lodge woodpile in a tattered plaid flannel shirt and patched jeans. Byron, in a navy summer suit himself, found him. "Mother says you vetoed the tux."

Cliff steadied a chunk of wood on the block, heaved his ax up high, then swung it down sharply splitting the wood neatly in two. "I tried it on. Looked like an ass. Tuxes aren't me, Brother."

Neither, Byron thought, were big weddings with hundreds of invited guests. "You own a suit?"

He picked up the two halves of cordwood, tossed them onto his growing pile. "Nope."

"Then what're you going to wear?"

"Clean clothes."

His brother, Byron could see, had withdrawn into himself to a perilous degree. "Cliff, what's going on?"

He set down his ax. Sweat poured down his temples and stuck his shirt to his back. Last night's showers had moved east, leaving southeastern Wisconsin under clear skies with warmer-than-average temperatures. Cliff and Liza couldn't have asked for a more perfect wedding day.

"I'm okay," Cliff said. "Guess I'd better get cleaned up, huh?"

"I guess so."

"Marrying Liza's what I want more than anything else in the world. If I have to do it in front of a crowd, then so be it."

In his mind, Byron had the bare inklings of an argument, but before it could take shape, Anne Forrester showed up at the woodpile. She was in her version of a mother-of-the-groom dress, meaning she'd opted for a plain blue wool dress instead of her usual tweed suit and had put on her best gold earrings. "There you two are. Cliff, I wanted to give you your wedding present. It's something...well, I'll let it speak for itself."

She handed him a small, flat, battered case that Byron doubted contained a dozen Waterford goblets.

Inside were about two dozen seashells, most of them broken, none of them worth a nickel.

"They're the ones you and Byron and Dad and I collected on vacations on Nantucket when you two were little boys," Ann said unnecessarily. "I wanted you to have something tangible of your childhood—something that would have meaning for you—to keep with you here in Wisconsin."

Cliff struggled visibly to retain his composure. "Thanks."

His mother laughed. "You're welcome."

And Byron's argument—his idea—took shape. He waited for his mother to go back inside. Then, walking slowly back to the lodge with Cliff, he and his brother talked, poured out their hearts, and plotted, coconspirators—really brothers—once more.

ALYSSA BARON GREETED Nora at the front door of her beautiful Victorian home on Elm Street, where Liza, bowing to tradition, had decided to get ready. Wearing a slim, silver-gray sheath with a matching beaded jacket, Alyssa looked radiant, calmer than she'd been in the weeks since the body was uncovered at her father's lodge.

"You look so wonderful!" she said warmly to Nora, who was dressed in a lovely burgundy silk dress she'd worn the night she was elected to the Tyler town council. "The orchids just arrived," she said, "and Amanda and Jeffrey and Dad are meeting us at the church." But she licked her lips, a hint of worry creeping into her eyes. "Liza's upstairs. I—I've never seen her so reflective. You know it's more like her just to plunge ahead. Nora... Nora, if this wedding isn't what she wants, if she's doing it for my sake, please tell her she's making a mistake. I only want what she wants. I mean that. I trust her."

"Isn't it a little late to be worrying if a big wedding's really what Liza and Cliff want?"

"No," Alyssa said, suddenly very sure of herself. "No, it's not too late."

"But people are already arriving at the church and the reception—" Nora broke off. "I'll talk to Liza."

Upstairs, Liza had put on her hand-sewn wedding dress, made from fifteen yards of silk organza and five-inch-wide lace that Gates had special-ordered for her from Paris. She was staring out the window overlooking her mother's backyard, fingering a simple clamshell she'd strung around her neck. "Cliff brought it from Nantucket with him. It's just a worthless shell— it isn't even pretty. But it's a part of who he is, where he's come from. God, I never thought I'd find anyone I love as much as I love him. I want… I want today to reflect who we are together and all that we can become. That sounds corny, I know, but it's true."

"Liza, it's ten o'clock," Nora said firmly. "You have to decide. It's up to you. Cliff is going to do what you want. If you want to go through with this big wedding, then let's get a move on. If not, then let's think of alternatives. Traditionally, weddings are much more the bride's responsibility."

"Mother—"

"Forget Alyssa. She wants what you want. She's told you, she's told me. Believe her."

Liza bit her bottom lip. Tears shone in her beautiful black-lashed eyes. "I want *her* to be happy, Nora. She seems so alone—and with all I've put her through over the years with my little rebellions, and now with this damned body stirring up painful memories…and Dad…" She exhaled sharply. "I just want to make up for some of what she's had to suffer."

"Then do it, Liza. Do it by having the wedding you want to have, because *that's* what your mother wants for you. That's what will help make her happy."

Turning back to the window, Liza said, "Last night I dreamed Cliff and I were married at the Lake—just him and me, you, our two families. It felt so right. It's where we met, where he's spent so many years healing. I'm not…we're not your traditional wedding types."

"Don't you think your mother and everyone else in town knows that?" Nora asked, realizing time was a-wasting and it was high time a decision was made.

"Cliff shouldn't have to be a spectacle, even if he gladly would for me. And it's such a beautiful day."

"Yes, it is."

"People are already arriving at the church."

"This isn't their wedding. It's yours."

Then Alyssa Baron was standing in the bedroom door, looking very maternal. "I've called Jeffrey. He said he can grab the preacher and meet us at the lodge. Amanda will get my father. They're waiting by the phone for me to give the word. What's it to be?"

Liza broke into a huge smile and ran to her mother, hugging her, even as Cliff Forrester, looking like a derelict, showed up in the doorway and announced that he wanted to get married at the lodge.

"Well, then," Liza said, laughing, "let's get a move on."

IT WAS ENTIRELY appropriate, somehow, that Liza Baron and Clifton Pierce Forrester were married in a short ceremony on the banks of Timber Lake, with a rotting dock in the foreground, a partially renovated lodge in the background. Liza wore her wedding gown, and Cliff, looking absolutely stunning, had put on the handsome tuxedo his bride had picked out for him.

It was one of the most beautiful and touching Wisconsin weddings Nora had ever attended. She stood beside Byron, slipped her hand into his, not caring if anyone saw, and cried. She always cried, if very discreetly, at weddings. This time she wasn't so discreet. She knew what she wanted, she knew who she was. If word got around Tyler that Nora Gates cried at weddings, well, that was fine with her.

Even Judson Ingalls admitted the lodge had been the right choice for his youngest grandchild. "But how're we going to explain this to all those folks waiting at the church?"

Byron stepped forward. "Nora and I will handle it."

They took her car, and Nora drove fast—ten miles over the speed limit, which, given her position in town as a business and community leader, she hated to do. But she wanted to get to the church not too much after the eleven o'clock ceremony was scheduled to begin. *And when this is settled, I'm going to tell Byron I want ours to be the next Tyler wedding.* She was suddenly very sure that was what she wanted. As sure as she'd been that warm August day when she'd been working on the back-to-school window at Gates and had spotted Byron for the first time and known he would change her life.

"Shame to let a good wedding go to waste," Byron said casually.

A chill went through Nora. Was he thinking what she was thinking? "Cliff and Liza will make an appearance at the reception. That will help. People will understand."

"I'm sure they will, but everyone loves a wedding. No question a lot of folks are going to be disappointed."

She gripped the steering wheel, taking a sharp curve. "Well, we can't cook up a replacement in the next five minutes."

Her heart was pounding. Because she knew they could.

Byron was silent. Then he said softly, "We could."

Nora nearly drove off the road. "Who?"

"Don't be dense, Nora. You know I'm talking about us."

"Us," she repeated.

He shrugged, confident, every inch of him a man she didn't want to live without. "Why not?"

"Because…" She pulled over to the side of the road, a few yards from Barney's pumpkin patch. She swallowed, but like Byron, she was suddenly confident, absolutely sure of herself and what she wanted. "No reason that I can think of."

"Do you love me?" he asked softly, his eyes penetrating all the way to her soul.

"Yes, Byron. Oh, yes, I love you. You've known that for a long time. You knew before I did."

He smiled, but she could see the relief—and the pleasure—in his dark eyes. "I knew before you'd *admit* you loved me. Nora… Eleanora Gates the Younger, I do love you. I always will. There's no going back." Then his smile broadened into a grin. "So let's get married."

"I've never done anything so impulsive in my life—"

"It's not impulsive. It's been three years in the coming. Look, we've got a church full of people—we won't even have to send out invitations. My mother's here, my brother, my sister-in-law. Couldn't be easier."

"You're serious?"

His smile vanished. "Yes."

"But Byron, where will we live? What will you do? What will *I* do?"

He sighed, hunching down in his seat, not looking the least bit worried about those particulars. "I'll remain on the Pierce & Rothchilde board. I called the appropriate parties this morning and resigned as president. I have a new idea for a series of photographs, but it'll take some time to accomplish—it won't, however, require a great deal of travel."

"No living in a tent?"

"I wouldn't ask a woman who needs her oatmeal and raisins every morning to spend the next umpteen years wandering from place to place and sleeping in a tent. Besides, that's not what I want."

"So you'll be a photographer—"

"As an avocation. I don't see it as my work. I'm also thinking about writing a book, teaming up with Henry Murrow."

"The literary novelist?"

"Yeah." Byron seemed very comfortable with the idea. "We're going to collaborate on a technothriller. He's tried one on his own, but it needs a ring of authenticity I can help provide, being my father's son and an ex-Air Force officer myself."

Nora didn't move. "A what?"

He laughed. "You sound so shocked. Yes, it's how I spent a part of my youth. I didn't make a career of it. I went to Harvard after I got out, then to Pierce & Rothchilde. Then I came to Tyler, Wisconsin, and met you and Aunt Ellie, and everything changed. I became a photographer and worked through what I needed to with regard to my past."

Nora felt a warm breeze against her cheek. "You're sure this is what you want?"

"Yes."

"We haven't…there's so much we don't know about each other, about our pasts."

"Well, we have to have stories to tell each other on cold Wisconsin nights. We know the important things, Nora. We know we love each other and that that's not going to change."

But she was staring at him, making sure. "Then you don't need to live in Rhode Island?"

"I haven't made that clear by now? No, I do not need to live in Rhode Island. It'll always be home. I'm sure I'll whisk you off periodically to Nantucket and visits to Benefit Street, but I'm already feeling as if Tyler's my home. I've followed in a lot of people's footsteps. When I came here three years ago, Aunt Ellie helped me realize I needed to find my own path so I could make my own footsteps. I've done that. Now I want to do it with you, Nora— I want us to find a place where our paths come together and become wide enough for us both to walk."

"We have," she said, as confident as he.

In five minutes, they were at the church in downtown Tyler. Byron jumped out while Nora went to park the car. When she came to the front door, Liza Baron Forrester was already there, handing her a bouquet of orchids.

"What're you doing here?" Nora asked.

"Are you kidding? I wouldn't miss this for anything."

Nora frowned. "I smell a plot."

"No one's ever said you were a dummy."

"Byron?"

"He's been thinking about international espionage—you should have heard him and Cliff plotting murder and mayhem last night over dinner, not to mention the millions they could make writing technothrillers. Though getting Tyler's own self-declared spinster up the aisle must've taxed him more than figuring out how to blow up the world."

"Liza…"

"Come on," she said, grinning, "we've got a packed house anxious for a wedding."

"Do they know what's going on?"

"Oh, they'll figure it out. People have been wondering for years when and if you'll ever get married. I think there are several pools going in town."

Two weeks ago, Nora would have been mortified. Now she laughed. "But, Liza, this was supposed to be your day—"

"It still is. But I want it to be your day, too." She tucked the second bouquet of orchids in front of her. "This time I'd rather not be the center of attention. You've always been there for everyone in Tyler, Nora. It's your turn to let us give you a party. Now, how 'bout I serve as your matron of honor?" She made a face. "What a yucky term. Any defense?"

"None. Let's abolish it. Just be my friend."

"Let's be sisters," Liza said, hugging her, and she whispered, "You're not alone anymore, Nora Gates."

And as she started up the aisle, Nora knew that she wasn't alone; indeed, had never been alone. Tyler was her family. Up ahead, Anne Forrester, looking as if she'd expected as much from her two sons, was in the front pew, waiting. Cliff Forrester moved next to his brother at the altar. The organ began to play, the crowd rose, and nobody seemed to bat an eye when it proved to be Nora Gates instead of Liza Baron who was the bride.

When she got close enough to Byron that he could hear her, Nora muttered, "You've been plotting this for *hours*."

"Nope." And he produced an antique ring from his pocket. "Belonged to my Great-grandmother Sanders.

I've been plotting this for days. I didn't know it'd be this morning, but I knew it would happen."

"What about a marriage certificate?"

"Already talked to the minister. He says we can get one Monday morning."

Nora was grinning. "I love you, Byron."

"Yeah. I love you, too. But I think what everyone's waiting to hear are a few I do's."

And they did, in a Wisconsin wedding that would surely go down in Tyler history.

EPILOGUE

ON A SNOWY morning a few weeks after the Forrester brothers had given Tyler a fresh jolt of gossip with their surprise marriages to two prominent town citizens, Nora was working on one of her famous Christmas window displays when she spotted Byron in the street. Her heartbeat quickened. Snowflakes were gathering on his dark hair. He waved at her and flicked a snowflake in her direction, always ready to tease.

She loved him totally. He'd continued to prove himself a man of excitement, surprise and change. He'd already talked to Joe Santori—Tyler's most eligible bachelor—about turning part of the garage into a studio for himself. The little twenties house was fast becoming not Aunt Ellie's, not Nora's, but a comfortable blend of the tastes and spirits of the woman who'd built it, the lonely girl who'd found herself there, the man who'd found love there. Together, Nora and Byron were becoming renowned as hosts. She was getting to know his friends from the East and all over; he was getting to know her friends from Tyler and the world of Wisconsin retail. That weekend, Henry Morrow—Hank, as he now preferred to be called—was coming to discuss technothrillers.

Byron pointed to the entrance to Gates Department

Store, indicating that he was coming inside. Nora finished what she was working on and joined him.

He was already on a stepladder, hanging the photograph of Aunt Ellie and Nora above the glass-fronted perfume counter where he'd taken it. Looking at the image of herself from three years ago, Nora realized Aunt Ellie had been right to encourage Byron to leave Tyler then. He'd needed the time, but so had she. Those three years had made today—and their future together—possible.

Byron climbed down and stood next to his wife. "Johnny Kelsey stopped by the store earlier," she told him. "Word's going out—they've identified the body found at the lodge as an adult female. Her size isn't inconsistent with Margaret Ingalls's."

"Does Liza know?" Byron asked seriously.

"I'm going out to the lodge now. I'll tell her myself."

He nodded. "I'll go with you. Thank God she has Cliff! With all he's faced, he can help her get through whatever she has to in the next weeks or months."

Nora looked up at the smiling face of her plain, beautiful great-aunt. "Aunt Ellie admired Margaret for being her own woman, even at the risk of having people disapprove of her."

"I wonder what she'd have said about this latest news."

"First things first," Nora said, quoting the woman who'd helped raise her, who'd guided her into adulthood and had helped her find her true self, even if she hadn't lived to see it all happen. She slipped her arm around her husband's solid waist, overwhelmed, as she still so often was, by how much she loved him, how tremendously lucky she was. "And she'd insist that Tyler's strong enough to face the truth."

"Your Aunt Ellie was a wise woman."

"She was," Nora said, "herself."

* * * * *

Books by Caro Carson

Harlequin Special Edition

Montana Mavericks:
What Happened at the Wedding?

THE MAVERICK'S HOLIDAY MASQUERADE

Texas Rescue

A COWBOY'S WISH UPON A STAR
HER TEXAS RESCUE DOCTOR
FOLLOWING DOCTOR'S ORDERS
A TEXAS RESCUE CHRISTMAS
NOT JUST A COWBOY

The Doctors MacDowell

THE BACHELOR DOCTOR'S BRIDE
THE DOCTOR'S FORMER FIANCÉE
DOCTOR, SOLDIER, DADDY

Visit the Author Profile page
at Harlequin.com for more titles.

DOCTOR, SOLDIER, DADDY

Caro Carson

With love for Richard,
who knew I would write this book long before I did.

Acknowledgments

I am indebted to my critique partners
for keeping me on track despite distractions and
obstacles. Thank you to my partners and friends,
T. Elliott Brown, Catherine Kean
and Nancy Robards Thompson.

CHAPTER ONE

River Mack Ranch, Texas

"You're letting a baby choose your wife?"

Jamie MacDowell chose not to answer that question. Instead, he contemplated the campfire as he let his brother's outraged tone roll off his back. Braden, his oldest brother, cared. That was the real emotion behind the outrage. Jamie had gotten much better at recognizing emotions in the past two years.

"Hire a nanny for the baby. You don't have to marry anyone." His other brother, Quinn, sounded less outraged—but more condescending.

The sounds of the Texas twilight settling over their parents' land filled the silence as Jamie stretched his legs out. He flicked a glance around the fire. It figured: he'd taken the identical pose as his brothers. Braden, Quinn and now Jamie sat with jean-clad legs stretched out fully, each man with his right cowboy boot crossed over his left. It was funny, really, the subconscious mannerisms families shared.

Two years ago, Jamie would have probably uncrossed his ankles, just to be different. But that was before Afghanistan. Before more than a year spent sewing up soldiers in an army hospital.

Before he'd brought his son, Sam, to the United States.

"A nanny can do the job perfectly well," Quinn continued. "You don't need a wife to take care of a baby."

"To take care of my son," Jamie corrected him. It was going to take his brothers some time to get used to the news that he was a father. He hadn't communicated much while he was deployed. Returning to Texas with a nine-month-old had shocked them all. "Not 'a baby.' My son."

"Right. He can be well cared for by a good nanny."

Jamie uncrossed his ankles. Neither of his brothers were parents. They didn't understand the impact, the complete sea change, of having a child. When he held Sam, Jamie knew that he was holding the most important thing in the world. It was a powerful emotion, one that ultimately made his life utterly simple. What his son needed, Jamie would provide.

His son needed a mother.

Not a nanny.

"I'm working in the E.R.," Jamie said. "You know the hours. What nanny is going to be available nights, days, whole twenty-four-hour periods without notice?"

"Get a live-in nanny." Naturally, Quinn had an immediate answer. He was a cardiologist. That particular species of doctor tended to be very math-oriented. Their world was physics. Pressure, diameter, beats per minute. Black and white.

In contrast, as an emergency physician, Jamie often had to wing it. Thinking on the fly, he came up with theories, tested and discarded them, until he'd diagnosed and stabilized whatever emergency had brought the patient to the hospital.

In Afghanistan, there'd been only one kind of emergency: injury. Some injuries were catastrophic, caused by explosives that destroyed so much of the body, Jamie raced the clock to stop the bleeding and keep the heart beating. Some were minor, a finger sliced open when a rifle was cleaned carelessly. All of them—*all of them*—required stitches. Sewing. Surgery. Jamie had performed more surgery as an emergency physician in the United States Army than many surgeons did in civilian life.

"What if I get deployed again?" Jamie asked both brothers. "Will the nanny guarantee her services for the length of my deployment? Will she write to me about Sam? Send me photos?"

Braden abruptly sat up from his lounging position. "I thought you were back to reserve duty, the one-weekend-a-month thing until your commitment was up. Did you sign a new contract?"

Jamie wanted to smile at the predictability of Braden's response. Like Quinn and himself, Braden was also an M.D., but he ran the research side of a massive corporation. He thought in terms of contracts and legalities, of facts on paper. Like Quinn, Braden saw everything as black and white.

The way their father had seen the world.

Jamie stopped lounging, too. With a firm thunk, he set his half-finished bottle of beer on the dry Texas ground by his chair. He wasn't like his father. Sam would have a better man to raise him.

"I'm in the reserves for another six months. I could be recalled to active duty tonight."

Now Quinn sat up abruptly. Jamie felt their tension as both men looked at him intently.

"It's okay," Jamie said quietly. "It's highly unlikely the army will send me back in the next six months."

Braden dropped his gaze to the crackling fire. "It's not that we aren't proud of you."

"I know. I'm proud to have served, too. There are times I've considered volunteering to go back. There's so much work left to be done there." Work that he'd seen one brave woman undertake. Work to promote literacy in the population. Work to provide health care to the poorest of the poor. Work to end the slavelike conditions in which so many Afghani girls were raised.

Work that had ultimately killed that one brave woman, leaving Jamie to raise Sam alone.

"A nanny's not good enough. I want a wife. If something should happen to me, Sam will still have a legal guardian. An American legal guardian."

"He's your son, Jamie. Do you think we'd let the state put him in an orphanage?"

"No." Jamie was touched. Braden had said *your son.* He, at least, was getting used to the idea of Sam being a MacDowell, not just a baby brought home from a war-torn country. "But Mom's getting a little old to start over again with an infant, and look at you. Both of you. A couple of bachelor doctors with insane working hours. Sam needs a full-time parent."

"Then hire a lawyer and make the nanny his legal guardian." Quinn was still seeing in black and white, apparently, but Jamie had already come up with that theory and ruled it out.

"It's easier to get married. A wife's custody is rarely questioned."

There had been no way to legally marry Sam's mother, not on the American base, nor in any Afghani court or mosque. In the end, after her death, that had meant no locals would claim Sam as their own, either. Jamie had been able to get Sam out of the country by mixing State Department regulations and medical necessity, but if the paperwork ever got scrutinized...

If. He wouldn't worry about that now. And if *If* happened, Sam belonging to an American husband and wife would be beneficial, compared to Sam being the child of a bachelor soldier.

Yes, Sam needed a mother. An American mother. Simple.

"I'm fine with a marriage based on practicality," he told his brothers. "I never planned on getting married for any other reason."

"You're sure about that?" Quinn asked.

Jamie sat back in his camp chair and picked up his beer. He brushed the sandy dirt off the bottom of the bottle. When he'd been in Afghanistan, he'd told himself the dry soil wasn't so different from Texas. He'd even been able to squint at the landscape and imagine himself home, if home had a lot of barbed wire and sandbag bomb shelters.

"I'm sure," Jamie said. "Doctors make lousy husbands—look at Dad. He had no time for Mom. No time for any of us. Without Mom, we wouldn't have had a parent at all. My kid needs a mother."

Braden studied the label on his own beer bottle for a moment. "You're not being fair to Dad. We had those fishing trips."

"Yeah, once a year we'd saddle up the horses and pack up the tents and come out here to spend, what? Four days? With a guy we barely knew."

"Still, he tried."

"Yeah, he would have made a fine uncle. Not my idea of a father. My son is going to have a real parent, someone there for him every day, not just for a camping trip now and then. If something happens to me, he's going to have another parent to finish raising him. I'll be damned if I'll leave him alone in this world. I'm getting married, and that's it."

"Slow down, Jamie. What happens if you find this perfect mother, but then you fall in love with another woman, someone you want for something besides mothering? Are you going to divorce the mother of your child to marry the woman you're crazy about? An affair won't cut it. I don't care what this 'perfect mother' agrees to, she's not going to be a Mrs. Mac-Dowell and willingly turn a blind eye to her husband having an affair."

"I'm not going to cheat on my wife, even if we aren't in that kind of a marriage."

"You need to think this through. I've been in love, Jamie." Braden rarely talked about it, but he'd been engaged once. "It can hit you like a lightning strike."

Jamie stood up and pulled the keys to his truck out of his pocket. "It already did, Braden, it already did."

"But, then—"

"She died. Her name was Amina. She was brilliant. Beautiful. An Afghani woman who translated for me on medical missions. She died during the birth and she left me a son."

Jamie dumped the rest of his beer onto a struggling scrub plant, then chucked the bottle into the bed of his pickup truck. "Lightning won't strike twice."

The shocked silence wasn't what Jamie had intended to cause. He clapped Quinn on the shoulder and used the side of his boot to push his still-full beer cooler toward his brother's camp chair. "You finish these for me this weekend. Mom's been watching Sam long enough. I'm gonna run."

Jamie had been away from his son for nearly two hours, and that was too long.

Braden followed him to the pickup. "Jamie. You never told us about the mother of the baby. Sam is really your child, then? Your biological child?"

Damn it. Even his own brothers hadn't believed Sam was his son. How would he convince the State Department? He needed to be married and have Sam legally adopted by his wife, in case they started asking.

"I'm not in the mood for a big-brother lecture, Braden." He loved his oldest brother. Braden had filled more of a father role for him than their father had, but when it came to his own life, Jamie knew what he was doing. He'd come to the ranch today to let his brothers know what his plans were as a courtesy, not so they could tell him he was wrong to want to secure a second parent for Sam as quickly as possible.

"I'm not lecturing," Braden said in a voice made for lecturing. "When do we meet this not-really-a-wife of yours?"

"I don't know who she is yet." Jamie opened the truck door and stepped up on the running board. "No woman I already know fits the bill."

"No woman will. I can't imagine who is going to want your son and not want you."

Ah, the blind loyalty of family. Braden was certain women would fall all over his little brother. He didn't know that most women gave up pursuing Jamie nowadays. His mourning for Amina showed somehow, he was sure.

His son was the only thing that brought a smile to his face now. As he thought of Sam, Jamie felt himself start to grin. "This isn't about me finding a wife. This is about Sam finding a mother. That's why I'm letting him choose her."

Jamie closed the truck door. As he drove away from the old homestead, a new feeling settled over him. A certainty that he was on the right course. Contentment, almost. He'd loved Amina, and now he loved their son. Building his life around his son's needs was the right thing to do.

He wondered whom Sam would fall in love with. He wondered whom his son would choose for him to marry.

CHAPTER TWO

KENDRY HARRISON WAS a general dogsbody. It wasn't the loveliest term, but it accurately summed up her career at West Central Hospital. She'd like to think that she was at least a gopher, but that would imply she worked for someone important who needed her to run errands. No such luck. She was just a general dogsbody, plugged into whatever entry-level job needed doing. Today, she was working in the pediatric ward.

Kendry loved the pediatric ward, even if it broke her heart half the time. Kids were kids, though, and even when they sported IV tubing and wore hospital gowns, they tended to be adorable. Kendry loved their earnestness when they described their little lives. She loved their willingness to play as hard as they possibly could, even when they found themselves forced to use their wrong hand or unable to climb out of a wheelchair.

Unlike the adult patients, the kids were still eager to grab life with both hands—unless they were in pain. Although an infant named Myrna was due to be discharged today, Kendry wondered if the little girl was in pain. Hour after hour, Myrna had been growing quieter and quieter. Kendry's shift was over in only minutes, but she couldn't leave Myrna without trying, one more time, to get the nurse to pay attention to the change in the baby's behavior.

She pushed the button to call the nurses' station. Again.

"What is it this time, Kendry?" The voice over the speaker was clearly irritated.

"I'd like a nurse to check on Myrna Quinones for me, please." If she kept her voice cool and factual, the way the doctors and nurses spoke, then she would be taken more seriously. Unfortunately, her nose was stuffy, and she barely grabbed a tissue in time for a sneeze.

"We've checked on her every hour. She's fine. She'll be going home when her mother gets off work today." And then, with the most sarcastic version of sugary sweetness the nurse could muster, her tinny voice came over the speaker. "And you're officially off work now, so go on home, darlin'. Take something for that cold, or you'll get all the children sick."

"I'm fine, thank you," Kendry said through clenched teeth. "It's just allergies."

She was the only adult in the pediatric ward's playroom, making it impossible for her to leave, but she resisted the urge to point that out to the nurse. Instead, she released the intercom's talk button and went to the sink to wash her hands for the fiftieth time of the day.

Every young patient who was able spent a good part of his or her waking hours in the ward's colorful playroom. There were hard plastic chairs and tables that could be sprayed down with bleach, plenty of floor space for children to play while they tugged along their wheeled poles with their hanging IV bags. A few of the children were not patients, but were the children of staff members. As long as the child wasn't contagious, staff members could pay a small fee to have their child spend the day in the playroom when their regular child-care fell through—a benefit that made West Central Texas Hospital one of Austin's top-rated employers.

For doctors, the policy was even more lenient. If it meant doctors would show up for every shift, the hospital was happy to provide childcare. These kids Kendry got to know well. One of them, a little charmer named Sammy, was demanding her attention now, as he often did.

Kendry scooped him off the floor and settled him on her hip. "That's right, Sammy. It doesn't matter if I'm off the clock, I'm not going home and leaving Myrna here in this condition, now am I?"

Sammy didn't get a chance to coo or babble an answer to her, because the person scheduled to replace Kendry had arrived and was listening in.

"Which one's Myrna?" she asked.

Kendry thought her replacement was kidding. For a second. One look at the woman's face—Paula, she remembered—revealed that she wasn't.

"Myrna is the little girl whose hand I'm holding. She was technically discharged because we were short beds, but her mother has to work, so admin said she could stay here." The little girl's belongings were packed in a plastic bag and her IV lines had been removed upon discharge, but her crib had been wheeled into the play-room until her mother could come to pick her up. Her room had already been filled by another patient.

"What time is her mother supposed to arrive?"

"Not for another hour. I don't want to leave Myrna like this."

Paula frowned at the baby in the stainless-steel hospital crib. "Like what? Calm and peaceful? Lord help me, I hope they all get like that and stay like that."

Kendry couldn't force herself to chuckle along with Paula's joke, although she knew that was what was expected of her. "Myrna's been here all week. Don't you realize this isn't her normal disposition?"

Paula shot Kendry a look. "Well, excuse me, Miss Know-It-All. There's a lot of kids in here, and they change every day."

Dang it. Now Kendry had taken the attention off the little girl and unwittingly put it on herself. Paula, unlike Kendry, was a certified medical assistant, a CMA. There was always a CMA on duty overnight. Paula was higher up on the hospital ladder, and Kendry had offended her.

"You're so right. The ward has been at full occupancy all week." Kendry could swallow her pride with the best of them when it came to helping a child. Heck, when it came to nearly every aspect of her life. "Myrna Quinones is acting like she's fighting an infection, maybe. Something is making her listless."

Paula pressed the call button for the nurses' station, announcing herself as she did so. "Hey, it's Paula here. Have you gotten a temperature on this Quinones child?"

The tinny response sounded exasperated. "Of course we have. Her vitals have been normal every single time we've checked them. Tell that orderly to go home. There's no budget for overtime around here. She should have clocked out five minutes ago."

Paula wasn't here five minutes ago, so I couldn't have clocked out.

Kendry spoke to Sammy, who sat on her hip as he

chewed his fingers. "Let's go for a walk, little guy. We'll clock me out, then come back to say bye-bye to Myrna."

The lively little boy on her hip cheerfully called, "Da-da!"

Sammy's dad was here. Kendry knew what *Da-da*'s voice would sound like. She braced herself for that educated, masculine timbre, that voice with just a hint of native Texas drawl.

"Hey, little buddy. How was your day?"

It didn't matter how many times she heard it, it still made her melt a little. Sammy kicked Kendry vigorously in happy response as she turned around to find Sammy's father, all six-feet-something of him, standing close enough to take his son out of her arms.

"Hi, Dr. MacDowell. Sammy's doing well today. He drank every ounce of formula. He seems to have an easier time taking his bottle when I have him sitting almost straight up. It makes me wonder if—"

"Good evening, Dr. MacDowell." Paula's voice had a different tone to it now. All peaches and cream.

Kendry stifled her frustration. She wanted to discuss Sam's ability to eat, but Paula wanted to...to...

Flirt. There wasn't a woman in the hospital who didn't know Dr. MacDowell was single. Never had been married, apparently. He'd returned from military service in Afghanistan with Sammy, so the rumor mill said, and had turned in his camouflage for a civilian career in order to spend more time with his son. Because no mother was in the picture, some people speculated that the baby was an orphan whom Dr. MacDowell had adopted. This only made women sigh with even more approval.

Sammy grabbed the tubing of Dr. MacDowell's stethoscope and tried to get it—and his fist—in his mouth. The doctor calmly pried the baby's fingers open, removed the stethoscope from around his neck and tucked it into the pocket of his white lab coat, all in one smooth move. Then he dropped a kiss on top of Sammy's head.

He was Sammy's father, all right. Who cared if the baby's hair was a darker black than his father's deep brown? Who cared if the child seemed petite compared to his strapping American father? This baby was loved. Kendry wished all the children that came through West Central were so lucky.

"You can go home now, Kendry," Paula said.

"What were you saying about Sam's bottles?" Dr. MacDowell asked.

"I'm wondering if—"

"I've got his daily sheet right here, with all his feedings listed," Paula interrupted. "Kendry, you need to go clock out. There's no overtime in the budget, and you don't want to tick off the supervisor."

Kendry wished her Irish heritage didn't make it so easy for her pale skin to blush. She hated being put in her place, but even more, she hated being so firmly reminded she was an hourly-wage orderly in front of Dr. MacDowell.

"I'll walk with you, Miss Harrison," Dr. MacDowell said. "I want to hear what you have to say."

Miss Harrison. He addressed everyone in the hospital by their proper names and titles. Still, she couldn't help but appreciate the respect he showed her. He wanted to hear what she had to say. He always did. He was the kind of doctor who would patiently listen to family members who anxiously brought someone to the E.R. He would listen...

Her gaze returned to Myrna, who was lying as she'd been for the past hour. She hadn't responded to Paula or Dr. MacDowell's appearance by her crib.

Dr. MacDowell would listen.

"Could you look at this patient for me? Her name is Myrna Quinones, she's nine months old, and she's due to be discharged today. She had surgery three days ago, and I'm wondering if she might have an infection or something. She's grown increasingly listless today, and I haven't been able to interest her in taking more than a couple of ounces from her bottle, but she's been off IV fluids since this morning. Maybe she's dehydrated?"

"Kendry, please." Paula sounded shocked. "You don't bother physicians with cases that aren't theirs. Dr. MacDowell, I assure you, the nurses on the floor have been checking on Myrna every hour. I've requested an update myself, and she isn't running a fever or showing any signs of infection."

"Thank you, Mrs. Cook."

Kendry bit her lower lip. Dr. MacDowell had said *thank you* in that dismissive tone doctors seemed to master, the one that said *when I want your opinion, I'll ask for it.* Kendry saw Paula call for the floor nurse with a press of a button. Once the nurses realized a doctor was checking the patient, they'd show up. Doctors were at the opposite end of the food chain from orderlies.

"Could you hold Sammy for me, please?" Dr. Mac-Dowell asked.

Kendry held out her arms for the little boy, who dove right into them. Dr. MacDowell took his stethoscope out of his pocket and slung it around his neck. As he walked the few steps to the hand sanitizer station, he asked Kendry questions briskly, impersonally.

Normal fluid intake? Number of wet diapers today? Normal activity level?

Then he was bending over the crib, opening Myrna's hospital gown, listening to her chest, running strong hands over the baby's limbs, feeling for pulse points. *Thank you,* Kendry wanted to say. *Thank you, thank you, thank you.*

The baby seemed fine, if unnaturally calm. The doctor didn't seem to be finding anything out of the ordinary. Kendry started to feel absurd.

"Is it possible to have an infection without running a fever?" she asked.

"No," Paula answered.

"Yes," Dr. MacDowell said. "Which procedure did this child have?"

Kendry waited a beat for Paula to answer, but Paula obviously didn't know and gestured toward Kendry with one hand.

"It was a kidney repair of some kind. I believe they opened a blocked tube, but whether it was going into the kidney or leading out, I'm not sure."

Dr. MacDowell opened the baby's diaper and palpated her pelvis and bladder. "Did you recently change her diaper?"

"It's been hours. I keep checking, but it's dry."

"Her bladder's distended. Mrs. Cook, I want this patient transported to the E.R. Get Dr. Gregory on the phone for me."

"Yes, Doctor."

Dr. MacDowell gently flipped the baby over and removed her incision bandages. Some unhealthy pus oozed from the tiny incision site. Kendry had never been so sorry to be proved so right.

Dr. MacDowell did not look happy. At all.

"I'm sorry," Kendry said. "I'm an orderly. I'm not allowed to remove a patient's bandage."

"No, but the nurses are," he said, and she didn't think she was imagining the quiet anger in his voice. "They should have, given your report."

For the first time in her memory, Kendry was suddenly glad she wasn't a nurse. No doubt Paula felt the same as she handed the phone to Dr. MacDowell. "Dr. Gregory on the line for you."

Kendry busied herself by packing up Sam's diaper bag with one hand as she held him on her hip with the other. Then she quieted another fussy baby, feeling soothed herself as she listened to Dr. MacDowell updating Dr. Gregory on the patient he was sending his way. One of her fellow orderlies arrived to wheel Myrna downstairs to the E.R.

Paula hissed in Kendry's ear as the crib was being rolled away. "Get off the clock before you get in trouble for going over."

"Here, hold Sammy then."

But Sammy wouldn't go to Paula. He clung to Kendry's neck as fiercely as any nine-month-old could, which was pretty darned hard.

Paula tried, anyway, pitching her voice to a falsetto coo. "Come on, Sam, let Miss Paula hold you." She started prying Sammy's small fingers off Kendry's neck, which only served to make the child more desperate to cling to the adult of his choice.

Dr. MacDowell hung up the house phone and came over to intercede. "Hey, buddy, come see Daddy."

Sam was in full-pitch tantrum mode now. He

wanted to cling to Kendry's neck, and by God, that's what he was gonna do.

"He usually comes to me," Dr. MacDowell said, frowning.

Kendry patted the baby's back and fought her urge to back away from Paula and Dr. MacDowell. She interjected a deliberate note of cheerfulness into her voice. "That's okay—it's okay. Shh, Sammy." She gave Paula's arm a pat to get her to stop clawing at the child's fingers, then started bouncing Sammy gently. "Just let him catch his breath. He'll be fine. He needs a second to decide what to do next."

Paula dropped her hand.

Dr. MacDowell spread his large hand over his son's back and stayed that way. "Okay, buddy," he said to Sammy. "Okay."

"I think he picked up on the tension. He knew I was worried about Myrna. Thank you again for taking a look at her."

"That was a good catch on your part. You were going to tell me something about Sam's bottles?"

From the corner of her eye, Kendry saw Paula turn away and start the closing routine for the playroom, although it would be a couple of hours before she'd bring the last children back to their regular beds for the night.

"It takes Sam a lot longer to finish a bottle than the other kids."

"It does?" His hand stilled on Sammy's back.

Kendry nodded. "I don't think he's just a slow eater. I think he has a hard time swallowing. I tried feeding him almost sitting up today, and he got that bottle down so much faster. You might want to try it yourself and see if that works for you."

"I will. Thanks." The man was really frowning now. Kendry could tell he was mentally recalling feeding sessions with his son, reviewing them for anomalies.

Such a doctor.

"I had no idea he was slower than the other kids," he said, sounding less like a doctor, more like an apologetic, perhaps a little bit defensive, father.

"I guess if you'd never fed another baby, you wouldn't." Kendry smiled at him, not wanting him to feel badly about himself. Sammy helped her out by choosing that moment to decide to turn his face toward his father. The steady, adult conversation had given Sam the chance to calm down enough to realize that he did, indeed, want Daddy.

"Da-da," he said, and twisted his whole little body away from Kendry to grab his father's lapel.

Dr. MacDowell easily took the child's weight from Kendry. "Hey, son. Let's go home. Can you say 'bye-bye' to Miss Harrison?"

But as Dr. MacDowell shifted a step back from Kendry, Sammy reached his hand out for her. "Me," he said. His little fist opened and closed, stretched out toward her. "Me."

"Bye-bye, Sammy. I'll see you again real soon." Kendry wished she could drop a kiss on his soft hair, but she wasn't supposed to kiss the children. It was against hospital policy, for health-related reasons. Besides, she'd end up with her face way too close to the doctor's face. She imagined the sensation of brushing cheeks with him—

That was best saved for another time.

No, that was best saved for never. It would never be a good time to imagine the feel of Dr. MacDowell's skin.

It would be warm.

Stop it.

Kendry settled for a smile, then bent to pick up her bag. When she straightened, Dr. MacDowell hadn't left, but looked like he was waiting on her. For a second, for one insane second, Kendry thought that the handsome man with that adorable child was waiting to spend more time with her.

"Can I walk you to your car?" he asked.

Kendry wanted to melt on the spot. He was such a gentleman. Too bad she didn't have a car for him to walk her to.

No, she was Kendry Ann Harrison, minimum-wage-earning hourly employee, the girl who rode the city bus because she'd once been too stupid to go to college when she'd had the chance. She didn't belong with the guy who'd devoted a decade of his life to learning all the medical know-how that allowed him to save people's lives.

"Thanks, but I have to go clock out. Have a good night."

She slung her tote bag over her shoulder and headed out of the room with what she hoped was a cheerful, unembarrassed, jaunty attitude.

"Me," Sammy said, drawing out the syllable in a high-pitched voice of distress.

Kendry almost stopped. She knew that when Sammy wanted something, he said "me" instead of "mine." But since she was Kendry, and his father was Dr. MacDowell...well, she wasn't his mother, and he wasn't her baby.

Still, she turned to blow her favorite baby a kiss over her shoulder.

THE JUGGLING ROUTINE never varied.

Jamie thought he ought to be getting better at it by now, but he still felt like a caricature of a single parent, the kind on TV commercials who dropped briefcases and seemed incapable of balancing babies and bottles. If only there were a solution at the end of thirty seconds of failure, like on TV. If only Jamie could press a door-opening button on the key to a certain car, or spot some golden arches that would magically make his day easier.

The juggling only got worse in real life. This evening, it was raining, but Jamie couldn't pull his car into the garage, which was still full of boxes from his deployment. He dashed with Sam from the driveway to the side door, but the door refused to open. The days of uncharacteristic rain had made the wood swell, so Jamie ended up kicking open the door while Sam cried and the rain pelted them both.

"I know, Sam, I know. We'll get you out of these wet clothes ASAP. They get cold real quick when they're wet, don't they?" Jamie kept his monologue running as he tried to keep the arm that was holding Sam inside the house while reaching out into the rain with his other arm to retrieve both his briefcase and the fallen diaper bag. "I can fix the clothes thing, son. Give me a second to shove this door closed, and I can fix that one problem. Thank God."

Sam didn't seem convinced, judging by the misery on his face and the volume of his cries.

Jamie applied some force to get the door to shut. In the still of the house, he could hear the rain dripping from the bottom of the diaper bag. The denim was soaked. One more thing he'd need to fix before his next shift at the hospital. Unpack the diaper bag, throw it in the dryer, repack it before work.

Damn. He let his head drop back to rest on the wall, let the denim drop onto the wood floor, which was wet, anyway.

His daily life wasn't difficult, really, just a constant to-do list of tasks. So why did he feel so overwhelmed by it all sometimes?

Maybe his brother was right. Maybe having a nanny waiting for him now would be the solution. A grandmotherly woman, ready to put the diaper bag in the dryer for him. A gray-haired lady who would have had the lights on in the house while she waited for him to come home. One of the nanny services he'd consulted had specified light cooking as an option in their contract. There could be supper waiting for him now, made by a sweet old lady.

Even when he was dripping wet and tired, Jamie didn't like the image. He didn't want a grandmotherly person in his house, someone to accommodate, someone to adjust to.

He wanted a partner, a peer, someone who would love Sam like her own, day after day, year after year, with no salary and no vacations. A mother for Sam, not for himself. Was it too much to ask?

Sam wailed.

"Right. It's just you and me, kid. Dry clothes, coming right up."

CHAPTER THREE

JAMIE STRUGGLED WITH his guilt while his son struggled with his bottle.

When all the little things went wrong, one after another, when Jamie's workday had been long and his baby refused to be comforted, memories of Amina brought him no comfort. On days like those—on days like today—instead of missing Amina, instead of wishing she were here to share the safe life of suburban America, Jamie would feel angry.

Amina could have shared this life. Amina could have seen their son growing day by day, but she'd chosen a different route, a path in life that had led to her death. She'd left Jamie alone to pick up the pieces, to protect her baby, to keep her memory alive for their son. And sometimes, damn it all to hell, Jamie was pissed off at the choices she'd made.

Being pissed off at a dead woman was unacceptable. The guilt was heavy on him now. It felt familiar.

He and Sam were dry, at least, both wearing white T-shirts and sitting together in the leather recliner. Jamie hadn't been able to find a rocking chair that fit his size comfortably, and the recliner did the trick when it came to relaxing with the baby until Sam—or both of them—fell asleep.

Tonight, though, as Sam worked his way through

swallowing and spitting up the contents of his bed-time bottle, relaxation seemed a long way off. Sometimes Jamie thought he'd never relax again—not for the next eighteen years, anyway. Not while he was the sole adult responsible for making sure Sam had all he needed for a good life.

Usually, these quiet moments with his son made everything fall into place. The troubles of his workday receded, unable to keep his attention when he held this baby and felt all the wonderment of a new life.

Usually, but not tonight.

As Sam grunted and sucked his way through the bottle, Jamie studied his son's face. Sam looked like Amina. His arrestingly dark eyes were undoubtedly his mother's. Jamie smoothed a hand over the soft, black hair on Sam's head—also Amina's. He let Sam curl his hand around Jamie's index finger. Those fingers didn't look like Jamie's. Nor his toes. Did they look like Amina's?

Jamie no longer remembered details like that, the shape of her thumb or pinky finger. He was forgetting. If he forgot Amina, there would be nobody to tell Sam about his mother. Amina had been the last of her family, the sole survivor when the rest had been wiped out by the war. For resisting the Taliban, her family name had been erased to the last distant cousin. Amina had only been spared by a matter of days, she'd told him, sent to school in London before the slaughter in her village had taken place.

Jamie wondered how the MacDowells would have reacted if the local sheriff suddenly had the power to walk onto their ranch and start shooting. His family probably would have been as defiant as Amina's family had been. Perhaps that was one reason he and Amina had hit it off so quickly. They were kindred spirits. She could have been a MacDowell.

She *should* have been a MacDowell.

Instead, even while she was pregnant with Jamie's child, she'd chosen to stay in a country where prenatal care was nonexistent. Hell, indoor plumbing was still a sign of personal wealth. Against Jamie's medical advice and personal plea, she'd obstinately traveled with a documentary film crew. In a remote village, she'd gone into premature labor while on her crusade to persuade Afghanis to let their daughters attend school. She'd died not from a Taliban bullet like the rest of her family, but from a lack of medical care, like too many women in her country.

Tonight, Jamie was angry at a woman who'd lost her entire family years before she, herself, had died.

More guilt.

Sam worked greedily at his bottle.

No, Amina's family weren't all dead. Sam was here, and Jamie would do everything to ensure one member of that brave family had a life that didn't end in tragedy.

Jamie bent his head as he lifted Sam's tiny hand and planted a kiss on the perfectly formed fingers. If they weren't his fingers and they weren't Amina's fingers, whose were they? A bit of DNA passed on from a great-grandparent? Or did those fingers, perhaps, come from another man, a man who had come into Amina's life before Jamie?

More guilt for even thinking such a thought.

Jamie had too much time to think about things in the safety of his quiet ranch house. Afghanistan had been intense—life outside the wire more so. Emotions ran high, bonds were formed quickly, and Amina, his unit's translator and general ambassador to the local population, had literally slipped into his bed after they'd worked together for only two short weeks.

At the time, he hadn't been surprised. They'd had chemistry and a connection from their first meeting. For the first two weeks, they'd spent nearly every moment together, seeking out the smallest villages and encampments, offering medical care to the local population. Amina's intelligence and her determination to better her fellow countrymen had made an impact on Jamie, if not on the villagers.

He hadn't been surprised that Amina was sexually experienced, either, because she'd lived in London longer than she'd lived with her family in Afghanistan. Her appearance was Afghani, but her personality was Western. He'd fallen for her and she for him. When, in the dark hours before dawn, she'd silently come into the hut he used as both clinic and bedroom, he'd had no doubts as she'd slipped into his bed.

Now, however, thousands of miles away and a year and a half later, he wondered. Had she already been pregnant? Had she wanted Jamie to believe he was the father, so that her son would have an American protector?

Sam gurgled down a few swallows of formula and patted Jamie's hand with his own. Jamie clutched the baby closer to his chest.

If Amina had wanted an American soldier to protect her coming baby, she'd gotten one. Jamie would never let Sam go, whether they shared DNA or not. The feel of this child in his hands was essential to his life.

It had been from the moment a local midwife who'd trekked miles on foot stood outside the barbed wire and handed him a dehydrated newborn and the news that Amina was dead. Dead and already buried, in accordance with their laws.

And so Jamie had sworn on a legal document that Sam was his biological child. He'd gotten the required signatures of others in his military unit, fellow soldiers and civilian contractors who could vouch that they'd seen Jamie working with Amina the eight months before the birth of the child, an appropriate period of time that could make it possible for Jamie to be the father. If any of those witnesses had wondered how an infant born at only eight months of gestation had appeared to be full-term, they'd kept that to themselves as they'd scrambled to help Jamie find formula and bottles—a futile search.

IVs had kept Sam alive those first critical days. Jamie had still had a week left on his tour of duty, but he'd literally wheeled Sam's stretcher onto the next medical flight to Germany. No one had questioned him. Jamie had gambled that forgiveness would be easier to gain than permission, and that gamble had paid off.

So far.

But in the quiet of nights like tonight, as Jamie looked at the son who looked nothing like him, fear crept into his chest. What if the State Department got around to that paperwork and a diligent clerk decided to order medical tests to prove the baby biologically belonged to the soldier?

The blood-type test would be ordered first. If the blood types were incompatible, then the soldier could not be the father of the child. If the blood types were compatible, it only proved that it was possible for the soldier to be the father, but the paternity was still in question.

Jamie knew his blood type. He knew Sam's. It was *possible* that he was Sam's father. But it was not a fact, not without further DNA testing, and if the State Department chose to order those tests...

He willed the fear away. Jamie sat Sam up to pat his back, hoping that air bubbles would come up but formula would stay down. It was a struggle at every feeding. The nurse at the hospital playroom had said that Sammy had more problems with the bottle than other babies in her care. That nurse seemed particularly bright, the one with the ponytail and glasses.

No—the young woman was not a nurse. She was an orderly. Jamie had noticed her before, when she'd worked in the emergency room. The orderly was certainly working in the right field; she had a natural talent for noticing patients' needs. She'd been working in the pediatric playroom more and more often, something Jamie had been glad to see. Sammy was in good hands when that particular woman was on duty.

"Come on, Sammy, give me a burp to make any college frat boy proud."

Instead, Sammy vomited a substantial amount of formula over the blanket that Jamie had laid over his lap. The formula wasn't curdled, not even partially digested. What went down came right back up, every feeding.

Sammy had been born with a birth defect, a hole in the wall of his heart. It would be repaired soon, and Sam would grow up never knowing it had been there. That particular birth defect shouldn't cause feeding issues. Jamie had assumed all this spitting up was normal, but now the orderly—Miss Harrison was her name—had said Sam needed to sit up to drink his bottle.

As he soothed Sam by rubbing his back, Jamie's medical training kicked in automatically. *Consider the options. Eliminate them one by one.*

What conditions caused a baby to need to be fed upright? Cleft palate? Jamie tapped his index finger to Sam's perfect, bow-shaped lips. Obviously, Sammy didn't have a cleft palate.

Jamie tried to feed Sam a few more ounces of formula, this time sitting him far more upright. It did make a difference. He could feel Sam's body relaxing as the ounces went down with less struggle. Was this how most babies fed, then? Settling in, relaxing, not fighting to get each swallow?

This time, when Jamie burped Sam, he slipped his finger in his son's mouth and felt the palate. The roof of the baby's mouth was there, intact. Of course, this had been checked early in Sam's life, part of the routine exam American doctors gave all newborns. Jamie had flashed his penlight down his son's throat more than once. The roof of his son's mouth was fine, intact on visual inspection. This time, Jamie pressed a little harder, moved a little more slowly, working his way toward the throat, millimeter by millimeter.

Sam objected, but Jamie concentrated as he would with any patient. He kept palpating despite Sam's whines and wiggles—and then he felt the roof of the mouth give. The palate wasn't formed correctly toward the back of the throat. It looked normal because the membrane covering the roof of the mouth had grown over it, but there was a definite cleft, hidden.

Miss Harrison had noticed a symptom that Sam's pediatricians and Jamie himself had missed. Sam had a cleft palate. A very slight, easily overlooked, but definitely malformed palate. One that hindered his swallowing.

Guilt.

If any parent should have figured that out, he should have. He was an M.D., but this was his first child, the first baby he'd ever given a bottle to, and it hadn't occurred to him that the amount of formula that came back up was greater than normal.

Like the doctor he was, his brain kept working despite the guilt. After the diagnosis, treatment options needed to be reviewed. As medical problems went, this one was simple. Sammy would have to go under the knife one more time, but it was fixable.

"Me," Sammy whined, reaching toward the empty bottle. "Me!"

"This is what you want, little buddy?"

Jeez, his kid was probably hungry, ready to eat more, now that he could get it down and keep it down, thanks to Miss Harrison figuring out the best position.

"Me."

"Got it. Coming right up." Jamie carried Sam into the kitchen, tossing the balled-up dirty blanket into the laundry room as he went, then started the process of opening the can of formula.

Jamie owed Miss Harrison more than a simple thank-you. He could write her a commendation, although the possibility for a raise or a promotion was slim when the hospital was under a strict budget.

"Me." Sammy grabbed for the freshly filled bottle.

Jamie chuckled to himself. "Yes, this is yours. Trust me, I don't want it."

At least his son did well communicating. He was advanced for his age when it came to expressing his needs verbally, as he was doing now. "Me" was an effective way for the baby to say he wanted something. He'd used it earlier today, when Jamie had come to pick him up at the hospital day-care center. Sam had wanted—

Jamie stopped in the middle of the living room.

Sam had wanted Miss Harrison.

CHAPTER FOUR

JAMIE MACDOWELL, EMERGENCY room physician and war veteran, very nearly chickened out.

Last night's revelation that Sam was attached to Miss Harrison warranted further investigation at his first opportunity, but when Jamie spotted her sitting alone in the hospital cafeteria, he felt like a boy in sixth grade, ready to turn tail and run rather than sit next to a girl.

The cashier charged the lunch to Jamie's account. Instead of looking toward Miss Harrison's table, Jamie made eye contact with the cartoonish scarecrow that was taped to the cash register for the fall. In four weeks, Jamie would be reporting to his reserve unit for two days of military training.

For the next six months, he'd report once a month, train for two days and come back home. Unless, of course, the medical unit was activated and deployed to Afghanistan, or any other corner of the world where they were needed. Jamie would go, and Sam would be left behind.

Sam needed a mother.

With a brief nod at the cashier and a fresh sense of determination, Jamie picked up the plastic cafeteria tray in one hand and turned toward Miss Harrison's corner of the cafeteria. Sam's favorite caregiver sat, alone, at one of the smaller tables. She was concentrating on her meal, so Jamie studied her face as he approached. He'd thought of her as plain, but she wasn't homely. If they shared a house, it wouldn't be a punishment to look at her across a dinner table. She had even features. Her mouth was compressed into a bit of a frown right now, but her lips were pink and not too full, not too thin.

Not that it matters. Mothers were always beautiful to their children, and this woman might make a good mother. He was here to find out.

"Is this seat taken?"

She looked up at him and froze for a moment, her spoon halfway to her mouth, before she glanced toward the entrance to the physician-only dining room.

"I'm not required to eat in the physicians' lounge." He smiled at her and stood there like an idiot, holding his tray. Middle school had never been this uncomfortable. "May I join you?"

She nodded, so he sat.

"Thanks," he said. "I thought you'd like to know how your dialysis patient was doing today."

"You mean Myrna?"

Jamie silently awarded her a point in her favor. She knew each child in her care by name. The patients were more to her than their pathologies.

"Was the incision site infected only near the surface, or had it spread outward from her kidney?" she asked.

"It appears to be localized at the incision site. Her kidneys are clear." Jamie was glad she understood the pathology, however, because his son had his share of medical issues. The kids whose parents were the best informed tended to be the kids who did well. Another point in her favor. "It was caught early, thanks to you."

"I'm glad to hear it, Dr. MacDowell."

"Call me Jamie."

For a split second, she looked at him like he'd just suggested they go somewhere and get naked. Dropping titles could indicate that kind of intimacy in a hospital setting, he knew. The next second, she turned her head and sneezed. Loudly.

Her nose seemed to be perpetually runny, although it was a nice enough nose, besides being red most of the time. She turned away from the table and blew her nose rather unbecomingly. With purpose. Force. Her bangs fell over her face, got tangled with the napkin she was using to mop up.

Jamie pushed aside his mashed potatoes and congealed gravy.

"Excuse me," she said, when she was done with a second napkin.

"No problem." Physical attraction to her would make their co-parenting awkward, anyway.

She was having soup and crackers. Lots of crackers. She had a tower of those little oyster cracker packets on her tray. He tried to see through them to the photo ID that hung on the lanyard around her neck, hoping to catch a glimpse of her first name. It seemed awkward to have to ask a woman her first name when she already knew his child as well as he did. Better than he did, in some ways. Her name tag stayed wrong way out.

"Have you worked here long, Miss Harrison?"

She turned away and sneezed again. At least it flipped her name tag around.

Kendry. Kendry Harrison. Jamie waited for a feeling of great portent to settle over him. Waited for a thunderbolt to strike, for a feeling of destiny, for something.

"Amina. Amina Sadat." She'd laughed, and in a voice that blended foreign tones with British enunciation, she'd said, "At least, that's the Westernized version of my name." She'd then recited a sentence-long string of syllables, her true Afghani name, one he would later learn included her father, her grandfather and nearly her whole family tree. Every syllable had sounded like exotic music...

Jamie cleared his throat. "Kendry? That's an unusual name. What country is it from?"

She dabbed at her nose with her crumpled napkin, an apologetic motion. "I think my parents made it up. They're kind of free-spirited like that."

Free-spirited parents? Not the kind of people he expected, somehow, to produce the plain, serious person in front of him.

"But to answer your first question, I've been working here for nearly six months."

Another point for her. She wasn't distracted easily. Which reminded him that he needed to keep his head in the game. He was here to gauge their compatibility. "Do you enjoy working in the hospital?"

"Yes, I do." Her eyebrows drew together, frowning at him as she met his gaze. Her eyes were sort of a nondescript greenish hazel. "Why do you ask?"

"I couldn't imagine working in any other environment, but not everyone feels the same."

"How does it compare to working in a hospital in the Middle East? Is it true that you were in the military?"

He hadn't intended to talk about himself, but fifteen minutes later, when Kendry stood and said her lunch break was over, Jamie realized she'd learned more about his life history than he had about hers.

"Can we do lunch again tomorrow?" he asked.

Her water glass rattled on her tray as she jerked to a sudden standstill. "Was there something else you needed to talk to me about? Something about Sam, maybe?"

He hoped his smile was casual. "Sam is my favorite topic. Let's meet tomorrow and discuss Sam."

She hesitated, looking oddly vulnerable in her plain green scrubs, holding her tray tightly with two hands. "Is there any trouble? Anything I should be aware of?" she asked.

"Trouble?" He hadn't meant to worry her.

"Am I doing something that could...that could mean I might be..." She took a deep breath and stoically asked, "Dr. MacDowell, am I in danger of losing my job?"

The way she asked it—the fact that she would ask such a thing at all—set some kind of alarm off inside him. Why would she jump to a conclusion like that?

Damn, he was going to have to hire a private investigator. It would have been the first thing his brother Quinn would have done, long before any kind of getting-to-know-you lunch. Jamie was a fool to begin by simply spending time with the woman his son preferred.

Kendry was waiting for his answer, her whole posture stiff and solemn.

"You're not in any trouble that I know of," he said. "Are you on probation for any misconduct?"

"I'd never do anything to jeopardize this opportunity. Not intentionally. But Paula told me I overstepped my bounds by asking you to check on Myrna Quinones yesterday."

Jamie leaned back in his plastic chair and studied her. Judging by the way her brows were drawn and her eyes watched him intently, she was either terribly concerned or terribly offended. The emotion brought a spark to her eyes, and he noticed now they were much more than a plain hazel. They were sharp, intelligent, expressive.

"I'm glad you did. You made a difference in Myrna's outcome. Any child would be fortunate to have someone like you watching out for him."

"Oh. Well, thank you." She stood there for another moment, tray in hand, and Jamie wondered if she felt as awkward as he had. "I've got to go. If I don't clock in on time, I really could be in trouble."

"See you tomorrow, then," he said, and he watched her walk away. She blended easily into the crowd of scrub-wearing personnel.

Yet, Sammy had singled her out.

Jamie glanced at the paper pumpkin decorations dangling from the cafeteria ceiling. Four weeks. He had four weeks to get to know Sammy's favorite caregiver. And maybe, just maybe, he had four weeks to persuade her to marry him.

WHAT ON EARTH had that been all about?

Kendry dumped her tray on the cafeteria conveyor belt and made a beeline for the elevators. She had to get to the hospital's basement and clock in within the next three minutes.

Her thoughts raced as she practically speed-walked down the corridor. Dr. MacDowell had eaten lunch with her. Sammy's daddy, the one who made her heart race when they accidentally touched while passing Sammy between them at pickup time. Physicians rarely ate in the main cafeteria, for starters, but for the hospital's most handsome and eligible doctor to single her out, to choose to sit at her table, was truly odd.

Kendry waved the bar code on her ID tag in front of the time clock's scanner with seconds to spare. According to the list tacked to the employee bulletin board, she was needed in the pediatric ward's playroom this afternoon. Dr. MacDowell had eaten lunch with her, so Sammy would be in the playroom. There was a silver lining to today's bizarre lunch.

She rode the elevator to the pediatric floor of the hospital, feeling her spirits rise at the prospect of spending the afternoon with Sammy and the other children.

Dr. MacDowell had wanted to update her on Myrna's condition. That was all. She wasn't in trouble. She hadn't broken any rules or done anything wrong.

Thank goodness. For a few heart-stopping moments, she'd been afraid Paula had been right, and she'd caused a problem by asking a doctor to check on a patient who wasn't officially his. She only had weeks to go until her insurance coverage as a hospital employee would begin, and heaven knew she needed that insurance. She wasn't ill, except for her annoying allergies, but she'd learned the hard way that living without insurance was risky, indeed.

She'd dropped her car insurance to pay her rent for one month, one lousy month after her previous job had crashed and her roommates had moved out without paying their share. It was perfectly legal in the state of Texas to not carry car insurance. The problem was, shortly after her job crashed, her car had crashed, too. Into a Mercedes-Benz. The judge had ruled her to be at fault, and until she paid for the cost of replacing that Mercedes, her money was not her own. It belonged to the state of Texas, practically every dime of it, thanks to the high monthly payment the judge had set.

The prospect of losing her hospital job was awful on every level, but the idea that she'd be fired just as she was about to have insurance was unbearable. She never wanted to be without insurance—auto, home, medical, dental, *any* insurance—again. The year she'd planned to take off before college had become the year that a lack of insurance had derailed her entire life.

By the time she walked into the playroom, her heart was pounding. Her thoughts were as much to blame as the speed-walking.

Relax. You're not losing your job. Dr. MacDowell is a polite man who knew you'd be curious about Myrna's health, so he filled you in and sat with you for twenty minutes. No big deal.

So why did he want to meet her for lunch tomorrow?

"Hi, guys," Kendry called to a trio of preschoolers as she entered the playroom. Paula sat at the tiny table, monitoring their serious coloring. Since the Myrna Quinones incident, Paula treated Kendry with more courtesy.

It was Sammy, however, who was really happy to see her. He pulled himself to a stand using the bars of his playpen, babbling his baby noises and bouncing in excitement.

"And hello to you, too, my special guy." Kendry scooped him up and gave him a squeeze, just as she caught sight of their reflection in the playroom's window.

"What's up with your dad?" she whispered. She'd never been what her grandfather called "a looker," but the stress of the last few years—the stress she couldn't blame on anyone but herself—had taken its toll.

She rested her cheek on top of Sammy's head. Even in the window's reflection, Sammy's black hair was glossy. Her own hair was a little dull. Her diet was pretty limited while she watched every penny, but she didn't think she was missing that many nutrients, not enough to make her hair less healthy, surely? She'd run out of shampoo and had been making do with bar soap to wash her hair. That probably made it dull, but still clean.

The dark circles under her eyes hadn't gone away in months. Even if she got enough sleep, she had terrible allergies, so the dark circles were here to stay. The bottom line was, she didn't look like the kind of woman a man went out of his way to spend time with.

Whatever lay behind Dr. MacDowell's sudden interest in her was a mystery.

None of it mattered, anyway. Her hair wasn't shiny, but it was clean. Her scrubs were faded, but clean. The important thing was, she was working in a hospital, where she'd always wanted to be. She wasn't a nurse yet, but she had a plan, and the first step had been to become a bona fide employee of the best hospital in Texas. She enjoyed being with the children so much, she might even specialize in pediatric nursing some day.

Sammy grabbed her glasses and succeeded in pulling them off. He chortled in glee. Sammy spent time with her because he liked her.

His father's motives were a mystery.

BE CAREFUL WHAT you wish for. You might get it.

How many times had Jamie wished for boredom on the job? While he was deployed, he'd fantasize about what his civilian life would be like. He'd work in an emergency room and treat patients whose medical needs were not truly emergencies, not like the carnage that he'd patched up after firefights. There would be a lot of children with runny noses and slight temperatures, a lot of adults with sprained ankles, and an affluent, overweight businessman getting the wake-up call he needed with a mild first heart attack. For an E.R. doctor, it would be monotony. While in Afghanistan, Jamie had craved monotony.

Now he was getting it. For two weeks, he hadn't had a single challenging case. He told himself that was good.

The E.R. at West Central Hospital had a small locker room for physicians. Off the main E.R. was a kitchenette for the staff, and off the kitchenette was a tiny space euphemistically called the physicians' lounge. It contained a plethora of lab coats, a few metal lockers that no one bothered to put locks on, and a cot that transformed itself from uninviting to nirvana when he had been on his feet for twenty-four hours straight.

At least Sam was happy today. Kendry had been on duty in the playroom, so Jamie could set his worried-parent hat aside for today's shift. She was still far and away Sam's favorite on the list of possible women. In fact, Sam didn't seem to have any particular affinity for any other nurse or medical assistant he came in contact with.

Jamie had made a point of speaking to each woman, anyway. He'd bought one nurse a cup of coffee, shared a slice of cold pizza with another woman while he worked the midnight shift. Quinn had made a point of introducing him to a nurse from the ICU. They were all the same, though, either flirtatious or flustered. The first he had no interest in, the second he had no patience for. He was starting to believe that Kendry Harrison was the only woman in the hospital who could carry on an intelligent conversation without batting her eyelashes.

Jamie half closed the door to the locker room, looking behind it for the dry-cleaning bag that held his white lab coats. Some women entered the kitchenette, and their voices carried into the tiny locker room. "He's a total hottie, even if he seems angry most of the time."

"Hot angry. *Hawt.* Where'd he come from?"

"He's from Dallas, I heard."

"I heard Austin."

"Whatever. He's a Texas boy, coming back after getting out of the army, or some say he's not out yet."

"The army? OMG, imagine him in camouflage and boots. Totally off the hotness scale."

Jamie jerked with surprise. They were talking about him. Had to be. Crap—now he was stuck in here. If he walked out, he'd embarrass the hell out of those women. He crossed his arms and leaned against the lockers. Looked like he was going to stand here and stare at the wall while they made their coffee. He had no choice but to listen to them talk about his *hawt*-ness.

"You didn't see his butt, Terry. He's always in his lab coat."

"I did so see his butt. In the parking lot. No lab coat, just a stethoscope around his neck as he got in his truck."

"Nothing but a stethoscope on? The man drives in the nude?"

Jamie rolled his eyes at the ceiling as the women giggled like girls. Still, it would have been gratifying to have one of his brothers hear him being drooled over. Jamie was the youngest. He was the baby of the three, four years younger than Quinn, six years younger than Braden.

That had been a huge age gap when he'd been in fifth grade while his brothers played high school football. The moms on the football stadium benches had cooed over Jamie, but his brothers had worn helmets and shoulder pads and attracted cheerleaders like flies. Jamie might have been in elementary school, but even then, he'd watched the cheerleaders in their very short skirts with their very long legs. They'd patted him on the head and watched his brothers.

It was an interesting switch, to be the big man on campus instead of the little brother. Apparently, at this hospital, he was the football star.

"Jamie MacDowell. Scottish sounding. Imagine him in a kilt."

"You're torturing us. It's no use. He's not interested in anybody. Dr. Brown even wore a miniskirt the other day, so it looked like she had nothing on under her lab coat. She looked like a freaking stripper."

"He didn't go for it?"

"Nope. She was pissed. It was one of my more entertaining shifts, I'll tell you that."

"Maybe he goes for men."

"I'd bet money he's not gay."

And you'd win. Now, could you ladies—and he mentally snorted in derision at that last word—*now could you ladies take your coffees and go?*

Jamie's cell vibrated silently. He checked the text. Time to get back to work. These women were going to hate him if he walked out of the room now, but the fifth-floor nurse needed alternate pain med orders for a patient he'd admitted.

"The only woman he ever talks to is some homely girl. I've seen him eat lunch with her in the cafeteria. He doesn't even go in the physicians' lounge. He sits at her table, wherever she is."

"Who? Do we know her?"

"She's nobody. An orderly or something."

They were talking about Kendry, of course. He should have anticipated that sitting with an orderly in the cafeteria would feed the grapevine. This particular grapevine didn't need to be fed further. He already didn't care for the tone of their gossip. Kendry might not be a nurse, but she still contributed to the well-being of this hospital's patients.

"What's this nobody got that Dr. MacDowell likes?"

She's kind. She respects children.

"I can't imagine. She's pitiful-looking. I swear, she wears the same scrubs every day."

"Oh—that girl. I think she decided to make herself over for the new doc. Did you notice she cut her bangs?"

Jamie glared at the door. He'd count to twenty, then

he'd leave this little jail cell whether those women were still here or not. He was feeling decidedly less considerate of their feelings.

"Ohmigod, yes. She had to have cut those bangs herself. With children's safety scissors."

"All right, guys, enough. You're being mean to the poor thing," one of the gossiping harpies cut in to defend the absent Kendry—about damned time. Jamie could tell they'd been revving up to pick her to shreds.

"She probably can't afford a decent haircut," the woman defending Kendry said. "She can't be making more than minimum wage."

"If I made minimum wage, I'd still work a couple hours extra, cut a coupon from the Sunday paper and at least get my hair done at one of those walk-in places. I think she just doesn't care."

"If she didn't care, she wouldn't have cut her bangs at all, would she?"

"Well, of course she cares about Dr. MacDowell. You can't be female and not notice him. Could you imagine them together, though? It'd be like a Greek god and a street urchin in bed."

"You're so mean!"

The nurse made it sound like a compliment.

"Maybe she turns him on, and we can't see why."

Listening to this crap was getting plain painful. True, Kendry didn't turn him on. But she didn't look like a street urchin, for God's sake. She wasn't *homely*. Who gave a damn about her haircut?

"Men have stooped lower. Look at some of the prostitutes we get in the E.R.—I can't believe men pay money to sleep with them. I'd say our soldier-doctor is on a mission to take that orderly on a pity date. Maybe an army buddy dared him to—"

"Yes. Maybe that's why he always looks so angry at the world. He got dared into giving that girl a mercy f—"

The nurses shrieked, literally shrieked, hysterically.

They were comparing Kendry, baby Sam's Kendry, to a prostitute. Jamie used the toe of his cowboy boot to give the door a nudge. It opened slowly as he remained where he was, leaning against the lockers, arms crossed over his chest.

"Oh, crap," said the nurse who saw him first. The other two audibly sucked in their breaths.

"Wanna know why I look so angry all the time, ladies?" Jamie asked in a deliberate, deadly serious drawl.

"Dr. MacDowell, I'm so sorry. I didn't know you—"

"I'm angry that three nurses are taking a break at the same time. That leaves patients lying out there, unattended."

"Yes, sir. We're done now."

Jamie wasn't done with them, however. "I'll tell you what else makes me angry. I'm angry that you'd take time away from patients in order to do nothing except trash a fellow employee at this hospital."

No one said a word to that.

"Her name is Kendry, and she's brilliant with sick kids. Next time you admit a child to the pediatric ward from the E.R., you watch real close if she's the orderly who comes to take them to their room. Watch and learn something about patient care, because she's one of the best we have at West Central. But right now, there are people out there who came to this E.R. for help, so put down your damned coffees and go."

"Sorry."

"Bye."

Jamie didn't move for a moment longer. He was angry, yes. Angry as hell, but also something else, some knot in his chest that made him want to punish something.

Himself.

That was it, damn it, he was mad at himself. For exactly what, he didn't know, but it had something to do with Kendry, with the woman his son loved.

CHAPTER FIVE

"IS THIS SEAT TAKEN?"

The bass voice sounded soothing in the cacophony of the cafeteria lunch rush. It never failed to send a pleasant shiver down Kendry's back.

"Hi, Dr. MacDowell."

"It's Jamie."

"Hi, Jamie."

The exchange was becoming a little tradition between them. Kendry didn't want to make more of it than it was, but it was nice to have their own private routine, wasn't it?

She smiled at Dr. MacDowell as he sat across from her.

"Soup again?" he asked.

Kendry willed herself to look nonchalant. For whatever reason, *Jamie* treated her like an equal. Like she had brains. Like her opinions mattered. When she spent all day being ordered to change linens and fetch ice, it was a relief to have a man like him to talk to. She wasn't going to shatter the illusion of equality with Jamie by confessing that soup was all she could afford. "Tomato's my favorite. I always get soup when it's tomato."

"I'll have to try it sometime."

The words were bland, ordinary, but he was looking at her…differently.

"Is something wrong?" she asked. Speaking used up air, naturally, so she breathed in again and caught a hint of his aftershave, that delicious, woodsy scent she'd noticed since the first time he'd sat with her.

She snatched a napkin in the nick of time as she turned away and sneezed. At least she'd cut her bangs so she didn't have to push them out of her eyes every time.

"You know," he said, "if I were a doctor, I'd probably give you a diagnosis of allergic rhinitis."

She rolled her eyes at him, but smiled so he'd know she wasn't upset. "I don't think I need to pay for an office visit to find that out."

"I take it that none of the over-the-counter pills are working for you. Do you need a prescription antihistamine?"

"No." Why was he asking about her personal health? They usually talked about other patients' health, not hers.

"I'll write you one." He already had a script pad out of his pocket and was writing away.

"Please, don't bother." She'd never be able to afford it, but she couldn't tell him something so embarrassing.

"It's no problem." He tore off the paper and handed it to her.

"Thanks." She reluctantly took the prescription. Why was he looking at her so strangely? Today's lunch was just…off.

She looked at the paper, so she'd stop trying to analyze his expression. His handwriting was amazingly legible for a doctor, maybe because he wrote in large letters, using up the blank space, filling it with dark ink. No faint scribbles for her to squint at hopelessly.

She only had to narrow her eyes a tiny bit to read his writing without her glasses.

This time, when she looked back up at him, he dropped his gaze to his plate. As if she'd caught him in the middle of—something.

"Did you hear something bad today?" she asked.

He looked up at her in surprise, as if she'd guessed right, but he didn't say anything.

"Myrna's not back in dialysis, is she? Or David?"

"No."

She hesitated before a burning need to know made her ask, "It's not about Sam, is it?" Her heart would break if anything happened to that little guy. *Please let it not be something about Sam.*

"No, nothing like that." To her surprise, he reached across the table and squeezed her hand. "Thanks for asking."

She took her hand off the table, grabbed another napkin, turned her head and blew her nose again. It would be nice to sit through a meal with the man without a runny nose.

Because then he'd notice how beautiful you are?

No, but it would be easier to pretend he did.

"I was wondering," Jamie said, "did you get your hair cut?"

"My—what?"

"Did you change your hair?"

"I trimmed my bangs a couple days ago. They were getting in my eyes." She hated this feeling, like she was missing a piece of a puzzle somewhere.

"You look nice."

Good lord, what was going on? Kendry felt herself turn ten shades of red.

Dr. MacDowell nodded once, like that was the end of that subject. Then he picked up his sandwich. "Have you met our new heart patient, little guy named Eric Raines? He came through the E.R. yesterday with a very unusual cardiac rhythm."

Thank goodness the conversation was going back on its normal track. They usually discussed any kids who had been admitted to the pediatric ward from the emergency room. Dr. MacDowell didn't mind teaching her about all kinds of medical conditions, and she found each one more fascinating than the last. She liked to think he was giving her a mini-internship, a taste of what her final year of nursing school would be like.

"His heart sounds were normal," he said, "but his—"

"Is this seat taken?" asked another deep voice. Without waiting for an answer, a tall man pulled out one of the empty chairs and sat, then leaned his arms on the table. He didn't wear a white lab coat like Jamie, just slacks and a dress shirt with the sleeves cuffed back, but the stethoscope slung around his neck screamed "doctor." He looked from Jamie to Kendry, who summoned a neutral, polite smile.

"Have a seat," Jamie suggested drily.

"Done."

"Kendry, this is my brother Quinn."

She'd already guessed that much. The two Mac-Dowell brothers were equally handsome and equally single. Before Jamie had arrived at the hospital, his brother had been the most eligible bachelor. Now there were two bachelors, and the hospital rumor mill had twice as much to speculate about. If she hadn't drawn enough attention to herself by having lunch with Jamie

MacDowell, today's lunch with both brothers was sure to do it.

"It's nice to meet you," she said, although she wished everyone in the cafeteria would stop looking over their shoulders at her table.

"Nice to meet you, too." Quinn turned to Jamie. "What kind of abnormal cardiac rhythm patient did you *not* refer to me?"

"Pediatric. Not your specialty. Kendry does a lot of work in the pediatric ward, though." Jamie hesitated, looked at his plate for a moment, then pinned his brother with a firm look. "Kendry is Sam's favorite caregiver in the playroom."

Quinn went utterly still for a second. "I see," he said, turning toward her with much more interest than he'd shown before.

What on earth was going on?

"What do you do here at the hospital, Kendry?" He emphasized her name slightly, like he was making a point of knowing it.

"I'm an orderly." When Quinn raised one eyebrow in unmistakable surprise, she lifted her chin and asked, "What do you do here, Dr. MacDowell?"

His lips twitched at her attempt to sound as condescending as he did. "Mostly, I'm in the cath lab, trying to open up coronary arteries."

"Mostly, he's at his plush private practice," Jamie corrected him. "He only comes to the hospital when he has to do some real work."

"How long have you been an orderly, Kendry?"

She tried to mask her surprise at the question. What was it with MacDowell men asking about her employment background?

"I'm getting close to the six-month mark." And then, because she couldn't help herself, she added, "Why do you ask?"

"Is this your dream job? Or do you have higher aspirations?"

"Quinn, shut up," Jamie said.

Apparently, Dr. Quinn MacDowell thought she was after his brother. A gold digger. Seriously, did she look anything like the kind of woman who attracted rich men?

Any men?

Irritated, she felt compelled to defend herself to the older—and really, much less handsome—Dr. MacDowell.

"For now, this is the best job. I'm working to earn enough money to get my CMA certification. If the hospital has an opening, then I'll have preferred status as an applicant because I'm already an employee here. The openings are few and far between, so I'm positioning myself to have the best shot at it."

"Your dream job is to be a CMA?" Quinn asked.

"It's a step in the right direction. I'm going to be a nurse. Once I'm a CMA, I'll be able to afford classes toward my bachelor's degree. I can be an RN eight years from now."

Quinn was silent, studying her for a moment. "That sounds like getting your RN the hard way."

"Sometimes that's the only option you have." Kendry toyed with her soup spoon, regretting the words the instant they left her mouth. No one at West Central knew she'd once tried to take the easy way, a year off to play more than work, the year she'd taken the foolish risk of dropping her car insurance. Until

she paid off the cost of that accident, she'd do everything the hard way. The right way.

Quinn glanced at Jamie, who was looking at her
oddly, then turned back at her. Kendry was definitely
missing something.

"I'll tell you what," Quinn said. "When you get that
CMA certification, you come see me. I pay more than
the hospital does, and I can always use someone with
drive and determination. With better pay, you can get
that RN degree sooner."

Whatever Kendry had been expecting, it wasn't a
job offer. She was certain she blew the good impression she'd apparently made by stumbling over her next
words. "Oh. Well. Th-that's very...very—"

"Kendry is interested in pediatrics, not cardiology,"
Jamie said firmly.

"Well," Quinn drawled, looking at his brother,
"since you're in emergency medicine and not pediatrics, you can't make her a better offer, can you?"

Jamie looked like he wanted to punch his brother.
Kendry looked from one to the other, as if she were
watching a tennis match. The two Dr. MacDowells
were fighting over her? It was insane.

"Maybe I can," Jamie said. "I'll have to see."

Kendry stood up. She nodded at Jamie. "I have to
go clock in. Excuse me, Dr. MacDowell." She nodded
at Quinn. "Dr. MacDowell." She grabbed her tray and
headed for the conveyor belt by the exit.

"WHAT IN THE hell was that about?" Jamie demanded.

"You can't be serious," Quinn said. "She's got some
spunk, no doubt, but she's as plain as can be."

"She's the one who figured out Sam had trouble eating. I still wouldn't have realized he had a cleft palate if it weren't for her."

"Admirable, but not a reason to marry anyone."

"I didn't say I was going to marry her, but she's not plain," Jamie said. "Considering the kind of relationship I want, it wouldn't matter if she were, but I'm sick of hearing people insult her appearance."

"For God's sake, her glasses are held together by tape."

"Kendry is fine the way she is. She's smart. Incredibly smart, and self-taught on medicine like you wouldn't believe. She'll fight for a sick kid with a passion. I've seen her do it."

"For what it's worth, I like her. As an employee. Be rational about this. Hire this Kendry to be the nanny. Hell, I would, after talking to her today."

"I'm not subjecting Sam to another series of nannies. He went through enough of that while I was on active duty. He's going to have a real mother."

Quinn pinched the bridge of his nose and closed his eyes like he was in pain. "When you fall in love and get married, then Sam will have a real mother."

The idea of hiring Kendry as some kind of temporary mother and then booting her out of the house when another woman came along felt wrong to Jamie on every level.

"What do I tell my son?" Jamie asked. "'Here's someone who loves you and cares for you, but say bye-bye now because I've found someone I want to sleep with'?"

Quinn opened his eyes and leaned forward to speak with forceful quiet. "You can't seriously plan on being celibate the rest of your life. You might be in mourning for your baby's mother right now, but one day you won't want to be buried anymore. You'll look around and what will you see?"

Quinn gestured toward the empty chair. "You're going to be tied to this…this…*girl,* and it will cost you half of everything you own to get the divorce you need, unless you have an ironclad prenup."

Jamie stood up, angry—the same kind of anger he'd felt when the nurses had cut Kendry to shreds.

He left the cafeteria through its outdoor dining area, planning to take a shortcut to the emergency room through the hospital's parklike courtyard. Quinn dogged his every step, still talking.

Jamie tuned him out. He didn't need legal protection against Kendry. Whomever he married would be providing *him* protection if the State Department should attempt to remove Sam from his custody. Removing a child from a stable, two-parent home would look bad. Jamie could leverage that in the press, if he had to.

If the State Department investigated. They might, because no child had been brought to the States from Afghanistan by an American soldier. He'd checked. No Afghani child had been adopted by a non-Muslim, period, just as no soldier had been granted permission to marry an Afghani.

If Sam wasn't his biological child. He might not be, because Amina had told him that life was short, that she lived to seize the day because you never knew when someone you loved might die. The rumor mill said there'd been someone she'd loved before she loved Jamie, someone who'd been killed in action.

If. Always *if* hanging over his head, a sword that, if it fell, could cut Sam out of his life.

"How do you plan on going from lunches with an orderly who calls you 'Dr. MacDowell' to proposing marriage?"

"Hell, Quinn, I don't have all the answers. I only know that Sam is attached to Kendry. She's pleasant, she's intelligent, and she seems to be attached to Sam, too. So, yeah, I'm having lunch with her every day."

An image flashed in his mind of Kendry in his house. He could see her holding Sam, standing in the kitchen, smiling the way she did when she talked about life with her unconventional parents. Jamie would not be alone. Someone would share his burdens.

"She'd be the one doing me the favor if she married me," Jamie said, stopping by a sumac tree.

Quinn was silent.

The leaves of the sumac were already starting to turn orange for fall. Less than two weeks were left before he reported to his new reserve unit for the first weekend drill. Sam was scheduled for his palate repair after that. Once that was healed, the hole in the wall of his heart would be repaired. Now that Sam was nearing his first birthday, the surgeons were willing to fix the things he'd been too frail to address earlier in his life.

Jamie rubbed his jaw, too tired to fight, too weary to explain.

Quinn filled the silence. "Kendry is the one, then?"

The world stopped. For a moment, everything was suspended. Slowly, Jamie turned his gaze from the orange leaves to meet his brother's eyes.

"Yes, she is."

Quinn shook his head. "Then I can't believe I'm saying this, but good luck."

Jamie walked the rest of the way to the emergency room before he remembered something important.

Amina.

He'd thought he'd marry Amina. Instead, he'd returned to the States with her child. *Their* child. Now he had to figure out how to ask a near stranger named Kendry to marry him, because Amina's child loved her, even if Jamie never would.

CHAPTER SIX

"YOU ARE MY favorite guy in the whole, wide world."

Kendry sat on the playroom floor and crooned sweet nothings to Sammy as he lay on his back on a blanket. Holding his little baby feet in her hands, she moved his legs like he was riding a bike.

"Where's that big, baby laugh?" She wiggled his feet. "I wanna hear that baby laugh."

Sam gifted her with his wide-open, mostly toothless smile.

"That's my guy!"

She loved this kind of day, when she was the only adult in the playroom and could lavish her attention on the children without feeling self-conscious. Sammy made her feel like a superstar. Everything she said was apparently what his little baby ears wanted to hear.

She stretched out on her side next to Sammy, propping her head up with one hand and tickling the baby's belly with her other. "Let's do this for a living. Forget all this bill-paying college stuff. We'll lie on a beach all day in Guatemala, like my parents."

Sammy cooed at her and grabbed his own toes.

"You're right. You need to live here. Stay in school, kid. It's harder than it looks to make ends meet without a degree."

She'd done some hard labor after work the previous evening, swinging at waist-high weeds with a ma-chete, of all things. The house across the street from her rented room had been foreclosed on, and the bank was trying to clean up the yard a bit before its auction. She'd earned twenty dollars, cash, by helping the yard crew for only two hours, sneezing all the way.

Now, however, she was paying a price in aching arm muscles. She flopped onto her belly on the cushy mat. She was horizontal, the playroom was quiet, and the cutest baby in town was lying safely next to her, as content and happy as he could be. If she wasn't care-ful, she would drift off to sleep.

Sam grabbed a fistful of her ponytail and yanked.

"Ow! I'm awake, Sammy. I swear."

"That's not how it looked to me," his father drawled.

"Eek!" Kendry pressed her hand on her chest as her heart skipped a beat.

"Didn't mean to scare you. Sam saw me coming and tried to warn you."

Kendry gave Sammy's belly a jiggle. "That's 'cause you're on my team, aren't you?"

When she moved to get to her feet, she nearly col-lided with Jamie, who was hunkering down on his heels to greet his son. The man was just so big. Not only tall, but wide in the shoulders, like he'd played football or something. This close, she could feel the warmth of him, smell his skin, and—

"Ah-choo!" Kendry barely turned her head in time to sneeze into her elbow.

"Did you get that antihistamine prescription filled yesterday?"

"Not yet." *Not ever.*

"You'd feel a lot better."

Not if Mrs. Haines kicked me out of her garage for not paying this week's rent, I wouldn't. I'm not going back to the homeless scene, not even for you.

Dr. MacDowell stood and looked down at her, frowning. "It's been a week since Sam broke those glasses."

Kendry picked up Sam and stood, too. "They're still wearable. Why get new ones if a toddler's going to whack them?" She grabbed the earpiece—the one without the bandage tape—and wiggled the glasses up and down, doing her eyebrows, too, like Groucho Marx. "These are now my special Sammy glasses."

Usually, Dr. MacDowell laughed at the jokes she made. They were the best way to deflect any comments that might lead to a more revealing conversation than she was willing to have. This time, he only smiled faintly. "But you did get new glasses? My offer to pay for them stands. My son broke them, so it seems only fair."

She waved a hand in the air breezily and hiked Sam up a little higher on her hip. "I'll get new ones. I've been busy. These aren't dead yet, anyway." It was time for a change of subject. "I've been reading up on cleft-palate repairs, so I'll know what to expect when Sam is with me afterward."

She had a hard time remembering the questions she'd wanted to ask about the surgery's recovery stages, because while she held Sam on her hip, Jamie started patting him on his back. The move made the three of them seem connected. It was intimate. It was unnerving.

As Kendry stumbled over her question, Sam squealed and grabbed her glasses. Thankful for the excuse to break the moment, Kendry laughed. "See? Sammy glasses."

"I see." He righted the glasses on her nose, and then Jamie MacDowell, M.D., the most eligible bachelor at West Central Hospital—the most eligible bachelor in Texas, she'd bet—smoothed a piece of her hair behind her ear, let his hand drift to her shoulder, and looked deeply into her eyes.

For that moment, the fantasy was real. Jamie was interested in her. Interested in *that* way.

Kendry dropped her gaze. *Too, too real.*

He squeezed her shoulder gently. "Some parents don't pay as much attention to their own children as you do to Sam."

This brought her gaze back to him. So that's what this was all about. He was warning her that she was too attached to a child that wasn't hers. She'd dealt with this kind of parent before.

"You're number one in Sam's world," she said. "Just because he likes me, that doesn't mean he doesn't love you."

The playroom door opened and her replacement came in, a CMA named Bailey who was wonderfully friendly to all—even orderlies. "Good evening, Dr. MacDowell. Hi, Kendry."

Kendry pushed Sam into Jamie's arms, turned away and sneezed. "Excuse me." She put a lot of distance between them, walking to the hand sanitizer dispenser and squirting the cold foam into her hand.

Jamie followed her, standing a tiny bit too close. "I meant that as a compliment. If I have to be at work, then I want Sam to be with someone he likes." His words were quiet and low, meant for her ears only.

She tried not to shiver at the goose bumps he raised. "Some parents don't feel that way. I've had at least one staff member who was jealous that her daughter would cling to me when she came to pick her up in the afternoons. That little girl doesn't come to the hospital's day-care center anymore."

"You're kidding."

"It's tough, sometimes. I thought that baby was a real sweetie, and now I'll never see her again."

"You'd rather stay with the same kid, year after year?"

There it was again, that intense look in his eyes. Kendry tried to deflect the question away from herself.

"Not just any kid," she said. Hoping to lighten the mood, she threw a comically exaggerated look over her shoulder, as if Bailey might hear something scandalous. "Let's be honest. Some of them can be a real pain. Not everyone was born as charming as your Sam."

"Our Sam."

"What?"

Jamie looked away. She watched him swallow nervously. *Nervously?*

"I meant," he began, speaking carefully, "that Sam seems to be as happy with you as he is with me." With a glance in Bailey's direction, he leaned near to Kendry's ear. "And I think that's very, very important."

Kendry had stopped rubbing the foam into her hands. That low voice drawling in her ear was...upsetting.

She tried to rub the sticky remains briskly into her palms as she headed for the crib where Sam had taken his nap. She picked up the denim diaper bag and turned toward Jamie, sticking her arm straight out to hand it to him from the great distance of her arm's length. Her tired muscles protested.

"Will you be back tomorrow?" Kendry asked.

Jamie took the bag from her without a trace of nervousness. Instead, he winked. "You couldn't keep us away."

As he left with Sammy, Bailey whistled quietly. "How did you do that?"

"Do what?"

"Get dreamy Dr. MacDowell interested in you."

"In me? You must be crazy."

"Did you not see the way that man smiled at you? I didn't know he had a dimple. Ye gods, if that man smiled more often, every woman in this town would come up with some reason to go to the emergency room."

Kendry hadn't known he had a dimple, either. But, *oh my,* he most certainly did, on the right side.

"Sit down here and tell me everything." Bailey settled into one of the two rocking chairs.

Kendry needed to sit down. "There's nothing to tell."

"Has he asked you out?"

"Be serious. Look at him. Look at me."

"Well… I don't know…" Bailey's certainty faded.

Kendry's certainty grew, the certainty that reading anything more into Jamie's smile tonight was foolish.

"He's happy that Sam is doing so well now that he's eating sitting up."

Bailey accepted her explanation, but as Kendry closed her eyes and rocked, she saw Jamie MacDowell's smile.

I wish we were more than friends.

She stopped rocking. The truth of that wish was powerful. Dangerous.

It was better to have Jamie MacDowell as a friend than nothing at all, just as it was better to be an orderly in a hospital than not work in medicine at all. Just as it was better to live in a converted garage than in a homeless shelter. Just as—

When had her life become a series of compromises?

When you wished for more than you had, and you ended up with nothing.

Wishes could be dangerous, indeed. If she wished for more than she had with Jamie MacDowell, she'd only raise hopes that would be dashed. She would end up not just broke, but brokenhearted.

That was too high a price to pay for any wish.

CHAPTER SEVEN

"DAMN IT, GET me a nurse!"

Jamie had thought his wish for a boring job had been granted, but it was one of those days in the E.R., the kind when a multicar accident and staffing cuts combined to make every moment a crisis.

"There are no more nurses, Dr. MacDowell. Everyone's tied up." His nurse sounded frantic, lying as she was on the patient's legs, trying to keep the half-conscious man from doing greater harm to himself.

Jamie kept his eyes on the gash in the patient's side, his hand pressing the severed vein shut, his other hand keeping the retractor in place. "An MA, then. An orderly. Anyone with two hands."

"How can I help?"

He recognized Kendry's voice immediately.

"They sent me down from peds," she said breathlessly, as if she'd been running, "and another orderly is on his way from ortho. I'm supposed to tell you the on-call doctor will be here in thirty."

Jamie didn't take his eyes off the vein. "Get this patient's oxygen back in place."

"Okay, it's on."

"Switch places with the nurse. Don't let those legs move." To the nurse, he gave orders for deeper sedation. He and Kendry held their positions until the patient went under. "Kendry, turn that suction on and get me a second laceration tray."

The tension in the back of Jamie's neck lessened a fraction. He could work with Kendry—and work they did. He barked orders, and she responded quickly. The nurse assisted him with the emergency surgery, but it was Kendry who made that possible by knowing where to find everything he needed, from surgical instruments to saline. When the patient was stabilized, it was Kendry who hand-carried Jamie's notes as she rolled the patient's bed to the regular operating room, where surgeons had been called in to take over the rest of the patient's care.

Hours passed as patient after patient made their way through the emergency room. Sometimes Kendry was with him, sometimes a different member of the staff. Every bed in the E.R. was full, from the privately walled cubicles to the spillover area, where beds were only separated by curtains. The waiting room was packed, several nurses had told him.

Jamie had signed a half-dozen discharge orders, but patients still occupied beds, waiting for their transportation either to regular hospital rooms or to the exit, whichever Jamie had decided was appropriate.

"Orderly!" Jamie barked at a very young man who was standing still in the middle of the rush. "I'm waiting on these beds to open up. Where's the wheelchair I asked for?"

"There aren't any more around." He fluttered his hands, helpless.

"Then go find one. Now. I want these rooms turned over."

Kendry passed Jamie at a half-jog, snagging the orderly's arm as she went. "Come on. You have to go to the parking lot and get the wheelchairs." Jamie caught her eye, and she made a face that clearly said, *Where do they hire these people?*

Jamie smiled to himself as he entered the next cubicle. Kendry could read his mind. Being married to her would be easy.

THE RAIN THAT had caused the night's car accidents hadn't let up. Neither had the volume of patients. Kendry had learned more during this shift than she'd dreamed possible. No wonder nurses and doctors had extensive internships. There was nothing like being on the scene, and tonight, the E.R. was like a scene from a TV show, intense and dramatic. Every time the glass double doors to the ambulance ramp slid open, the damp night air whooshed in with another patient.

One stretcher had been wheeled into a cubicle by two paramedics while a third paramedic straddled the patient, pumping hard with two hands on the prone man's chest. While Kendry had replenished oxygen masks and blankets across the hall, she'd heard Jamie's calm command, "Clear," before the unmistakable sound of defibrillator paddles. It was dizzying to realize that a life was being saved just feet away from her.

She often heard Jamie call her by name. "Kendry, grab a lumbar-puncture tray and meet me in room three." She'd learned about the importance of the bevel on the needle and how the manometer worked, even as she'd smiled for the woman getting the spinal tap and tucked a warm blanket over her shoulders to counter the cold of her exposed lower back.

She'd had to gown up in protective gear in order

to peel the mask, gown and gloves off Jamie after he'd stabilized a bloody patient. "You keep that gear on while you clean this room," Jamie had said to her sternly as he'd left her for the next patient, instructions that weren't necessary, but that made her feel like he was watching out for her.

Always, when a child was involved, his tone was softer. She learned that he called the little girls "princess," every one of them. "Okay, princess, I brought you someone special. This is Kendry, and she's going to take you and your mommy to get a picture of your arm. Your mom can climb on board and Kendry will push your whole bed. You have to be in a hospital to get a cool ride like that."

Then suddenly, the pace slowed. Kendry stood near the central nurses' station and checked off each room in her mind. Each one was occupied, but not one case was critical. Most patients were in a holding pattern until test results came in. Jamie was standing at the nurses' station, updating chart after chart. If she had been half in love with him before, she was a goner now. The man was the real deal: handsome, skilled, calm in a storm.

Kendry glanced at the clock. Six hours. She hadn't stopped running for six hours. She'd been called down from the pediatric ward only after the E.R. had been swamped for some time. That meant Jamie had been running even longer than she had. The decisions he'd been making, the responsibility on his shoulders—shoulders which, even now, looked strong enough to carry them and more—

Yes, she was a goner.

Who watched out for him? Shouldn't the leader be

taken care of, so he could take care of everything else? With that thought in mind, she took a Popsicle and a carton of milk from the supply kept for patients, then returned to the nurses' station. She waited patiently while Jamie dictated notes into the hospital phone.

He noticed her immediately, finished speaking into the phone while he kept his eyes on her, and hung up. "What's up?"

She held up the Popsicle and the milk carton. "Which do you need more? Sugar or protein?"

He shook his head and smiled with that one-sided dimple. "I'll take both. You are my favorite person in this entire hospital."

She nearly blushed. "Nah. Sam's upstairs, remember? He's sleeping. I peeked in on my way back down from ortho."

"Did you?" His smile started to fade, although he didn't look angry or upset. Just...intense. Again. He told the nurses he was going on break. "Take a walk with me?" he asked Kendry.

"Sure."

He led the way outside the sliding glass doors to the ambulance ramp, where an admin clerk was startled in the middle of a forbidden cigarette. The entire hospital grounds were designated as a no-smoking area, but with the pouring rain, no one wanted to cross the street for their smoke break. The covered portico had sheltered more than a few smokers tonight.

"Sorry, Dr. MacDowell," the clerk said, quickly crushing out her cigarette. She narrowed her eyes at Kendry, looked between her and Jamie, and shook her head slightly. "See you inside in a few."

Jamie sat on a metal bench and gestured for Kendry to sit beside him. "Tired?" he asked.

"I'm afraid I will be if I stop moving. This has been crazy, but time sure flies when it's this busy. Getting six hours of overtime isn't bad, either."

"It isn't always this busy. It's amazing how a hard rain guarantees a car accident or two, every time."

"Do you like it when it's busy?"

"That's a trick question. How can I say I enjoy seeing people in pain and need?" Jamie crunched the last mouthful of Popsicle off the wooden stick. "I'll tell you the truth. If the intensity of the rush didn't make me feel alive, then I wouldn't be an emergency physician. People either welcome that adrenaline, or they don't. The ones that don't shouldn't choose this specialty."

He downed the milk in a few gulps. With his head thrown back and the carton at his lips, his thirst seemed almost carnal to Kendry. She watched him, feeling that schoolgirl crush mature into something more physical.

And equally hopeless. Be happy that he's your friend. Don't wish for more.

Without standing, Jamie pitched the empty carton and the naked Popsicle stick into the nearest trash can. Then he angled himself toward her, stretching his arm across the back of the bench. "How about you? Would you like to be an E.R. doctor after tonight?"

"I really want to be a nurse. I'm more about the patient care than I am about the diagnosing."

"Would you want to be an E.R. nurse, then?"

Kendry turned away to better see the rain coming down beyond the overhang. Better to keep a few inches between her back and his hand. "I have a long time left to decide." She ducked her chin a bit, then slid him a glance. With a grin, she confessed, "But I was kind of loving that adrenaline in there tonight."

Jamie laughed. "I knew you were. You're either cut out for it or you're not. You've got what it takes."

His praise made Kendry want to burst with pride, but she tried to play it casual, crossing her arms over her chest and shrugging. "I've also got what it takes to fall asleep on a playroom floor with your son."

"I've got that, too."

They both laughed, and then Jamie placed his warm hand very firmly on her shoulder. This was no casual brushing of body parts. He was touching her on purpose, laughing with her.

Don't wish for more.

"Kendry, don't you see it? What a good pair we are?"

"We…" The sound of the rain was nearly drowned out by the sudden buzzing in her head. "We are?"

"In the middle of all this adrenaline, you stopped and checked on Sam, too. He's on your mind, like he's always on mine."

"I wanted… It was just a habit, really. I see him almost every day, so…"

"You're the closest thing to a mother he's got."

"I am?"

Jamie tightened his grip on her shoulder. "Kendry, listen to me. You can skip the CMA thing and go straight to nursing school. You should be a nurse. You have amazing instincts when it comes to patients."

The rain kept falling, and Kendry kept feeling lost by the conversation. "Are you—are you offering me a scholarship?"

"I have enough money for anything you need. Tuition, books." He paused and flicked a glance at the bandage that kept the earpiece of her eyeglasses together. "Glasses."

"I never heard of a scholarship that included glasses."

"I'm not talking about a scholarship."

"Then what are you—"

"Marry me."

For one second, Kendry was shocked. The next, she was hurt. Jamie didn't know what he was playing with. He couldn't know how hard she was working toward that nursing degree. Still, to joke about marrying someone was odd. "You had me going there for a minute. I thought you were serious about the nursing school."

"I've never been more serious. Marry me, and my money becomes our money. And our money can certainly be spent on your education."

"Marriage? We're barely friends."

"We're definitely friends."

"But—" She groped for the right thing to say. What she was hearing was so far from what she could possibly have expected. "You don't marry someone because you're friends."

"You are more than just a friend to me, Kendry."

She swallowed hard. She'd wished he saw her as more than a friend, and now here he was, about to tell her that her wish had come true. It didn't seem right. It didn't seem possible.

"This is an awfully big leap," she whispered, "from friends to marriage. You've never taken me on a date. We've never kissed."

At that, he seemed almost surprised. He let go of her shoulder and brought his hand to the back of his neck, kneading the muscles there in something of a nervous gesture. "I wasn't thinking of that kind of marriage."

"I see." She saw nothing. What other kind of marriage was there?

"I want a wife who'll be my partner raising Sam. I want my marriage to complete my family. I didn't mean that I wanted something, uh, romantic." He gestured between them with his hand. "We don't have that kind of thing. You know that."

No kind of chemistry between them? It was nothing more than she'd expected, that Jamie didn't see her as girlfriend material, let alone wife material. He said it bluntly, in a tone that made it seem like he was stating something obvious. She felt sick to her stomach.

Jamie ducked his head a little, looking at her face, not letting her break eye contact. He chuckled. "I've sprung this on you a little too suddenly, huh? I'm not doing this very well."

Jamie picked up one of her hands in his. "I didn't plan on asking you here, but didn't tonight prove how well we work together? You're perfect for the kind of marriage I'm offering. The fact that we get along so well is an incredible bonus, as far as I'm concerned, because the most important thing is that Sam loves you."

Kendry looked down at their loosely joined hands. Jamie ducked down to make eye contact again. "Sam does love you. There's no doubt of that."

Two women came from around the corner. They must have been outside for a smoke break, standing around the corner this whole time. They'd barely passed Kendry when they made those horrible sounds people make when they are trying to hold their laughter in.

The rain had stopped. Kendry hadn't noticed it stopping, but the silence was now oppressive. "You keep bringing up Sam. How about Sam's mother?" she said, jerking her hand away. "Maybe she'd like to fill the role."

"She died during his birth." Jamie let her hand go. "I thought you knew."

Poor Sam. Now her heart hurt along with her stomach for poor little Sammy, and the poor woman who had never had the chance to cuddle her baby. Jamie was trying to fill the hole that woman must have left. Not the emptiness she'd apparently left in his heart, though. Only the empty space where a mother for Sam should be.

Or maybe her heart hurt because she felt sorry for herself. Poor little Kendry, so undesirable that a man thought she'd marry him without a kiss.

She stood up, which seem to startle Jamie, because he stood up, too, and stepped closer to her. "Do you need some time, maybe? Do you...do you want to talk about it?"

"No, I understand everything now. The lunches, meeting your brother, the way you kept asking for me tonight whenever the patient was a child. It was all an audition. You've been looking for a woman who would agree to a loveless marriage, and you think I'm that woman."

"Not loveless. I want Sam to be raised in a home where his parents love him madly. Both of them."

A *sexless* marriage. That's what she didn't have the guts to say. She was the perfect woman that an intelligent, caring man like Jamie MacDowell thought would jump at the chance for a sexless marriage.

No other man has made you any offer at all. Have you looked in a mirror?

The glass doors slid open and stayed open as some paramedics strolled out with an empty stretcher. Kendry didn't want to speak in front of any more witnesses. Heck, she didn't want to speak ever again. She didn't want to be here.

But she and Jamie stayed where they were, silent, until the sounds inside the emergency room reached her ears. Snatches of voices. "I swear on a stack of Bibles. He asked her to marry him." Snippets of conversation. "Not that kind of marriage." Shrieks of laughter.

This was it. This was the price she'd now pay for reaching above herself and imagining that she was someone besides the girl who counted pennies. She'd had a grand future planned for herself at West Central Hospital. Now she wouldn't be able to hold her head up.

"It doesn't matter what other people think," Jamie said stiffly. He must have heard every word she had. "If our arrangement works for us, who cares?"

"I care. I care that everyone in this hospital thinks I'm a joke. I thought you were my friend. You're not."

"Kendry." He reached out to touch her arm, but she backed up.

"I have to go clock out now. Goodbye, Dr. Mac-Dowell."

With her head held high, Kendry walked through the E.R. to the bank of elevators. She hoped her broken glasses hid the tears in her eyes.

CHAPTER EIGHT

WHERE THE HELL was Kendry?

Two nights ago, she'd clearly been upset when she'd left the E.R. The patient load had prevented him from following her, but he'd told himself it was okay. They were okay. After all, the gossip had hurt her feelings, but Jamie had only said nice things to her about how much he wanted her in his life. She couldn't have meant it when she said he wasn't her friend.

When he'd brought Sam to the playroom on his next shift, a medical assistant he didn't know had told him that Kendry was already gone for the day. Kendry normally worked the day shift, but Jamie had taken the swing shift; that was why their paths hadn't crossed.

Today, he was back on the day shift. He'd been counting on finding Kendry in the playroom. Sam fussed when Jamie left him with a stranger.

The playroom had been full, as it usually was in the mornings. The two women on duty were not Kendry, however. Sam had cried when Jamie left him, which always tore at his nerves. He was determined to find Kendry in the cafeteria at lunch.

So where was she? He stood in the center of the dining area and turned in a slow circle, ignoring everyone who watched him. He checked the line of people waiting for the cashier. Nothing.

They'd met for lunch every time they'd both been working at the hospital. Every single day for nearly a month. She had to know he'd be looking for her, so why was she being so hard to find?

She has no reason to avoid me. I told her she was perfect for me. I told her my son loved her. I promised to send her to nursing school. I proposed to her.

But she hadn't said yes. She'd been embarrassed by some gossip and had taken off running. She couldn't blame him for that, could she?

Apparently, she could.

Okay, so his proposal had been clumsy, and it hadn't occurred to him to sweep the area for eavesdroppers, but that wasn't a good reason for her to avoid him now. His relationship with Kendry was better than that. Without any romantic ties, they could just be friends. Friends didn't avoid each other.

By the time Jamie found her in the courtyard, he was feeling decidedly unfriendly. He'd walked past her twice without seeing her. For one thing, she had her back to the cafeteria and was seated on the farthest possible park bench. For another, she was wearing bright pink. He'd been looking for traditional green scrubs, the kind she always wore.

But it was Kendry, all right, taped glasses in place, mopping her nose with a fistful of napkins, as usual. "There you are," he said, not attempting to keep the accusation from his tone.

She jumped like a startled bird and blinked up at him from under her bangs. She hadn't been sneezing, he realized. She'd been crying. Was still crying.

All his anger and irritation fled in an instant. "Kendry, what's wrong?"

She hid her face in her napkin immediately and shooed him away with one hand.

Right. Like he'd leave his friend like this. Jamie sat on the bench. Kendry scooted a few inches away from him. With each snuffled breath, her shoulders shook a little bit. Helplessly, he waited while she caught her breath, watched as she trembled in her stiff clothes.

She looked frail. He'd known she was thin, of course, but the pink scrubs emphasized how thin. They were obviously new, still creased from their packaging. He wished she'd say something. He wanted to help; her tears were distressing.

Of course they were. Tears pretty much equaled distress, but Kendry's tears seemed somehow worse to him. Maybe because she was usually so sharp, so enthusiastic about her job. About Sam. About life.

He patted her on the shoulder, lightly, the way he patted Sam when he needed soothing.

"I'm sorry," she finally said, pushing her bangs aside with the back of one hand. "I didn't think anyone would find me here."

"You did make it a challenge. I've been looking for a while. What's wrong?"

"Nothing, really. Just having a pity party."

She wasn't going to say any more, he could tell. She threw the last bit of a saltine at the base of a tree, for the squirrels or birds or ants.

"What's the occasion, then, for the pity party?"

"Oh—" She flicked the back of her hand toward the tree, a sign of general irritation with the air. "It's nothing."

Jamie felt a little irritated himself. In his experience, women didn't cry over nothing, despite popular male opinion to the contrary. But also in his experience, if a man asked what was wrong and then sat patiently and asked a second time—not that he thought he deserved a medal for it or anything—then the woman would be glad to share her reasons for crying.

Not Kendry. She crumpled the cellophane cracker wrapper in her fist and sat there, napkin in one hand and wrapper in the other.

Was he supposed to ask a third time?

He looked from her clenched fists to her face. She was looking away from him, which allowed him to study her profile. Her glasses were halfway down her wet nose, so he could see that no fresh tears were falling from her mostly green eyes, but her lashes were wet.

Really thick lashes.

Really irrelevant thought. The important thing was, she was upset, and she wouldn't explain why. His eyes dropped to her mouth, as if he'd find a reason why words were failing to appear there. Her lips were pressed together, hard, with a tremor. She didn't want to cry around him.

Whose shoulder did she cry on, then? Frankly, he didn't like the idea that there might be someone else she felt more comfortable with. The background check he'd ordered on her had come back clean. No criminal past, only a single court appearance for a traffic accident. She'd earned a GED after sporadic school attendance, which Jamie knew was due to her parents' travels. She'd never been married, and there was no indication that she had any man in her life, or that she did much besides work and go home to someplace she rented, for no property was in her name.

In other words, Kendry had no other person's shoulder to cry on.

And so, for a third time, he asked her.

"Kendry, what's wrong?"

THE MAN WAS PERSISTENT. In a good way, if she were honest with herself. Persistent like a friend would be.

She sniffed in the last of her teary, sloppy self. Blew her breath upward to puff her bangs out of her eyes and tipped her head back to look at the sky. It was crisscrossed with the branches of the sumac tree. Very pretty. Picturesque.

"Nothing's really wrong. I got thrown up on by one of the kids in the playroom. I had to get these new scrubs."

"I know you can handle the sight of blood, but vomit can be something else entirely, can't it?"

I'm not going to cry. I'm not going to cry. No matter how nice he is to me, I'm not going to cry.

Jamie kept being nice. "I'd understand if it grossed you out to be thrown up on, but why the tears?" He was trying to make her smile. Her heart broke a little more. Could she have dreamed up a more perfect man? Too bad she was barely even a female to him. He'd made that clear.

I didn't mean that I wanted something romantic. We don't have that kind of thing. You know that.

She looked down at the too-sharp crease in the too-crisp pants. "They made me take these scrubs. I didn't want them."

"Why not? You don't like the color? C'mon, Kendry, talk to me. Something's gotten to you, bad."

"These are too expensive." She said it very quietly

as she used the index finger of one hand to trace the crease. Cracker crumbs from the cellophane in her palm left a little trail. "It's my fault. I should have had a spare set on hand, but I didn't, so my supervisor ordered me to put these on."

"Ordered you to buy scrubs? They could have loaned you a set. The E.R. has stacks of them."

"For their department. Departments don't share that much, you know. All we have at peds is a supply of tiny gowns that don't close in the back." She spared him a quick glance. "Seriously, you don't realize how easy it is to ask for something when you're a doctor. I can't pick up the phone and call surgery or emergency and ask them to send me a pair of scrubs."

"Your supervisor could have called."

Fresh tears sprang to her eyes. Tears of frustration, this time. "You have no idea what life is like at the bottom of the totem pole, Dr. MacDowell."

"It's Jamie, remember?"

He shifted closer to her, studying her. Kendry regretted her words already, and the scrutiny they were causing. She had her pride. It would be awful for him to know how tempting his offer of marriage had been from a purely financial standpoint.

"Call me next time," he said, "but if I know you, you'll always have a spare set on hand now."

"I only have one set, if you haven't noticed."

"No, I didn't."

That almost made her smile. "Typical man."

"All scrubs look alike," he countered.

And you don't notice my appearance.

"My supervisor said I needed a second pair, anyway. I do wash my scrubs, you know, every single night. They're clean."

It was such a struggle, day after day, getting those scrubs in the sink, working the soap in, rinsing and rinsing and rinsing until the suds all came out. Hanging them up so they'd be dry by her next shift. It was a daily necessity, and she hadn't failed, not one day, to get it done. She greeted her children in clean clothes every morning.

She shifted in the scratchy new scrubs.

"Of course they're clean," Jamie said, and she could practically hear the frown in his voice.

"Thank you." Kendry sniffed again, sucking the tears back in an unladylike fashion, but she refused to weep anymore. "But my supervisor doesn't think it's possible for a person to wash her scrubs every single day, I guess."

She looked at Jamie fully for the first time since he'd sat down. The concern in his expression just about made the weeping start again, so she went back to looking up at the tree, focusing on the beauty of the branches against the sky. "It's okay. They'll dock my pay a little every week for the next eight weeks. I can survive eight weeks."

Desperation—fear—crawled up her throat a little bit, but she pushed it back down. She'd been told to clock out early today. Those extra six hours at the E.R. couldn't be paid as overtime after all, so she had to go home to prevent her time sheet from going over its weekly forty hours.

Still, even with her pay being docked for the cost of these scrubs, she'd pay the rent. That was most important, not to end up on a sidewalk, unprotected. Not to go backward, back to the homeless shelter.

She was so busy coming up with a new budget for the next eight weeks that Jamie caught her utterly, completely by surprise when he cupped her cheek in his hand and turned her to face him.

Her first thought was *his hand is so warm*.

Then, *his hand is so large*.

And as her eyes closed, so she wouldn't have to look into his and their unbearable concern, she thought, *his hand is so gentle*.

It was her undoing. Tears ran down her cheeks, no matter how hard she scrunched her eyes shut, but Jamie's warm, large, gentle hand drew her head to his shoulder. She leaned her forehead against the smooth cotton of his dress shirt, pressed her face into the male muscle underneath and sobbed.

Her careful plans had come undone. She'd nearly had enough saved to take the last course to become a certified medical assistant. Nearly. She thought longingly of the envelope labeled *school* that she had taped to the inside of her dresser drawer. She'd been managing to put five dollars in it, every week, on a schedule to start classes in February.

For the next eight weeks, though, her paycheck was going to get docked. She quickly did the math in her head, something she'd gotten good at. Her rent was an even one hundred dollars per week. These scrubs, with their contrast piping, were fifty dollars. Six dollars and twenty-five cents would be missing from her paycheck every week. There went the five dollars for tuition, plus another dollar and twenty-five cents that would have to come out of which envelope?

Food. There was no other choice. The court-ordered payment took more than half of her paycheck, but it was not negotiable.

She gulped and hiccupped, but couldn't stop a fresh waterfall of tears. Jamie's shirt was going to get soaked, but the weight of his hand was keeping her head on his shoulder.

She had to keep the tuition money. She had to. She'd never get out of debt if she didn't have the qualification for a better-paying position.

She could keep the five dollars for her tuition if she skipped lunch three or four days each week, but lunch was all she had. She always saved her plastic bowl and refilled it before leaving her shift, getting two meals for the price of one. Although Kendry had learned that she didn't need to eat much, even she couldn't get by without three days of meals.

Maybe she could drink the juice and eat the Popsicles that were kept on hand for the patients. Her conscience objected, though. She felt guilty enough today for eating the crackers that came with the soup when she hadn't bought soup. She could go without food one or two days a week, couldn't she?

Probably not. She would have to delay her classes. Again.

"I'll be okay," she said out loud. For Jamie's benefit, and her own. There was no law that said she had to start the CMA class in February. June would be here before she knew it.

She lifted her head, but Jamie pressed her back down into his shoulder and put his arm around her. "Be still for a moment," he said. "Relax."

Relax? She almost laughed. First, she was too anxious about money to relax. On top of that, Jamie was too damned handsome for a woman to think of relaxing in his embrace—and no matter how he viewed her, she was quite aware that she was a woman whenever he was near. He smelled good, warm and woodsy, and the shoulder she rested her forehead on was all muscle. It would be terribly easy to turn her face toward his throat and taste his skin. Since kissing him was out of the question—and would result in a humiliating scene for her—she faked relaxation as best she could.

Mostly, she wanted to run away from this man who was everything she wasn't.

"Don't let this supervisor get to you," Jamie said, his breath warm on her hair. "It sounds like she threw her authority around a little, but it's only a set of scrubs."

He thought her feelings were hurt, then? He thought this was an issue of pride?

Her own conscience prodded her: *Isn't it?* She was too proud to admit how poor she was, how far in debt she'd dug herself. The hole had been of her own doing; it was up to her to dig her way back out. Jamie was right. She was too proud to tell her supervisor why she couldn't afford the scrubs.

"Let things like that roll off your back. It doesn't matter what people say. You know your clothes are clean. I think your bangs look nice," he said.

That startled her into raising her head a little. She wiped her cheek with the back of her hand. "Excuse me?"

"Your bangs." He gestured toward them with one hand, nearly touching them, but not. "I think they look nice, even if you cut them yourself. Don't let the gossip get to you."

"I—I—" She had no idea where this new informa-tion fit in. "I don't understand." But she did. People in the hospital must have been making fun of her home-made haircut. Jamie had heard them.

Her humiliation was absolute. Everyone saw through her charade of respectability. Everyone scorned her at-tempts to act like she had a normal life and a normal job at this hospital. Everyone except Jamie.

Instead of scorning her, Jamie pitied her. For a month, she'd eaten lunch with him and let herself be-lieve he was her friend, but the truth was, he pitied her. A man didn't ask a woman to be his celibate wife if he didn't think she was rock-bottom hopeless.

Kendry sat all the way up, and this time he let her. Then he sat up, too, straightened his tie, and dusted her cracker crumbs off his lap. The cellophane wrapper she was still holding must not have been empty, after all.

Embarrassed, she tucked that fist into her own lap. "Sorry."

"No big deal. Sam makes a much bigger mess than you do."

"A big mess," she repeated. She forced a little laugh. "That about sums it up. I'm a big mess."

"I didn't say that."

Oh, but he had. It was the truth, and it hurt to hear. She'd made a mess of her life, and she knew it.

"Your hair looks nice. Your clothes are clean. You are never late to work, and you are exceptional at your job. You're not a mess, Kendry, and I don't want to hear you think that way about yourself."

Kendry didn't want to think about anything at all. She was exhausted. She bent to grab the plastic bag at her feet that held her dirty scrubs, the ones she had to go home and clean in a tiny bathroom sink that she shared with three other people, the sink she had to clean first, before she could clean her scrubs in it. She threw her trash in the bag.

"My life is a mess, Jamie. It's the truth. Sorry if it offends you."

"It's not that you offended me," he began, but then he stopped and practically glared at her. "Check that. Yes, you did offend me. I asked you to marry me. Do you think I'd ask a 'big mess' to be the mother of my child?"

There was no other kind of person he could have expected to say yes. Pain made her lash out.

"You want to secure some kind of permanent nanny for Sam. Your proposal wasn't what Prince Charming said to Cinderella, was it? 'Come to my castle and take care of my kid.'"

"I'm offering you much more than that. We'll be a family."

"You have a family. You need a babysitter. If you'd asked me to be your babysitter, I might have said yes. It depends if you pay better than the hospital."

Jamie stood abruptly. "It's not about money, and it isn't about babysitters, but if that's what it boils down to for you—"

She looked up at him, dry-eyed, angry. "That's exactly what it boiled down to, Jamie. You offered me marriage to get yourself a free babysitter. You thought I was so pitiful I'd take you up on it. Well, the answer is no."

"No? You're turning me down?"

She couldn't believe he still thought she'd say yes. Was she that pitiful, then?

Look at yourself. Crying over fifty-dollar scrubs. Eating free crackers. He must have thought you were a sure thing.

Pride kept her chin high and her voice even. "I'm not as desperate as you think, Dr. MacDowell. Of course I said no."

He left. Without another word, he walked toward the hospital with his usual stride. Purposeful, swift. Not a backward glance. Not a goodbye.

As she watched him walk away, her heart hurt even more than her empty stomach. Jamie wasn't heading for the E.R. He was going toward the tower that held the playroom. Kendry understood perfectly. She wished she could hold sweet Sam, rest her cheek on his perfectly soft hair and feel loved.

Instead, she had to go wait for the city bus.

With filthy scrubs in a trash bag.

With the horrible knowledge that she'd picked a fight with a man who didn't deserve it.

CHAPTER NINE

JAMIE WANTED HIS motorcycle back.

It was completely and utterly impractical for a father. Sam couldn't be transported on it, so Jamie had sold the bike to Quinn. He regretted that sale when he needed to clear his mind.

Kendry didn't want to be married to him. Kendry didn't want to be Sam's mother.

Twice in his life, Jamie had asked a woman to marry him. Twice, he'd been told no. At least Amina had chosen to stay in Afghanistan, where marriage to him was legally impossible, because she'd wanted to help her countrymen. But Kendry—

Jamie pushed the door open to the physicians' lounge in the E.R. with too much force, making it bang against the wall.

Kendry hadn't given him any reason at all. She'd sat on a bench and bawled over a set of new scrubs, and he'd felt sorry for her. *Sorry* for her, as if getting her feelings hurt fell anywhere on the same scale as saving children in a third-world nation.

Jamie rifled through the lab coat he'd left in the locker, looking for his truck keys. Quinn would use his truck while he used the bike, no questions asked. If Jamie had any hope of restoring a sense of calm, he needed to feel some speed and some wind and let his asinine, ridiculous feelings about Kendry get blown away by the highway.

That little scrap of a girl had insulted him. Kendry thought he was a simpleton for suggesting that her supervisor could have called the E.R. for fresh scrubs. *You have no idea what it's like to be at the bottom of the totem pole.*

Fine.

She didn't think his proposal was good enough. *Come to my castle and take care of my kid.*

Fine.

Jamie dug the motorcycle's key out of Quinn's gym bag, put his truck keys in its place and slammed the locker shut.

He'd said her hair looked nice, damn it. Wasn't that what women wanted to hear? Hell, he deserved an Oscar for his performance, trying to make her feel like she wasn't a big mess.

She *was* a big mess. She refused to do anything about her allergies, she was forever eating crackers and trailing crumbs, and she didn't care about getting new glasses.

Still, she'd turned down his marriage proposal. Life with a successful, decent man like himself hadn't been good enough for sloppy, messy Kendry Harrison.

He started to walk through the kitchenette, his gaze going to the coffeepot where the three nurses had smugly laughed at Kendry after calling her...

He stopped.

Calling her exactly what he'd just thought. He hadn't said "homely" or "street urchin" like they had, not exactly, but he was focusing on the surface things, on her physical appearance, when he'd asked her to marry him for deeper reasons.

He stared absently at the coffeepot, then at the wall behind it, automatically reading the piece of paper taped to the wall, the flyer that food services put out every week.

This Week's Specials:
Enchilada Casserole
Vegetarian Lasagna
Free refills on soup, Monday through Friday

Pieces started falling into place. Bits of information, coalescing into a new theory. The taped glasses, the refusal to buy over-the-counter allergy medicine—it all came together.

Free refills on soup, Monday through Friday.

He was an idiot. Blind. How many times had he teased Kendry for loving soup? Free refills—it was all she ate, all he ever saw her eat. God, she probably ate soup all day long.

Except today. She'd had no soup bowl on the picnic bench. Crackers, always the free crackers, but nothing else. Not when they were docking her pay for the cost of her scrubs.

He'd chalked up her tears to chafing under a supervisor's orders, but she'd been worried about the cost. He'd sat next to her on a picnic bench and lectured her about being too sensitive while she'd exchanged her lunch for scrubs she hadn't wanted.

Kendry wasn't some college kid, living on student loans. Kendry lived in poverty.

It was like a punch in the gut. He thought highly of

Kendry, very highly. She had every quality that would be important if she became Sam's mother. He enjoyed being around her. He thought of her as a friend.

And he, he who had grown up on a prosperous ranch, he who'd banked the military bonuses for being a doctor and for being in a combat zone, adding those extra thousands to the accounts he'd already inherited from his father, *he* had spent a month watching his friend, too thin as she was, eat bowl after bowl of free soup refills.

Jamie headed outside toward the park bench. Kendry wasn't there, and he'd already learned from the playroom staff that she was done for the day. He started running toward the parking lot, aware that he was turning heads. It didn't matter. He needed to find Kendry and make things right. Now. Her shift was over, so she'd be going home, and he had no idea where her home was.

Did she have a home?

He'd failed her. The woman was going to eat nothing today, nothing except crackers. With every pound of his foot on the pavement, the thought repeated in his mind: *I failed her.* He'd offered her marriage, confident she would accept, but he hadn't made sure she had a damned sandwich to eat.

Every moment it took to find the bike, to don the helmet, to fire up the engine, was another moment away from Kendry. Jamie drove the motorcycle through the labyrinth of hospital buildings, looking for one woman among the pedestrians, since it was now painfully obvious to him that Kendry couldn't afford a car.

He caught a glimpse of her—her hair, plain and

brown, her scrubs, new and pink—as she boarded the
city bus at the next corner. He shouted her name, but
his voice only bounced around inside the motorcycle
helmet.

The bus was easy to follow. It was harder to dodge
the black exhaust that bellowed out every time the bus
merged back into traffic, but Jamie stayed immediately
behind it, watching to see if Kendry was one of the pas-
sengers who stepped onto the pavement at each stop.

It was hardest of all to dodge his own thoughts.
He gave up trying. He deserved every mental lash he
gave himself. Every scrap of a memory that caused
him pain, he deserved.

*Just leave your tray, Dr. MacDowell. I'll take it up
with mine.* He'd walked away and never looked back
to see that she was undoubtedly buttering the roll he
hadn't wanted, or finishing the apple pie he'd only
eaten half of.

What kind of man let a woman starve in front of
him? The bus belched more black smoke, and he put
the motorcycle in gear to follow.

Primitive, caveman feelings he hadn't felt in ages
came to the fore. He was male and she was female.
He was bigger and stronger; he ought to have been
protecting her.

In Afghanistan, he—and probably every soldier
there, male and female alike—had felt the frustration
of not being able to protect the helpless, the children,
the women who still hid in their burqas, afraid to trust
that the Taliban would not return to power. They'd
all done what they could, both as soldiers and as individuals.

There had been native Afghanis willing to fight for

the helpless, as well. People like Amina. Near the end, as her pregnancy became obvious and the local situation deteriorated, he and Amina had fought, every day, about her desire to keep crusading and his desire to bring her to the States, to London, to anywhere safe. They'd never reconciled their goals as an unmarried, doomed couple.

In the end, none of it had mattered. Jamie hadn't been able to save Amina from the same thing that killed an appalling number of women in Afghanistan: childbirth.

He'd failed to convince Amina to stay with him.

He'd failed to convince Kendry.

He faltered, letting go of the motorcycle's throttle. The bus moved on without him.

He couldn't go through this again. He couldn't chase a woman and beg her to let him protect her, plead with her to stay where he could keep her safe.

He couldn't, he wouldn't, endure the heartache when the woman refused his offer of help.

Don't lose it, Jamie. This is Kendry you're thinking of, not Amina. Kendry isn't going to die if she refuses to live with you.

No, but she'd go hungry. Jamie would be damned before he'd let Kendry go hungry any longer.

The feelings were new, yet familiar at the same time. He'd felt this way about Amina when she'd told him she was pregnant, an absolute surety that he accepted the responsibility for one woman. He couldn't feel this protective of Kendry, too.

Sam's second mother? You don't think you should feel protective of her?

Put that way, it made perfect sense that he needed to

take care of Kendry. If they married, he'd be the provider, after all. He felt protective of Sam, so he was feeling protective of Sam's new mother.

Jamie turned the throttle, caught up to the bus. This possessive feeling was completely different than his feelings for Amina.

His cell phone vibrated in his pocket again, as it had at least a half dozen times during this low-speed, pollution-filled pursuit. He wouldn't answer it while he was in traffic. He'd sewn up the aftermath of too many drivers checking their cell phones while on the road.

At last, in an obviously low-income neighborhood, Kendry stepped off the bus.

She looked as pitiful as the hospital grapevine said. The new pink scrubs hung too loosely on her frame. Her eyes were downcast, her ponytail drooped, and it looked like raising one hand to shield her eyes from the Texas sun took all her energy. Jamie felt a twisting emotion, deep inside.

He pulled over to the curb and silenced his bike. She'd turned on the sidewalk and was headed toward him, so he took off his helmet and waited until she came closer. She didn't see him, shading her eyes the way she was. It sickened him to realize she couldn't afford sunglasses.

"Kendry."

"Dr. MacDowell! What are you doing here?"

For a second, his mind went blank. He was here because she was here—but that wasn't what he was supposed to say. He'd come to tell her one hundred things. He started with the most important one. "I'm sorry. I'm so sorry, Kendry. You were right. My proposal came out all wrong."

She walked closer to him, so he stayed seated on the bike, keeping their faces on the same level.

"You didn't have to follow me home for that," she said. "I knew you'd change your mind. You'd have to be crazy to really want to marry me for any reason." She held her bag of old scrubs away from her body.

"I haven't changed my mind about anything." Homeless people leaned against the wall of the gas station behind her, making an apathetic audience. "Sam hasn't changed his mind about you, either. I still want you to marry me."

She made something of a little squeaky sound at that, and looked away. The incessant vibrating of his cell phone was getting to him, so he impatiently took it out of his leather jacket's pocket, glancing at the screen as he silenced it.

Sam.

Jamie had left him safely at the hospital's playroom, of course. He wasn't due to pick him up for hours yet, because he'd been scheduled for an after-lunch staff meeting—a meeting he'd blown off to follow a city bus. The message on the phone's screen made his heart stop for a second. Finances and soup and scrubs were wiped from his brain.

"What's wrong?" Kendry asked.

"Sam," he managed to say. "He's in the E.R."

"Oh, God."

"Let's go." He gestured toward the back of the bike, and Kendry only hesitated for a second before she got on. It was all so obvious. He needed to be with Sam, and he needed Kendry to be there, too, by his side—or rather, his son needed Kendry to be by *his* side.

He handed her the helmet. "Put that on." He stood to kick-start the bike.

Over the roar of the engine, Kendry hollered, "You wear it."

He shook his head impatiently. It wasn't against the law to ride a bike without a helmet in Texas; it was just a foolish risk. Desperate times called for desperate measures. As imperative as it had been to get to Kendry, it was now to get back to Sam—but he was taking Kendry with him, no question. He'd not leave her to starve for the rest of the day.

"Put the helmet on, damn it."

When she tried to balance her plastic bag on her thigh in order to take the heavy helmet, he picked the bag up and hurled it toward the gas station's open trash can. "I'm getting you new scrubs."

He was a jackass for giving her orders. He shrugged out of the leather jacket, then twisted toward her, holding it open so she could put her arms in it. "Please. Put this on, please." She was fragile. He didn't want her hurt. Period.

"Be extra careful," she said, as she tentatively set her hands at his hips.

"Hold on tighter. Like this." He pulled her hands all the way around his stomach, then let go and pulled away from the curb, hands on the handlebars.

Hang in there, Sam. I'm on my way. Kendry and I are on our way.

CHAPTER TEN

KENDRY CLUNG TO Jamie hard and prayed even harder. They were parking under the eaves by the E.R.'s sliding glass door in half the time it took the city bus to get there. It was startling how close she lived to the hospital, really. Commuting by bus took so much time, Kendry had always felt so far away.

Jamie had not sped nor broken a single traffic law the entire way back, but Kendry had felt his tension in her body, pressed as she'd been against his back. There was nothing she could do to comfort him, nothing she could say to reassure a man whose child was in his own E.R. Maybe she'd kept her arms wrapped around him a little too tightly, wanting things to turn out okay for him. Maybe he'd assumed she'd been scared to fall off the motorcycle.

The security guard leaped up to stop him as Jamie headed through the sliding glass doors like he owned them. With a curt nod at the guard, Jamie kept walking. Kendry wasn't swift enough, so the guard held out his hand and stopped her before she could enter the building. "Who's he?"

"That's Dr. MacDowell," Kendry answered, looking through the glass door, watching Jamie's back recede as he strode swiftly down the linoleum aisle toward the nurses' station. Toward Sam. She felt ill with worry.

"And who are you?"

Kendry hesitated, unsure what to say. Confessing she was an off-duty orderly who was unrelated to any patient in the E.R. wasn't going to get her anywhere.

The security guard crossed his arms over his chest in something of an aggressive stance. "You can't leave that bike here."

Kendry still wore Jamie's leather jacket. It swallowed her whole rather than lend her any biker swagger, but she decided to act like Jamie, anyway. She nodded once at the guard like Jamie had. "I'll tell him to move it," she said, and walked toward the doors like a woman with a purpose.

It worked. The guard didn't reach out to stop her, the doors whooshed open, and Kendry walked purposefully down the aisle, shrugging out of the leather coat as she went. She got close enough to Jamie to almost make out what the nurse was saying to him, picking out words like *cyanotic* and *oxygen*.

"Which bed?" Jamie demanded impatiently.

Kendry wanted to shake the nurse. *He's not this baby's doctor; he's his father. He wants to hold his son, not hear a medical report.*

Jamie headed for bed three. So did Kendry, but another hand reached out to stop her. "There you are," the nurse said. "We're low on linens."

"I'm sorry, but I'm off the clock." Kendry watched Jamie disappear into one of the private cubicles that had a door. Bed three.

The nurse was looking at Kendry's scrubs and frowning. "Where's your ID?"

"I'm off the clock," she repeated. "I'm sorry, but I've got to go see a patient."

"Who?" the nurse asked, as though it were a fantastical improbability that Kendry might know a single patient personally.

It burned. Kendry had never felt so impatient in her life. Sam was here, sweet little Sam, and she had no idea how he was doing. Jamie wanted her to be with him—with Sam, that is. The guard and now the nurse were stopping her.

"Sam MacDowell," she said through gritted teeth. "He was brought down from the peds ward."

The nurse frowned harder. "His father just got here. It's family only back here. You know that."

"But…it's Sam. I want to see him."

"If you're not here to work, you can leave through the waiting room. HIPAA regulations are very clear about—"

"Kendry." The voice that spoke her name was quiet, authoritative, male.

She and the nurse turned toward Jamie. He was standing just outside the door of bed three, his hand held out to her. Feeling like the out-of-place orderly she was, Kendry thought he wanted his jacket back. She put it in his outstretched hand.

Jamie frowned at her, like the guard and the nurse, but he took the jacket and very deliberately held out his other hand. Kendry ignored the heat in her cheeks as she put her hand in his. His fingers closed around hers, warm and firm, and he tugged her with him into the room.

Sammy, so tiny, lay in the middle of an adult-sized treatment bed. The side rails had been raised, and some additional padded buffers had been placed around him to keep him from rolling off.

Sammy didn't look like he was in any condition to roll anywhere. One of his arms was being held straight by a green plastic splint, a tiny needle and thin IV tube coming out of the crease at his elbow. A pediatric-sized oxygen mask still looked too big on his little face, covering his nose and mouth—and his whole chin, too.

"Oh, Sammy," Kendry cooed, tears blurring her vision as she dropped Jamie's hand and bent over the bed, clutching the rail's cold metal in both hands. "How's my favorite guy?"

Sammy turned toward the sound of her voice immediately. After one blink, his mouth opened wide in a big, mostly toothless smile behind the clear oxygen mask. Kendry thought her heart would burst at his cheerful attitude in his dismal situation. She couldn't help it; she had to touch him.

"I'm so glad to see you, too," she said, trying to keep her voice even as she placed her hand on his belly. Sam wriggled a little and lifted his splinted arm a fraction, but the effort apparently reminded him that he was somewhat pinned down, and he frowned.

Just like his father. As clear as day, Kendry saw Jamie's facial expression on little Sammy's face. Her favorite little guy looked just like her big dream guy. Emotions filled her, too many to name.

Jamie cleared his throat. "I think he wants you to pick him up."

As she'd done a hundred times for other patients, Kendry dropped the side railing to the bed. As she had never done before, she picked up the patient, kissed him on his soft hair and closed her eyes in gratitude that she could hug him close. "You scared us, Sammy." She kept her eyes closed for a moment longer, then stole another kiss. Sam settled into her heavily, and she could tell he'd be asleep in moments. She sat on the bed with him in her arms.

Not looking up from Sam, she asked Jamie, "Why is he here?"

"Respiratory distress."

"But he's breathing okay now?"

"Time will tell. Someone left him on his back in his crib with a bottle."

Appalled, she looked up at Jamie. "That's against policy for all the infants, let alone one with Sammy's swallowing problems."

"I know." The mattress gave a little as Jamie sat down next to her, their thighs touching as he patted Sam's back. After the motorcycle ride, she found it wasn't so unnerving to be near him physically. It was even comforting. Sheltering. It made her feel better when the sight of Sammy in his medical gear had her shaken up.

Jamie gently took the oxygen mask off Sam. "He probably choked on the formula. He may have inhaled a bit of it into his lungs. Between the choking and the coughing, he was screaming, of course. Given his heart defect, he started to turn blue from lack of oxygen."

"Oh, Sammy." Kendry rested her cheek on the top of his head. She didn't want to put him down ever again. "What happens next?"

"We wait and see if he develops pneumonia from the formula getting in his lungs—if it got in his lungs. His coughing and gagging may have kept it out, like reflexes are supposed to. The respiratory distress could have been from the heart defect, not from liquid in the lungs. We'll find out this week. The hard way."

"Poor baby," Kendry whispered. "If only I had been on duty."

Jamie raised his eyebrows a little at that. "If only I *hadn't* been on duty." He surprised Kendry by standing suddenly, looking like he wanted to pace. The treatment room was too small for a man his size to take more than a half step. "Don't start feeling guilty about anything, Kendry. It will eat you up. God knows I've already screwed up enough things for ten parents to feel guilty about."

"You didn't screw up anything." She kept her voice low as Sam fell asleep. "It's not your fault someone gave Sam a bottle while he was lying flat on his back."

Jamie nearly laughed. "Yeah."

"This isn't your fault." Kendry studied him, worried. He looked a little wild, a little bit like a man on the brink, not like the controlled doctor she knew.

"I should have caught that cleft palate the day he was born."

"Don't be ridiculous. I'm sure—" She stopped, catching herself as she was about to blunder into what was probably painful territory.

"You're sure of what?"

"I'm sure that had to have been the least of your worries the day he was born." Kendry bit her lip and watched him anxiously, but Jamie didn't seem fazed by her statement. She'd only learned two nights ago that Sam's mother had died during his birth, but Jamie had been living with that horrible knowledge for nine months.

"Sam shouldn't have been born in that situation to start with. I got *him* out of Afghanistan, at least, and I've been pretending I know what I'm doing, but hell,

Kendry... I don't know anything. I've failed him in a million ways. I didn't know how to hold him to feed him, for God's sake."

"But you learned. That's the important—"

"I haven't been able to get his Social Security number yet. I know he needs these surgeries, but I keep putting them off, because I don't know how to handle his recovery and my job at the same time. Hell, my family thinks I'm crazy not to hire someone else to take care of him. Maybe they are seeing the obvious. Maybe they can see that I can't take care of a baby."

"You can so. You're a wonderful parent."

"I can't give him all he needs. He needs so much. He needs a mother, too, not just me, but I—" He gestured toward her. "I can't even make a friend without screwing everything up for her. I've made you the object of gossip. I threw away your clothes an hour ago."

The scrubs were going to be a problem, but she wasn't about to lay her burdens on this man. "I'll deal with it, Jamie."

"I don't want you to. Can't you see that?"

He loomed over her, intense and serious. She kept Sammy in her arms between them.

"I don't want you to handle it," he said. "I want to take care of it for you. I want to take care of Sam, to provide for both of you, to do something right for once. I'm so tired of things going wrong. The war, Amina getting pregnant when she shouldn't have, dying when she shouldn't have, Sammy needing emergency care when he shouldn't, you needing a damned meal when you shouldn't. If I was half the man I should be, none of that would happen."

"Oh, Jamie." Kendry hadn't realized his pain, the

depth of his feeling of letting everyone down. The past year of his life had to have been harrowing. Like everyone on earth, he needed a break. He needed something to go right.

"You have a wonderful little boy here," she began.

"Yes, I do," Jamie said, and the old Jamie was back. At least, the determined and confident man was back, the one who saved strangers' lives in the E.R. Only now his cool and clear focus wasn't on a patient. It was on her.

"My son is a wonderful boy. He's fallen in love with you, because you are a wonderful woman. Whether you marry me or not, Kendry Harrison, you are not going to go hungry again, and you aren't going to struggle for material things, because you deserve better than that. Sam thinks so, and so do I. But I'd rather marry you. I want to do something right. I want to be normal, and have a family, and have the legal and moral right to care for you and Sam, to build something real."

He moved toward her, as if he wanted to pull them both into his arms, but stopped short and instead stood over them, arms open, empty.

"But you're not in love with me." Kendry whispered the words as she met his clear gaze, wishing with all her heart she weren't stating a simple truth.

Very slowly, very slightly, Jamie shook his head. "My heart was buried with the woman I gave it to."

He reached out to lift her face with a touch of his warm fingers under her chin. "But that doesn't mean I'm not offering you something good. Something real. I'm offering you all I have left in me to give, and that includes my son."

Jamie dropped his hand to lightly touch Sam's hair.

"I'm not offering you an easy child to love. I'm offering you one with a lot of health problems. A future of surgeries and therapies and rehab. The more you love Sam, the more it will break your heart when he's in pain. But I—I think he's worth it. I can't imagine living without him."

Her heart stopped when Jamie stopped touching Sam's hair and instead cupped her cheek. "And lately, I keep imagining a life with you. Kendry Harrison, I want to marry you."

He hadn't really asked a question, but she answered him anyway.

"Yes."

He didn't love her. He'd never love her.

But she loved him.

CHAPTER ELEVEN

"YES."

Kendry had said yes. The rush of adrenaline had been instant. Unexpected.

It was all Jamie could do to play it cool and wait by the motorcycle for Quinn to show up with his truck, when he wanted to grab Kendry by the hand and run to the courthouse before she could change her mind.

Quinn pulled up in Jamie's practical extended-cab truck and parked it under the eaves. He had the engine off and was rounding the hood when he spotted Kendry holding Sam and stopped short. Jamie stayed where he was, leaning on the motorcycle, arms crossed over his chest. As he watched Quinn take in the scene, he started to grin.

"I believe you've already met my wife to be, Kendry."

Quinn lifted a brow in question, looking so much like their father that Jamie felt a brief pang.

"Well." That was it. That was all Quinn could come up with.

Jamie would have enjoyed the moment of Quinn's speechlessness longer, but Kendry was looking acutely embarrassed. "It's not like we're—"

Jamie put his hand on Kendry's shoulder—God, she was all bones—and dropped the bike keys in Quinn's hand. "We've got to run. Thanks for bringing the truck back so quickly."

"I had no desire to continue to drive around town in a truck with a baby's car seat in the backseat. It could've killed my reputation with the ladies."

"Or it could've made it. Babies are chick magnets. Sam caught me a wife, see?" Jamie nodded toward Kendry, willing her to not look scared to death of his brother.

Before Jamie could think of the right thing to say to put her at ease, Quinn snapped out of his shock and proceeded to give Kendry a bear hug, despite Sam in her arms, and a kiss on the cheek for good measure.

"Welcome to the family, then, sis."

Good old Quinn, the mathematical cardiologist. Like their father had always done, Quinn neatly categorized everything he encountered. If Kendry was Jamie's wife, then that made her family. Family got a hug and a welcome. Plain and simple.

Dad would have acted like Quinn.

Somehow, the idea that his father would have accepted Kendry as his daughter-in-law made the knot in Jamie's gut feel just a little—just slightly—looser. Which made no sense at all, because Jamie was trying to be a different kind of father than the one who'd raised him. Or rather, different than the one who hadn't been there much at all to raise him.

Impatiently, Jamie snapped Sam into his car seat in the back bench of the pickup truck. Whether his father would have approved or not was irrelevant. If his father had taught him anything, it was that if a boy didn't have a mother, he'd be a lonely child, indeed.

It was time to get Kendry Harrison to the courthouse.

KENDRY SAT IN the backseat of the truck's cab so she could keep an eye on Sam. Her little guy was sleeping hard, exhausted from his afternoon of choking and coughing, but he was otherwise fine. Kendry couldn't help looking at him every two minutes to reaffirm that fact.

Jamie didn't need her beside him, anyway. During the few minutes they'd waited for Quinn to arrive with the truck, Jamie had used his phone to learn everything he needed to know about getting married in Austin.

They'd breezed through a fast-food drive-through on the way to their first stop, since Jamie insisted she needed a burger and a shake. Kendry felt a little guilty for not putting up much of a fight on that point. Then they'd driven on to the Travis County Clerk of Courts, which wasn't in the main courthouse, but rather in a one-story plaza in an unremarkable part of town. Unremarkable, if she didn't count the building on the opposite side of the street, a warehouse whose sign was a two-story-tall candy cane with a lamb dangling from it. The candy cane looked to be leaning away from the old candy factory it marked, cantilevered at a crazy angle with its motorcycle-sized lamb dangling by a thread…

It was all so bizarre. This whole day was bizarre. Kendry slurped the last drop of the shake as quietly as she could. She looked at Sam. He was sleeping peacefully, but it was quite possible that his lungs were battling an infection while she sipped a strawberry shake.

The clerk's offices weren't empty, but it seemed all the people they ran into were on their way out of the building. Perhaps the good citizens of Austin were in a rush to get back to their jobs after running an errand on their lunch hour. Whatever the reason, she and Jamie and Sammy were the only ones eager to go into the government building, rather than out of it.

Eager? Was she eager to reach the marriage license window?

This was not, ever, the way she'd imagined getting married. Not in a rush. Not wearing scrubs that still felt stiff and itchy in their newness. Not lugging a sleeping baby in his car seat, and not with a man who wasn't in love with her.

But he did love her, in some small way. Or rather, he loved the idea of making her Sam's mother. He loved the idea of being a settled, married man. He was grateful to her.

And she, Kendry Harrison, was settling for less than she really wanted. Again. An orderly instead of a nurse. A mother instead of a lover. She should stop this marriage.

"The marriage license is seventy-one dollars. We only take cash."

The clerk was more concerned with the cash than she was with verifying that the two people standing in front of her were eligible to be married. A casual look at their driver's licenses was all it took for the paperwork to cross the counter.

"You have to wait three days before you can get married," the clerk explained.

Kendry saw Jamie's pen stop in midstroke on the paperwork.

"Three days?" he asked.

"There's a seventy-two-hour waiting period."

Three days. This crazy idea that today, a random Thursday in September, would be her wedding day, ended. They had time to come to their senses. Jamie surely would change his mind, and she would not be his wife.

She looked at the set of his jaw, at his close-cropped hair, military in its style, at the way he kept one hand on Sam's car seat, always keeping that baby safe, although the seat was securely sitting on a wide desk.

Suddenly, she didn't want to wait. Jamie would change his mind, and she would lose him. And lose Sam. And lose the feeling of being wanted and needed.

She was worried about compromising, about settling for being Jamie's platonic wife. But when faced with not being his wife at all, she realized this was one compromise she was willing to make. She wanted, more than anything, to get married on this Thursday to this man, while wearing brand-new pink scrubs and holding her brand-new sleeping son.

"Three days will be Sunday," Jamie said.

"Yep," the clerk said, after dutifully checking her desk calendar.

"I'm in the army. I have to report to my new unit tomorrow night. Friday."

"Oh," the clerk said, brightening. "If you're active-duty military, you don't have to wait. Just show your military ID to the justice of the peace. The closest one who might do a wedding today is at the courthouse on Guadalupe Street."

Jamie looked as relieved as Kendry felt. Briskly, he held the door open for her, then drew her to his side as they headed for the truck. "Let's go right now. Today."

He really wants to marry me.

Kendry smiled at him.

He didn't smile back but gave her the smallest of squeezes before letting go. "I have to turn in my active-duty ID when I report to my reserve unit tomorrow night. We made it in the nick of time."

Or maybe he was just an efficient kind of groom.

EFFICIENT WAS AN understatement. Her actual wedding had been a blur, a handing over of paperwork and IDs, a local judge who was willing to spend his break between scheduled hearings to earn an extra hundred dollars, and a civil exchange of vows. The judge skipped the part about exchanging rings and pronounced them man and wife. Jamie had quickly thanked him before the judge could say anything like, "You may now kiss the bride," so that part was eliminated as easily as the rings. Minutes later, Jamie was checking his watch as he opened the passenger door for Kendry.

"I think Sam's going to sleep a little longer," he said. "Let's go replace those scrubs I threw away."

Kendry began her married life at a big-box store, pushing a shopping cart and keeping an eye on Sam. He slept in the car seat, which snapped into place on the cart's handle. On their way to the back of the store, Jamie passed a display for the melt-in-the-mouth kind of allergy medicine. "This one works fast," he said, "so take it now, and you'll be feeling better by the time we leave."

She meekly obeyed the doctor's orders, especially after the man opened the package and put the pill in her hand. They had to pay for the opened package, so there was no sense arguing. She could practically see Jamie checking an item off his imaginary mental list: *Treat allergies. Check.*

In the uniform department, Kendry carefully selected one set of scrubs in her size. Jamie grabbed

four more sets and tossed them in the cart. He made a
beeline for the shoe department. "I don't think Sam's
going to sleep long enough for me to get you something nicer, but these will be better than nothing for
work tomorrow."

Kendry looked down at her sneakers. Compared
to the new pink scrubs, they looked horribly worn.
She wanted to point out that these would last another
day, but Jamie was already halfway down the aisle of
women's shoes. It took her longer to try on sneakers
than it had to say "I do," although she only tried on two
pair. When she said, "These fit fine," Jamie produced
a pocketknife, cut the tags off the new ones and threw
her old pair into the box and then the cart.

It was embarrassing to see his hands handling her
battered sneakers. She gave up pretending this was
a normal shopping trip on a normal day, and silently
followed Jamie through the store, mustering a smile
and a nod when he asked her if she needed socks, too.

Get the orderly outfitted for work tomorrow. Check.

Jamie was practically in full E.R. doctor mode, a
man on a mission, and he didn't need her input. He led
the way to the baby aisle. Kendry kept calculating how
much it would all cost. The diapers and formula alone
were enough to pay her rent. Jamie didn't seem to care.
In fact, he kept adding more baby items to the cart,
more concerned with which brand of teething biscuits
Sam would enjoy than with which brand cost the least.

Kendry hadn't set foot in a major supermarket in
a year. It was too time-consuming and expensive to
switch buses to get from the inner city out to the sub-
urbs, so she bought things like cereal in overpriced
gas stations. She'd forgotten how colorful the super-

stores were, how high the ceilings, how many different brands of everything filled shelf after shelf. It was dazzling. It made her want to cry.

Sam began to cry instead. Kendry unbuckled him from the seat and held him close, grateful for the comfort she received from comforting him. *He* was important. *He* was what it was all about.

"Here, let me hold Sam while you get what you need." Jamie lifted Sam off her hip with a "hey, buddy," and waited patiently by the cart.

Kendry looked around, then felt herself blush. She'd followed Jamie into the cosmetics aisle.

"I don't wear makeup." She tried not to squirm when Jamie automatically looked at her face—not at her, but at the surface of her. Her skin and stuff. She couldn't stand it; she put her hands on her blushing cheeks. "I probably should, I know, but—"

"Why should you?"

She dropped her hands. "I don't know. It gives women a more professional appearance, I guess." As soon as she said that, she thought of her hasty, homemade haircut and tugged on her bangs.

Jamie spoke to Sam. "Do you think Kendry needs to look more professional?"

Sam cooed and stuck his fingers in his mouth.

"Me, neither," he said, smiling at Sam before turning back to Kendry. "We like you just the way you are. If you want makeup, go for it. If you don't, that's fine, too." He nodded at the shelves behind her. "You at least need some shampoo and items like that."

"Oh! Shampoo!" She whirled to the shelf behind her. She'd been using one bar of soap for her face, body and hair for so long now, she'd forgotten the luxury of having separate products. Soap was soap, and they all did the same job, but Jamie would think she was weird if she didn't use shampoo, wouldn't he? She didn't want him to think she was weird.

That was her excuse to start touching the bottles. She even picked up a couple, popping their caps open for a quick sniff of heavenly fruits and flowers. Thanks to that tiny allergy pill, her nose was actually drying up enough to smell something. The ginger and lemongrass shampoo smelled so good, she held it up for Sam to smell, too. Then she put it back on the shelf and bent down to pick up the economy-sized bottle of the store-brand shampoo.

"Okay," she said, placing the bottle in the cart. "Next aisle."

"Kendry." Jamie sounded hoarse. He looked angry.

Her hand hovered over the bottle. "I'm sorry, is it too much? I wasn't thinking—I mean, it probably looks greedy, doesn't it? But it's cheaper per ounce and it won't expire—"

"Kendry." But Jamie didn't say anything else. Instead, with Sam in one arm, he grabbed the ginger-lemongrass shampoo off the shelf and placed it in the cart. Then he grabbed the matching conditioner, too.

She was going to cry. It was humiliating, being so poor, making do, pretending you didn't want all the products you couldn't afford. Sam started fussing and reaching for her, wriggling to get down from his father's arms. Children had a way of picking up the tension around them.

Jamie handed Sam to her. "Money's been tight for you, I can tell, but we're a family now. Sam deserves the best I can give him, and Sam's mother deserves the same. Please, pick out whatever you need."

He touched her under the chin, a move she was certain he meant to be comforting. Maybe, like Sam, Jamie could sense that she was on edge. For the first time in hours, he smiled at her. "We'll still be able to send Sam to college, I promise."

She smiled back, because she wanted to pretend everything was okay, that she wasn't the most pitiful bride ever, and this wasn't the least romantic wedding day in history. Then she threw into the cart a facial cleanser and a lotion that had sunscreen in it.

Just as they were leaving the aisle, she grabbed a lip gloss and tossed it in with the rest, telling herself it had nothing to do with the warmth of the man's fingers as he'd lifted her chin.

CHAPTER TWELVE

THE TRIP TO the superstore landed Kendry in an optometrist's office. She'd paused at the rack of reading glasses that looked like the ones Sammy had broken. Jamie's interrogation had begun, and he'd insisted she get a proper prescription. She'd agreed to make an appointment. Soon.

Jamie's idea of soon was to call a friend, an optometrist who immediately made room in her schedule for them. Kendry suspected the optometrist, who was very pretty and very blonde, wasn't terribly thrilled to find out she was helping a female friend of Jamie's and not Jamie himself.

If she finds out Jamie is no longer a bachelor, she's really going to be unhappy.

She didn't find out. When they were alone in the exam room and the optometrist needed Kendry's last name for the vision prescription, Kendry said "Harrison" without thinking, and that was that.

Next patient.

When the staff member who was supposed to help Kendry select new frames for that prescription began fetching frames from displays labeled Versace and Gucci, Kendry had to protest.

"I need something for everyday. Nothing fancy. I'm with babies all day, and I'm not always fast enough to dodge them, you see?" She waved the old taped frames, which she held in her hand, hoping her explanation accounted for dime-store plastic in this shiny world of designer frames.

Thanks to the dilating eye drops Kendry had been given, the office grew brighter as her vision grew blurrier. By the time Kendry was persuaded to order the wire-thin, flexible frames that a child could bend without harming, along with invisible lenses that were supposed to be nearly impossible to break, a headache was clearly starting. The saleswoman placed the taped-up old frames in a new case and assured her they'd put in a rush order—as a professional courtesy, of course.

Kendry tried to muster a smile before returning to the waiting room. She was grateful that the office provided disposable sunglasses, a thin rectangle of plastic brown film with paper earpieces.

Jamie was talking quietly to Sam, who sat in his father's lap and waved his empty bottle in the air, turning it this way and that with serious concentration. Kendry was content to stand, unnoticed, and watch Jamie and Sam, together. It was the first time Jamie had looked relaxed since...

She racked her brain. Since the night they'd worked together in the E.R.? The night he'd sat on the bench with the rain falling beyond them, right before he'd told her they didn't have *that* kind of relationship?

Kendry watched him a moment more. Somehow, when a big man held a little baby, it made him look all the bigger and more masculine. Jamie smiled while Sammy babbled at him as if he were speaking in complete baby sentences, explaining something fully, and

Kendry could see the traces of laugh lines at the corner of her new husband's eyes.

Yes, he'd been unhappy since that rainy night, but now that they'd gotten married, he looked relaxed again. Her heart did a little flip. Being married to her mattered to him.

Sammy spotted her, promptly let go of his bottle so that it clattered onto the floor, then held up both arms with his little hands open. "Me."

Jamie looked her way immediately. Like watching something bad happen in slow motion, Kendry watched a frown take over Jamie's expression. Maybe even anger.

Her heart fell. He'd never been angry with her, not until today. Their wedding day.

"You need sunglasses," he said, scooping the bottle up with one hand, hiking up Sam in his other arm. He practically stalked toward her.

"O-only for the next couple of hours," she said, alarmed. "These drops wear off fast."

"This is Texas. You need sunglasses. Good ones, to protect your eyes from UV rays." He gestured for her to go ahead of him, back toward the frames and mirrors, then pulled the chair out for her. She sat.

I'm not your patient, she wanted to say. *I'm not your employee.* But because the saleswoman was eagerly standing by, Kendry held her tongue.

Jamie removed the disposable plastic rectangle from her face and started slipping sunglasses on her himself. He was quick about it, focused, like he was choosing the right needle for a medical procedure. The pair Jamie liked best cost more than three weeks of her rent. They were still cheaper than the other sunglasses that made his cut, so Kendry agreed with his choice.

As Jamie handed his credit card to the receptionist, Sam started his fussy cry, the one that said he'd had enough and this wasn't where he wanted to be or what he wanted to be doing. Kendry bounced him on her hip as she waited by the exit. "Me, too, honey, I feel just the same," she whispered.

Jamie walked up and reached around her to push the door open. For a moment, the three of them brushed bodies as Jamie gestured for Kendry to leave first. Sam grabbed for her new sunglasses.

"No," she said, jerking her head an inch to dodge his inaccurate fist. "We can't afford to break these."

Jamie spoke quietly in her ear, words that sounded measured, but like he said them through clenched teeth. "Yes, we can."

Kendry squeezed Sam a little tighter as they walked to the car. Sam was tired. She was tired.

Jamie was angry.

This wasn't where she wanted to be or what she wanted to be doing, so she took a breath and dared to speak her mind.

"I think it's time for me to go home."

HOME. THE WORD paralyzed Jamie for a moment.

Today was the first day of making a new home for his son and himself. Could a man make a home with a woman he didn't love?

Sudden doubt filled him.

Sam protested being set in his car seat, although Jamie had parked the truck in the shade of a tree, and the Texas heat wasn't unbearable in September at this late hour of the day. Out of the corner of Jamie's eye, he could see Kendry standing with her shoulders and her ponytail drooping, waiting to get in the backseat next to Sam.

"Let's go get something to eat first, before we go home." He just needed time. Just a little longer before he brought Kendry to his house. Permanently.

Did you carry a bride over the threshold when you were going to be parents and partners, but not lovers?

"Aren't you worried about Sam?" she asked.

Jamie glanced through the open door at Sam, who had settled into his straps. "I'm always worried about Sam," he said.

Now I'm worried about my wife on top of that.

He couldn't say that out loud, not to a woman who was clearly too thin beneath her new scrubs and sneakers and sunglasses.

Kendry rubbed her forehead as she looked at Sam, too. "Maybe he needs to get home so he can sleep in his own crib. What if he's fighting off pneumonia at this very second? What if we expose him to more germs at a restaurant? What if—"

"I don't waste a lot of time on if. There's always another if waiting to happen."

Kendry looked away from him quickly.

Jamie looked in the other direction. That had sounded kind of harsh, he supposed. Kendry had no idea that the main reason Jamie had wanted to be married was to prevent a big State Department *if* from happening. She could become the key to Sam staying in Jamie's custody, if...

Jamie was glad to have Kendry on his team and by his side, yet here he was, making a mess of their first day together. He still hadn't found his balance after chasing down her bus at lunchtime. He'd practically forced her back to the E.R. with him, then to the licensing office, the courthouse, the grocery store, the optometrist. He hadn't stopped to catch his breath, which meant she hadn't had a chance to, either. "Let's go somewhere we can sit for dinner. Sam will be fine."

She looked back at him then, but he couldn't read her expression behind the sunglasses. Her shoulders rose, then fell slightly, and he imagined he'd heard her sigh as she waited patiently for him to give her further instructions. She was so good at that, at waiting patiently while nurses and doctors and patients made their demands.

He didn't want his wife's life to be that way. When they were off duty, he wanted her to be his partner. Instead, he'd been dragging her in and out of buildings all day, telling her what to buy. Hell, he'd even chosen those sunglasses, and now he was informing her that she would eat in a sit-down restaurant...

"Unless you want drive-through?" he asked, feeling ludicrously unsure of what to say next.

"I have a headache, and I'd like to go home." Kendry said it simply, as politely as a schoolchild. Her demeanor said she held as much hope as a student might when suggesting that a teacher change his plans.

"Maybe you have a headache from hunger. There are a couple of different places to eat near my house."

Her eyebrows lifted a little, shifting the bangs that brushed the top of the dark frames. "I meant my home, not your house. I'd like to go to my home now. Unless... you aren't working the night shift tonight, are you?"

Jamie shook his head, silently. They'd only been

married a few hours, and she wanted to be alone. She wanted to leave him. And Sam. She wanted to leave *them*.

She had her own life to get back to, her own agenda. It was like arguing with Amina all over again. They weren't on the same team; they didn't share the same priorities. His head swam, but he tried to listen to Kendry's next words.

"Then if you don't need me to watch Sam tonight, you can take me to my place." She said it patiently, so very patiently, like she was speaking to a child.

He was no child. He was her husband. Her husband, damn it.

"You're not the babysitter. We're married. It goes without saying, we now live together. We'll get something to eat, then we'll go to my house."

Kendry didn't move. She just stood there, wilting in the setting sun, unreadable in her sunglasses.

Jamie felt like a jerk for what seemed like the millionth time that day. "We can stop at your place and pack up your things first, although I thought we bought enough stuff to get you through the night and to work tomorrow."

"You bought that stuff."

"What?"

"You did. You decided we would go to the store. You decided which store, and you bought that stuff. You decided to get me glasses. You decided which shampoo I would use—"

"Because you were going to buy the cheapest thing—"

"Because I don't have any money! I was being reasonable. Rational. Responsible."

"You have money now. Pardon me if I don't want

my wife to wear plastic film on her face when she needs sunglasses."

"I don't have a dime. I'm not bringing anything to this marriage. Pardon me if I don't feel easy about spending someone else's money on myself. And—and—and pardon me for needing all this stuff in the first place. I'm sorry your wife embarrasses you with her taped-up glasses, but I didn't ask you to fix me. This is our first day of marriage, and I thought this was going to be all about Sam. Instead, all you've done is fix me."

Jamie was speechless. Had he just been thinking that Kendry was too patient, too willing to take orders?

She tapped her new sneaker at his silence. "You've been angry at me the whole day."

"I'm not angry at you."

"You've spent the entire afternoon with your jaw clenched, biting out your words at me. Now you've got me angry, too."

"I'm not angry at you." His words bounced off the asphalt and the metal side of the truck, vibrating in the air.

Kendry crossed her arms over her chest. "I'm glad we got that cleared up. I don't know how I could have thought you were angry."

Her sarcasm surprised him, but her next words, spoken softly and seriously, cut him to the quick.

"Honestly, Jamie, sometimes a plan sounds better in theory. Actually marrying me seems to have you in knots, so let's go undo it. I don't want this."

The pain was startling. This hurt every bit as much as arguing with Amina about leaving Afghanistan. This hurt every bit as much.

He was older now. Wiser. Passionate shouting

matches didn't solve anything. Hell, passion didn't solve anything. He and Kendry had always been able to talk, but now here she was—

Yes, here she was. Kendry hadn't thrown her hands in the air dramatically and stormed off to her own living quarters on a military base. She was standing right here, close enough to touch. Certainly close enough to talk to without shouting.

"You don't want this," he said, quietly affirming her words. "I do. I need this."

Kendry leaned against the truck, took off the sunglasses and rubbed her eyes. "You need to fix me?"

"Not at all. I like you the way you are. I need a partner. I need you, because you are the one I…" He hesitated, unsure how to put his feelings into words. "You're the one I trust. If I'm coming across as angry, it's because I'm mad at myself for not realizing sooner that you needed money. When I think of how much soup I watched you eat, I hate myself. I'm sorry."

She opened her eyes and looked at him. Jamie had a moment to notice how bright the green of her iris was compared to the black of her pupils.

"It's not your fault that I'm on a tight budget," she said. "In a way, it's a compliment that you didn't notice." She scrunched her eyes closed a second later with a muttered "ouch" and hastily put her sunglasses back on.

"I'm sorry for dragging you into an eye exam," Jamie said, and he leaned against the truck next to her, feeling worn out but hopeful at the same time. She was still here.

She was still here.

"It didn't occur to me that getting new glasses meant

you'd be spending your wedding day with your eyes dilated."

"It's okay," she said, and with a wave of her hand, dismissed all the inconvenience of the eye exam.

That's the way Kendry was, never carrying a chip on her shoulder, always ready to move past any obstacle. She was one of the nicest women he'd ever met.

It was why he'd married her. It was something Sam must have felt in her arms.

Jamie wanted to give her a hug. He really did.

He crossed his arms over his chest.

KENDRY STOLE A glance at the man leaning against the truck with her, the man whose arms looked tanned and strong, muscles flexed, pulling his dress shirt taut as he crossed his arms over his chest.

"How would you have preferred to spend your wedding day?" Jamie asked.

I would have preferred to have you smiling at me in my white gown in a garden. I would have preferred to have you scoop me up with those strong arms to carry me to a white bed in a quiet room.

She hadn't agreed to that kind of marriage. She had no right to expect that kind of day.

She couldn't lie and tell him she wanted anything else, either. She was a terrible liar, so as usual, she deflected his question.

"I have a headache. I'm worried sick about Sam. I know that whether or not he gets pneumonia doesn't depend on if we take him home right this moment. I know he's sleeping just as soundly in his car seat as he would in a crib, but if I could have anything I wanted, I would go home and stretch out on a blanket on the floor next to him and fall asleep. I know being next to him won't prevent pneumonia, either, but that's what I really want to do."

"In my home?"

She heard the tentative note of hope in his serious question. She wasn't imagining it. He wanted her to say yes. He wanted her to live in his house. He wanted to be married to her. Her head hurt, but her heart lightened.

He spoke before she could answer. "Or did you want us to come to your home?" He didn't sound like a doctor anymore, no longer sounded like he was her boss. "Do you have room for us at your place? I'm not sure where you live, but if you want, Sam and I could crash at your house."

"Oh, no." She didn't want Jamie to see her place, ever. She didn't want little Sam to lie on the cement floor of the converted garage she rented by the week. "My place isn't, uh, child friendly…" Now it was her turn to trail off awkwardly.

"Jeez, we're a pitiful pair." Jamie said it with a bit of a smile on his face. He pushed away from the truck. "Let me think. What was it the prince wasn't supposed to say? 'Come to my castle and take care of my kid'?"

He rubbed the back of his neck with one hand for a moment, thinking. "Let me try this instead. Mrs. MacDowell, would you like to come to my castle and take a nap on a blanket with my kid? You can keep an eye on him, and I can cook you an omelet. I'm pretty sure the castle is low on everything except baby formula and a dozen eggs."

Kendry knew she was blushing ten shades of red. Her headache wasn't any better, but her husband's teasing eased the tension in the air. She didn't know how many times she'd already said it that day, but she said it once again: "Yes."

CHAPTER THIRTEEN

HER WEDDING NIGHT was sensual, in its way. She stared up at the ceiling in the darkness and felt the cold air from the vent fall on her face. The pillow was plump and deep, and smelled of fabric softener. Her stomach did not growl, and her teeth felt clean and smooth and minty. She wore her new husband's T-shirt as her nightgown. The rough cotton covered her shoulders and felt coarse on her stomach and tickled the tops of her thighs.

It wasn't the sensuality of a man, but of a man's shirt. Kendry Harrison, or rather, Kendry MacDowell, was once more settling for what she could get. She was married to a man, but she was having no wedding night. She was a guest in a bachelor's spare room, sleeping in a bed that shared space with some weight-lifting equipment and an oversize stereo.

She heard the snuffle and quiet mew of a baby. Sam. Her baby. Kendry waited a moment, but she didn't hear the sound of Jamie's footsteps going to check on the baby.

In this one area, then, she didn't have to compromise. If Sam was her baby, then she'd go check on him.

She tiptoed into the hallway, feeling like an intruder. Jamie's house was enormous. Never in her life had she lived in something with so much square footage. Her parents had sometimes bunked with friends. Kendry could remember sleeping in the back of a minivan, the Woodstock-era Volkswagen type. She'd been cozy, squashed between Mom and Dad, at least until she'd gotten older and had been to school another semester or two in America and figured out that not everyone lived that way. In fact, no one else lived that way. No one except Kendry Harrison and her wacky, hippie parents.

But as a preschooler, it had been cozy.

Would Sam ever know that kind of coziness? Never. She couldn't see herself sleeping with Jamie MacDowell, their baby tucked between them, van windows open to the night sky—

"—and the night bugs," she whispered to herself as she sank her bare toes into the plush carpet. It hadn't been that idyllic. Sam wouldn't be missing out on too much with his parents' platonic marriage.

Sam's room was next to the guest room. It was softly lit with a nightlight. There was, however, no baby in the dark wood crib. The snuffling baby sound didn't seem to come from the direction of the master bedroom at the end of the hall, either. That door was wide open, but Kendry wasn't about to tiptoe into Jamie's bedroom to check on him.

Sam was her guy, not Jamie. She wanted to find Sam.

Kendry entered the family room, her way lit by the glow of the television screen. A twenty-four-hour sports channel was on, its volume so low as to be barely noticeable. Jamie was sprawled in a brown leather recliner, all six-feet-whatever of him, sound asleep. Sam was in his arms, fussing his way into a more comfortable position against his dad's chest.

My guys. They are both mine to have and to hold, for better or worse.

She bit her lip. It didn't seem possible, but here they all were, the MacDowells. Two asleep, one awake. What was a wife and mother supposed to do in this situation?

Kendry started small. She picked up the bottle from the end table and walked it into the kitchen, then she returned to the family room. The guys looked comfortable enough. Frankly, she didn't think she'd be doing anyone a favor by picking Sam up and taking him to his crib.

Instead, she went into Jamie's bedroom and pulled a blanket from the foot of his bed, then returned to tuck it around the baby. Feeling as self-conscious as she possibly could, she lifted the edge of the blanket and pulled it down to cover Jamie's bare toes. He had nice feet, she could tell in the glow of the TV.

She felt her cheeks redden and tried to laugh at herself. She wasn't a blushing bride. She wasn't a virgin. She'd lived on a dozen beaches where people of both genders and all ages walked around half-clothed. Yet, seeing Jamie in sweatpants and bare feet felt so incredibly intimate.

I'm going to have to get over this if I'm going to live with the man for...

For how long? Had Jamie thought beyond his son's upcoming surgeries, or past Jamie's own time in the army reserves? If she was Sam's mother throughout his childhood, what would they do once Sam grew up and moved out of the house? Would they stay friends and quietly get a divorce once Sam got his college diploma?

Am I wife for a year? For a decade? Forever?

She didn't know.

Kendry turned off the TV and went to bed. Alone. In the guest room of her husband's house.

KENDRY GLANCED AT the institutional clock on the playroom wall. She only had a few minutes left on her shift, and she still hadn't found a way to tell Bailey that she'd gotten married. It was a hard thing to work into conversation.

Hey, pass me those diaper wipes, please. So, yesterday after work, I went to the courthouse with Dr. MacDowell—the E.R. one, not the cardiologist—and got married. I think Susie needs the crayons.

"I'm gonna take your temperature now," Bailey said to the preschool-aged Susie. "You don't even have to stop coloring."

As a medical assistant, Bailey had the duty to take each child's temperature. The task was a piece of cake with the latest device that let her swipe each forehead for a few seconds.

"No Sammy here this morning," Bailey said conversationally.

This was the opening Kendry needed. She liked Bailey, and she wanted to tell someone her world-changing, life-changing news. This weekend, she planned to write her parents a letter and mail it to the last tropical address they'd given her, but that wasn't the same thing at all.

"Too bad for us, huh?" Bailey continued. She wrote the child's temperature on her chart.

Kendry chickened out. "Y-yes. Sammy is my favorite."

"Sammy is everyone's favorite. If Sammy's here,

we get to see his daddy at pickup time, and Daddy is definitely a favorite. Man candy. Yummy."

"I like candy," Susie announced.

"Can you draw me a picture of candy?" Bailey asked. "I know Miss Kendry likes candy, too."

Kendry pushed her taped glasses into place with one finger. "Well, I don't know about that."

Bailey waved her thermometer at Kendry. "We all like candy."

Kendry cleared her throat. "So, about Sam…"

Bailey put her hand out and grabbed Kendry's wrist. Hard. "Oh, my God."

"What is it?" Kendry looked at each child in the room, searching for the one who was in trouble.

"I'm gonna die right here. Right now. Check out the new wrapper on that candy."

Kendry turned to see a soldier approaching the playroom's glass door. He wore camouflage and walked with a purpose. He carried a baby, and when he made eye contact with Kendry through the glass, he smiled.

"I'm gonna faint," Bailey whispered.

"Me, too." Kendry covered her mouth, but it was too late. The words were out. Bailey giggled and nudged her as Jamie opened the door.

"Hi, Kendry," he said. "Are you ready to go?"

She used the fingertips covering her mouth to give him a little wave.

He handed a willing Sammy to her. Jamie greeted Bailey with a nod and a smile. In fact, Kendry thought he looked awfully smiley for a man who'd spent the night sleeping in a chair. The recliner must be comfortable.

Bailey smiled right back at Jamie. "I know Kendry

is Sammy's favorite, but he and I will get along just fine when she has to leave. Don't worry about a thing, Dr. MacDowell."

Jamie glanced at Kendry with one brow raised in question. "Thanks, but Sammy and I are here to pick up Kendry. We've got some errands to run before I report for drill this weekend."

Bailey stared at Jamie for a moment. "I see."

Clearly, her tone said she did not. Kendry cleared her throat and made a halfhearted gesture toward Jamie. "I didn't get a chance to tell you yet, but Dr. MacDowell and I…kind of…got married yesterday."

Bailey stared at her. "Seriously?"

Kendry patted Sam on the back. "Yes, so I could be Sammy's mommy. He's got some surgeries coming up." Saying it out loud made it sound odd. No one got married because they had a surgery coming up.

Then Jamie took a step closer. His arm encircled her shoulders, the surprisingly smooth material of his uniform sliding across her back. The heat of his body competed with the shock on Bailey's face for Kendry's attention.

"I only had to ask her a half-dozen times," Jamie said.

"No, he didn't. Just twice." Kendry wanted to explain things to Bailey so that it all made sense, but Jamie's nearness was distracting.

"Just twice," Bailey repeated. "You got married yesterday?"

"It's not like that." Kendry stopped talking abruptly when Jamie squeezed her shoulder in a kind of warning.

"I wasn't going to let her change her mind once she finally said yes," he explained. "We eloped."

Silence followed that statement. Silence, except for the pounding of Kendry's heart. *Eloped* was such a dramatic way to describe their civil vows. Such a romantic way to describe them.

"Miss Bailey, my crayon's broken."

The child's voice seemed to break the spell Bailey was under, because she threw her arms open wide. "Well, congratulations!" She tried to close her arms around Kendry, but Sam and Jamie were there.

Bailey laughed and hugged Kendry as best she could, anyway. "Why didn't you tell me? We could have had a bachelorette party, or at least I would have bought you a cinnamon roll for a wedding cake this morning."

"Oh, I made sure she got fed this morning." The way Jamie said it made Kendry want to drop through the floor. He made it sound like he'd fed her while she was stark naked in bed or something, when they'd really stopped at a pancake place on the way to the hospital.

Bailey gave Kendry a playful shove in the shoulder, which moved Jamie and Sam, too. "You sly thing, I didn't even know you two were dating."

For the life of her, Kendry couldn't think of a thing to say. Bailey had gotten the completely wrong impression, and Jamie had made sure she did.

Bailey made a shooing motion with her hands. "Go on, get out of here. Clock out and enjoy those *errands*."

IT TOOK KENDRY at least five minutes to think up and then discard fifty-five ways to broach the subject on her mind. Finally, she blurted it out. "Why did you do that?"

"Do what?" Jamie looked curious as he drove toward their first errand, whatever it was. Curious, and calm, and completely in control. The camouflage only made him look that much more in charge.

He looked that much more out of her league. No wonder Bailey had been so shocked.

"You made Bailey think we were really married."

"We are really married."

"I mean, like we got married because we were in love." There, she'd said it. She'd gotten that monumental word out there.

Her soldier-husband shrugged as if the L-word didn't matter. "Most people will jump to that conclusion anyway."

"I don't think they will."

That seemed to bother him a little. "Why not?"

He had to be pretending he didn't know. It was kind of him, but it was unnecessary. "We don't look like a couple. Most people don't even see me to start with, but, Jamie, look at you. You're the hottest bachelor at the hospital. You must know it." She paused deliberately, wanting him to acknowledge the truth.

He shrugged again. "Quinn doesn't know it. He thinks he's the hot one."

Kendry burst out laughing. "True enough."

Jamie pulled into a car dealership and parked. He turned in his seat to focus on her. Kendry found she couldn't hold his gaze.

She clasped her hands in her lap. "The point is, you don't have to pretend we're in love. I'm not vain. It's not going to hurt my feelings when people say how shocked they are that you married me. They'll guess that you needed someone to watch over Sam, and that's okay."

"That's not okay." Jamie placed one warm hand over her two tightly twisted ones. "As part of my family, you're important to me, and I don't want to see you get hurt. I'm not going to stand by and do nothing if someone acts shocked and you feel embarrassed."

"Bailey isn't mean. She wasn't trying to embarrass me."

"I know, but others will do it on purpose. If I can tell a true story, and believe me, it feels like I asked you a hundred times before you agreed to marry me, or if I can hold your hand and make gossip stop, then I'm going to do it."

Kendry should be firm in this. She should insist that they not pretend to anyone, because no one's opinion mattered. Jamie's plan was unnecessary.

Unnecessary, but tempting.

Jamie wanted to touch her in public. He wanted to tell people things about her that sounded romantic. She'd compromised in every area of her life, it seemed. This compromise, at least, would allow her to live a little bit of her fantasy. For a few moments at work, whenever they encountered gossip that Jamie wanted to silence, she would be treated like a woman who'd enthralled a man. Not just any man, but Dr. Jamie Mac-Dowell, who drove a motorcycle and saved lives and wore a soldier's uniform.

She took a deep breath and looked Jamie in the eye. "If that's the way you want it, then okay."

Jamie gave her hands a brisk pat, then opened his door. "Great. Let's go get you a car."

CHAPTER FOURTEEN

IN THE END, of course, she compromised. She didn't
want a car. Rather than tell Jamie that she didn't trust
herself behind the wheel, she'd pointed out that the
gossip would surely say she was a gold digger.

Jamie had countered with some disappointingly reasonable logic. "My unit drills in Dallas. I can't leave
you stranded at the house all weekend. You'll need to
get groceries. You'll want to go back to your place and
pick up some clothes. What if Sam starts running a
fever and you need to take him to the hospital?"

Kendry had let Jamie rent her a car to use while he
was away. Before she signed the rental contract, she
triple-checked that they'd added the optional insurance. On that, there was no compromising.

In the rental-car company's lot, Jamie pulled a large
box out of the back of his truck and proceeded to in-
stall a new baby seat in the back of the rental. Then
he handed her a new iPhone, showed her how to send
photos with it, and told her that he, Quinn, his mother
and an older brother in New York named Braden,
whom she hadn't known existed, were already pro-
grammed into the speed dial. He put two hundred dollars "for groceries" into her hand, along with the keys
and rental-car paperwork.

All these things he handed over to her easily. Sam

took a moment longer. After a kiss on the top of his son's head and a squeeze that might have been tight enough to make Sam protest a bit, Jamie handed Kendry his son.

"I won't be gone that long," he said. "Just two nights. The time will fly."

"I know." Kendry wasn't sure if Jamie was trying to convince himself or her.

His hand drifted from the top of his son's head to her chin, as he'd done before. After lifting her face to look into her eyes, his hand drifted over her shoulder briefly, almost like he was connecting his son and his wife together in his mind with one gentle sweep of his hand.

He stepped back and nodded, then spoke in a husky voice. "Thank you. If I can't be with him, then I'm glad he's with his new mom."

He walked away. Kendry lifted Sam's hand to wave as his daddy drove off, back to the military career that had ended with a lost love and a new baby.

"He's not going to lose you, too, Sam. I'm going to take good care of you."

She drove the rental car back to Jamie's house like an actress who set the perfect example in a driver's-education movie. Considering how badly her hands were shaking once they parked in the driveway, Kendry was grateful she only dropped the car keys twice, and not the baby.

FRIDAY NIGHT EVENTUALLY became Saturday. The long, late-September Saturday turned into Sunday. As the time passed, Kendry discovered that taking care of

Sam around the clock, day and night, for every feeding and for every diaper change, was…

…a joy. There was something empowering in being able to comfort a baby. Whether he needed food or a toy, whether he needed to be soothed or entertained, Kendry was able to make Sam's world better. In return, he paid attention to her like she was the center of his universe. For this weekend, she was. Sam snuggled into her like she was the most comfortable place to be.

Kendry herself couldn't remember the last time she'd been so comfortable. The shower with its modern rainfall spray was sinful, and she sinned whenever Sam napped. Her lemongrass shampoo made her hair feel almost as soft as a baby's. She'd found some disposable men's razors under the sink, so now her shaved legs were nearly as soft as Sam's, too.

The refrigerator dazzled her in stainless steel, and the ability to open the double doors wide and see shelf after shelf of brightly lit, icy-cold food was a luxury she hadn't had in years. Jamie had said they were low on food, but there were two kinds of breakfast cereals in the pantry—a pantry! A whole room just for food!—as well as a loaf of bread and a package of lunch meat in the fridge, so there was no need. She organized all the bottles of ketchup, mustard, mayonnaise, pickles.

The washing machine was the best of all, a miracle of technology after hand-scrubbing everything she owned with a bar of soap in a tiny sink. Kendry gathered up Jamie's T-shirts and sweatpants, cut the tags off the last set of her new scrubs and put everything in the machine. She pushed a few buttons and walked away. Kendry had never had this luxury.

Never. Certainly not during her childhood, living with parents who enjoyed rustic living to the extreme. Her parents had thought if they were going to learn pottery techniques from natives in a rainforest, then they should live in a wooden, thatched hut like the natives, too. When the Harrisons had returned to the States for the odd school year, beat-up Laundromats with their rusted carts and change machines had seemed the height of modern convenience.

Jamie had married her and brought her to his palace, indeed. Kendry napped, she slept, she played with Sam. She was on vacation in a luxury resort.

She only had her new scrubs to wear in the luxury resort, but that was okay. It made it easier to justify eating the man's food and showering in his house if she felt like a hired nanny in professional scrubs.

The rental car stayed in the driveway. Kendry had no desire to go to her own place and bring her old clothes into this paradise. She wanted to enjoy this fantasy a little longer. It was so much easier than deciding how to tell Jamie that his real wife had a really messed-up life.

THERE WERE SOME things a man shouldn't tell his mother over the phone. Jamie's marriage was bound to come as a shock, so the least he could do was tell his mother in person that he was now a married man. It would be easier to explain face-to-face why he'd taken a woman he'd known for a month to the local courthouse and bound himself to her.

Quinn gets it. Dad would have gotten it. Mom will understand when I explain it.

That's what he told himself as he traveled the last graveled piece of road that led to the River Mack

Ranch. The truth was, as the grand white house came into view a few acres in the distance, he felt like a little kid about to explain to his parent that the detention slip in his backpack was not as bad as it appeared.

The ranch was located nearly an hour and a half outside of Austin. Jamie hadn't had enough time on Friday to stop by on his way to reporting to his reserve unit in Dallas. Now, on his way home, he had no excuse not to stop and reveal to his mother who, exactly, had been watching Sam for him these past few days.

He'd tell her the good news that he was married, and then he'd leave. He was impatient to get home. The entire weekend he'd been texting Kendry, and she'd been using her new iPhone to send him all the photos of Sam he could want. Her photos were funny and quirky, like a close-up of a messy baby hand along with the caption, *Where there's a will, there's a way. I can't use a spoon, but I can feed myself oatmeal.*

It had seemed natural to start sending back photos of where he was, what he was doing, whom he was with. He'd sent her a photo of the tasteless substance that passed as cake in the army's dehydrated, portable meal system, and had promised to pick up fried chicken on his way home. They'd have to pretend it didn't taste like heaven, so Sam would be content with his oatmeal while they devoured the Colonel's original recipe.

Soon. He'd be home soon. But first he had to tell his mom he had a wife. She'd obviously seen his truck coming up the road, because she was waiting on the porch, looking as if she'd been expecting company in blue slacks and a crisp white shirt. Like many Texan women of her generation, she always had her hair and makeup done, just in case.

"Well, this is a pleasant surprise," she said. "Where's the baby?"

"He's home. How are you feeling?"

"I'm fine. I could have taken care of him for you."

Jamie gave his mom an extra hug. "I'm glad to hear you're feeling up to it. Which rheumatologist did you end up seeing?"

"Oh, some new kid. He looks younger than you, and all he offered to do was run a bunch of tests."

"Mom, that's what we docs do. I'd rather he ran tests than guess why you've had these periods of weakness."

Her personal physician as well as Jamie and his brothers were all certain she had an autoimmune disease, one of those poorly understood conditions that would flare up, then nearly disappear. Just when everyone stopped fearing the monster, it would rear its ugly head and remind them that Mom was not invincible. She was getting over the worst of a flare now. Taking care of a baby all weekend would have wiped her out.

Still, she had some homemade sweet tea in a pitcher in the fridge, and she insisted on serving Jamie while he sat at her kitchen table. Affection warred with exasperation as he watched her moving a little too carefully to fill his glass with ice. "Mom, let me do that. You sit."

"I'm just fine. I can pour a glass of tea. If you'd told me you were coming, I could have had dinner in the oven, too."

"I can't stay for dinner, but I wanted to talk to you."

She set his tea down, then set herself down in the chair across from his. "Well, this sounds serious."

She looked at him with 100 percent of her atten-

tion. She'd always been like that. No matter how little
he'd seen of his dad, he'd always known his mother
was there for him, like Sam would now always have
Kendry.

"Mom, I got married."

She blinked. "My goodness. I didn't know you were
dating someone. Do I know her?"

"She works at the hospital. I think Dad would have
approved."

"It sounds like you think I won't. What makes you
think your father in particular would have approved?"

"Quinn approves, and he thinks like Dad. I needed
a wife, and I found a woman who fit all my needs, so
I didn't waste any time about it."

"It sounds more like you hired someone than like
you fell in love."

"We're not in love, not the way you're thinking. But
she's everything I was looking for." He used the side of
his hand to make neat little karate chops on the kitchen
table, punctuating each point. "She's smart. She can
handle a sick child. We work together well. Done deal.
Problem solved."

"What problem?" She sounded a bit faint.

"Sam needed a mother. I'm nearly as busy as Dad
was. I chose the same career. I know I won't always
be there for Sam. If he doesn't have a mother…" He
reached across the table and touched his own mother's
hand. "I can't imagine what my childhood would have
been like without you."

She started to tear up. Jamie thought she was tear-
ing up at the compliment, so her sudden disapproval
caught him off guard.

"Your father was devoted to you. He loved you

every bit as much as you love Sam. How can you say he wasn't there for you?"

Jamie didn't want to bring up ugly memories. He wanted to break the news that he was married, and then he wanted to go home, to the new family he was making with Sam and Kendry. "I'm sorry, Mom. Forget I said anything."

"Tell me how your father wasn't there for you."

Jamie felt his frustration build. He'd opened this can of worms. He only had himself to blame if he was late getting home. "Maybe because he missed entire football seasons when I was playing. Maybe because when he was home, he was always on the phone."

"Oh, Jamie. Have you been thinking that your whole life? Your father hated missing your games. Hated it so badly, he gave up part of his own salary to get the board to hire another physician. The board took six weeks to approve a replacement, and I thought he was going to blow a gasket at the delay. Once they got the new doctor in, your father was at every one of your games."

Jamie swallowed sweet tea as he thought back. He remembered running onto the field, completing a play, looking up at the stands, spotting his mother. Had his father been sitting right next to her? He supposed he had been, some of the time.

"I hated those camping trips." To his own ears, he sounded like a sullen adolescent.

"Oh, those camping trips." She drummed her fingers on the table, distracting the doctor in Jamie with the demonstration of dexterity that proved she was well into remission. "I tried to speak to your father about juggling his roles. We didn't have work-life balance and all those catchphrases when you were little, but we faced the same issues. Your father, though, was all or nothing. He'd realized that being near a telephone meant he was always answering calls instead of spending time with you boys. His solution was as extreme as yours."

She made little karate chops on the table, imitating him. "If the phone was a problem, then he'd take his boys where there was no phone. Problem solved."

Put that way, Jamie was uncomfortably aware that maybe Quinn wasn't the only MacDowell brother who thought like their father. Maybe Jamie tended to make decisions the same way.

He gently pressed his mother's karate hand flat on the table. "I'm having more sympathy for Dad now that I'm in his shoes. Quinn wants me to do more, to take over the medical director position from him next year, or at least chair the emergency department. But every career yes is a Sam no."

"Did you decide to say yes to the career? Is that why you married someone, to gain a full-time nanny for Sam? I don't think you should criticize your father, then. Your solution is more extreme than anything he ever came up with, and it puts work before family, which he never willingly did." She stood abruptly.

Jamie stood, too, defensive and more emotional than he wanted to be. "That's not why I got married. I'm still refusing to take on more work, because I want to spend every minute I can with Sam. Marrying Kendry wasn't extreme. It was rational."

"Your father didn't marry me because it was rational. He married me for love. Crazy, passionate love."

Jamie winced. "Mom, please."

"It's true. You need that in your life."

"I had that in my life. How do you think Sam came about?"

The memories came back to him in a rush, vivid and emotional, now that he'd opened the door a crack to discuss earlier days. He saw Amina clearly, dark eyes flashing, daring him to take everything she had to give. He covered his eyes with his hand and waited for the wave to pass.

It took a moment to be able to breathe again. "I will never, ever love anyone the way I loved Amina."

His mother hugged him. "I'm sorry, son. I don't want you to settle for anything less than that."

Jamie took a deep breath, dropped his hand, blinked at the kitchen he'd grown up in. "Yes, well, *that* is gone. I'll never feel for another woman that way."

His mother frowned. "Not that precise way, no. But that doesn't mean you'll never fall in love again." She pushed Jamie into the chair she'd been in, then pulled out the chair next to him. She put her hand on his knee. "The longer you stay married to this girl, the easier it will be for her to win alimony. Your share of this ranch could become hers, if her lawyer is good enough. Will she put up a fight, or can you end this quickly and quietly?"

Jamie froze at the thought of losing Kendry.

No.

All his earlier caveman instincts came back, full force. He'd lost Amina. No way in hell was he going to lose Kendry. He needed her, and she was his now. His.

"I'm not ending my marriage. Ever."

"Oh." His mother let go of him immediately, as if

she'd gotten an electric shock. "I thought you married a girl you weren't passionate about."

"She's not a girl. She's my wife, and she doesn't want this ranch. She doesn't know it exists." His mother was so off base, it was laughable. So, Jamie tried to laugh.

"Tell me about her, then."

"What do you want to know?"

"You could start with her name."

"Kendry Harrison." And then, because he'd learned the information on the marriage license, and because his mother was still looking at him strangely, he told her more. "Kendry Ann Harrison. She'll turn twenty-four in December. That might sound young, but she grew up all over the world. She's seen a lot. We eat lunch together, which is usually the only bright spot of sanity in my workday. There are times at that hospital when I'd swear Kendry is the only person I can talk to, the only person who gets me."

His mother was silent.

Way to go. Way to hurt your mother's feelings.

Tiredly, Jamie stood. His mother stood, too, using the table for leverage. Jamie saw tears in her eyes. They might have been from pain because her joints had stiffened while she sat, but he feared it was worse than that. He'd made her sad.

"Don't cry, Mom. Please, I didn't mean it that way. I know I can always talk to you, too."

She accepted his hug, resting her head briefly on his shoulder. "Oh, I hope you did mean it, son. I hope this woman is the one who understands you. It's very special when you find someone who doesn't try to change you."

She stepped back, keeping her hands on Jamie's arms, and gave him a little shake. "So tell me, is she pretty?"

Jamie rolled his eyes. "I can't tell you how sick I am of people talking about her appearance. She loves Sam. That's what matters."

His mother only raised an eyebrow at him. He could practically see the wheels turning in her head. She'd never reminded him more of Braden.

Aw, damn it. Braden. He'd forgotten to tell Braden he was married. That was going to have to happen by phone. Jamie wasn't going to fly to Manhattan when there wasn't a thing Braden could say that would make him change his mind about Kendry.

Kendry. He wanted to go home, to his house, to his wife, to his child. Now.

"Okay, Mom. The top of her head comes to about here on me." With the side of his hand, he touched his jaw. "She's got brown hair, and she wears glasses that make her eyes look kind of hazel. But when she doesn't have them on, if you brush her bangs away, her eyes are actually green. She's waiting for me, Mom, so I've got to go now."

His mother didn't move, except to tilt her head a little as she continued to study him.

"She's waiting for me. So…okay?"

"Okay. Go home to your green-eyed wife, then. I can't wait to meet her." His mother walked him outside to his truck. She seemed pretty happy now, and Jamie was relieved enough that he wasn't going to question why.

He hadn't backed up his truck five feet, however, when his mother waved at him to stop.

She leaned in the window, one hand on the ledge like she'd keep the truck in place that way. "You let me know when you're coming with her. None of this dropping by without giving a person notice. Not when I'm meeting my new daughter-in-law for the first time. I've got to have a cake ready at the very least."

"Yes, Mom."

"You promise?"

"I promise."

Jamie breathed in the late-afternoon air as he drove down the ranch road, watching the familiar scenery of his childhood roll by. He was exhausted by the conversation. Exhausted by the whole weekend. Yet he was leaving here with less anger toward the memory of his father, and a strange feeling that his mother agreed that the detention slip in his backpack wasn't so awful after all.

CHAPTER FIFTEEN

KENDRY HEARD SAMMY wake up with his usual cry. Not a cry of distress, but the one she thought sounded like he was saying, "Hey, I'm bored in here. Come and get me."

"I'm coming, my little alarm clock," she muttered to herself as she stretched briefly in bed. She felt great after another night of satiated sleep, this time with a belly full of fried chicken.

Kendry swung her legs over the side of the bed and stood up, marveling as she did every morning at how rich the plush carpet felt under her arches. She tugged Jamie's T-shirt into place and walked into Sammy's room with her eyes still half-closed.

Jamie was already there, wearing his sweatpants. Nothing else. His back was to her as he bent over the crib, and the movement of his shoulder muscles under an acre of smooth, male skin penetrated her sleep-fogged brain in the most delicious way.

He's got no shirt on, because I'm wearing it. It was a silly thought, of course. Jamie must own dozens of T-shirts, yet it seemed as if between the two of them, they were sharing one outfit. He was bare on top. She was bare on the bottom.

Her eyes popped open. She was really, really bare on the bottom. She tugged the hem of his shirt another inch lower on her thighs at the moment he turned around with the baby in his arms. "Good morning," he said, flashing her an easy, friendly smile, clearly oblivious to her state of undress.

She only had one pair of underwear in the house, the pair she'd been wearing when Jamie had whisked her away from the city bus stop on his motorcycle. Every night, she'd been washing them and putting them in the dryer. Every morning, wearing nothing but the man's T-shirt, she'd gone into the laundry room and put the freshly cleaned pair back on. No big deal, to sleep in a T-shirt only.

Only today, the T-shirt's owner was standing three feet away from her, smiling, and she felt practically naked. He *looked* practically naked.

Kendry started backing out of the room, tugging the front of the T-shirt down while she swore she felt a breeze on her bare backside. "Yes, um, good morning. I'll just, uh, go get ready, since you've got Sam."

She backed up into the hallway bathroom and shut the door. Her heart was pounding. Her face felt hot. She glanced in the mirror. The T-shirt came all the way down to the middle of her thighs. Jamie couldn't possibly have seen whether or not she was wearing underwear. She should have been more worried about her hair, which was falling in an uncombed pillow-mess down to her shoulders.

It only took a few moments to go through her morning routine. Teeth brushed, face washed, hair brushed and ponytail holder twisted into service, she cracked the door open again, hoping to get into the laundry room and back to her bedroom without any more awkward *good mornings*.

She stepped into the hall when the silence was interrupted by the unmistakable sound of the washing machine lid being opened. Good lord. The man did his laundry first thing in the morning. Kendry hurried through the kitchen toward the laundry room.

"Wait," she called. "I'll get my things."

Too late. The release mechanism for the clothes dryer's door made a distinctive noise. Kendry jogged the last steps into the laundry room. There Jamie stood, in all his bare-chested glory, with a handful of wet camouflage clothing in one hand and, in his other arm, a baby who was using his father's naked shoulder as a teething ring. Jamie was staring in the dryer.

"Here, let me get my stuff." Kendry nearly elbowed him out of the way. Sure enough, although she'd thrown her bath towel in with her unmentionables, her bra and underwear rested on top, in plain view. She snatched the clothes and held them to her front. "Sorry."

"Sorry," Jamie said at the same time. He gestured with the wet clothes in his hand. "Thought I'd get these uniforms washed before work."

"Sure. My stuff's all done." Kendry retreated to her bedroom and didn't emerge until she was fully dressed. Fully. From her old bra and underwear to her new socks and scrubs. Sneakers on, laces tied. Completely dressed.

When she walked into the kitchen, she saw that Jamie was dressed, too, in boots and slacks and a dress shirt. She seized the opportunity to talk about anything except laundry. "You're expecting a slow day today, aren't you? On nights and weekends, you wear scrubs."

"You are one very observant wife." Jamie had placed Sam in a bouncy chair and was shaking up a bottle of formula. He was an efficient man, all right. She supposed he'd had no choice, being a single parent.

He looked over his shoulder at her. "You're wearing your wedding scrubs."

"I guess they are, aren't they?" Kendry was wearing the pink pair that had set off her tears the day they'd gotten married. Her old glasses were firmly in place, still serviceable until the new ones came in.

"I didn't realize you had to work today." Jamie checked his watch. "What time does your shift start?"

"I'm off. I kind of assumed I'd be home with Sammy." They should have discussed this over fried chicken. Instead, they'd told each other amusing stories about their separate weekends.

"I think Sam wants to be with you whether you are in the playroom or at home." Jamie sat Sam upright in his lap and started to give him his bottle. "If you don't have to go to the hospital today, why are you in scrubs?"

"They're comfortable." Kendry had been wearing his T-shirt and her scrub pants when he'd gotten home the night before, and Jamie had jumped to the conclusion that she'd gotten ready for bed early.

"You never went back to your place this weekend, did you? Not even to get some clothes?"

"No, I didn't feel like it."

Jamie seemed thoughtful as he watched Sam drink his bottle. "You didn't go to the grocery store, either. We're out of bread and cereal."

"I'm sorry. I should have saved you some for breakfast today."

"That's not the problem, Kendry. I can grab something at the hospital. The problem is, what are you going to eat for breakfast if you're not going to work today?"

"Oh, don't worry about me. We've got mashed potatoes left over from last night."

Jamie sighed, then stayed silent.

Kendry bit her lip. It was hard to read his thoughts as he watched Sam finish his bottle, but Jamie clearly wasn't relaxed or happy or any of the things she wanted him to be now that they were married.

"I like mashed potatoes," she said. "Honest."

Jamie looked up at her. "The real problem is trying to figure out why you stayed in this house for two and a half days. Do you feel like it's not your place to use the money I gave you for groceries?"

Surprise made her hesitate. "I can do the grocery shopping if you tell me what you like. Do you want the same brand of cereal again?"

"You live here now. This is your house. You should buy your favorite cereal, not only mine."

"I can't just barge in here and take over. That's not the way I am."

The corner of his mouth lifted. "That's too much the way I am. Last time we went to a store together, I took over. As I recall, my wife didn't appreciate it." Jamie put the empty bottle down and started patting Sam's back. He kept his eyes on her, however. "Tell me the truth, Kendry. How badly do you hate to drive?"

Dang it.

She gave up and sat down. "Really badly."

"There's no bus stop around here. I'll drive to the grocery store, but you have to take a few laps around the empty part of the parking lot so that you get more comfortable behind the wheel. Deal?"

Her little fantasy weekend in the castle was over. "Deal."

The compromising resumed.

JAMIE WAS POURING himself a cup of coffee in the E.R.'s kitchenette when it hit him. He'd bought her scrubs and he'd bought her socks, but he hadn't bought Kendry any underwear. Underpants. Panties. Whatever the hell they were, there had been one clean pair in the dryer, one scrap of pale blue, plain cotton, which meant—

He shoved the stainless-steel pot back onto the burner. So, she slept commando. When she'd been standing there in Sammy's room, with her hair loose and her glasses gone, she'd been bare-assed under his shirt. He hadn't thought about it at the time. He'd only been surprised by how fluffy her hair was when it wasn't scraped back in a ponytail.

But Kendry had been aware of it. Their odd tango in the laundry room, the way she'd backed out of Sammy's room with quick, small steps, it all made sense now.

It was funny, really. An amusing little bit between roommates.

Jamie didn't feel like laughing. He had a sudden vision, a piece of a remembered dream, of a woman's legs silhouetted against the glow of the television and a blanket drifting down over his feet. The memory was uncomfortable. Almost erotic.

"How's married life treating you?" Quinn's big voice crashed into Jamie's thoughts.

He grunted at Quinn, took a sip of his coffee. "Did you come here on my bike or in your truck?"

Quinn reached across him for the coffeepot. "It's

my bike. If you want to buy it back, it'll cost you. But I've got the truck today."

"Good. I need you to help me move Kendry's stuff into my house."

Quinn took out his phone and flipped through a few screens. "I can make Wednesday a half day."

"Tonight. She needs clothes."

"You sure about that? This is your honeymoon, after all." Quinn leaned against the counter with his coffee and looked like he was settling in to enjoy a series of jabs.

Jamie pitched his voice low, conscious now of eavesdropping staff. "It's not like that, and you know it. She needs her own clothes. She can't keep wearing mine—and don't try raising that eyebrow at me like Dad."

A nurse peeked in the kitchenette. "Dr. MacDowell? We've got an MI on the way. Two minutes. Radio says he coded."

Jamie set down his coffee, tamed the adrenaline rush as he headed toward the room they kept ready for the most serious cases and tried not to feel too grateful for the distraction.

"Six o'clock?" Quinn called after him.

"Six. Thanks."

CHAPTER SIXTEEN

KENDRY WAS BACK in her old neighborhood. Despite her objections, Jamie was with her, driving the pickup truck that he erroneously thought was needed to move all of her belongings from her place to his.

He'd even come home tonight with Quinn and a second truck, as if she needed a convoy of pickups to haul all her worldly possessions. Quinn had been pressed into babysitting Sammy instead.

"Are you sure Sammy's okay with Quinn?" Kendry asked. "Make a left here."

Jamie flicked on the turn signal. "He can thread a wire into a man's heart. He can tape a disposable diaper over a baby's bottom."

One more left turn, and they were there. Kendry's home. Her heart sank as she tried to see it for the first time, the way Jamie was seeing it. The driveway they parked on was choked with weeds, and the bushes grew wild all around the dingy home exterior. The house still stood despite the neglect, probably because it had been built of brick.

When Kendry had found this neighborhood, she'd noticed how sturdy the block of brick houses were and had thought it a point in their favor. She'd had no choice but to overlook the signs of neglect, the furniture left to rot in the front yards, the chain-link fences allowed to rust away. Kendry was glad she'd swung that machete to tame the foreclosed house's weeds not long ago. The street looked better for it.

"This is your house?" Jamie's voice was obviously, painfully, neutral. Nonjudgmental, when there was only one judgment possible. Kendry's heart squeezed in her chest in gratitude.

"I rent the garage, actually."

The truck cab felt stifling, the air thick with silence. There was nothing Jamie could say without making her feel worse, and he probably knew it.

She took her glasses off and looked out the window. It was nearly seven, and people were starting to loiter in the streets. During the day, the place was a ghost town, but at night, people came out of their houses. Neighbors started sharing beers, laughingly taunting one another. It took a few hours for the camaraderie to turn vicious. Kendry didn't leave the safety of her brick-walled garage at night.

"I should have used the rental car and moved my stuff out myself. I didn't want to bring Sam here, I guess." *Not even in the daylight.*

Jamie opened his truck door. "Come out on my side. That bush is blocking your door." He gave her hand a tug as she slid across the bench seat. Once she was out, he didn't let go while he used his free hand to grab an empty cardboard box out of the truck bed. They crunched their way over rocks and weeds toward the garage's side door.

Inside, the temperature was easily over a hundred degrees. Kendry tucked her taped glasses into the breast pocket of her scrubs. She lowered the half window on the door and turned on her little electric fan.

"This will cool things off. It's amazing how much a fan helps."

"I know. It was the same way in Afghanistan." Jamie dropped the box onto the concrete floor. "We should put the bigger stuff in the truck first, like that chest of drawers."

"The furniture isn't mine. The apartment came furnished." She'd always called it her apartment. It had a tiny, dorm-sized fridge and an electric hot plate, so she had a kitchen. The twin bed and chest of drawers were her bedroom. It was just a quick hop across the yard to the utility room of Mrs. Haines's house, which had a sink, toilet and microscopic shower stall. All the components of an apartment were here.

"Did you write to your parents yet?" Jamie's question was unexpected.

"No. Why do you ask?" Kendry pulled open the lowest drawer and took out her favorite sweatshirt, which was wrapped around one of her parents' pottery pieces, and set it carefully in the box.

Nearly done packing.

Jamie was still on the topic of her parents. "I need to find a way to send them money without offending them. We could fly them back to the States under the pretense of celebrating our marriage. I've got enough to help get them on their feet, if they want to live here."

"Get them on their feet? Jamie, my parents aren't poor."

He went very still. "Don't tell me they have money."

"They have all they want. They're fine."

"They're fine," he repeated in his flat voice. Suddenly, he shoved her one and only chair away with his boot. "Then what the hell is this? Some kind of sink-

or-swim lesson? They cut you loose to live on your own in a gang neighborhood?"

"I'm almost twenty-four years old, Jamie. I'm not their responsibility." Pride made her pretend she was the proud owner of this place. "It may not look like much to you, but I'm really doing fine."

"This neighborhood is dangerous. You've been starving. What kind of parents let their child starve if they have money?"

"They're good parents, Jamie. I came back to the States with money for college and everything. It wasn't their fault I blew it, so I haven't asked them for more." She sank onto the end of her bed while Jamie paced one lap around her one-car garage.

He returned to the bed and sat next to her. "If they're good parents, they have no idea about what part of Austin you live in, do they?"

Kendry shook her head. "It's only temporary, so why worry them? It might take me eight years, but I'm going to be a college graduate with a nursing degree. The end result will be the same."

"What happened to your college fund? You're the most responsible person I know. Were you robbed?"

Kendry shook her head.

"Were you in over your head, involved with a bad crowd? Drugs?"

"No."

Jamie would find out everything, sooner or later. If they were still married on September thirtieth, she couldn't keep it a secret. She stood and walked to the door. The fan pushed the hot air past her, out the window she'd been so proud to rent. Even the view of overgrown shrubs had brought her pleasure, because they were an improvement over her previous circumstances.

Jamie's opinion of her had always mattered. Maybe she could make him see how much progress she'd made on her own. But first, she had to tell him how stupid she'd been.

"We were never rich, but during the times we lived in the States, we usually rented a real apartment. We had a TV. I had shoes. My parents wouldn't have let me wear worn-out sneakers, either." She looked down at her new sneakers and flexed her foot.

"And then?" Jamie stayed on the bed, giving her his full attention.

"And then I got my GED right before I turned twenty. Finally. The diploma arrived while we were living in Mexico. My high school years were mostly spent overseas, so I got too old to keep enrolling whenever we came back for a few months. It's embarrassing to be an eighteen-year-old sophomore. Anyway, when the GED arrived, my parents surprised me with this nest egg they'd saved for me. They left Mexico for Peru, and I came to Austin, ready to enroll in the community college."

"Why Austin?"

"I'd made friends who were from here, people my age who were vacationing in Mexico." Kendry remembered their fun-loving confidence. She was an American high school grad, too, like they were—or so she'd reasoned.

"I moved in with two of them, sharing rent on a great house. Three bedrooms and a swimming pool in a gated community. The guy had one bedroom, which he shared with his girlfriend. The girl had one bedroom, which she shared with her boyfriend. I had the third all to myself. The four of them got me a part-time job where they worked. I was thrilled to be waitressing at this high-end, trendy restaurant, bringing home hundreds in tips.

"My share of the rent was in the hundreds, too, though. I did the math and decided if I worked full-time, I could keep living with my friends and save a little more for college, as well. If I worked for two semesters instead of going to school, then I'd have enough to skip community college and go straight to a university for all four years."

"Knowing you, it was probably a solid plan."

"I kept pushing that college entry back. I decided I could buy a car if I worked for three semesters, and then go to university." She rested against the doorjamb, watching the shrubs blow in the evening breeze. It was nearly dark outside, and she tried to remember if Jamie had locked the truck.

"The guy and the girl decided they loved each other instead of their roommates, and they ran off. I was left with a weeping ex-girlfriend and an angry ex-boyfriend who didn't want to pay their share of the rent. After a week, the two of them had a fight. They broke a window. I thought I'd been robbed, until the girl returned to get her clothes. She left. He left. I was alone when the bills for the month came in. Electric. Water. Satellite. Internet. Rent."

She kept her arms wrapped around her stomach, feeling sick at the memory. There'd been so many bills, arriving in the mail one after another.

"Half my savings were wiped out in one month. Half. Then a new restaurant opened up, and our trendy place stopped being trendy. Within a week, my tips plummeted from hundreds to tens. No one I knew could afford to move in with me."

She wanted Jamie to understand. It had all been one domino falling after another, one huge downward spiral. "I panicked when the rent was due again. Four weeks came so fast. I let my car insurance lapse to pay the bills, but then I got in an accident. I rear-ended a car. I got the ticket."

"And you got the medical bills?" Jamie sat forward on the bed and rubbed his face with his hands. "God, Kendry. How long were you in the hospital?"

"Not a minute, thankfully. I wasn't going fast enough to trigger the air bags, but I'd hit the other car at a little bit of angle, they told me. Just enough to throw the frame out of whack. I totaled a Mercedes."

Jamie frowned at that.

Kendry was getting used to him frowning at her now that they were married, but she didn't like it. He'd always been so nice to her when they were just friends, talking to her easily over cafeteria lunches, listening to her stories. Of course, she hadn't told him stories like this one.

She went back to staring out the window. "It's that easy to go from having a little bit of savings to using the public library's free computer to look up homeless shelters."

"You lived in a homeless shelter," he repeated in that carefully neutral voice, the voice that didn't fool her. There was only one judgment to make.

"Look, I know it was a stupid gamble, to go for a month without car insurance. You know the law in Texas. If you break it, you have to pay for it, whether you have car insurance or not. That's fair, but it hasn't been easy. For two years, I've been buying a Mercedes-Benz, one paycheck at a time. I've got twelve payments to go. I'll make the next payment on September thirtieth."

"The judge expected you to pay off a Mercedes in three years?" In the corner of her eye, she saw Jamie stand up. "Kendry, most people who buy a Mercedes get a loan that lasts far longer than thirty-six months. Did you appeal?"

"Appeal what? I hit them from behind."

"Your sentence was outrageous."

Kendry had nothing to say to that. She'd been living with it so long, it seemed normal to her. "The good news is, the thirtieth is also my six-month anniversary at the hospital. I'll have health insurance for the first time in my life, and I get a raise. Another fifty cents per hour."

Outside, a bird twittered near her window. People called out to each other across the street.

A single gunshot rang out.

Jamie tackled her. His arms came around her as he landed with her on the ground, hard. Her head would have bounced off the concrete had he not cradled it in his hand. She gasped into his neck, tasted the salt of his skin as she panted in fear.

"A car," she breathed, as soon as she was able. "A car backfired. S'okay."

He was heavy on her, clasping her to his chest. "It's gunfire." He rolled off just enough to slide them both closer to the brick wall, away from the wooden door.

"No, I've heard that sound before. People have old cars around here, and they backfi—"

Several gunshots sounded, a dozen within a second, sounding like an automatic machine gun. A woman screamed. Kendry was instantly smashed underneath Jamie again.

Long moments passed. Outside, everything had gone utterly silent. No birds. No people. Inside, she could hear only her own heart pounding in her ears, her own shallow, rapid breathing. She wanted to take a deeper breath, but Jamie was holding her too tightly. His breathing seemed steady and even, but her face was pressed against his neck, and she could feel his pulse, strong and quick.

"You're right," she panted. "That was gunfire."

Jamie didn't say anything, and she remembered his earlier comment about Afghanistan. Perhaps he was going through a kind of post-traumatic stress episode. Concerned, and more than a little shaken herself, she lifted her hand and combed her fingers through his hair. "Jamie? Are you okay?"

He eased up far enough to look into her face. Their breaths mingled. "You've heard that sound before?"

She nodded, feeling very small and very inexperienced in the arms of a man who'd lived through a war.

"And what did you do? Did you lie there on your bed, telling yourself it was a car? A bullet could have shattered that glass. You could have been killed where you lay. How could I protect you from that?"

Kendry recognized the look in his eyes, the slightly wild look he'd had in the emergency room when he'd talked about Amina and Sammy and her. About the responsibility he felt. About the normalcy he craved. She felt like she'd deceived him, agreeing to marry him when she'd known all along that she would add to his burdens, not lighten them.

"You don't have to protect me."

"The hell I don't."

"I'm not stupid. I wouldn't just lie there if bullets were flying."

He gave her a little shake, his face so close she felt the air vibrate with his voice. "Bullets *were* flying. You stood by the window."

"You didn't give me a chance to move!" She wasn't helpless. She wasn't a mess. She'd worked damned hard to live in these brick walls.

The wind had been knocked out of her by the man who was even now squeezing her too tightly, smashing her glasses into her breast. She'd been lying on the floor long enough for the concrete to start hurting her shoulder and hip. She wriggled, pushing at his arms, but he was too big for her to budge.

"Let me up." Tears of frustration filled her eyes. "This hurts."

It was the wrong thing to say. Or maybe it was the right thing. He rolled to his side, taking his weight off her. As she took a deep breath, he started running his hand over her arm, her waist, her leg.

"I'm okay," Kendry said, but his hand wasn't quite steady, not quite the touch of a doctor. He smoothed his way clumsily up her ribs, brushed the side of her breast. She inhaled quickly.

"It hurts where?" Jamie said roughly. She couldn't take her eyes off him, the way his lips were firm, the way the muscles in his neck were tight with tension.

"Just—no. My glasses were in the way—"

His fingers were on her breast, dipping into her

pocket, pulling out her glasses. He tossed the taped frames away. As they skittered across the concrete, his hand returned to her breast, fully cupping her this time, hot and sure, sliding his thumb over the peak in a single, experienced stroke.

Her gasp was captured by Jamie's mouth as he kissed her, one searing meeting of his mouth on hers. Her thoughts froze, until Jamie parted her lips, tasting her fully, and Kendry came alive in a burst of sensation. She whimpered with need, overwhelmed by the rush of want.

He pressed his hand, his mouth, his whole body into her. She melted underneath him, hotly returning his kiss.

Abruptly, he rolled away.

Kendry lay on the floor, panting for air, feeling dazed and alone. She wasn't aware of Jamie sitting up, but his strong arms lifted her by the shoulders, and then she was cradled with her back against his chest.

"My fault," he murmured into her hair. "My fault. Forgive me. I should never have...not with you."

Not with her? Not with his wife, who loved him terribly?

Then with whom?

She wanted to howl the question, but the answer came to her too quickly.

With Amina.

The gunfire. The desire to protect a civilian. Beyond a doubt, it all had combined in his mind with yesterday's military training to remind him of Amina, Sam's mother. Sam's real mother.

Kendry was, and always would be, second best for Jamie.

This kiss had changed nothing.

She'd married him for one reason: to make a family for Sam. As awful as it was, Sam had never known Amina. Unlike his father, Sam didn't miss Amina, but he would miss Kendry if she walked away.

I would miss him, my favorite little guy. I'd miss both of my guys.

She couldn't jeopardize this marriage and her chance at motherhood.

She dashed her tears away and blew the bangs out of her eyes. She smiled brightly at the mattress of her bed, just to get her facial muscles working, then turned around to face Jamie.

"No big deal," she said.

Jamie seemed a little startled at her chipper tone.

"You were remembering Amina, I know. If all the soldiers who returned from war kissed the way you do, then I don't think there'd be so much research into post-traumatic stress disorder right now." She patted his shoulder and stood up. "Let's get my stuff and go. We still need to hit the grocery store."

CHAPTER SEVENTEEN

JAMIE KNEW HE'D broken the rules. He'd crossed the line. He'd mauled Kendry on the floor of her old apartment, and she'd forgiven him on the spot for mistaking her for Amina.

The hell of it was, he hadn't been thinking of Amina. Not for one second. He'd known full well it was Kendry in his arms. Everything about her was different than Amina, from the shape of her to the scent of her skin and the taste of her mouth. He'd known it was Kendry he was kissing. Kendry he wanted to toss on the bed.

Four weeks had passed, and it was still Kendry he wanted in his bed.

If she knew, she'd hate him. She admired him for staying devoted to Amina. She'd married him only after he'd promised her that his feelings were buried.

They were.

This wasn't love. It was lust, an unfortunate part of that caveman satisfaction he felt toward all things Kendry. It was undeniably gratifying to watch the changes marriage made in his wife. She no longer sneezed and sniffed. The dark circles under her eyes were gone, and her new glasses with their barely there frames let her look at the world without squinting. She was no longer gaunt, but fit and slender. The doctor in him appreciated how healthy she now looked.

The caveman in him did not appreciate how the other doctors looked at her, but Jamie buried that emotion with grim determination. Jealousy. Lust. Love. He would allow none of them to destroy what he had with Kendry.

Sam was blossoming in the new family they were making. Between Kendry's personal history and her true interest in medicine, Jamie understood why she hadn't wanted to quit her hard-won job at the hospital, but he'd been touched when she cut her hours down to one day per week. On most days, Jamie came home to find her on a blanket on the floor with Sam. Sam had started crawling, early for a premature baby. All that blanket time with Kendry was paying off.

Jamie would be a fool to lose everything for the sake of a purely physical tumble with Kendry. She'd think less of him for betraying Amina, and she would be right to think so. How could he love another woman, when he'd loved Amina?

Jamie would leave the blanket time to Sam. If the phrase conjured visions of a tousled Kendry amid tangled blankets on his bed, that was his personal problem. He would never risk his family for something purely physical.

THE ANXIETY KENDRY felt during Sam's first surgery made her feel like a real mother. The threat of pneumonia had passed, and Sam's doctors had decided to repair the hole in his heart first. It was, as Jamie had warned her on their wedding day, not easy when a child she loved was scared and in pain.

The repair was a relatively simple procedure, performed in the cardiac cath lab. A wire was threaded through an artery, then positioned over the hole between the upper chambers of the heart. Between beats, a patch was unfurled through the same wire and set in place over the hole, where it stuck by the force of pressure within the heart itself. Within months, Kendry was told, the heart tissue would grow over the patch, making the repair permanent.

To Kendry, it was a miracle. To her husband and her brother-in-law, it was routine. Still, Jamie held her hand during the two-hour wait, and she knew that it wasn't a ploy to silence the hospital gossips.

He took a few days off to be with Sam during his recovery, holding Sam most of the time to limit his activity for the first forty-eight hours. Jamie did everything himself, even turning down Kendry's offer to change Sam's diaper.

"I want my son to know I'm always here for him," Jamie explained.

"You make changing a diaper sound very noble," she joked in response, but for the first time, Kendry started to wonder if it was a bit obsessive. By the third day, Kendry realized Jamie stuck like glue to Sam because he had nothing else to do.

She didn't, either, so she decided to tackle the stack of boxes that prevented them from parking the truck in the garage. She'd expected to uncover winter clothes, or perhaps a kitchen gadget. Instead, she discovered mementos that revealed the man Jamie had been before she'd met him. A whole life existed in the boxes, one that Jamie had evidently packed up before leaving for Afghanistan. One he had never picked up again.

"I didn't know you rode horses," she said over dinner, watching Jamie patiently spoon mushed-up bananas into Sam's mouth.

"I don't anymore. Sam's too young."

After dinner, Kendry brought in a framed football-team photo. Jamie was the team doctor, crouched in the front row with the coaches. The team had written thanks for his volunteer work in black marker. "We should hang this somewhere. Who is the team doctor now?"

Jamie looked at the photo like it had nothing to do with him. "One of the kids' dads took over when I was deployed."

She found a motorcycle helmet and snowboard gear.

Jamie had nothing to do with any of it.

The Jamie she knew returned to work the next day, then came home and cared for Sam. The Jamie she knew had never done anything else.

In his quest to be a great father, he'd given up too much. He was expecting Sam to fulfill all his needs. That couldn't be good for him, or for Sam. No baby, no matter how cherished, could meet an adult's every social, mental and emotional need.

In fact, Kendry was feeling a little stir-crazy herself. She couldn't hire a babysitter, though, and take her husband on a date. As nice as her new mother-in-law had been when they'd visited with Sam, Kendry couldn't ask her to watch the baby for a weekend while she took her husband snowboarding in nearby New Mexico.

They didn't have that kind of marriage.

She was, however, the only wife Jamie had. Like

a million wives before her, she decided it was time to manage her husband—for his own good.

KENDRY DECIDED TO start small: a family outing to a high school football game. Quinn had told her he'd never seen Jamie take Sam anywhere except their mother's house. It was appalling to her that the people who'd known Jamie his whole life hadn't met his son yet. If she'd had this adorable baby, she'd want everyone to meet him.

"Easy-peasy, lemon-squeezy," Kendry sang to Sam as she snapped the bottom of a red Onesie over his fresh diaper. The high school's colors were red, white and blue, so Kendry added blue overalls to complete Sam's school spirit outfit. "What's the point of having a gorgeous baby like you if we don't get to show you off? Your daddy is going to bask in your reflected glory tonight."

Jamie was going to enjoy fatherhood, by golly, and Kendry was going to make sure of it, even if she had to kidnap him tonight to do it. Unfortunately, she was pretty sure that was exactly what she was going to have to do.

Kendry buckled Sam into his car seat and headed the truck toward the hospital to pick up Jamie, doubt assailing her every mile of the way. She was more nervous to take Jamie to a football game than she'd been to marry him. She'd been certain Jamie wanted to marry her. She wasn't at all sure what he would do when she drove him to his alma mater's stadium.

Of course, showing off his son meant Jamie would be introducing his wife to old friends, as well. How many times at the hospital had Jamie put his arm around her shoulders, silently defending her when any member of the hospital staff raised their eyebrows in surprise that she—plain Kendry Harrison—was his wife? How many times had Jamie repeated his "Sam and I like you just the way you are" line?

She was supposed to be lightening Jamie's load, not adding to the burden. Superficial or not, having people think his wife looked pitiful was, well, pitiful. The new glasses helped, of course, and at the hospital, everyone wore scrubs, so that was a certain equalizer. But this morning, as she'd stood in front of the bathroom mirror, scissors in hand, ready to trim her bangs for tonight's outing, she'd wondered if there was more to her routine than being thrifty and frugal. Perhaps she was being plain stubborn, refusing to change because she was too proud. Perhaps it had been easier these past two years to pretend that everyone else was shallow, rather than that she had fallen into poverty.

She tossed the scissors down and picked up the phone. She wasn't doing Jamie any favors by sticking to her old routine. It was hard to spend someone else's money on herself, but in this case, she was spending it to make Jamie's night a little less stressful. That made all the difference.

It was amazing how easy some things were to accomplish once she set her mind to it. Bailey had answered the phone, and Kendry had arrived at Bailey's stylist within two hours. Sam had reveled in cooing female attention while Kendry let the stylist have his way. He'd cut long layers into the rest of Kendry's hair to blend it with the long bangs, gushing about "sexy beach waves" the whole time.

Kendry's experiences with beaches were that they

were sandy and left her hair a tangled mess, but when the stylist had turned her toward the mirror to see the final result, she'd decided to skip her ponytail for the evening. She looked like the carefree coed who'd worn a mini while waitressing in the latest Austin hot spot. Kendry had almost forgotten that person.

Now, sitting in the truck, waiting at the last red light before the hospital, Kendry fluffed and finger-combed her hair. Maybe Jamie meant it each time he said he liked her just the way she was. Maybe he didn't want Sam's new mother to look different. When he said she should spend money on herself, maybe he meant on her education, not on something frivolous like a hairdo.

Enough. The money had been spent. The damage, so to speak, was done.

The light turned green. She'd find out what her husband thought soon enough.

CHAPTER EIGHTEEN

AS SOON AS she saw Jamie headed from the E.R.'s ambulance entrance toward the truck, Kendry's heart sped up. As usual, he'd changed from scrubs to jeans. The October air was crisp in the evening, so he wore his leather jacket. He looked like a movie star with his military haircut, handsome, tall and strong. Memories of that hot kiss on the floor were never far away.

Stop it.

Her husband was her friend, a caring man, one who'd given her that same jacket to wear for her own safety. He was devoted to his son. Knowing Sam was in this E.R. without him had torn him up that day.

Jamie flashed a quick smile as he came up to the truck door, and Kendry was right back to square one: her husband looked like a movie star. Her *platonic* husband, the devoted father...

Lord, she needed to keep it all straight.

"Hi." She waved as Jamie walked up and opened her door. She gripped the steering wheel and delivered her first, carefully constructed line. "Why don't you let me drive tonight? You look tired."

He actually looked very alert at the moment, openly checking out her clothes. She'd spent a little more money on herself in that department, too. Football in Texas was big, an Institution with a capital *I*. Her new red sweater, worn over a good pair of jeans and boots, would take her anywhere in Austin before, during or after the game, according to Bailey.

"What's the occasion?" Jamie asked.

Kendry let go of the steering wheel with one hand and ran her hand down her thigh. "I don't think wearing jeans calls for an occasion."

Jamie raised his gaze from her boots to her face and quirked one eyebrow. "I meant, what's the occasion, because you are choosing to drive. Are those new jeans? They look good."

Kendry put her hand back on the wheel. "You could sit in the back with Sam, if you wanted to."

"Wow. What did you do to your hair?" Jamie ducked his head a bit to look into the cab.

"I got it cut."

"It's...really different."

Some feminine part of Kendry felt put out. Just a tiny bit. Couldn't he say something besides *it's different?* It was bad enough he'd thought her choice to drive was more noticeable than her new outfit.

Jamie rounded the hood of the truck and jumped in the front seat, but he kept staring at her.

"It's not that different," she said, putting the truck in gear.

"It's nice. Really nice."

Jamie rested his arm across the back of the bench seat, and she felt him finger a curl near her shoulder. The sensation of being touched in such a personal way crossed the line from friendly to intimate. Maybe nice wasn't so boring. If he felt the desire to touch her hair, then Kendry could love nice.

Jamie gave her hair a slight tug. "I bet Sam has been yanking on this all day."

Lesson learned. She was Sam's mother in Jamie's eyes. They were pals. Co-parents. If she'd expected a new hairstyle to be a turning point in that relationship, then she wasn't keeping real life separate from her fantasies.

"It gives him something to grab besides my glasses," she said. Out of the corner of her eye, she saw Jamie smile at her dry joke.

She took a deep breath before her next rehearsed line, inhaling the traces of Jamie's woodsy aftershave, enjoying it more than ever, now that it didn't make her sneeze. It smelled masculine and inviting. "I want to take you somewhere special to eat."

Lord, that had come out all wrong. Too husky. Too serious. She changed her tone to flippant. "Ask me what's for dinner."

"What's for dinner?" They'd come to a red light. Jamie let go of her hair and turned around to interest Sam in a toy.

"Stadium nachos."

He stopped jiggling the toy. "Nachos?"

"Doesn't that sound delicious?"

"That sounds hard to swallow."

"For a baby? Yes, which is why I already fed Sam. Quinn told me you graduated from Sam Houston High, so I looked them up. They've got a home game tonight, and I thought this would give you a chance to go somewhere besides the hospital and the house."

"My work schedule keeps me away from Sam too much as is."

"Well, you'll notice he's coming with us."

Oops. That had sounded a little more irritated than cute, but she'd been anxious with the light turning yellow as she'd entered the intersection. She came to a halt at the next light, stopping a full length behind the car in front of her, and tried again. "You must like football. We have that picture of you volunteering to be the doctor for a team."

"That was before Afghanistan. I had more time then. I couldn't begin to volunteer for the football team now."

"You don't have to. You were going to make time to eat dinner tonight, right? I'm just asking you to eat dinner at the stadium."

Friday night rush-hour traffic was taking all of Kendry's concentration. She couldn't recall her carefully persuasive phrases and the gentle arguments she'd lined up.

"I thought you understood," Jamie said. "With Sam's medical concerns, he's my only after-work concern."

A driver cut in front of Kendry, and she tapped the brakes a little too hard, angry at the stranger's carelessness. "Sam isn't sick," she bit out through clenched teeth.

"I can't believe you said that." Jamie sounded stunned. "Are we talking about the same kid? He was born prematurely, with a bad heart and poor swallowing reflexes. We have to track his development. He's—"

"He's not sick. He's got a couple birth defects that are being fixed, but in the meantime, he's not sick."

"We dodged that pneumonia bullet. We were lucky."

"Yes, we were, but you know what else, Jamie? His immune system overcame that challenge. He's not an invalid. He's actually pretty normal, and he and I want to *do* something normal tonight. We want to go to a football game at his dad's old high school."

Jamie was silent. Kendry couldn't take her eyes off the road to gauge his facial expression. One second of inattention was all it took for an accident to happen and a life to be altered.

"I don't think of Sam as an invalid," Jamie said. "I just don't think a football game is a great place for a baby."

"I brought him a bottle and some cookies. If he gets fussy, we can leave, okay? But I think Sam is going to love his first real live football game."

Right on cue, like a little gift from heaven, Sam squealed in happy agreement.

When the silence continued, she added softly, "Maybe I'm the one who needs to see something besides the hospital and the house."

Jamie only grunted. Kendry finally stole a peek at his profile. He didn't look angry, just resigned.

"Was that grunt a manly sound of agreement?" she asked, trying to lighten the mood.

Jamie sighed dramatically and leaned against the headrest. "That," he said, gazing at the roof above him, "is the sound of a man who has lost his first argument with his wife."

Kendry welcomed the little bubble of happiness in her chest. "Was it so bad?"

Jamie rolled his head from left to right. "That depends."

"On what?"

"On whether or not the Sam Houston Huskies win tonight. I'd hate to go through one humiliating defeat only to watch another."

The little happiness bubbles multiplied. "In that case," she said, joining the long line into the stadium parking lot, "go team, go."

JAMIE HAD NEVER seen Kendry so excited. He had to admit, the bright stadium lights against the night sky stirred a certain something in the soul. The sound of the marching band warming up under the bleachers and the smell of the gooey, artificially orange cheese substance on the corn chips were a combination he hadn't realized he'd forgotten.

Kendry was loving it. It was obvious in the bounce in her step and the smile on her face. "Isn't this great?" she kept asking. "It's so All-American, you know?"

Jamie was reminded how different his upbringing had been from Kendry's. He hadn't missed a home game in four years of high school. Kendry hadn't made a complete semester in America. She carried Sam and the nachos as she led the way from the snack bar to the bleachers. Jamie followed with the empty car seat and the drinks, wondering how the scene looked through her eyes.

He'd never considered all that Kendry had missed because of her unconventional upbringing. Not being part of a sports team, for example. He looked at her speculatively as she led the way up the bleachers' metal stairs. What sport would she have played, if she'd had the chance? He had no idea what she enjoyed. With her slender build, she looked like she'd run cross-country, maybe. She wasn't too tall, but in those jeans, it was easy to tell that she was all legs.

At that moment, Kendry looked over her shoulder at him, an automatic move to see if he was still following. He was, and damn if he didn't feel like he'd been caught checking her out. His own wife. As if a man would check out his own—

Well, yes, he supposed most men did check out their own wives. That's how women became wives in the first place, wasn't it?

That wasn't how Kendry had become his wife. It seemed wrong to start checking her out now, not when they'd made promises to each other for a different kind of relationship. Theirs had been entered into from a logical standpoint, knowing they would be compatible, having similar values toward family and shared interests in things like medicine.

It was the kind of relationship a woman might hope for if she lived in a country like Afghanistan. The kind of relationship a woman in that part of the world would trust her family to contract on her behalf. The kind of relationship Amina had probably grown up dreaming about.

Jamie had given Amina's dream to Kendry.

He stumbled on the next step and caught himself, looking down at his own jeans and well-worn boots. He was a born and raised Texan, as Western as a man could be. Kendry, in her red sweater and blue jeans, looked as American as a slice of apple pie in a suburban high school stadium.

Neither one of them was from Amina's world, yet he expected his American bride to keep to an Afghani-style commitment to family, not to romance. Slowly climbing the stairs with a hundred other people, listening to the marching band playing a fight song as the announcer directed his attention to the home team running onto the field, Jamie felt like he was in the right place for the wrong reasons.

Yes, he should be at his alma mater's game with his wife and his child. But should he be in a relationship where admiring the way his wife sashayed up a set of bleachers was off-limits?

That's what you offered. That's what she accepted. You can't change the rules now. You'll embarrass her by checking her out.

But Jamie couldn't keep his eyes off her now. It was like being told not to think about a pink elephant. He was trying not to think about his wife's body, trying not to look at the swish of her hair, trying not to admire the glimpses of her face as she searched the rows for available seats.

She turned to talk to him again, making Jamie feel like he'd been caught with his hand in the cookie jar. Jeez, this was ridiculous.

"Is this high enough, do you think?" she asked, beaming with excitement. "I want to see everything."

A man's voice, unexpected but instantly recognizable, called out behind him. "Jamie MacDowell. Heard you were back from overseas. Good to see you."

"Luke." Jamie greeted his old football teammate, someone he'd once spent four hours a day with, five days a week, during Austin autumns like this one. "Good to see you, too."

He meant it. It had been two years since Jamie had left for Afghanistan, but Luke was looking good as always, still physically fit, unlike too many of their friends who'd become desk jockeys at office jobs. They shook hands.

"You've been a stranger."

"Just busy," Jamie said, an automatic excuse to answer the unspoken question. He and Luke and the rest of the crowd all moved up another step.

Jamie couldn't ignore his wife and baby standing a few steps above him. Introductions had to be made. Ready or not, Jamie was about to drop some big news on his old world. "I'd like you to meet my wife, Kendry."

"Your wife?" Luke looked shocked, the same reaction the hospital staff gave. Luke's gaze zeroed in on Sam. "You've got a baby, too?"

"Told you I've been busy. Kendry, this is Luke Waterson. We went to school together."

"How do you do, ma'am?" Luke whipped out his Sunday manners and greeted Kendry with a proper Texas twang to his tone.

Jamie knew what was coming next. He and Kendry had been through it often enough with coworkers. People would look at Sam, then at Jamie, and they'd nod to themselves, as if they understood his marriage. *Oh, he needed someone to help him take care of the baby.* Jamie didn't want to go through it. Not here. Not now. Not again.

Instead, Luke asked something no one at the hospital ever did. "How did you two meet?"

Kendry hiked Sam an inch higher on her hip. In the split second before she answered, Jamie had the horrible intuition that she was going to tell the truth, that Jamie had sought her out because he needed a mother for Sam.

Jamie didn't want the truth. He didn't want anyone to know that his marriage was different than everyone else's. He was essentially a widower, unlike any of his friends. He had a baby who could be deported, a situation none of his friends could imagine. His marriage might be right for him, but tonight it seemed out of place, wrong for this setting and this part of his life.

"We met at the hospital," Kendry said, smiling at Luke like she was enjoying herself. "We both work there."

God, that sounded so blissfully normal, Jamie could have kissed her in relief.

"I'll bet he didn't give you a chance to say no once he'd set eyes on you."

Kendry shook her head immediately, dismissing the compliment. She was so easily flustered by compliments.

Luke must have caught her embarrassment, and being the stand-up guy Jamie would never admit out loud that he was, Luke changed the subject slightly. "I know you're not from around here, because I would have scooped you up first. How long have you been in Austin?"

As Kendry answered, Luke listened with real interest. For once, Jamie's wife was getting all the attention, not his son. He felt something fill his chest, something dangerously close to pride. Luke Waterson, one of his oldest friends, was clearly seeing what Jamie had always seen. Kendry was interesting to talk to, world-traveled and an intelligent woman. It was good to have someone else appreciate his wife.

Luke turned to him. "You kept her out of my sight

until you got a ring on her finger. Smart man. You know I've always had a soft spot for redheads."

A redhead? Jamie looked up at her again. Sure enough, lit by the stadium lights from above, his wife was a dazzling full-color woman against the black night sky behind her. Her hair shone more red than brown, thick and wavy.

Sexy as hell.

Back in the day, he and Luke would have fallen all over themselves trying to catch the attention of a woman like this.

Kendry laughed at something Luke said, and her smile lit her green eyes. Although she held a baby, men were still taking a second glance as they passed her on the bleacher stairs.

She looked as sexy as hell, and damn if that didn't make Jamie as uncomfortable as hell. He tore his gaze away and nodded at the parents around them. "We better take a seat before kickoff, or all this Texas friendliness will disappear real quick."

"Football is serious around here," Luke said to Kendry. "No one knows that better than 'The Doctor.'" He clapped Jamie on the shoulder. "Hey, you really are a doctor now, aren't you? That there's what you'd call ironic."

"Clever as always, Waterson. You sitting with us?"

"Can't. Got a date. High maintenance, and I expect it's already gonna cost me dearly for making her sit alone this long." He nodded at Kendry again. "Good to meet you. *Great* to meet you." To Jamie, he said, "You know I'm going to hound you for more details. Jamie MacDowell is a married man, and my momma is gonna want to know everything. You know how it works."

"I know how it works." Jamie's arrival at the stadium with a woman and a baby was going to top everyone's list tomorrow morning when they recapped the game with family and friends. Unless, perhaps, the team did something astounding on the field.

Go team, go.

CHAPTER NINETEEN

"LUKE SEEMED REALLY NICE."

His wife spoke conversationally while they completed a complex exchange of items that ended with Sam in Jamie's lap, nachos in Kendry's lap, a car seat on the bench below them, a diaper bag in the car seat and two cups of icy soda set carefully under the metal bench they sat on.

"What did he mean when he said it was ironic that you were a doctor?" she asked.

Sam lunged for the nachos, so Jamie dug around in the diaper bag for Sam's cookies. "It was a nickname I had in school. The Doctor."

"Because your dad was a doctor?"

"It started sophomore year. I was the backup quarterback and got called in for the fourth quarter. We won." He shrugged. "Coach said the team was dying, and I'd brought them back to life. The Doctor. Maybe it did have something to do with my dad."

"Stop." Kendry looked like she was in shock. "Stop."

"What?"

"Are you telling me you were the high school quarterback?"

"I wasn't the starter until junior year, but yeah."

"I married the high school quarterback? Are you kidding me?"

Jamie couldn't tell if this was a bad thing or a good thing. Kendry was absolutely wide-eyed. She'd grabbed his arm in her intensity.

"Is this significant somehow?" he asked. "We're talking about twelve years ago."

Kendry threw back her head and laughed. "Oh, my gosh. My mom is going to flip out. I'm about to flip out. Me, little old me, married to the high school quarterback."

Jamie watched her laugh and listened to her go on for a moment. Who knew that Kendry had a thing for quarterbacks? He shook his head and spoke to Sam. "She's gone off the deep end, son."

"You don't understand. My mom hated the cold weather. I spent every fall and winter taking correspondence courses under coconut trees on whatever island called to my parents that year. But deep down, my dearest secret wish was to cheer on guys in shoulder pads.

"When I did go to high school, it was a tiny place that had kindergarten through twelfth grade in one building. Still, even at that little country school, even in the spring when the season was over, the quarterback was the Big Man on Campus. I didn't stand a chance with him. But you," she said, gesturing from his chest to the stadium at large, "at this practically NFL stadium, you were the quarterback of a real team. And I married *you*." Kendry nearly squealed the last word and thumped his arm for good measure.

"You're telling me I can still get mileage with girls for being a high school has-been quarterback?"

"I'm your wife. I'm the one who gets mileage for snagging the quarterback." Kendry popped a chip in her mouth and winked at him.

Winked at him? Serious Kendry, so interested in kidney-function tests and lumbar punctures?

Jamie wasn't certain he could resist this new version. Sexy hair, tight jeans, flirting and laughing. The desire to sleep with her had never been stronger.

The familiar guilt returned. Lust wasn't the same thing as love. Amina should be the one sitting next to him in the bleachers. Amina should be handing a cookie to Sam.

Amina hadn't wanted this life.

Jamie looked around the stadium. The Huskies were winning. The band was in full regalia, filing out of the stands and lining up behind the end zone, preparing for the halftime show. Parents and fans filled the stands, cheered their boys, called greetings to each other.

Kendry scooted an inch closer to him on the metal bench. She still held his arm, and squeezed it in excitement. "Look how big the marching band is. This is like something out of a movie. I love your school."

Kendry thought his life was wonderful. Everything Amina had rejected, Kendry wanted.

What he had was good. It really was. Amina hadn't been the right woman for his life.

And that thought, that one unacceptably disloyal thought, was enough to kill his joy in the evening. What was wrong with him? He'd loved Amina. They'd created a child together—something else it was disloyal to doubt—and he couldn't blame her for not wanting to leave her mission and her world. If she hadn't died in childbirth, they would have worked things out, somehow. They hadn't been able to find a way during the eight months before Sam was born, but they would have come to some compromise, had she lived.

The woman sitting next to him now hadn't asked for any compromise. Kendry had agreed to live with him on his terms, wholly.

He looked down to see Kendry's hand, plain and unadorned, touching his thigh to get his attention. Amina had refused to wear an engagement ring for fear of alienating the local women she wanted to help. Rings symbolized romance. Amina found that immodest. Kendry had married him without one.

"Are you okay?"

"Fine." He looked into her eyes, sometimes hazel, sometimes green, but always pretty and full of true concern. "Thanks for asking."

Thank you for wanting what I have to offer.

He leaned over and kissed her cheek. Gently, gratefully, unrushed. He lingered for a moment, feeling the softness of her skin under his lips, the brush of her hair on his face.

He wasn't breaking any rules. As he'd told her, he couldn't love her like he'd loved Amina. But that didn't mean he couldn't value the tenderhearted woman he'd made his wife.

Kendry leaned forward to fuss with the diaper bag, breaking their contact. Her hair hid her face as she pulled out a blanket for Sam.

Sam was the reason he'd made this woman his wife. For a minute, Jamie had forgotten that this was all about Sam. It had almost felt like it was all about his marriage.

"We can go now, if you're tired," Kendry said. "It's getting colder."

"Sam's happy where he is. Let's stay. You want to see the halftime show pretty badly, I'll bet, even if the quarterback doesn't do a thing in it."

Her grin bloomed into a full smile under the white lights. "How'd you know? I hope they have baton twirlers and flag wavers and all that stuff."

"They do. You are about to see a true-blue, all-American halftime show, Mrs. MacDowell. Enjoy."

He gave her bare hand a squeeze.

I'm going to buy her a wedding ring.

It didn't mean his heart wasn't still with Amina, but he shared a life now with Kendry. For better or worse, he and Sam were living an American life, and this Mrs. MacDowell, the one he'd actually married instead of the one he'd planned to marry, should have a wedding ring.

THE MORNING AFTER the football game, Kendry and Sammy waited by the front door in their pajamas before Jamie left once more for a weekend of army reserve duty.

"It's only one night this time," Jamie said. "The time will fly."

Kendry smiled at his words, so similar to what he'd said in September. She'd wondered then if he were trying to convince her or himself. She knew him better now; he was trying to convince himself that he wouldn't be gone long.

"Hardly more than a long day at work," Kendry said, trying to keep her voice upbeat as her two guys hugged. Her heart broke a little as Jamie pressed his forehead to his son's for a long moment. They were so different, a large man and a petite baby, but they so clearly belonged together.

Kendry was certain the main reason Jamie had married her, the reason she could call these two guys her own, was to care for Sam if Jamie got called to active duty and sent back to war indefinitely. She prayed she'd never see these two part for more than a weekend's drill.

"Okay, buddy. Time for you to go with Mommy."

At the word *Mommy,* Sammy turned toward Kendry and pointed.

Kendry's breath caught. She felt electric, like she was watching a winning touchdown.

"Mmah," Sammy said, savoring the long *m.*

"That's right," Jamie said, sounding as excited as Kendry felt. "That's Mommy."

"Mmah." Sammy dove toward Kendry with all the justified confidence of one who knew he'd be caught.

"Oh," Kendry said, kissing his cheek as she settled him on her hip. "Just…oh." She felt tears well up.

"I think he said '*Mom,*' don't you?" Jamie smoothed his hand over Sammy's back.

"Yes!" Kendry laughed at the squeak in her own voice.

As he had the last time he left them, Jamie let his hand drift from Sam to her chin. His fingertips didn't slide down to her shoulder and away. This time, he brushed her hair away from her cheek, burying his hand in the tumble of her hair, cupping the back of her head gently.

He's going to kiss me.

She didn't move. Didn't breathe. But her heart

pounded, and she felt everything vividly. The warmth of his hand, the weight of Sam in her arms, the brush of Jamie's camouflage pants against her pajama bottoms.

The heat of his lips, surprisingly soft, achingly gentle against her own, for one brief, perfect moment.

Then he was stepping back, picking up his heavy duffel bag, and not quite making eye contact with her as he opened the front door.

"You two have a good weekend."

"Be safe," Kendry said. "Come home tomorrow."

"You couldn't keep me away." With a wink, he headed for his truck.

The way he said it jogged her memory. Only two months ago, when Jamie had come to the playroom to pick up Sam after work, he'd told Kendry that he'd be back tomorrow, that she couldn't keep him away. Bailey had been certain—for about five minutes—that Jamie was interested in Kendry.

Kendry had wished it were true.

Maybe it was safe now to wish for more. She hoped so, because she couldn't stop herself from wanting to be so much more than her husband's friend.

CHAPTER TWENTY

JAMIE CAME HOME hours earlier than Kendry had expected, but she'd been ready. She'd washed her hair, then blown it dry in its beach waves, and then fretted that it looked too obvious that she'd done her hair. She wore a cheerful yellow sweater over her jeans and boots, then worried that the boots gave away how deliberately she'd chosen her outfit, so she went barefoot. She cleaned her glasses. She put on lip gloss, then decided the lip gloss was too much for a woman who was supposed to be hanging out in her own house on a Sunday.

It was all in vain, because the man who came home was not the same man who'd kissed her before he left.

Jamie said hello, as if he'd just returned from a day at the hospital instead of a weekend in the army. He didn't ask where Sam was, although Kendry supposed it was obvious that he was still napping.

"How was your weekend? Was it full of exciting, top-secret army stuff?" The drill weekends were routinely dull, according to Jamie, but she wanted to cajole him into talking.

Jamie flipped through Saturday's mail, which she'd carefully piled on its usual corner of the kitchen counter. He pushed aside the top pieces, looked at the bottom pieces, and then...stood there.

Something was definitely wrong.

Kendry tried to smile naturally. "Did you notice the college catalogs? Every nursing program in the city sent me their materials. It's going to be exciting to read through it all."

Jamie looked at her briefly, and a ghost of a smile passed over his mouth. "That's good."

Then he reached into the cargo pocket on his camouflage pants and pulled out a handful of tattered white business envelopes. He added them to the pile.

"We had mail call this morning. Things sent to my last unit finally caught up to me."

The addresses were lines of letters and numbers, with forwarding stamps and more handwritten numbers. No wonder they had taken months to catch up to him. They looked official, because they had the kind of government seals in the upper left corner that her mail from the court usually bore.

Then he pulled out a padded manila envelope. The square outline of a DVD case had rubbed through the worn surface.

Kendry bit her unglossed lip. Jamie's face was expressionless, unnaturally so. She wanted to touch him. She reached a hand out and tapped the padded envelope instead, taking in the return address at a glance. "Who do you know in London?"

"It's not really from London. It's from Afghanistan." He held the padded manila envelope a moment longer, then put it down. "Do you think Sam will sleep much longer?"

"Yes. He went down about twenty minutes ago."

Jamie rubbed the back of his neck. "I need to watch

this DVD and get it over with. I'll shower while I charge my laptop and…" His words drifted off.

Kendry had never seen him so unfocused, so distracted.

"I'll watch it in my bedroom."

Kendry made one last, lame attempt at a joke. "So it's actually top secret, then?"

Jamie grabbed the envelope in a decisive motion, his face as grim as if he were being forced to declare a patient dead. "It's about to be shown all over the world, actually. It's the documentary they were filming the day Amina died."

SAM'S SECOND SURGERY was scheduled toward the end of the week. Kendry knew it would be more involved than the heart patch. Repairing a cleft palate required scalpels and stitching, and the recovery was going to be painful for her child. The surgery itself was scheduled to take longer than the heart procedure, too. This gave Kendry time to sit next to the silent man whose name she shared, the man who hadn't smiled in days.

Sam had been understandably fussy as they waited for his surgery, since no eleven-month-old child could understand why he had to be fasting. Despite the demands of keeping Sammy as calm as she could, Kendry had noticed Jamie's peculiar tension. He'd hedged his answers to the hospital registration clerk, providing the same written statement that he'd attempted to get a replacement copy of Sam's birth documents from the embassy in Kabul. Attempted, but not yet succeeded.

Without the embassy's report of birth, Sam still had no Social Security number. So far, Jamie's health insurance had been covering Sam as his dependent, but for this surgery, the clerk had asked Jamie to sign an affidavit that he'd pay all expenses in the event that coverage was denied.

In the surgical waiting room, Kendry and Jamie settled into side-by-side chairs, which lasted about two minutes. Jamie stood. He paced. He walked over to the coffeepot, then walked back again without pouring a cup. He sat. Just as Kendry put her hand on his shoulder, he stood and started the whole process over again.

She was ready for him when he returned to the chair. She waved the paging device in her hand. "Let's go for a walk. They'll let us know when he's in recovery."

"No, thanks."

A piece of the old Kendry, the dutiful orderly, wanted to sit silently and be a good, obedient girl. But another piece, a stronger piece, felt she had the right to make this decision for the two of them.

Maybe because she was worried about her child, or maybe because she'd been referred to as "Mrs. Mac-Dowell" all morning, or maybe because she knew that whatever was wrong had everything to do with Jamie's military mail call and nothing to do with her, Kendry stood and reached for Jamie's hand, tugging him with her. "Let's walk."

Kendry kept up the small talk as they made their way to the park in the center of the complex. "That room was too small for you to pace in. Besides, you were scaring the other families. You were scaring me, and I know this is a minor operation, not a heart transplant."

He gave her hand a quick squeeze in agreement.

Kendry slowed their pace once they were outdoors. The October days had been quite warm, but this close to dawn, at the early hour surgeons seemed to prefer to work, there was a definite chill in the air.

She and Jamie probably looked like a contented couple, he in his leather jacket and she in the red pea-coat she'd purchased as a fall-to-winter staple. They stayed on the meandering path that led past the glorious autumn colors of a large sumac tree as Kendry headed for the most private bench in the park, the one she'd thought would hide her when the cost of her pink scrubs had derailed all her careful plans.

She didn't care about those plans anymore. Those meager hopes and dreams no longer existed. She wasn't Kendry Harrison, a solo woman focusing on a sole career goal. She was Kendry MacDowell, in a nontraditional marriage that still formed the basis of a traditional family.

She dreaded the conversation she was going to have with Jamie when they reached the bench, but this was her family and her life. She needed to know what was going on, for better or worse.

"I DON'T THINK you're mourning Amina."

Kendry's voice was soft but firm, familiar to Jamie in a way that soothed. It took a moment for the actual words to sink in. Not so soothing. Jamie's first response was surprise at the sudden topic. His second was to be offended. "Of course I'm mourning Amina. I will always mourn her."

With that knee-jerk declaration out of the way, Jamie had nothing else to say. The two of them never discussed Amina. They discussed Sam and their work at the hospital. They talked about nursing schools.

Lately, they'd mentioned getting a dog, but they never spoke about Amina.

Jamie changed their grip, threading his fingers between Kendry's. He wasn't ready for this. He'd never be ready for this.

Kendry apparently was. "I thought seeing that DVD must have refreshed all your memories of Amina. I was hoping it would be at least bittersweet for you."

Kendry would hope such a thing. What other woman would hope he'd remember good things about a former love?

Not former. Forever. He still loved Amina. He did.

"You've been so withdrawn, though, that I assumed seeing that DVD must have intensified your grief instead. I tried to put myself in your shoes. If I'd loved someone like you loved Amina, what would I do when his memory became painful?"

It was a rhetorical question. He wasn't expected to fill the silence that came after. Thank God.

They sat on the bench. She angled her whole body toward him, her knee brushing his thigh, their hands interlinked. "If I were missing someone, I would have clung to the baby we created together. I would have taken comfort in the miracle my lover left behind."

The miracle my lover left behind. That was Sam. Jamie wanted to tell Kendry she'd gotten it exactly right. He wanted to thank her for putting it into words for him.

If he spoke, he might choke on this sudden emotion. He couldn't speak.

Kendry could, and she did. Deliberately, carefully, logically. "But you've been very distant from Sam this week. You look at him with such longing, Jamie, but you don't hold him every second that you can, not anymore. It's like there's a pane of glass between you, and you are looking at something in a store window that you want, but you can't have."

It was frightening to have someone see him so clearly. Frightening to know he could no longer hide.

It was time to tell Kendry, whether he was ready or not.

CHAPTER TWENTY-ONE

KENDRY SAT ON the bench, studying Jamie's face while he studied their hands. She heard the siren of an approaching ambulance carry over the hospital walls.

"I don't know how to have this conversation," Jamie said. He let go of her hand and stood up, shoving his hands in his jacket's pockets. "There's a dinner event here in Austin, soon. A fund-raiser that goes with the documentary. We'll all be seeing it on the big screen. If that mail had taken much longer to catch up with me, we'd have missed it."

"We can still miss it. You aren't required to relive anything in a movie theater." Kendry didn't want to see it herself. She didn't want to know Amina better. As a vague, faceless ghost, she was already too much competition. "We can pack the DVD away for Sam. Someday, he will treasure that film of his mother."

Jamie kicked a few tree leaves off the sidewalk with the toe of his plain, black boot. "I have to be there. I owe them."

"You owe whom, what?"

"They were filming forty miles away when Amina went into labor. That may not sound like a great distance, but over there, it can be days of trekking on foot. The crew gave a ride to the midwife who was left with Sam. She never would have made it to the base before

Sam died of dehydration, otherwise. The cameraman and the producer stayed. They wrote letters attesting to the fact that I was the father of Amina's baby."

"Is that some kind of Afghani tradition?"

"It's an American legal requirement. If I can provide proof of paternity to the embassy, then Sam's a U.S. citizen."

Kendry remembered those other redirected envelopes, the ones with the official seals. At this morning's patient registration, Jamie had denied that he'd gotten a reply from the embassy.

Maybe he hadn't. "When do you have to give this proof to the embassy?"

"I did, when Sam was born. Actually, a whole group of us did. At our base, there was no way to feed Sam. No formula. No wet nurses among the locals. We kept Sam on IVs, but time was running out. Guys in my unit spent their internet minutes to read State Department regulations instead of emailing their families. Everyone helped put together a packet with the witness letters and my statement. We did a quick blood-type test. Then Sam and I got out on the next plane to a U.S. base in Germany. I had to trust the film crew to deliver the packet to the embassy in Kabul. It's not the kind of thing you can drop in the mail." He reached up and yanked a leaf off the tree. "There is no mail in Afghanistan."

"Is that the problem? They didn't deliver the packet?"

"They did. Amina was their friend, and they knew her baby had no chance as an orphan in Afghanistan. There is no adoption in that country. Officially, there are no orphanages."

Jamie dropped the leaf, then reached up and yanked another one off.

Kendry stood and took the leaf out of his hand. "What is on that DVD that has to do with this paternity paperwork?"

"Another man." She watched Jamie force the words through a tight throat and clenched jaw. "There was another man."

"Another man who did what?" The obvious answer came to her before Jamie could form a reply. Kendry's world tilted. She grabbed Jamie's arm. "But Sam is yours. There were blood tests."

Jamie steadied her with a strong hand on her other arm. "Blood tests can rule out paternity, but they don't prove it. Our blood types only mean it's possible that I'm the father."

Numbly, she sank to the bench with Jamie.

"I'm sorry," he said, rubbing her arms briskly. "I don't know how to make this less of a shock for you."

Anger exploded inside her. How dare Amina deceive Jamie? How dare this woman lie to Jamie about carrying another man's child?

"Oh, Jamie," Kendry managed to choke out, despite the fury clogging her throat. "That DVD must have been devastating."

Her husband had fought so long and so hard for his son, only to learn this week that Sam's mother might have been unfaithful to him. Kendry wanted to defend Jamie, but against what? A dead woman's betrayal? She couldn't fix that. Tears of helplessness stung her eyes. She cupped Jamie's face in her hands, his strong jaw warm in her palms. "I'm so sorry."

"No, it wasn't like that." Jamie took her hands and held them close to his chest, inside his open jacket. "I'm not explaining this right."

Although Kendry was practically vibrating with outrage, she could feel Jamie's heartbeat through his shirt. Steady, strong—this wasn't a shock to him.

"I've always known there was someone before I met Amina, another soldier who was killed in action. She didn't cheat on me the way you're thinking."

Kendry drew in a shaky breath. "Then what does this other man have to do with Sam?"

Jamie's voice remained steady, that of a man who gave commands during crisis, but the anguish in his eyes was unmistakable. "Haven't you noticed, Kendry? Sam looks nothing like me."

"He must look like Amina."

"He's supposed to be premature, but he's hitting all his milestones on time. I had no doubts, none whatsoever, throughout the pregnancy. None during those first six months in Germany. But lately, the possibility that Amina was already pregnant when I met her has been getting harder and harder to ignore."

"You said there was no adoption in Afghanistan. Even if Sam isn't biologically yours, you would never send him back there."

Jamie pressed his hand over hers, keeping it near his heart. "I've got a lawyer who specializes in immigration, but we're in uncharted territory. There's never been a case like this. I was supposed to bring that packet to the embassy in person, for example. We had to get a judge to rule for an exception on that. I've got to make that original packet suffice. Anything to prevent a DNA test, in case my suspicion is right. I can't let Sam be deported to Afghanistan."

Deflated from the rush of anger that apparently hadn't been called for, Kendry pulled her hands back and leaned forward, resting her arms on her knees, letting her hair hide her face. "When were you going to tell me all this?"

"Never." The wooden bench shifted as Jamie stood again, ready to take action, although there was none to take. "The embassy would acknowledge Sam's birth, and I'd never tell you there was a chance Sam wasn't really mine."

Another leaf was plucked, crumpled, tossed. "Sam is mine. He is, damn it, in every way that counts."

Kendry shut her eyes at the fierce pain in his voice. Losing Sam would devastate her, but she was afraid it would destroy Jamie. Afraid, because anything that caused Jamie pain would hurt her, too.

She loved him. He'd married her for horribly practical reasons, but she'd married him because she loved him.

So she lifted her head and shook her hair back. "What can I do to help, Jamie?"

His hand froze in midair. The leaf he'd been reaching for dangled, brilliant orange, on its branch, and then Jamie was down on one knee before her, so close that she had to widen her knees to give his body room.

"How can you help?" he repeated, as if he hadn't heard her right. His hands were in her hair as he lifted her face and kissed her forehead, her cheek and then, a pause. He kissed her other cheek. "I don't deserve you, Kendry. My God, you should be furious with me."

"For what?" If her voice shook, it was because she had so much Jamie, so close. He was big, vital, startling her with his hands in her hair and his kisses on her face.

"I asked you to help me care for Sam. I told you it wouldn't be easy, but I didn't tell you every possibility."

"Jamie." She smoothed back a piece of his hair, something she'd only done once before, on the concrete floor of a garage. "No one knows every possibility when they get married. I promised 'for better or worse,' and that's that."

Jamie's eyes lowered as he focused on her mouth.

He's going to kiss me.

But he didn't. He closed his eyes briefly, then took her hands in his as he settled back on his haunches. With their hands clasped and their heads bowed, they might have looked to any passersby like they were praying.

He touched his forehead to their clasped hands. "We may go broke paying legal fees, even on a doctor's salary."

"Been there, done that. Could do it again." She wanted to lighten the mood, at least a little, so she sighed with deliberately theatrical loudness. "But I warn you, it sucks."

Jamie chuckled and lifted his head. "Kendry Mac-Dowell, I love—" He stopped, but kept his half smile in place. "I love the way you make me smile."

He came to his feet, so Kendry stood, too, trying not to wish that he'd finished his sentence differently.

Jamie picked up the paging device and pulled her to his side as they headed back toward the waiting room, walking in sync.

Her husband valued her more than ever, but this wasn't what Kendry had wished for. Not at all.

CHAPTER TWENTY-TWO

TEN DAYS LATER, Jamie's wait was over. He came home from just another day of work on an unremarkable November evening. He walked into the kitchen to find Kendry sitting at the table, feeding Sam his dinner. Sam now ate jars of baby food with great gusto as he recovered rapidly from his palate repair.

"You got a package from a law firm. It came by private courier." Kendry sounded breathless as she gestured with the baby spoon to a flat, plastic document case on the table.

Sam tracked the movement of the spoon with his entire body, keeping his mouth wide open, all his attention on the food that had taken a detour away from him. It was a classic, comical baby moment.

My God, they are precious. Perfect. I want this in my life.

Jamie looked at the courier case. For eleven months, during a rushed exit from Afghanistan, a frustrating series of nannies and doctors in Germany and the relatively peaceful routine of life in Texas, Jamie had worked and waited, battled and prayed, for one document to arrive from the State Department.

He picked up the plastic case. Inside, he'd find out if the embassy had demanded further proof of paternity.

I could lose it all.

He was a trained soldier, a physician who handled trauma. He didn't hesitate to break the seal and remove the papers inside, no matter how tragic the news could be. No matter how tight the knot in his gut.

"What is it? What does it say?" Kendry's attention was riveted on Jamie, the spoon in her hand frozen in midair.

Sam thunked his heels against his high chair and babbled a string of indignant consonants at the spoon. Jamie felt a smile tug at the corner of his mouth and the center of his heart. Still standing, he placed the paper he wanted Kendry to see on the table, took the spoon from her hand and fed Sam some mushy peas.

Kendry picked up the certificate, a work of art in shades of blue, which trembled in her hand. "This is it. 'Consular Report of Birth Abroad of a Citizen of the United States of America.' Jamie, you did it."

Jamie scraped peas off Sam's chin with the soft spoon and gave his son a second chance at them.

"This calls for champagne," Kendry said. "You're home free now. Passports, Social Security numbers…"

Jamie let her words rush over him in a soothing cascade.

"Isn't it icing on the cake that you got this news now? The premiere is the day after tomorrow. You'll be able to tell the film crew that their trip to Kabul was worth it. Do we have champagne in the house?"

Sam was hungry, mouth open and ready for more. He could eat so easily now, less than two weeks after the operation. The difference was astounding. Sometimes a person only realized how bad something had been once it got better.

Jamie slipped a plain business envelope from the

case into his back pocket and handed Kendry the spoon. "I'm going to get some air."

He watched Kendry's smile fade.

It's not you. You're perfect.

"I need a moment." He slapped the light switch for the outdoor lighting as he slid open the glass door and walked onto the back deck. He stood at the railing and looked over the lawn, nearly an acre that sloped gently away from the house, ending at a creek that served as the property line.

Jamie had bought this house because of the backyard. He'd thought it the ideal place to raise a boy. The creek was shallow enough to wade in, full of rocks to build dams. The lawn was sloped just enough to give a young football player some downhill speed if he tried to dodge a dad who had to run uphill to catch him.

But had Jamie stood next to the real estate agent and dreamed of playing ball with another man's son?

He took the envelope out of his pocket and set it on the deck railing. From the moment the ugly suspicion had whispered in his head, he'd told himself it didn't matter. Amina's past lover was dead and buried. Jamie had been the one to support her during the pregnancy. Someone had to raise Sam. Someone had to *love* Sam, forever, and Jamie was honored to be that man.

That damned DVD.

Jamie had known who the man was the moment the camera had shown Amina speaking to him. The documentary was careful not to show any of the women interacting with men in a manner that strict Afghanis could label as improper, but as Jamie had watched Amina speaking across the expanse of a table with a man identified as Corporal Anthony Schroeder, he'd known. There'd been something in Amina's smile, a look in her eyes that Jamie recognized, because she had loved him, also, after that corporal had died.

Jamie unfolded the report. Because of that DVD, the dead man had a face. A name. And now, according to the private investigator Jamie had asked his lawyer to employ, Corporal Schroeder had a grave in South Carolina, two grieving parents and a sister. A family who might want their dead son's living, breathing baby.

My baby, damn it. Amina wouldn't have deceived me.

Amina might not have known. She would have only been weeks along. Maybe days. This Schroeder guy had died not knowing. His family had no idea.

Through the glass door, Jamie saw Kendry lift Sam out of his high chair and swing him high, celebrating the supposed safety of his citizenship.

Kendry had forgiven Jamie everything so far. She'd accepted all his terms and done all the compromising, but she was a woman of definite standards and proven strength. She didn't need him to build a good life for herself. He didn't think she'd stay with him if he gave their child away.

Life without Kendry?

God, no. He needed her. She was quick to forgive, eager to be happy. She was his best friend. His sanity.

Sam laughed at the woman who'd become the center of his world. Kendry, the beautiful woman with the long legs who spun in circles on his kitchen tiles, was the woman Sam had chosen. The woman Jamie was falling in love with. Hard.

Jamie was probably Sam's biological father. There was no need to ever find out for certain. No one except he knew the Schroeder family might be missing out on a grandchild. He crumpled the report in his fist and hurled it into the darkness.

Eventually, the sliding glass door slid open with barely a sound. "Is everything okay out here?"

Jamie clenched the porch rail.

"I know you're a soldier, but it is kind of chilly and you've been out here for a while." Kendry draped the blanket from his bed around his shoulders.

"Thank you," he said, the weight of her kindness heavy on his shoulders. "Where's Sam?"

"He's in his play saucer. I can see him from here." Kendry leaned her backside against the railing, facing him. "Did you lose a patient today? You're looking pretty grim."

"I had some thinking to do."

She tugged a corner of the blanket over his forearm. "I forget that every success with Sam must remind you that Amina is gone. But you've done right by her child. That will help, I think, if you give it time. You've jumped through a million hoops—or maybe you've pushed them all out of the way—and you've kept Sam safe."

"Don't make me out to be a hero. Please." He took the blanket off his shoulders and wrapped it around hers. "I'm not as good as you think I am. You're going to hate me, Kendry, but I need to get that DNA test."

"But why? You love that baby." The grief in Kendry's cry and the stricken look on her face made Jamie wrap his arms around her without thinking. As if he, the source of her pain, could also soothe it away.

He spoke into the warmth of her hair. "That DVD changed everything. I can't stop thinking that it could just as easily have been me. I could've been the one Amina loved first. I could've driven over that IED and died."

"Don't say such a thing." Kendry clutched him tightly, and he loved her all the more for hating the thought of him dead. He hated himself for what he was about to put her through.

"If I'd died, how would my family have welcomed the news that I'd left a child behind? I've been so narrow-minded, doing everything to keep Sam. It never occurred to me I might be denying another man's family the chance to know their son's child."

He was damn near close to sobbing. Damn close, but Kendry sobbed for him. He pressed his cheek against her hair.

"I have to order that DNA test. I'm so sorry, but I have to do it."

She stayed in his arms for longer than he would have expected, but finally, she stepped back. "You said you weren't the man I thought you were, but, Jamie, you are exactly that man. You have the courage to do the right thing, even if it hurts you."

He didn't deserve her. Even now, Kendry could see something worthwhile in him. "I don't know what I'd do if—"

"Don't worry about that yet. Maybe never."

Jamie let her silence him. He'd started to say he didn't know what he'd do if he lost her, but it wasn't the time to be placing more burdens on her. It was enough that she loved Sam. He had no right to expect her to love the man who was about to take a step that could cause them all unimaginable pain.

IN THE MORNING, they went together to a private lab that ran DNA tests. The lab tech casually informed them that the results could be ready in as little as twenty-four hours. They might get the news the day of the documentary's showing.

Kendry and Jamie agreed the timing was good. If Sam was not related to Jamie, they could confirm with the crew that Corporal Schroeder and Amina had been a couple. Jamie was going on a hunch, and they couldn't ask the surviving Schroeders to take a DNA test without knowing for certain.

She and Jamie agreed that if Schroeder wasn't the man, they needed to get the right name from the film crew. Everything was discussed politely and logically, calmly and rationally, from morning to evening.

By midnight, Kendry was exhausted from the strain of suppressing her emotions. She was sick with sympathy for what Jamie had to be feeling. She was scared to death that Sam would lose the only parent he'd known.

She was selfishly, oh, so selfishly, worried about herself. The reasons Jamie had married her were disappearing, one by one. Sam's health challenges were all but gone. He'd sailed through his two surgeries. He was eating and crawling now, babbling up a storm and didn't need any kind of extra therapy. The embassy had recognized Sam's citizenship. Jamie's military commitment was nearly over. They'd made it through two drill weekends, and he only had four more to go.

She'd be completely unnecessary four months from now. If this DNA test came out badly, she wouldn't even have that long before Jamie notified the family in South Carolina.

She didn't want to lose this new life she lived. She'd

learned to be content with what she had, and what she had was the regard of a good man. If that man never stopped mourning his lover, then so be it. She'd thought they were moving toward something more, reading too much into each kiss, but that had been foolish of her. She had his friendship. They loved Sam. It was enough.

Sam was rustling around in his crib, so Kendry tiptoed down the dark hallway to his open door. She sucked in a whispered "oh" at the sight of Jamie's bare back, golden in the soft nightlight. He was bending over the crib, shirtless, as he'd been that first weekend. This time, she was wearing proper pink pajamas instead of Jamie's T-shirt, but he...dear God...he was still a picture of male strength.

Her eyes drank in his smooth skin, stretched over defined muscles that tapered in a delicious symmetry down to the low waistband of his loose flannel pants. Her entire body woke, responding to the sight. She felt warm, and her pajama top felt too heavy against her skin. Her own muscles felt the need to stretch and move, to wrap themselves around the male heat of Jamie.

He was humming quietly to his son as he rubbed his back. She watched them for a while, her two guys, one sleeping, one soothing. If the sight of Jamie made Kendry's mouth water and her body ache, then the sound of him humming to a baby made her heart no longer her own.

I could lose everything tomorrow. If Sam belongs to another family, then Jamie doesn't need me, not even for four more months.

Jamie straightened and turned toward her. Their eyes met immediately, as if he'd known she'd be there.

I'd be losing something before I really had it. And she really wanted it. There was no denying that.

His joined her in the hallway, shutting the bedroom door behind him. In a husky whisper, he said, "He's sleeping."

She drew in a breath, deliberately controlled, but the scent of warm, clean man undid her. She wanted to press herself against that bare chest. She wanted to be comforted, to be held. She wanted to be made love to.

"You couldn't sleep, either?" Jamie spoke quietly, standing so close that she could feel his body heat.

Kendry lifted her chin to look at him. "Too bad you can't rub my back and put me to bed, too."

She saw his eyes narrow, his gaze sharpen, studying her to see if she'd meant it the way it sounded. She didn't look away.

Jamie literally turned her away. Taking her by the shoulders, he turned her to face the wall, but he didn't let go. Instead, he brushed her hair aside, exposing her neck, and started kneading her shoulders. His strong hands made her feel weak as her muscle tightness was released with firm strokes. She touched the wall with her fingertips to steady herself.

Their bodies almost brushed as his hands slowed, pushing deeper. "Did I ever tell you what my plan was, if the embassy said no?"

Kendry couldn't form the right syllables, so she only shook her head.

"In the middle of nights like these, I would see myself grabbing Sam and running. Out of the country. I'd put my money in overseas bank accounts, something I could access from a tropical island."

His breath touched the back of her neck. "You've

lived on a lot of islands. Tell me which one, Kendry. Tell me which one would be a safe home, and we'll run away."

His hands worked lower, his fingers pressing firmly into her flesh, following her spine.

She swallowed hard and whispered into the dark hallway. "You don't mean it."

"Don't I? Name your island, Kendry."

His hands reached her lower back, thumbs touching her skin under the hem of her pink pajama top.

She shivered.

"Say the name, and we'll fly out tomorrow. We'll go somewhere sunny and hide from the world." His lips brushed the back of her neck as he spoke, so lightly she might have imagined it. "We'll sleep in the shade of a coconut tree, warm on the sand of a beach."

Oh, how she wanted him. He was only toying with her, spinning a little fantasy that he thought was harmless.

"You would never really do it."

"You might be surprised at what I'd do. Why wouldn't I go to your island?" His hands slid around the bare skin of her waist to the softness of her stomach.

Enough.

She turned around to face him, making his hands stop their sensual play. She shook her hair back from her face and looked him in the eye. "You would never do it, Jamie, because the beaches on my island are too warm, and everyone there is bare. I'd be topless under that coconut tree, and you don't want that. You don't think of me that way."

She had the length of a heartbeat to see the look in his eyes turn dangerous.

"Oh, I think about it," he growled. Then his hands were in her hair, tilting her face up as his mouth came down on hers.

His body crowded hers against the wall, chest to chest, his hard hips against her soft waist. On her gasp of breath, he invaded her mouth, his tongue velvet, the slide smooth and sure and certain. When he broke off the kiss to speak against her lips, he sounded angry. "I know exactly what I think about. I've been imagining it since the first night we were married."

"Don't lie." Her thoughts were jumbled and further words wouldn't come, but she shook her head with a tiny, quick movement of denial.

Jamie moved one hand to her back, holding her close as he spoke and kissed his way down her neck. "You were lit from behind by the television." He licked her skin lightly. "Your legs were bare. You put a blanket over me."

Had she? She couldn't think straight, not in the arms of a man who so clearly desired her. She was being ravished, devoured, and she had no defense. She wanted none.

"Two months of imagination, Kendry. Two months of knowing you'd think less of me." His words were whispered, fervent, desperate. Her pajama top had a loose neckline, exposing her collarbone, and Jamie's hot mouth caressed the upper curve of her breast.

"I want you to put on those old glasses. I want your hair in a ponytail and your body hidden by scrubs. Anything to tame my imagination. The hell of it is, it won't work. I know you, Kendry. I know you, and I want you, and nothing you change on the surface of you will undo that. It's too late. I want my wife."

He bent his head lower. Through the thin cotton of her top, she felt the heat and the moisture as he took the peak of her breast in his mouth, moving the rough cotton over her sensitive skin as he stroked the tip with his tongue.

He hadn't really asked her a question, but she answered him anyway.

"Yes."

CHAPTER TWENTY-THREE

KENDRY WOKE TO the sound of a baby crying, the same as she'd done every day for two months. This morning, however, she woke in Jamie's bed.

His empty bed. For a delicious moment, she thought Jamie had gone to get the baby, and she smiled into the pillow that smelled of his aftershave. He could bring the baby back to the bed and they could laze around, admiring the perfection of Sam's fingers and toes as he drank his bottle between adoring parents.

Not today. Jamie was gone. She had a fuzzy memory of rolling over in bed to see him standing in the darkness by his tall dresser, already wearing scrubs and fastening his watch. At the sound of her stirring, he'd come to her side and kissed her lightly. "Stay asleep," he'd whispered. "I have to go in. Gregory's swamped."

It was hardly the good-morning lovemaking she might have hoped for, but it was the reality of being married to an emergency physician.

Sam reminded her he was still stuck in his crib.

"I'm coming, my little alarm clock." Reluctantly, she left Jamie's bed.

When Kendry didn't hear from Jamie by midmorning, she knew he was probably still swamped. Last night had apparently been a doozy for the city, and the E.R. was undoubtedly still treating Friday night's patients well into Saturday morning.

Kendry put Sam in his stroller and went for a long walk, wondering how Jamie could concentrate at work. She could hardly think of anything except last night, of the exquisite thrill of being able to touch him without reserve, the nearly unbearable intimacy of him moving inside her, the incredible feeling of being kissed like every square inch of her skin was delicious.

She managed not to worry until lunch came and went. Either the E.R. was still ridiculously busy, or Jamie was waiting to hear the DNA results from the lab before calling her.

Couldn't he call just to tell me he...

He loved her? He hadn't said that last night.

That quickly, the terrible truth hit her: nothing had changed for him. Jamie didn't usually call her from work, so why should he call today? They'd been friends yesterday, and they were still friends today. Friends with benefits, now.

She hated the term. It was touted as highly civilized, a bit of harmless fun even, to have friends with benefits, but Kendry had never understood the philosophy. She wondered now if Jamie did.

Stop it. You'll make yourself crazy. He's probably reluctant to call until he's heard from the lab.

The DNA test. The possibility of losing Sam. Yes, Jamie had more to worry about than calling her to see if she'd enjoyed herself in his bed.

Sam drank his afternoon bottle lazily, taking his time and getting drowsy. Kendry made the effort to

block out thoughts of lab tests and friends with benefits, so that Sam wouldn't be held by tense arms.

Then, finally, Jamie texted her.

Want to talk to you. E.R. slammed. Will call as soon
as I can. No lab results yet.

She put Sam down for his nap. Kendry stood in the
hallway and touched her fingertips to the wall. They
had made love, hadn't they? It had been more than just
sex. More than tension-relieving, stress-reducing sex
between two consenting adults.

She glanced down the hall toward the bed they'd
barely reached. Actually, they'd gone at each other
like starving people at a feast. He was a man, one who
hadn't taken a woman to bed in a year of mourning, a
man whose world hung in the balance of a lab test, a
man in desperate need of mindless relief.

Here Kendry had stood, female, healthy, willing.
She'd dared him to imagine her undressed in the trop-
ics.

A second, more terrible possibility arose. Instead of
treating her as if nothing had changed, maybe Jamie
hadn't called because he didn't know what to say to a
woman he regretted sleeping with.

They'd mindlessly crossed a line he'd never meant
to cross. He'd never wanted them to be lovers. He'd
never wanted there to be "that kind of thing" between
them.

Whether last night had been casual fun or a horrible
mistake, one thing seemed certain: Jamie would have
called if last night had made him fall in love with her.

KENDRY COULDN'T FIND Jamie in the crush at the premiere. He'd sent her one more text as she was dressing for the event:

Austin gone crazy. Will have to meet you there. Quinn picking you up. No labs yet.

The hotel's conference space had been turned into a movie theater and cocktail lounge, with tables and chairs grouped before a giant screen and bartenders serving drinks from kiosks in every corner. It wasn't yet dark outside, only five o'clock in the evening, but inside, it looked like midnight.

Kendry had chosen her dress with modesty in mind, knowing many of the film crew were native Afghanis. When Kendry thought of women in Afghanistan, she pictured women who peeked suspiciously from behind scarves held over their faces.

Over Bailey's objection, Kendry had chosen a plain burgundy dress with bracelet-length sleeves and a below-the-knee hem. The round collar and the wide cuffs were trimmed in burgundy sequins, adding a subtle sparkle that saved Kendry from having to buy jewelry.

She'd guessed, correctly, that Afghani women would be present tonight, their heads covered with scarves, but they were far from plain. Colors and patterns swirled around the room, and the women looked exotic in their brilliant blues and emphatic oranges and yellows. Kendry felt dull in comparison.

At last, she saw Jamie. His back was to her, but she knew the height and breadth of him, filling out his tuxedo. She waited a step behind him as he finished his conversation, then tapped his arm.

He turned around. Not Jamie. A handsome man who smiled at her, but not Jamie.

"I'm sorry," she said. "I thought you were someone I knew."

"Who? Quinn or Jamie?" Almost immediately, as if he'd answered his own question, he called out, "Jamie."

Kendry spotted her husband cutting his way through the crowd. He wore his formal military uniform, the dark blue coat decorated with medals, the epaulettes of gold thread shining with his rank.

"Braden," Jamie said, sounding surprised as he came within a step of them. Before shaking hands or hugging his brother, Jamie stepped close enough to Kendry to kiss her cheek.

Her cheek.

Introductions followed. "I need to steal Kendry away for a moment, before the movie starts. We'll catch you at the table. Thanks for being here." They did the manly clap-on-the-shoulder thing, and then Jamie guided Kendry toward the exit with a hand on her back. "I've got news."

A man stepped into their path. "Captain Mac-Dowell, so good to see you, sir." More men gathered around. As Jamie introduced her to the film crew, Kendry struggled to control her patience. Jamie had news, but was it good or bad?

The lights dimmed three times. The film's producer escorted them to the front of the room and sat with them at a reserved table where Braden and Quinn already waited. Another gentleman walked to a waiting microphone to address the crowd.

Kendry leaned over to Jamie. "Did you hear from the lab?" she whispered.

Jamie nodded, then stood. Surprised, Kendry looked around and realized other uniformed personnel in the audience were also standing. She felt foolish for not paying attention to the speaker.

After a round of applause, Jamie took his seat. "They won't give results over the phone. I got there just before they closed. That's why I was so late, but—"

The speaker gestured toward their table, and all eyes turned to them. Kendry, sitting between Jamie and the producer, assumed a neutral, attentive expression until the moment passed. She grabbed Jamie's leg under the tablecloth. "But?"

With his eyes on the speaker, Jamie leaned back in his chair to whisper in her ear. "Sam's mine."

Two simple words. Two incredibly important, life-altering words. Tears filled her eyes. She was happy, so happy, for Sam. He belonged with Jamie, and that was where he'd stay, loved and cherished his entire life.

The speaker finished as the movie opened with a soaring view of Afghanistan's landscape and the sounds of lush ethnic music. As the camera came in closer and closer, first to one valley, then to one village, then to one house, the music became quieter and simpler, until only one instrument was playing and one woman was laboring in a hopelessly dry garden plot.

Jamie whispered to her. "I'm sorry I put you through this. You didn't need to be dragged into it. I shouldn't have doubted her."

And then Amina filled the screen, vibrant and alive. She was young, so young, unveiled and full of energy. Long moments passed before Kendry could focus on Amina's words. They were intelligent, articulate.

Passionate.

Jamie bowed his head.

Nausea crawled up the back of Kendry's throat, fear and pain making themselves felt. This was the woman Jamie loved. How could she, plain Kendry Harrison, have ever thought to replace her?

You didn't need to be dragged into it.

Jamie would have gotten that DNA test without her. He would have survived the overnight wait without her in his bed. Perhaps he was feeling guilty for sleeping with Kendry when he loved Amina.

The film moved on, showing scenes of young girls' lives, images Kendry could hardly absorb while she studied Jamie's profile each time Amina appeared. Kendry couldn't fool herself. She was second best for Jamie. She always had been, and she always would be.

She could no longer bear to live her life that way.

When she wiped away a disobedient tear, one that refused to be blinked back, the film's producer nodded, apparently believing her tears were evoked by his people's plight.

She felt like a fake.

She had to leave. Now.

"Kendry!"

Jamie's voice cut through the night air. Kendry winced and hugged her arms more tightly around her waist. She wanted more time to brood out here alone, on the hotel's pool deck. She needed more minutes to breathe the cool November air and listen to the calming sound of the muted downtown traffic.

Jamie called her name again.

She couldn't hide from Jamie any more than she could hide from her feelings. This sparkling blue pool, brightly lit in the night but deserted at this time of year, was as good a place as any to end a marriage.

Solemnly, she stepped out from behind a concrete arch. Jamie came toward her immediately, pushing a deck chair out of his way. She nearly smiled, remembering the way he'd shoved her garage apartment's chair aside, angry when he'd thought she was a neglected child.

She wasn't neglected, and she was no child. She was done living a compromise.

"Are you all right?" The concern in his voice was genuine.

"Jamie, we need to talk." He was the kind of man who would listen. He always had been.

"Only if by *talk,* you mean this." He pulled her to him as if she didn't have her arms wrapped protectively around her middle and kissed her without hesitation.

Her body was a traitor, responding immediately, eager for more of last night's bliss. It was so easy to give in, to let him open her mouth and taste her. Her body tried to overrule her mind. It nearly won the battle, but as the kiss built in intensity, Kendry turned her head sharply to the side. "Stop. Please."

"Why? Why on earth—"

"I need to end this before it goes any further. For my own sake."

Jamie's breathing wasn't perfectly controlled. The hand in her hair wasn't steady. "And by *this,* what do you mean?"

She bit her lip. This was going to be hard, finishing something that she shouldn't have started. "Last night was my fault. I gave you the wrong impression."

Jamie let go of her slowly, letting his hand graze the length of her hair before he took a step back.

"I'm not a friends-with-benefits kind of girl." Now that the first words were out, the rest could follow. "I can't have sex now and then with a man I'm so in—that I'm such good friends with. It ruins our relationship."

"I won't do anything to ruin what we have. If you don't want me to touch you, then I won't touch you."

The words were meant caringly, but they also confirmed what she'd known, deep down. Sex with her was a take-it-or-leave-it situation for him. She'd been willing and available, nothing more.

She uncrossed her arms and shook her hands out, cramped as they were from holding all her tension in. "I can't keep living with you."

"We've had no problems until now. I'll do whatever it takes to make you comfortable again. Our family is everything to me. Everything."

"You won't lose that. Sam is yours, safe and sound." She gestured in the general direction of the ballroom. "You've got Quinn, and Braden, and your mom. Your family will always be yours."

He caught her hand and brought it to his chest. "Not my family. Our family. Our family is everything."

She felt the hard rectangles of his medals pressing into the back of her hand while he used his free hand to search his pockets.

"If you don't believe me, then believe this." He held up a band of plain gold. "I bought it for you after the football game, and I've been carrying it around ever since. I couldn't find the right time to give it to you, not after the DVD arrived. It's not the kind of thing you can give a woman while she's praying the State Department won't put up a fight."

This was too much. He was making it too hard on her. Kendry started shaking her head no, no, no.

She must have backed away because he caught her hand again, her left hand. "I couldn't give it to you while we were waiting for DNA results. Tonight isn't ideal, either, but I want you to know how serious I am about keeping us together. This is for us, you and me and Sam. Our family."

Jamie slid the ring on her finger.

Just yesterday morning, the ring would have been enough, proof that her choice to marry a friend instead of a lover was the right one. "You wouldn't risk this to sleep with me again?"

He didn't answer her. After a long moment, he dropped his gaze to her finger and rubbed his thumb over the gold band.

She placed her other hand over his. "I know I'm crazy to give you up. Having most of Jamie MacDowell is probably better than having all of someone else, but I can't do it."

"I love you, Kendry."

Her heart tripped, but the reality was that he loved her as his friend, as family. She tried to drop her hand, but he held firm.

"I love you," he said again. "If you need to leave, then I won't stop you, but I will follow you. What I said about never touching you again was a lie. I'm going to try to touch you as often as possible, Kendry. I'm going to do everything I can to make you want me, and when you do, I'm going to make love to you until you're helpless with pleasure. Then I'm going to bring you back home and continue loving you, forever."

Her body responded with an immediate, aching desire. Her heart cried yes, but she let the first thrilling shiver pass and kept her mind clear. "I'm nothing like Amina. I'll never be like her."

"Amina?" He was taken aback, so surprised that she was able to pull her hand away. "Of course you aren't. I don't expect you to be."

She gestured again toward the ballroom. "I understand now, Jamie. I get it. She was a truly special person, one of those charismatic people that aren't afraid of anything. You'll never forget her. How could you, when you have Sam? But even if Sam didn't exist, you'd never get over her. That makes your next lover second best."

"That's not true."

"There's nothing you can do about it. She was once in a lifetime. I get that, too. But I know me, and I know my heart, and it will tear me up to stay married to you and know that I'm second best."

"Second best? Is that how you see yourself?"

She stepped closer to the pool. The light under the water reflected upward, catching the sequins of her dress in a muted way after sparkling through the water first. "I'm just me. Pretty simple. Not too interesting."

"You're amazing. Always. Every time I look at you, I see something new. Right now, your eyes look blue. You're a brunette in this moonlight."

"I'm always a brunette."

"No, you're not. You were a redhead in the stadium. Your hair was black silk on my pillow last night."

She felt her cheeks flush.

"Do you know what color your eyes were when we met? They were hazel. When you hold my son, they're green. Do you know what I thought when I sat down across from you during that first lunch?"

She shook her head.

"I thought to myself, 'I could look at her across a kitchen table for the rest of my life.' It's not a matter of hair and eyes. They're just a reflection of you, a woman of depths and layers, a woman who fascinates me."

When she turned away in disbelief, he caught her shoulders and turned her back to face him. "It's true, Kendry. I was falling in love with you from that first day, even when I told myself it wasn't possible."

"Because you loved Amina."

"Yes. But you were Kendry, and I couldn't not love you. The more I knew you, the more I wanted to know you. You are always interesting, always surprising, but you are always, always my Kendry."

With a gentle touch, he brushed her hair behind her ear. "I'm not offering you the old love I had for someone else. What I feel for you is whole and new, a love for you. Only you."

Jamie dropped to one knee.

The night must have moved on. The city must have continued its business, but for Kendry, her entire world was the man before her.

He took another ring out of his pocket, one with diamonds that caught every glimmer of available light and then threw it back into the night tenfold.

He reached for her hand and kissed the plain gold band reverently. "I realized a wedding ring wasn't enough. It's only part of our lives. That ring says we're a family, Kendry, but this ring..." He slid the circle of faceted light onto her finger, letting it touch the gold. "This ring says I love you."

He hadn't really asked her a question, but Kendry answered him anyway, laughing through tears as joy filled her heart.

"Yes."

"Let me ask you. Kendry Ann Harrison MacDowell, will you be the love of my life?"

"Yes," she said again, so he'd stand and hold her and kiss her like a woman wanted to be kissed by the man she loved.

Jamie stood, but as she tilted her head back for his kiss, he asked her one more question. "Will you let me take you on a honeymoon? I've got a vision of you under a coconut tree that's driving me out of my mind."

"Yes," she whispered, and then he kissed her exactly as a man wildly in love with his bride should.

* * * * *

We hope you enjoyed reading

WISCONSIN WEDDING

by *New York Times* bestselling author

CARLA NEGGERS and

DOCTOR, SOLDIER, DADDY

by

CARO CARSON

Both were originally **Harlequin®** series stories!

Discover more heartfelt tales of family, friendship and love from the **Harlequin Special Edition** series. Romance is for life, and these stories show that every chapter in a relationship has its challenges and delights and that love can be renewed with each turn of the page!

SPECIAL EDITION

Life, Love and Family

When you're with family, you're home!

Look for six *new* romances every month from **Harlequin Special Edition!**

Available wherever books are sold.

www.Harlequin.com

"The dog wasn't the silver lining." He tapped one finger on the top of the box. "You and pie are the silver lining. I hope you have time to have a piece with me." He leaned in. "You know it's bad luck to eat pie alone."

She made a sound that was half laugh and half sigh. "That might explain some of the luck I've had in life. I hate to admit the amount of pie I've eaten on my own."

His heart twisted as a pain she couldn't quite hide flared in those caramel eyes. His well-honed protective streak kicked in, but it was also more than that. He wanted to take up the sword and go to battle against whatever dragons had hurt this lovely, vibrant woman.

It was an idiotic notion, both because Francesca had never given him any indication that she needed assistance slaying dragons and because he didn't have the genetic makeup of a hero. Not with Gerald Robinson as his father.

But he couldn't quite make himself walk away from the chance to give her what he could that might once again put a smile on her beautiful face.

"Then it's time for a dose of good luck." He stepped back and pulled out a chair at the small, scuffed conference table in the center of the office. "I can't think of a better way to begin than with a slice of Pick-Me-Up Pecan Pie. Join me?"

Her gaze darted to the door before settling on him. "Yes, thank you," she murmured and dropped into the seat.

Her scent drifted up to him—vanilla and spice, perfect for the type of woman who would bake a pie from scratch. He'd never considered baking to be a particularly sexy activity, but the thought of Francesca wearing an apron in the kitchen as she mixed ingredients for his pie made sparks dance across his skin.

The mental image changed to Francesca wearing nothing but an apron and—

"I have plates," he shouted and she jerked back in the chair.

"That's helpful," she answered quietly, giving him a curious look. "Do you have forks, too?"

"Yes, forks." He turned toward the small bank of cabinets installed in one corner of the trailer. "And napkins," he called over his shoulder. Damn, he sounded like a complete prat.

Don't miss
A FORTUNE IN WAITING by Michelle Major,
available January 2017 wherever
Harlequin® Special Edition books and ebooks are sold.

www.Harlequin.com

HARLEQUIN®

SPECIAL EDITION

Life, Love and Family

Save **$1.00**
on the purchase of ANY
Harlequin® Special Edition book.

Available wherever books are sold, including most bookstores, supermarkets, drugstores and discount stores.

Save $1.00

on the purchase of any Harlequin® Special Edition book.

Coupon valid until February 28, 2017.
Redeemable at participating outlets in the U.S. and Canada only.
Not redeemable at Barnes and Noble stores. Limit one coupon per customer.

52614499

5 65373 00076 2   (8100)0 12239

NYTCOUP1216

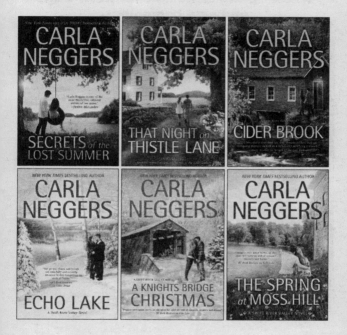

New York Times bestselling author

CARLA NEGGERS

returns to charming Swift River Valley, where spring is the time for fresh starts and new beginnings.

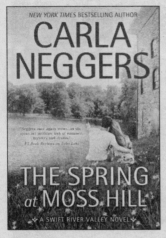

Kylie Shaw has found a home and a quiet place to work as an illustrator of children's books in little Knights Bridge, Massachusetts. No one seems to know her here—and she likes it that way. She carefully guards her privacy in the refurbished nineteenth-century hat factory where she has a loft. And then California private investigator Russ Colton moves in.

Kylie and Russ have more in common than they or anyone else would ever expect. They're both looking for a place to belong, and if they're able to let go of past mistakes and learn to trust again, they just might find what they need in Knights Bridge…and each other.

Available now, wherever books are sold!

Be sure to connect with us at:
Harlequin.com/Newsletters
Facebook.com/HarlequinBooks
Twitter.com/HarlequinBooks

www.MIRABooks.com

MCN1867

We hope you enjoyed reading
Best of My Love
by #1 *New York Times* bestselling author
Susan Mallery

If you liked this story, you will love
Harlequin® Special Edition!

Discover more heartfelt tales of family,
friendship and love from
Harlequin® Special Edition series.

Look for six new romances every month!

SPECIAL EDITION

Life, Love and Family

www.Harlequin.com

SEBPA1216

THE WORLD IS BETTER WITH

Romance

Harlequin has everything from contemporary, passionate and heartwarming to suspenseful and inspirational stories.

Whatever your mood, we have romance when you need it, wherever you are!

♦ HARLEQUIN®

A *Romance* FOR EVERY MOOD™

www.Harlequin.com

#RomanceWhenYouNeedIt
